To Paddy

With best wishes

John

TURTLE WAS GONE A LONG TIME

TURTLE WAS GONE A LONG TIME

Volume Three

ANACONDA CANOE

John Moriarty

THE LILLIPUT PRESS
Dublin

Copyright © 1998 John Moriarty

All rights reserved. No part of this publication
may be reproduced in any form or by any means
without the prior permission of the publisher.

First published 1998 by
THE LILLIPUT PRESS LTD
62-63 Sitric Road,
Dublin 7, Ireland.

A CIP record for this
title is available from
The British Library.

ISBN 1 901866 02 5

Acknowledgments
To Anne Garvey for her composition.
The Lilliput Press receives financial assistance from
An Chomhairle Ealáion/The Arts Council of Ireland.

Set in 11 on 13 Bembo by Sheila Stephenson
Printed in Ireland by Betaprint of Dublin

Introduction

SERVING AS BOTH PROLOGUE AND EPILOGUE

At the end of the last volume all seemed well. Approaching it on a Maidu raft, we set foot on Buddh Gaia. Now, however, we find ourselves ascending the primeval river. And not only that: we find ourselves ascending it in a theriomorphic canoe. Or is it a theriozoic canoe which might at any moment turn upon us and constrict us? What has happened? In the synapse between these volumes, what has happened? Have we regressed?

Let us take our bearings. In the last volume, vicariously in Ahab, we harpooned our way out of Time into Tehom. As the evolving narrative would soon disclose, this meant that we had harpooned our way to humble beginnings, to destitute beginnings, to Maidu beginnings:

In the beginning there was no sun, no moon, no stars. All was dark and everywhere there was only water. A raft came from the north, and in it were two persons – Turtle and Father-of-the-Secret-Society ...

In Turtle, again vicariously, we endured the age of the world's night. We endured the abyss. Eventually, we came ashore, we set foot on Buddh Gaia, but you will I think agree that we didn't do so in a mood of Rousseauistic optimism. The hope is that this side of Nero's fiddle and Hitler's jig we know ourselves better than that. But we don't only live this side of the Coliseum and Auschwitz. We live this side of Gethsemane and Golgotha. In a redemptive sense, all geological ages live this side of Gethsemane and Golgotha. And that means we can come ashore in a way we previously didn't. It means we can come ashore at Punta Alta. It means that, bringing all of what we phylogenetically are with us, we can ascend the river. Be it Congo, Amazon, Rio Negro or Rhine, we can ascend it not into the heart of darkness but into Tenebrae.

In other words we dare to hope that Anaconda Canoe is Kundalini Canoe; that for all its terrors the river is in some sense the earth's sushumna. And that is why, in Part 3 of this volume, we think of Linn Feic as a chakra. And what else but the crown chakra is Nectan's Well?

INTRODUCTION

Are you, in all of this, continuing in a direction set for us by D.H. Lawrence in his poem called 'Snake'?

I'm attempting to continue in a direction set for us by Christ in Gethsemane. It was here, in agonized resignation, that we realigned ourselves with evolution. From now on we would seek to emerge not from but with the earth. And since, as I see it, we can hope backwards as well as forwards from the Triduum Sacrum, I invite you, seeing it with your mythic imagination, to behold a wonder: Horus, the young sungod of ancient Egyptians, ascending the Nile in Apophis Canoe. That is Good News from below. It is Good News from the phylogenetic foundations of our psyches. It allows us to hope that the great reconciliation and integration that occurred in Christ can occur in us. Not overnight of course, and not to all of us all at once. Horus ascending the Nile in Apophis Canoe does not mean that we can now expect an end to bad dreams. Nor does it mean that the wolf will now lie down with the lamb. And yet Old Man is right. Among some of the native peoples of North America, the creator or maker of all things is known as Old Man. His work finished, and ready now to retire from view, he had this to say:

Now if you are overcome, you may go to sleep and get power. Something will come to you in your dream, and that will help you. Whatever those animals who come to you in your sleep tell you to do, you must obey them. If you want help, are alone and travelling, and cry aloud for aid, your prayer will be answered – perhaps by the eagles, or by the buffalo, or by the bears. Whatever animal answers your prayer you must listen.

There is a way of being in the world that enables the world to be on our side.

This we know from some of our oldest fairy stories.

This we know from 'The Rime of the Ancient Mariner'. An emanation as it were of the favouring world, the albatross made a favouring breeze to blow.

We know it from the Book of Job. Undergoing his agony, Job became heir to a promise:

For thou shalt be in league with the stones of the field and the beasts of the field shall be at peace with thee.

At some level of his being and of our being, Anaconda is at peace with us. At some level of his being and of our being Apophis is at peace with us. At some level of our being and of their being Apophis is willing to be our Mesektet boat, Anaconda is willing to be our canoe.

It's as if waking up one morning in his house in South Molton Street,

INTRODUCTION

Blake were to find that Tyger had left a medicine bundle behind.

However dangerous it is, however dangerous it will continue to be, the primeval can be on our side. Inside ourselves and outside ourselves, it can be on our side. Anaconda Canoe can be Mucalinda Canoe, Mucalinda protecting us as he did the Buddha.

In the course of his voyage on a whaler called the *Acushnet*, Melville went ashore on the Encantadas, an archipelago of volcanic islands better known to us nowadays as Galapagos. Reflecting on the hissing, reptile life that he encountered there, he concluded:

In no world but a fallen one could such islands exist.

But supposing Melville had gone ashore on those islands in the way that Old Man would go ashore on them?

Supposing Old Man's state of mind were to become our state of mind?

Could it be that the pre-cosmic raft of the Maidu is a lifeboat drawing alongside the *Acushnet*?

Could it be that Anaconda Canoe is a lifeboat drawing alongside Sputnik?

Or, if it is indeed a fallen world we live in, will anything less than the Triduum Sacrum be lifeboat to us?

Did you write this book in the belief that it is time to lower the lifeboat?

Given so much that is so appallingly true of ourselves and our world, it has always been time to lower the lifeboat. And if it is the Triduum Sacrum you are talking about, it is of course God not Lenin who lowers it. And it isn't just onto the surface of our red, revolutionary square that he lowers it. And, given a frightful recalcitrance in things, our voyage from here on won't be all plain sailing.

It is above all I suppose when we look at an image of Mucalinda Buddha that we in the West can see what Lawrence saw, that we have missed our chance with a Lord of Life, that we have something to expiate. In the pit in Lascaux, our oldest garbhagriha, we must expiate it. In the dust of Esagila we must expiate it. On the wake of the *Pequod*, our Marduk Street at sea, we must expiate it. And if we should ever wish to acknowledge that it isn't just a pettiness that we must expiate, then, the better to picture it, we might imagine Ishmael reading *Moby-Dick* to the Fisher King. In particular, we might imagine Ishmael reading a chapter called 'The Cassock' to the Fisher King. Listening, the king will see that it is our collective protarchos ate, repeated now again in our day, that he is wounded with.

INTRODUCTION

Shiva Linga
Taurs Linga
Cetu Linga

Moby-Dick is our modern Enuma Elish. And the wake of the *Pequod* isn't only Marduk Street at sea. It is Fifth Avenue at sea. It is the Champs Elysées at sea. In a tragic sense, and all our revolutions notwithstanding, our Eiffel Tower and our Empire State are ziggurats: not even in desire has either one of them raised its head above our continuing Babylonian captivity. And, be he a Napoleon or a Lenin, the modern liberator must confess – if only in his dreams he must confess that his Marseillaise hasn't brought his medulla with it. And that's what this book attempts to do. Or rather, the Christ you encounter in this book, that's what he sets out to do. Only it isn't Christ's fault if, having brought eohippus-anthropus to the Kedron, he can't make him drink.

Anyway, the very title of this last volume suggests that we've taken our biblical foot off the Serpent's head. But in case anyone should conclude that this is an invitation to instinctive anarchy, let us be quite clear that it is on the contrary an invitation to Gethsemane.

To come forth by day is not to come forth into another world but into another way of being in this world. And so wherever we settle, it will not for the moment be safe for a sucking child to play by the hole of the asp nor for a weaned child to put its hand in the cockatrice's den. To be at peace with the beasts of savannah and sea does not mean that they won't menace us or kill us. This side of redemption expect blessedness but also the 'rush dreadful' of tiger and lion on God's holy mountain. Expect terror. Expect that your bed will sometimes be a *Liz de la Mervoille*. Expect a continuing need for Kwakiutl firelight. And yet the mind altering alters all. Ordinariness is tremendous. The universe is as stupendous in a daisy as it is in a galaxy. And evenings there are when we see, in a seeing not blinded by practical eyesight we see, how unworldly the world is. And any philosophy that isn't a Song of Songs and any geology that doesn't sing with the earth and any astronomy that doesn't sing with the stars is defamation.

Early in the second volume we encounter Narada. Early in this volume we encounter Yaje Woman. The least we can say of them is that they are philosophically disruptive visitors to our shores and it is likely, isn't it, that we will find it as difficult to welcome them as Montezuma found it difficult to welcome Cortez?

This question falls I think within the ambit of a larger concern in the book. I've gone over the ground elsewhere so I hope that on this occasion a less

INTRODUCTION

elaborate response will suffice.

Let us begin with Aristotle. 'The more solitary and retired I become,' he says, 'the more I love the myth.' In this mood, deliberately echoing the word philo-sophos, meaning lover of wisdom, he coined the word philo-mythos, meaning lover of myth. His thinking was as follows: philosophy has its origin in wonder, in mind come into a state of wonder. Myths are instinct with wonder. Like nothing else perhaps in our culture, they uncompromisingly mediate the difficult strangeness of self and of world. Therefore the philomythos has as good a chance of reaching and living in the Truth as the philosophos has.

Hegel was surely right to insist that the familiar, precisely because it is familiar, remains unknown.

Coleridge would concur:

In poems, equally as in philosophic disquisitions, genius produces the strongest impressions of novelty, while it rescues the most admitted truths from the impotence caused by the circumstance of their universal admission. Truths of all others the most awful and mysterious, yet being at the same time of universal interest, are too often considered as so true, that they lose all the life and efficiency of truth, and lie bed-ridden in the dormitory of the soul, side by side with the most despised and exploded errors.

Elsewhere he considers the need to awaken our minds from what he calls 'the lethargy of custom' and the 'film of familiarity'.

How unknown, because of our familiarity with them, are our myths?

Don't we occasionally need an exotic myth or two to awaken something in us?

Maybe Yaje Woman will open our minds and eyes in ways that Morgan Le Fay no longer can.

Maybe Yaje Woman ascending the Dee in her very strange canoe will reawaken the folklore lobes.

It will of course seem to be going too far but I'll say it anyway: with or without Aristotle's approval, I welcome *The Mabinogion* as my *Treatise of Human Understanding*, because, ever and again, it is while I am reading it, not while I am reading Hume, that I find myself at home in the wonder of self and of world. I have often yearned for a philomythic *Mabinogion*, a suite of myths, traditional or modern, that would mediate the highest truths to us. I am persuaded that myths can bring the whole psyche into conformity with their apprehensions in a way that arguments, however cogent, cannot. If this book can be said to be in any way philosophical, it is philomythically that it is so.

Something that Yeats said is relevant here:

INTRODUCTION

There is for every man some one scene, some one adventure, some one picture, that is the image of his secret life, for wisdom first speaks in images ... and this one image, if he would but brood over it his whole life long, would lead his soul, disentangled from unmeaning circumstance and the ebb and flow of the world, into that far household where the undying gods await all whose souls have become simple as flame, whose bodies have become quiet as an agate lamp.

Could it be that Narada coming through the pass at Thermopylae is such a scene or image? Could it be that Yaje Woman ascending the Rhine in her Anaconda Canoe is such an image? Could it be that Yaje Woman and King Soma standing either side of Christ as he looks down into Adam's empty skull is such an image?

As I've suggested elsewhere, this book is a Trojan Horse of such images. Think of Tiamat giving sensuous suck, chakral suck, to six marvellous mornings. Think of Prometheus undergoing re-education in Blue Thunder Tipi. Think of Bright Angel lifting his lamp, as Liberty lifts hers, at the mouths of the Yukon and the Hudson, at the mouths of the Dordogne and the Tiber. Think of Eo Fis in Linn Feic. Think of Nectan's Otherworld Well. It is in that well that the seven rivers of Ireland have their source.

In the hope that they will help us in the way that Yeats says they can, this book is a rosary of such recurring images, it is a mother tongue of such recurring images, it is a Hozhonji song of such recurring images, and who knows, they might have it in them to bring us to where we are, they might have it in them to bring us to Buddh Gaia.

Arnold tells us that the strongest part of our religion today is its unconscious poetry. That's why this book relies so much more on myth, metaphor and parable than it does on logic, dialectics or discursive reason. That's why, instead of Kant's arguments, we have Vishnu revealing the secret of his Maya to Narada. That's why, instead of Schopenhauer's persuasions, we have Yaje Woman ascending our river in Anaconda Canoe. Narada's story and the story of Yaje Woman could, with some concessions to local colour, claim unobtrusive inclusion in a philomythic *Mabinogion*, or, dare I say it, in a philomythic *Critique of Pure Reason*.

The claim that Yeats makes for the contemplation of images does not, of course, contradict the need of mystics to go beyond images into what Christians call Tenebrae, into what Hindus call nirvikalpasamadhi.

But why, from among all the parables available, did you choose the Narada parable? And why, from among all the myths available, did you choose the myth of Yaje Woman?

x

INTRODUCTION

There are in our culture many myths in which the phylogenetically thinking depths of our psyches are in seance with us. The myth of Andromeda menaced by Ketos or of Cretan civilization menaced by the suppressed Minotaur come to mind. Because they help us to articulate and picture ourselves to ourselves, these myths comfort us in a way that his comforters couldn't comfort Job. Because there was no pre-existing myth that could speak to his condition, Job had to become the myth, he had to be willing to be lived by the myth, that could comfort him. And there are few situations so lonely as this. Think of Jesus in Gethsemane. Knowing their own limits, any Middle Eastern or Near Eastern myths that came with him malingered this side of the Torrent. They most certainly malingered this side of Golgotha.

Strange to say, there are in our culture hardly any myths of immediate epistemological import. The few that Plato invented read like inventions. Perhaps the best we can expect in this regard is the odd parable and the odd story.

And so, there they are, Narada and Yaje Woman, and I sometimes think that, meeting him before he crossed the Torrent, they might have had something to say to Jesus. Meeting him as he crossed into Good Friday, they might have been able to say something to him, something helpful but not immediately comforting about the nature of mind.

Relentlessly, in almost all of its sects and schools, Mahayana Buddhism asks and answers questions about the nature of mind. And in this regard, particularly in its continuing advaitavedanta phase, Hinduism is no less tireless. And there was a morning when Chuang Tzu asked a disturbing question not just about the nature of mind but about the nature of self. During the night he dreamed that he was a butterfly flitting from flower to flower. When he woke up he couldn't decide whether he was Chuang Tzu dreaming that he was a butterfly or a butterfly dreaming that he was Chuang Tzu.

But it isn't only in the Orient that questions about the nature of mind have been asked and answered. In much of what some Christian mystics have to say there is an implicit philosophy of mind. It is when we are drawing close to God in contemplation, it is when we go beyond mental activity into the cloud of unknowing or into the dark night of the soul or into Tenebrae, that the nature and limits of mind become clear to us. It isn't hesitatingly that St John of the Cross tells us what he knows:

O wretched condition of this life wherein it is so dangerous to live and so difficult to find the truth. That which is most clear and true is to us most obscure and

INTRODUCTION

doubtful and we therefore avoid it though it is most necessary for us. That which shines the most and dazzles our eyes, that we embrace and follow after though it is most hurtful to us and makes us stumble at every step. In what fear and danger then must man be living seeing that the very light of his natural eyes by which he directs his steps is the very first to bewilder and deceive him when he would draw near unto God. If he wishes to be sure of the road he travels on he must close his eyes and walk in the dark if he is to journey in safety from his domestic foes which are his own senses and faculties.

The light of our natural eyes bewildering us and deceiving us – our senses and faculties charged as it were and arraigned as our domestic foes – that, surely, doesn't fall far short of the Hindu or the Buddhist diagnosis. How far are we here from a doctrine of maya, from a doctrine of mind-maya? How far are we here from Mayashakti or Yajeshakti ascending our river in her serpent canoe, in her ropesnake canoe?

Morgan Le Fay. Fata Morgana.

Had Morgan Le Fay evolved with an evolving mysticism, or had she evolved with the evolving articulation of a mysticism, she might now be our Mayashakti, our Yajeshakti. What I'm trying to say is that Yaje Woman isn't as exotic to our culture as she might at first sight seem to be.

Yaje Woman ascending our river is a question about the nature of mind ascending our river. Seeing her, we might well ask is she our Cortez? Is she our epistemological conquistador? Does her coming signify our philosophical Year One Reed?

What will it mean or what might it mean for Plato and his philosophy when Narada knocks on his door?

Towards the end of *Timaeus*, Socrates says:

Now, when a man abandons himself to his desires and ambitions, indulging them incontinently, all his thoughts of necessity become mortal, and as a consequence he must become entirely mortal, because he has nourished his mortal part. When on the contrary he has earnestly cultivated his love of knowledge and true wisdom, when he has primarily exercised his faculty to think immortal and divine things, he will – since in that manner he is touching the truth – become immortal of necessity, as far as it is possible for human nature to participate in immortality.

The highest of our faculties heightening and brightening its awareness of the highest and brightest objects of thought – that, Plato believes, is how we will regain the life of transcendent dignity and glory we have de-clined from. Not a few mystics would disagree, their testimony leaving us in no doubt that in the course of their return to Divine Ground they crossed into a state beyond all objects of thought and all thinking about them.

INTRODUCTION

This state beyond thinking, imagining, remembering, this state beyond mental activity, Hindus call nirvikalpasamadhi. The classic statement is in the Chandogya Upanishad:

Yatra na anyat pasyati, na anyat srinoti, na anyad vijanati, sa bhuma.
Where nothing else is seen, nothing else is heard, nothing else is thought, there's the Infinite.

Thinking eclipses Divine Ground. And thinking about an angel eclipses it as much as thinking about a sod of turf does. It isn't thinking that makes us immortal. We are immortal because of immortal ground in us.

To say, however, that thinking eclipses Divine Ground is not to say that, mystically therefore, thinking is dispensable. On the contrary, the mystical journey will normally involve us in thinking of the most daring kind, persistently pursued. It isn't thoughtlessly that we come to stand beyond thought.

Both as map of reality and road map, Plato's map is seriously flawed. And Narada knocking at his door is the Chandogya mahavakya knocking at it. It is the single Sanskrit word, jneyavarana, knocking at his door.

Jesus crossed the Torrent and, falling silent, all of Plato's dialogues ceded ground to the nocturnes of Tenebrae.

Imagine it: St Paul setting up a Tenebrae harrow in Plato's Academy. At that moment, no Leonidas and his men opposing him, Narada walks through the pass at Thermopylae. At that moment, even here in Athens, metaphysics gives way to metanoesis. At that moment, a ghost herself now, Atossa calls out to her husband and son: where thousands failed, at Marathon failed, at Salamis failed, a single one has won. And Aeschylus too, with ghostly eyes he sees it:

> Seven against Thebes,
> One against Athens.
>
> But lo, the one who comes has no sword, no shield, no torch.
> The one who comes only has his own story.

Waiting alone in the theatre of Dionysus, Melpomene takes off her tragic mask and welcomes him to ground haunted by Clytemnestra, Electra, Oedipus, Hippolytus, Orestes, Agave, Pentheus, Phaedra, Medea and Jocasta.

Hearing Narada's story, they know that they too can wake up from the plays they have for so long been so ignorantly trapped in. And far away in Thebes, in the silence of her underground tomb, Antigone hears what seems for the moment to be a very strange question:

> Did you bring the water?

INTRODUCTION

With that question the stasima of her play, of all Greek plays, become the nocturnes of a mystical rite of passage.

It's the Hindu way of asking the apocalyptic question, isn't it?

Yes, and I've often thought that we should be confronted by it at the beginning, not at the end, of our holy book.

Are you replacing the Dionysian and the Christian grapevine with the Desana yajevine?

No. As I've indicated, I'm concerned with the nature of mind. And what I am saying is this: my spinal cord is more like a yajevine than it is like a grapevine. And on Golgotha we come down totally from the veiling consciousness it gives rise to.

Anaconda Canoe is in some sense a ropesnake canoe. And a good day it will be for us all when it ascends our river. A good day it will be for Christianity when it ascends the Jordan, the Ilissus and the Tiber. On that day it is as Tenebrae harrow that the Grail will enter the hall at Camelot.

This last volume opens with six stories. You have elsewhere referred to them as a hexameron of stories. This suggests a likeness to the six days of creation with which the Bible opens. If there is such a likeness, is it seriously intended?

When I think of beginnings I think not of creation but of emanation, and yet, since it would I believe be an irreverence to do so, I am careful not to let this preference degenerate into a doctrine or a dogma. Some days, sitting among mountains, the only good way to pray is to call all our thinking about them back from them and let them be. But this isn't entirely germane to your question, so I'll put it this way: working with the biblical story of origins, there is, in there somewhere, a yearning that the six days of cosmic creation would continue into six days of culture creation. In this view of things, cosmos and culture can be a continuum, a single emanation in an unbroken series of pulsations out of Divine Ground.

What I'm attempting to say is very different from Vaughan's vision:

> I saw Eternity the other night,
> Like a great ring of pure and endless light;
> All calm as it was bright
> And round beneath it, Time in hours, days, years,
> Driven by the spheres
> Like a vast shadow moved; in which the world
> And all her train were hurled.

INTRODUCTION

Time isn't beneath Eternity. There is no objectively existing gulf that separates Time and Eternity. And when you go and sit among the mountains and are finally as silent as they are, then you will know that *world* doesn't rhyme with *hurled*.

In one sense, but only in one sense, these stories are a Native American *Mayflower* that might one day bring us to vita nuova here at home.

As I understand it, vita nuova implies that we needn't forever be victims of the calamity remembered and depicted in the pit in Lascaux. It implies that cosmos and culture can be what they aboriginally were, a continuum. It implies that Uvavnuk's song not Vaughan's song will be the sea shanty of our voyage to the Mundus Novus we were born into.

Are we back to Job?

Yes. His addiction to his civic day so forcibly and so terribly overcome, Job walked abroad. Within as well as without he walked abroad, and now again culture is out of Divine Ground, now again when we come to build our temple the stones of mountain and canyon will be in league with us and the beasts of savannah and sea will dream our dream with us. Job coming home is Old Man coming home.

He isn't cast down by the sight of Leviathan.

In our biblical vision of him, Leviathan has seven heads.

Un-biblical it will be to say it, but I'll say it nonetheless: sinking down, in a swoon sinking down, onto the floor of an Eastern ocean, Ahab dreams that Moby is his Mucalinda, dreams that with each of his seven heads he sings the song that Tiamat sings, she singing it in the beginning, singing it, she also, with her seven heads.

Transformed archetypes imply the possibility of transformed culture. Alternative archetypes imply the possibility of an alternative culture. It is as important for ancient Egyptians as it is for us that we would imagine Yaje Woman ascending the Nile. For us and for them it is important that we would imagine her ascending it in a cobra canoe – the same cobra which, as Uraeus, transfixes us from Pharaoh's brow. Already in this ascent, the Pharaoh's cobra is becoming the Pharaoh's Mucalinda, his Mucalinda Canoe. Already, with this ascent, the Egyptian Book of the Dead is beginning to read like the Tibetan Book of the Dead.

Alike for ancient and modern peoples, the new epistemology is the new *Mayflower* that will bring us to a new understanding of ourselves and our world.

Yaje Woman ascending the Nile in her cobra canoe will give to religion and culture an ethos and an orientation very different from that given to them by Mary, mother of Christ, standing as crushingly as she does on the biblical head of our biblical serpent. Mary standing on the head of the serpent gives religious recognition to repression. Undergoing an agony in Gethsemane, Jesus gives religious recognition to integration. And here it is that cobra canoe, apophis canoe, Anaconda Canoe become available to evolving humanity. In this we must of course be careful not to assume that evolving humanity is synonymous with those relatively recent peoples who have become addicted to making history. Looked at from Bright Angel Trail, history might well be hiatus.

That Narada and with him the mysticisms of the Orient might walk through the pass at Thermopylae is one thing. Altogether more menacing is the possibility that Pleistocene or Arctic shamans would dance their buffalo or caribou dance on the Plain of Marathon. Your defence of them notwithstanding, I put it to you that these six stories are a threat to the values of Classical-Christian culture.

Almost thirty years ago now I spent a summer in Mexico. Partly I suppose because I had read so much about it, I was everywhere aware of the old Aztec and Toltec world. Even where nothing of it was visible I was aware of it. In Chapultepec Park Museum, which I regularly visited, it was almost as threateningly real to me as it was to Bernal Diaz listening to the big, booming drum that announced and accompanied the sacrifices to Huitzilopochtli and Tezcatlipoca. Listening to that drum, listening to it in my imagination, I was tempted to take refuge in a simple answer: an old and very powerful priest ate the *psilocybe* or *stropharia* mushrooms, he had a bum trip and by sheer force of his personality he institutionalized his delusions.

For the first time in my life, wilfully and with full consent, I was heir to the Greek enlightenment. How glad I was to walk with Socrates to the Ilissus, to walk with Aeschylus to Areopagus Rock. How glad I was that someone had questioned and again questioned my inherited habits of feeling and thought.

Here, however, on the summit of a pyramid in Tenochtitlan, the Aztec capital, here where hot human hearts were fed to the awful apparitions of the Smoking Mirror, here I had to acknowledge a common humanity with the priests who so sanguineously served this Pantheon. I acknowledged a not so un-common proclivity to derangement and delusion – to these as they looked back at me from sun, moon and stars, to these to the extent that they had become cosmologies.

Here, in the most literal sense, the snake in the rope was a bloodthirsty pantheon in the rope. It was a hunger for still palpitating, still hot

INTRODUCTION

human hearts in the rope. As Geoffrey Hill has it:

> By blood we live, the hot, the cold,
> To ravage and redeem the world:
> There is no bloodless myth will hold.

Is it so?

Given the carnivorous savagery of the world, given our own carnivorous dentition, is it so that there is no bloodless myth will hold?

Will the Buddha sitting uncarnivorously in lotus position not hold?

Will Krishna playing his flute in the immemorial Hindu night not hold?

Will St Francis singing to Brother Sun and Sister Moon not hold?

Will Christ preaching the Beatitudes not hold?

> Odour of blood when Christ was slain
> Made all Platonic tolerance vain

The Kwakiutl open a sacred ceremonial door to a Being they call the Crooked Beak of Heaven, and Hindus have long acknowledged the terrible as well as the lovely face of Divinity.

> *Ghora murti*: the terrible face
> *Sundara murti*: the lovely face
>
> Nature in *ghora-murti* mood
>   Therefore
> Divinity in *ghora-murti* mood
>
> Nature in *sundara-murti* mood
>   Therefore
> Divinity in *sundara-murti* mood

Our own *ghora-murti* moods we project into the rope.
Our own *sundara-murti* moods we project into the rope.

We know what Coatlicue looks like in terrible mood. What does she look like in lovely mood?

Religion must be able for the terrible. Christianity is able for the terrible and yet, standing on the pyramid of the sun, I nonetheless yearned for a religion without blood-letting. I yearned for a Christianity in which the chalice had given way to the Tenebrae harrow.

Golgotha is more like Borobudur in Java than it is like the pyramid of the sun in Teotihuacan.

Whatever else it is, Golgotha is our ascent into the Cloud of Unknowing, it is our ascent into Tenebrae.

INTRODUCTION

With Aeschylus we came, bringing our religious inheritance, to Areopagus Rock.

In Jesus we climbed in our human condition to the summit of Golgotha-Borobudur.

Good Friday is our exodus from Golgotha as pyramid of the sun to Golgotha as Borobudur.

And yet Golgotha isn't only Borobudur. It is Golgotha-Borobudur.

What I'm saying is, the Classical-Christian tradition isn't immutable.

How could it be, given Aeschylus and Christ?

How could it be, given Areopagus Rock and Golgotha?

There are times when we go to Thermopylae to resist. There are times when we go to make welcome.

To welcome change from within as well as change from without.

As I understand them, the six stories you have such difficulty with could be the lost, last chapters of the Book of Job. Certainly, it wouldn't be altogether inappropriate to imagine that Job's agon opened a door to them.

There is a Leonidas who defends the pass. There is a Job who suffers in it. In the end, deepened and opened by his sufferings, he is himself the pass. He is our biblical Thermopylae. In him the tradition suffers. In its myths and in its metaphors it suffers. In every book of its holy book it suffers. In its rituals it suffers. In its vision of God it suffers. And then, his agon over, Job walks through. Unopposed by Moses, he walks through the pass into a changed religion.

In what way changed?

Changed so as to meet the needs of a people who have come ashore at Punta Alta. Within himself, Nietzsche came ashore there and was ever afterwards in more trouble than he could handle.

Right there on the shore at Punta Alta, what happened to Hippolytus happened to Nietzsche.

What happened to Nietzsche can happen to Anthropus.

And so, knowing how phylogenetically implicated in the evolving earth we have been and are, what do we do?

Either we come ashore, it seems to me, or we become extinct.

Either Nietzsche can integrate his phylogenetic awareness of himself or we go the way of trilobite and dinosaur. Integrating this awareness is the next great step in evolution.

And now again I come back to Gethsemane.

As I understand them, Gethsemane and Punta Alta are one and the same ground.

INTRODUCTION

Christ in Gethsemane is Christ coming ashore.
Christ in Gethsemane is Anthropus coming ashore.

In Christ we have come through the evolutionary challenge. And what we need is a Christianity that can watch with Jesus as he comes through.

To watch with Jesus is to watch with evolving humanity.
To watch with Jesus is to watch with the evolving earth.

And now we are ready to ascend the primeval river, are we? But how sure can we be that this time also the adventure won't end with those terrible words, 'The horror! The horror!'

Inland at night we will know what Blake knew:

The roaring of lions, the howling of wolves, the raging of the stormy sea and the destructive sword are portions of eternity too great for the eye of man.

And yet we must run the risk of commonage consciousness. And that is why this volume includes two stories that I think of as sacraments of reconciliation with animal and plant. Having these sacraments, we have now no need to excavate a labyrinth or to build a city wall. City wall and labyrinth became extinct in Job. In Job, right there at the heart of the biblical world-view, animals and plants began to draw shamanically close to us. There is a good and a blessed way of being a brother to dragons and a companion to owls. There is Old Man's way. There is the way of St Francis.

Also included is a story that celebrates our reconciliation with Takanakapsaluk, the mother of sea beasts, she who lives sometimes shut up in anger on the floor of the ocean or if you like on the floor of *Anima Mundi*. Since Coleridge so misconceived it, this story needs re-telling. And thinking of Takanakapsaluk's anger, it might be timely to suggest that it isn't only a dead albatross that must fall from the neck of our European humanity, the terribly wounded bison bull in the pit in Lascaux must fall from it also. This is how I imagine it happening: at a time of famine in the Pleistocene a girl, still adolescent in her thoughts and feelings, climbed a rock-wall in the Dordogne. Seeing a herd of bison shimmering darkly under a red horizon, she called out or was it that she heard herself calling out: if you will come and be food for my people, I will marry your Chief. The Bull that led her away that night had a spear through his anus, bowel and penis. Up from the pit in Lascaux he had come. He was the Chief, not just of bison. He was Pasupati, lord of animals. It was by his leave that all other animals came and went. It was by his leave that one of them, or two of them, or a few of them would consent to be killed by us. And then

INTRODUCTION

we speared him. At sea we harpooned him. Famine followed. And he only fell from our necks when we learned to say 'we' where formerly we said 'us and them'.

Given his biblical attitudes, it was difficult and very dangerous for Mistah Kurtz to attempt to ascend the primeval river. As for ourselves, all we can do is hope that our attempt will bring us, not into the heart of darkness in which we are overcome by the snake we project into the rope, but into Tenebrae.

Our roots in Time are roots in Eternity. And for as long as we are in the world a blessed way of being reconciled to Divine Ground is to be reconciled to all that has emerged from it. Inside and outside, the primeval can work with us. And this brings us back to the voice of Old Man.

It brings us back to the medicine bundle that Tyger might yet leave behind in a house in South Molton Street, or that Stegosaurus might leave in Anaconda Canoe.

Or that the bison bull might leave in the pit in Lascaux?

Or that Moby might leave in the Whaleman's Chapel in New Bedford. The Whaleman's Chapel is a Christian continuation of the pit in Lascaux. Our Palaeolithic spear embedded in the Bull is our modern harpoon embedded in Moby. It is a terrible tableau, Taurus Dei, Agnus Dei, Cetus Dei, all three of them speared and, sad though it is, the centuries of the Grail Quest and a century of psychoanalysis have left us more or less as we were – not knowing what question to ask and having as a consequence to live with our Amfortas wound. In this book we go down into the pit and in the hope that it will be sacramentally efficacious to do so, we tell the Native American story of our re-entry or re-initiation into commonage consciousness. That's us attempting to live this side of Nietzsche's discovery, of Conrad's discovery. That's us attempting to ascend the Dordogne into our lost Serengeti on a new first morning of the world. It is in six stories, become six sacraments in the telling, that we begin to ascend it.

Those six stories are our canoe. They are Anaconda Canoe transforming itself into six ascending rites of passage. It is by rites of passage not by steamboat that we seek to ascend to civilization and culture.

But we don't only need a religion that will help us to live this side of Nietzsche's discovery or, if you like, this side of the voyage of the *Beagle*. No less urgently, we need a religion that can help us to live this side of Kant's *Critique of Pure Reason*. The religious correlative of that *Critique* is Tenebrae, a ritual quenching, as though they were candles, of our senses and faculties. Not everything is quenched when our senses and faculties

xx

INTRODUCTION

are quenched. It's as if mind is no longer blinded by mental activity. It's as if a kind of miraging were out of the way. And this reminds me of a faded fresco in a thirteenth-century church in France. It depicts the temptation of Eve. Astonishingly, in so far as we can make it out, the Serpent is coiled not about a big, broad-leaved, fruiting tree but about an *amanita muscaria* mushroom. Without warrant, of course, I take it to mean that the Fall was a bum trip. It was a wandering out of Unity into awareness-of-self-and-other-than-self. As the Mandukya Upanishad might have it, it was a wandering out of Turiya into experience of Duality. By this reading, the fresco is a philosophy of mind. And so, Yaje Woman isn't so exotic after all. Naturalized in our culture, we could call her Amanita Muscaria Woman.

> Before colours caused
> Or curved my eyes,
> I was curved
> Where the moon
> Pulls its red face from:
>
> Red and green
> And by Circe swined,
> I was pulled from the roots
> Of my mandrake mind.
>
> My split-level skull
> Divided my mouth:
> As its witch and high priest
> I served cauldron and cup.
>
> And tonight by the sea
> I'm awash, I'm aware
> I am barnacle boned
> And my skull opens up.

We have wandered into the world of Mayashakti, Yajeshakti, Mandragorashakti, Who-Has-an-Illusion, Tatei Hikuri and Grandfather Teonanacatl, all of whom Jesus must resist and walk past on his way into his transtorrentem destiny.

We have wandered into the Kalahari Desert where, his voice like wind in withered scrub, a Bushman tells us that a Dream is dreaming us.

How long till we hear the great question:

> Did you bring the water?

How long till we see that, having Tenebrae, we have the great answer.

Erat autem fere hora sexta et tenebrae factae sunt in universam terram usque in horam nonam. Et obscuratus est sol: et velum templi scissum est medium.

INTRODUCTION

The Gospels have no special claim to the Christ who has come this far. Christianity has no special claim to the Christ who has come this far.

It is for the religions of the world to attempt to comprehend what it means to come this far.

Amanita Muscaria Woman has come to stay, has she?

Her coming among us only means that questions about the nature of mind are now being asked, and answered maybe, in another way. In an Oriental way.

In spite of everything you have said, it isn't yet obvious to me why there is such a sense of heavy foreboding about our attempt to ascend the river.

George Steiner likens the will to scientific discovery to a will to open doors in Bluebeard's Castle. Knowing that, no matter what, we must and will open the final door, he is alarmed:

The real question is whether certain major lines of enquiry ought to be pursued at all, whether society and the human intellect at their present level of evolution can survive the next truths. It may be – and the mere possibility presents dilemmas beyond any which have been in history – that the coming door opens on to realities ontologically opposed to our sanity and limited moral reserves ... it may be that the truths which lie ahead wait in ambush for man ...

It is my belief that in so far as human inwardness is concerned all doors have long ago been opened. Here for a certainty, the next truths are old truths and it isn't today or yesterday that they first ambushed us.

They ambushed us in the Psalmist:

> I am fearfully and wonderfully made.

They ambushed us in Sir Thomas Browne:

> There is all Africa and her prodigies in us.

They ambushed us in Nietzsche:

I have discovered for myself that the old human and animal world, indeed the entire prehistory and past of all sentient being, works on, loves on, hates on, thinks on in me.

They have ambushed us in Hopkins:

> O the mind, mind has mountains, cliffs of fall
> Frightful, sheer, no-man-fathomed. Hold them cheap
> May who ne'er hung there ...

INTRODUCTION

They have ambushed us in Conrad:

The mind of man is capable of anything – because everything is in it, all the past as well as all the future.

Such self-apprehensions have brought us into canyon country. Into inner canyon country. To back out is not the way out. The only way out is through. And that's what I mean when I say we must attempt to ascend the primeval river.

To attempt to ascend the primeval river is to run the risk of total exposure to all that is phylogenetic in us, and as Nietzsche discovered, even in civil surroundings the phylogenetic is neither dormant nor inactive.

> *Seig heil*, the first rose:
> Were it not for that day
> And the robin's first song,
> The Rhine might have shovelled
> The Dark Ages away.
>
> Although God's Gulf Stream
> Flows all night long
> He was Israel's unclean pig,
> The one all Europe would eat
> Between Nero's fiddle and Hitler's jig.

This is a poem about the heart of our European darkness. Not one of our well-known, well-loved rivers but reaches into it, and when we yet again attempt to ascend into it, as far into it as the pit in Lascaux, as far into it as the quarterdeck of the *Pequod*, as far into it as Sophie's choice, it isn't only the possibility of regression that should give us pause. As well as all that we phylogenetically are, we are spirit, and in us therefore is the possibility not just of regression but of Fall.

Neither Nebuchadnezzar nor Lucifer is irrelevant to our condition.

Kurtz didn't only become a Nebuchadnezzar of the place. He became a demon of the place.

'How many powers of darkness', Marlow asks, 'claimed him for their own?'

And if they claimed Kurtz, how sure can we be they can't also claim us? As individuals claim us? Claim us collectively? Claim us to such an extent that the collective life becomes *Mein Kampf* life?

In one of his sonnets to Orpheus, Rilke says:

> Everything perfect reverts
> To the primeval

INTRODUCTION

Civically perfect or nearly so, Job underwent such a reversion. He came home inwardly and outwardly enriched beyond what was normal or normative in his religion and culture.

The question is: is there in the primeval some essential nourishment without which individuals and civilizations will sicken and die?

Contact with the primeval, let alone a reversion to it, is not without stupendous risks, of course.

Talking about his steamboat ascending the Congo, Marlow says: 'Where the pilgrims imagined it crawled to I don't know. To some place where they expected to get something, I bet! For me it crawled towards Kurtz ...'

In this volume we can only hope that it is towards St Kieran in his cluain, not towards Kurtz in his clearing, that we are crawling.

Our journey through Bluebeard's Castle is but a journey through the outer courts of an Interior Castle. Travelling inward by degrees of orison, Teresa of Ávila travelled farther than Kurtz, travelled farther than Freud.

Will all our attempts to ascend the river in a steamboat fail? Will we only ever successfully ascend it in a zoomorphic canoe? Will we only ever successfully ascend it, in other words, when the primeval itself is with us? When, specifically in this case, Anaconda is with us?

Most certainly, Old Man would not attempt to ascend it in a steamboat.

And it wasn't by mechanical movement-local that Job ascended it.

Yet again, the Book of Job is the great alternative to our Western *polla ta deina* way. Way of fantastic tricks. Way that makes the angels weep. Way that has ended in those terrible words, 'The horror! The horror!'

In his contact with behemoth and ostrich and hawk and horse, Job is our contact with our lost Serengeti. There where it underlies our city, where it underlies our eighteenth-century park, he is our contact with Lucy's savannah. Astonishingly, he became neither a Nebuchadnezzar of the place nor a demon of the place.

In his contact with 'Leviathan the crooked serpent, even Leviathan the piercing serpent', Job is our contact with the primordial.

Job is a sacrament of openness to savannah and sea we should annually enact.

That openness the Kwakiutl enact and celebrate in Tsetsekia.

In that openness of our temple door to savannah and sea, our civilization is beginning to have a chance.

As you have imagined it, to ascend the river is to ascend into canyon country. It is to ascend beneath and between all the old seafloors of earth and psyche. Am I right

INTRODUCTION

in thinking that it is your view that we can only survive this awakening to all that we phylogenetically are if it is accompanied by another simultaneous awakening, an epistemological awakening, a Narada awakening?

Think of how ancient Egyptians prepared themselves for their post-mortem journey through the underworld. Forgetting for the moment all other awe-full hazards, there was in that underworld a long river which the wayfarer must ascend. It was called the River of the White Hippopotamus.

The Egyptian Book of the Dead assumes that in our post-mortem ascent this hippopotamus exists independently of our perception of him. The Tibetan Book of the Dead assures us, over and over again, that we need not fear him, the reason for this being that he is a creation of our karmically conditioned minds.

It is because I incline to the epistemology of the Tibetan Book of the Dead rather than to the epistemology of its Egyptian counterpart that this volume begins where it does, with Yaje Woman ascending our river in Anaconda Canoe or, if you like, with Narada ascending our river in Ropesnake Canoe.

And if it is the Amazon we are ascending, then we might one day come among the Uitoto. In their story of origins the creator or maker of all things is called Who-Has-an-Illusion:

Was it not an illusion?

The Father touched an illusory image. He touched a mystery. Nothing was there. The Father, Who-Has-an-Illusion, seized it and, dreaming, began to think.

Had he no staff? Then with a dream-thread he held the illusion. Breathing he held it, the void, the illusion, and felt for its earth. There was nothing to feel. 'I shall gather the void,' he said. He felt, but there was nothing.

Now Who-Has-an-Illusion thought the word 'earth'. He felt for the void, the illusion, and took it in his hands. Who-Has-an-Illusion then gathered the void with dream-thread and pressed it together with gum. With the dream-gum iseike he held it fast.

He seized the illusion, the illusory earth, and he trampled and trampled it, flattening it. Then as he seized it and held it, he stood on it, on this that he'd dreamed, on this that he'd flattened.

As he held the illusion, he salivated, salivated, salivated, and the water flowed from his mouth. Upon this, the illusion, this, as he held it, he settled the sky roof. This, the illusion, he seized, entirely, and peeled off the blue sky, the white sky.

INTRODUCTION

Now in the underworld, thinking and thinking, the maker of myths permitted this story to come into being. This is the story we brought with us when we emerged.

It is my belief that the Uitoto and the Desana can help us to ascend our river. Thanks to them we have two myths that will light our way in the heart of our modern epistemological and phylogenetic darkness.

For religion, as for philosophy, questions about the nature of mind are, in the literal sense of the word, crucial.

Narada ascending the Rhine in Ropesnake Canoe is an invitation to Kant to cross, in Good Friday imitation of Christ, from metaphysics to metanoesis. It is an invitation to him to cross from *Prolegomena to Any Future Metaphysics* to *The Cloud of Unknowing*, from the *Critique of Pure Reason* to *The Dark Night of the Soul*.

It is in this crossing over that our Copernican revolution in philosophy will complete itself.

All of this notwithstanding, there are times in your book when you talk like a naïve realist. Are you aware of this?

Yes, I am. And the reason is simple: I am a naïve realist. By moral imperative, categorical in its demands upon me, I am a naïve realist. Let me try to explain.

In the presence of Jesus in Gethsemane or on Golgotha, it would never occur to me to attempt to console him by telling him that he should think of his sufferings as the unreal sufferings of an unreal ropesnake. Nor would it occur to me to recite Emerson's jingles to a raped woman. It is Brahma who speaks in his poem:

> If the red slayer thinks he slays,
> Or if the slain thinks he is slain,
> They know not well the subtle ways
> I keep, and pass, and turn again.
>
> Far and forgot to me are near;
> Shadow and sunlight are the same;
> The varnished gods to me appear;
> And one to me are shame and fame.
>
> They reckon ill who leave me out;
> When me they fly I am the wings;
> I am the doubter and the doubt,
> And I am the hymn the Brahmin sings.

INTRODUCTION

> The strong gods pine for my abode,
> And pine in vain the sacred seven;
> But thou, meek lover of the good!
> Find me, and turn thy back on heaven.

If Longinus thinks that he has speared Jesus, and if Jesus thinks that he has been speared, then look at me, Ralph Waldo, transcendently wise, emerging unperturbed and refreshed from a siesta which, Brahma be praised, continued from the sixth to the ninth hour. Good heavens! All this Good Friday turbulence! It is so uncivil. No need at all, I say, for a Lamb of God who takes upon himself the sin of the world. Do but climb to the summit of the nearest hill and you will see that the shame of child abuse is in no way different from the fame of St Francis of Assisi's sanctity.

No. I'm not a Docetist.

There is an epistemological way of being Judas not just to Dr Johnson's hurt toe but also to the stone he has kicked.

Under God, and in conscience, the demands of morality overrule the permissions, if that's what they are, of epistemology.

The Christian Borobudur is Golgotha-Borobudur.

And some of the most resplendent of our Christian mahavakyas are agonistic in character:

I have chosen suffering for my consolation and I will gladly bear this and all other torments in the name of the Saviour for as long as it shall please His Majesty.

Thou seemest, Lord, to give severe tests to those who love you, but only that in the extremity of their trials they may learn the greater extremity of thy love.

God felt, God tasted and enjoyed, is indeed God, but God with those gifts which flatter the soul. God in darkness, in privation, in forsakenness, in insensibility, is so much God, that He is so to speak God bare and alone.

Since suffering is real, I conclude that the world in which it occurs is real, even if its reality is best described as will and representation, even if its reality is a dream from which we will one day wake up:

> *Oubli du monde et de tout hormis Dieu.*

So yes. I am, for moral reasons, a naïve realist. And yet, without permission from the Christian *consensus gentium* I have welcomed Narada and Ropesnake into Christian Good News.

Having come to the Hill of the Koshaless Skull, Jesus is Thales to an alternative philosophical tradition. Down the centuries, this tradition has fostered metanoesis not metaphysics.

The Tenebrae harrow is the mystic's Holy Grail.

INTRODUCTION

Big Mike in the first volume, Ishmael in the second and, if only as a haunting possibility, Kurtz in the third. Is this a counter movement to the movement from Paradise Lost to Paradise Regained that you talked about in the general introduction?

Somewhere in the text I explicitly say: if you open the door wide enough to let in God you open it wide enough to let in the devil; if you open it wide enough to let in the light you open it wide enough to let in the dark; if you open it wide enough to let in heaven you open it wide enough to let in hell; if you open it wide enough to let in the great sanity you open it wide enough to let in the great insanity.

In saying this I am neither proposing nor promoting a Manichaean dualism. But it is true that, very shortly after the heavens opened above him in Jordan, Jesus was confronted by Satan. It does seem that no sooner do we wake up spiritually than there he is, the Great Adversary. Whether or not this Great Adversary is a creation of our own terror is not, for the moment, the issue. No one who has encountered him, as the Buddha did on the night of his enlightenment, as Mahavira did in incarnation after incarnation, will be tempted to make light of his numinous enormities.

In the Book of Job he is called the King of Terrors.

King of Terrors. King of Illusions. King of Delusions.

There are Japanese Zen Buddhists who will talk to you about makyo, a realm of devil's illusions you can wander into or be lured into. And it wasn't only once in the course of his conjurings that Yeats was perturbed to find that his via sacra had become a Hodos Chameleontos.

People who in Conrad's phrase live between the butcher and the policeman in a well-trodden, tamed land will tend not to credit this, but

They that go down to the sea in ships, that do business in great waters, they see the works of the Lord and his wonders in the deep …

Wonders and works they see and seeing them they cannot believe that the Lord, their Lord, had any hand in creating them. And that's when the trouble begins:

> Ne wonder if these did the knight appall;
> For all that here on earth we dreadful hold,
> Be but as bugs to fearen babes withall,
> Compared to creatures in the sea's entrall.

Big Mike, Ishmael and Kurtz did business in great waters. Ishmael knows what can happen:

Alone, in such great waters, that though you sailed a thousand miles, and passed a thousand shores, you would not come to any chiselled hearthstone or ought

INTRODUCTION

hospitable beneath that part of the sun; in such latitudes and longitudes, pursuing too such a calling as he does, the whaleman is wrapped by influences all tending to make his fancy pregnant with many a mighty birth.

It recalls the old Anglo-Saxon Seafarer:

min modsefa   mid mereflode
ofer hwaeles ethel   hweorfeth wide

In Pound's translation it reads

my mood   mid the mereflood
over the whale's acre   would wander wide.

I am trying to draw attention to the dangers of extravagance, to the dangers, in the literal sense of *extra-vagare*, of wandering beyond.

Big Mike was extravagant. So in their different ways were Ishmael and Kurtz.

Ishmael warns us: consider them both, the sea and the land; and do you not find a strange analogy to something in yourself? For as this appalling ocean surrrounds the verdant land, so in the soul of man there lies one insular Tahiti, full of peace and joy, but encompassed by all the horrors of the half-known life. God keep thee! Push not off from that isle, thou canst never return!

Big Mike came home to his island.

And where Kurtz whispered 'The horror! The horror!', Big Mike one night called out:

> The fishing is good.
> The fishing is very good.
> The fishing, not fishing at all,
> Is blessedness, is bliss.

The two Udanas, one of despair and one of hope, that continue to haunt extravagant humanity.

To Big Mike not to Kurtz belong the last words about our prospects.

But Kurtz remains a dreadful possibility.

For the seafarer in particular, for the extravagant one, he remains a dreadful possibility.

It is only in total surrender to divine good-shepherding that we will come through our wide-wandering in the whale's acre.

It is only in total surrender to divine good-shepherding that we will come through the dissolution of our rock of faith into the abyss of faith, into the Tehom of faith, into the Tao-Tehom-Turiya of faith.

INTRODUCTION

And yet, for all the dangers that wait upon our efforts to regain it, Paradise can be regained.

Big Mike called out, sang out, his Udana in the first volume. Why did the book not end there? Why the next two volumes?

However many and various his metamorphoses, the hero of this book is a culture hero, he must bring home the boon, and that is a much more difficult task than it might at first sight seem. It isn't with a simple wave of a wand that he will institute his wisdom. It isn't overnight and without opposition that he will bring his people with him. Just think of how expectantly long he might have to wait for the necessary metaphors, the necessary myths. Just think of how expectantly long he might have to wait for the necessary rites of passage. Just think of how expectantly long he might have to wait for a vision of the centre that will hold. The hero's anodos into social significance will very often be as difficult as his kathodos.

Concerning the kind of Christianity or, indeed, concerning the type of religion that emerges in your book: am I right in thinking that it is much less concerned with obedience to divine command than it is with assimilation to anterior archetype, biblical and non-biblical. In it, even Jesus himself is assimilated to A'noshma enduring the abyss in the age of the world's night, to Vishnu recumbent on the coils of Ananta and to Venus rising from the sea. Such assimilation to archetype is the clear contrary, isn't it, of our modern emphasis on the inviolable uniqueness of the individual?

First, in regard to archetypes biblical and non-biblical, may I remind you of something Blake said:

The antiquities of every nation under heaven is no less sacred than that of the Jews ...

Not all ancient, sacred traditions are equally enlightened, of course. A Toltec priest who sets out to climb the Pyramid of the Sun in Teotihuacan in Mexico will have very different expectations from those of a Buddhist monk who sets out to climb Borobudur in Java. And yet, in spirit if not in achievement, this book is a kind of panethnic walkabout, and this is so because the Christ we encounter here is neither culture-bound nor bound by the master metaphors of any particular religion. He is himself panethnic. It is pan-ethnically that he underwent our transtorrentem destiny, and it is drawing on the illuminating resources of no matter what religion or culture that we will deepen our understanding of what occurred in him. Hence the seemingly outlandish figurations:

INTRODUCTION

A'noshma Jesu
Jesu Anantasayin
Jesu Anadyomene

To say Jesu Anadyomene is not to imply that the anodos of Jesus is in all ways identical to the anodos of Venus. Nor is it to imply that Jesus, being the newcomer, is the one who is being assimilated to a transition that first realized itself in Venus. In this, as in so much else, archetypal priority is a function not of temporal precedence but of profundity.

Archetypally, Christ is prior to Persephone, Horus and Tammuz. He is prior to all who came back from beyond or below, and this is so because in him anodos is not anodos out of but anodos with. In him, however slowly, the whole of our underworld is coming forth by day.

Let us call it

The Pananodos

St Paul would have us live baptismally:

Know ye not, that so many of us as were baptized into Jesus Christ were baptized into his death. Therefore, we are buried with him by baptism into death: that like as Christ was raised up from the dead by the glory of the Father, even so we also should walk in newness of life.

To live baptismally is to participate willingly and with full, gracious consent to the anodos of all things.

To live baptismally is to be willing to be divinely goodshepherded into and through our transtorrentem destiny.

To live baptismally is to be willing to undergo our final evolutionary transitions:

Gethsemane
Golgotha
Garden of the Sepulchre

As important as the process of individuation that Jung talks about is the process of archetypalization that St Paul talks about.

D.H. Lawrence claimed that the adventure is gone out of Christianity. And when he proposed a new venture towards God, he presumably believed that Christianity will have as little part in it as it has had in the adventure of science in the modern West. If, like astrology, Christianity has had its day, doesn't it follow that your book is an oddity, already outmoded at birth?

INTRODUCTION

Having regard to humanity generally, I have elsewhere asked three questions: are we AIDS virus to the evolving earth? Are we the iceberg into which the voyaging earth has crashed? Have we lost or have we ever acquired evolutionary legitimacy?

If, given the evidence against us, these can be admitted as prosecuting questions, then we mustn't seek to evade conviction by entering the plea that, in virtue of the religion or race we belong to, we are mere oddities.

I'm attempting to remind you that Lawrence didn't only talk about the end of the Christian adventure, he talked about the death of our era, the doom of our white day:

> Our era is dying
> yet who has killed it?
> Have we, who are it?
>
> In the middle of voluted space
> the knell has struck.
> And in the middle of every atom, which is the same thing,
> a tiny bell of conclusion has sounded ...

This would suggest that it isn't only Christians who are outmoded. But Lawrence isn't downcast:

> There are said to be creative pauses,
> pauses that are as good as death, empty and dead as death itself.
> And in these awful pauses the evolutionary change takes place.
> Perhaps it is so.
> The tragedy is over, it has ceased to be tragic, the last pause is upon us.
> Pause, brethren, pause!

Lao Tzu has long ago told us how we should be within that pause:

> Blank as a piece of uncarved wood
> Yet receptive as a hollow in the hills.

Could it be that, more by providence than by chance, a raft and a canoe will be waiting for us within that pause? Could it be that something more profound than the primeval is on our side? Could it be that the shape of the universe is the shape of Shiva's abhaya mudra?

You have, as if by a kind of sleight of hand, by a kind of sleight of mind, evaded my question.

Ironically, in view of how you posed that question, it is astrologically that Lawrence announced the end of Christianity:

INTRODUCTION

> Dawn is no longer in the house of the Fish
> Pisces, oh Fish, Jesus of the watery way,
> Your two thousand years are up.
>
> And the foot of the Cross no longer is planted in the
> place of the birth of the Sun.
> The whole great heavens have shifted over, and slowly
> pushed aside the Cross, the Virgin, Pisces ...

I cannot imagine that the heavens will ever push aside metamorphosis in insects or puberty in persons. Neither can I imagine that they will cut us off from our transtorrentem destiny. To do so would be to terminate the evolution of the hitherto evolving earth.

And as for Christianity having lost its original will to adventure: is it not we, the peoples of the West, who have lost that will? And have we lost it because we have lost the vision that would inspire it? Here at home on earth is the place of our farthest voyaging. No one will ever journey more deeply into the universe than Jesus did in Gethsemane.

If a real, worthwhile journey is what you desire, then board a Hozhonji song, not the Greyhound Express.

I'll say that again. I will say it more elaborately: if a worthwhile voyage is what you desire, then board the Triduum Sacrum, not a spaceship.

Let us recall the opening, great sentence of a recent, great adventure:

After having been twice driven back by heavy south-western gales, Her Majesty's ship *Beagle*, a ten-gun brig, under the command of Captain Fitzroy, R.N., sailed from Devonport on the 27th of December.

A Darwin who boarded his baptism would have set out on an altogether more stupendous voyage than the young naturalist who boarded the *Beagle*.

In the course of his voyage on board the *Beagle* Darwin observed the fact of evolution. In the course of his voyage on board his baptism, evolution might well have undergone its final transitions in him.

For as long as Western history hasn't caught up with the Triduum Sacrum and organized itself in sacramental participation around it, for so long will it continue to be an evolutionary oddity. A vanity.

Speaking of Oddities. Of all the odd ideas in your book there is none so vainly odd as the assumption that the past can be changed. Encountering this idea, it is hard not to conclude that instead of following Bright Angel in broad daylight we have fallen asleep and are following White Rabbit, to a very mad tea-party.

With your leave, I'll follow White Rabbit awake:

INTRODUCTION

The Babylonian story of origins is named from its first two words, *Enuma Elish*. This is how it begins:

> When there was no heaven, no earth,
> no height, no depth, no name,
> When Apsu was alone,
> he, the sweet water, the first begetter; and Tiamat
> she, the bitter water, and that
> return to the womb, her Mummu,
> when there were no gods —
>
> When sweet and bitter
> mingled together, no reed was plaited, no rushes
> muddied the water,
> the gods were nameless, natureless, featureless, then
> from Apsu and Tiamat
> in the waters gods were created, in the waters
> silt precipitated.
>
> Lahmu and Lahamu
> were named; they were not yet old,
> not yet grown tall ...

Lahmu and Lahamu, the first silts, the first precipitations of earth and psyche — to these we must always keep the trail open, with these we must always stay in contact.

It is on clay tablets made from these first silts that we, the new Sumerians, should inscribe our new Enuma Elish, our new story of origins.

For as long as we assent to it, our story of origins isn't only a tale told. It is forms of our sensibility and categories of our understanding. It is our way of being in the world. It is who we religiously and culturally are.

From these first silts, from these first precipitations of earth and psyche, we make the bricks with which we build our first temple. A temple that houses the Divine Silence when there was as yet no heaven, no earth, no height, no depth, no name.

In it the Divine hasn't yet become goddess or god. It is therefore anterior to rite. It is too sacredly silent for acts of worship. And we don't go into it.

We might call it our Turiya Temple.

Lahmu and Lahamu are the outer and Tiamat and Apsu are the inner doorkeepers of its great portal.

In and with this temple, we are giving ourselves a new Sumer and a new ancient Egypt. In it and with it we are giving ourselves a new ancient Middle East, a new ancient Near East.

INTRODUCTION

From it a new West might emerge.

The question is: how can we be well in our Lady Chapel if we aren't well in the Lascaux that underlies it? How can we be well in our eighteenth-century park if we aren't well in the Serengeti that underlies it? How can we be well in Old Compton Street if we aren't well in the canyon that underlies it? How can all be well with us in our relationship to a Lord above if all isn't well with us in our relationship to Lords Lahmu and Lahamu below?

How until Bright Angel Trail is aisle can we say we are well? Can we say we are on the way to being well?

As I see it, the song evolution sings in a Silurian sea it sings again in Gethsemane. Scandalously, in the sense that it will scandalize Darwinians, I believe that the Gunflint cherts, Galapagos, Gethsemane and Golgotha are verses of the same song and the song is such that any one verse of it has in it all other verses, whether before or after. However vast the expanse of apparent time that separates them, the Gunflint cherts are simultaneous with Golgotha and Gethsemane is simultaneous with Galapagos. In Gethsemane, Jesus is Vishvayuga. In him the karma of all the ages is conciously integrated. In him nature in all its ages and strata encounters grace. In him, nature in all its ages and strata passes through the purifying fire, and that is agony. The agony in the Garden belongs to the same evolving story that the Gunflint cherts do, and they are happening together.

> Time present and time past
> Are both perhaps present in time future
> And time future contained in time past

The trail is aisle. The Rose Window is retina to Stegosaurus. In Modern, Medieval and Mesozoic time now, it is retina to evolution and lens to our Hubble telescope. And it is only because this is so that we are seeing the universe as it so gloriously is.

Thinking now again of the stories with which this volume begins: Ted Hughes has said that a mind that has many stories is a small early Greece. Have you told these stories in the belief that they have in them the potencies of alternative beginnings?

I take the point about a mind that has many stories, but why in particular should such a mind be a small early Greece? Why not a small early Amazonia, a small early Australia, a small early Siberia, a small early American Southwest? Why not a small Aurignacian Dordogne?

Much as a very bright and very excitable schoolboy might, Nietzsche believed that in matters of culture all other peoples were horses and chariots to the Greeks. Holding the reins, Greeks were the leaders, Greeks were the drivers, Greeks knew the way.

Just listen to him:

And so one feels ashamed and afraid in the presence of the Greeks, unless one prizes the truth above all things and dares acknowledge even this truth: that the Greeks, as charioteers, hold in their hands the reins of our own and every other culture, but that almost always chariot and horses are of inferior quality and not up to the glory of their leaders, who consider it sport to run such a team into the abyss which they themselves clear with the leap of Achilles.

Let us imagine it:

The *Iliad* arrogating to itself the right to be charioteer to the *Mahabharata*.

Plato's *Timaeus* arrogating to itself the right to be charioteer to the Maori story of origins.

Aristotle's *Nichomachaean Ethics* arrogating to itself the right to be charioteer to the Tao Te Ching.

Socrates arrogating to himself the right to be charioteer to Black Elk.

The Parthenon arrogating to itself the right to be charioteer to Byodo-in.

The story of Ariadne and the Minotaur arrogating to itself the right to be charioteer to the story of the Blackfoot maiden and the bison bull.

Sophocles' Theban plays arrogating to themselves the right to be charioteer to the Triduum Sacrum.

Standing under a hole in the ozone layer, it isn't altogether an ingratitude to remember that the bronze charioteer in Delphi is left holding a broken reins.

To look at him is to wonder whether civilization ever dawned so confidently as it did in him.

Yet now, a Pythia, who is also a ventriloquist, might have him whisper: 'The horror! The horror!'

Being a small early Greece, or a small early Israel, or a small early Rome, mightn't be the most auspicious of beginnings.

There is a dream in which, manure fork in hand, you do what Job did, you walk out of civilization into the savannah that underlies it. You do this, very deliberately it would seem, in all three volumes. Why?

The sacred stories that you come upon in this book aren't only tales told. They are enabling sacraments. If you like, they are rites of passage, they are initiations. In them and through them and by them we approach the

INTRODUCTION

earth and set foot on it. In them and through them and by them we become Earth Initiates. In this regard, there is in the book a clear difference between the way Noah approaches the earth and the way Neil Armstrong approaches the moon. Neil Armstrong didn't, I imagine, become a Moon Initiate. Setting foot on it in the way that he did is of no value to him or to us. It is by rite of passage that we should voyage. Hence, the dream. Stand back a little from that dream and you will see that in it we ascend the river. In it, walking home alone from his funeral oration, Pericles turns into Old Compton Street.

It isn't, in other words, because of our victories at Marathon and Salamis that our city is safely founded. It is safely founded only when Pericles has successfully undergone what Job underwent. Indeed it is safely founded only when everyone who lives in it has successfully undergone what Job underwent.

Pericles turning into Old Compton Street.

Ishmael turning into Rue Dauphine.

That's the dream. And the dream is repeated because: *gyrans gyrando spiritus vadit*.

Also, our walk with the dreamer into the savannah and our walk with Vishnu into the desert are reaches of a single songline. The hope is that in our religion and culture this songline will take over from the wake of the *Pequod*.

And here, an opportunity having presented itself, may I suggest that this is a book of songlines. Its songlines are spiritual-psychological, are epistemological, not geophysical. In this sense the Book of Job is a songline. Christ's passion and death and resurrection are a songline. Orestes walking to Athens is a songline. Oedipus walking to Colonus is a songline. Our walk with Newton, Hume and Kant is a songline. And, be he Nebuchadnezzar, Pericles or Job, the dreamer walking into the savannah under his city is a songline. Our efforts to ascend the primeval river, the karmic river, is a songline. Collectively, all these songlines are a single songline. Bright Angel Trail is the songline this book would walk. However unconsciously, it is the Trail we walk when we walk Marduk Street in Babylon, Rue Dauphine in Paris, Old Compton Street in London.

H C E Here Cometh Everyone, manure fork in hand.

The opportunity to acquire evolutionary legitimacy remains. Indeed, the opportunity to find and negotiate the evolutionary channel remains.

And we didn't need a Galahad to draw the manure fork from the stone.

When, in the Maidu story of origins, Earth-Initiate needed a rope and a stone, there they were, he only had to reach for them.

At a depth of ourselves and our world, the world is on our side.

INTRODUCTION

And we didn't set out to charm the monster as Orpheus would. And we didn't set out to club him to death as Hercules would.

The grid goes up, and that is Gethsemane.

Gethsemane is evolutionary good news.

Have you, without explicit prompting, expected us to conclude that the dreamer with his manure fork has taken over from Hercules with his club?

Here I must enter a most serious caveat. We sometimes talk about the dreamer of a dream when we should, in reverent self-removal from all claim to authorship, talk rather about the seer of a dream, the epoptes of a dream. The only thing that is asked of the epoptes of a dream is that he or she would self-effacedly report it. Further to what we have already said about it, we can say of the dream you refer to that it is a Tsetsekia enacted by the psyche within the psyche, and I therefore incline to the view that it has transindividual significance. I will leave it to yourself to imagine the vast cultural consequences that would ensue were we to substitute Tsetsekia for the killing labours of Hercules or, more pertinently perhaps, for the killing labours of Theseus on his way from Troezen to Athens. To kill Hydra is not to be liberated from Hydra. To kill Sinis is not to be liberated from Sinis. All the killing wounds that preceded civilization and culture are also wounds to ourselves. Not one of them but came to the surface in Jesus, killing him, on Good Friday.

Better Hercules Hydrasayin than Hercules with Hydra hanging from his neck.

So yes, the book does substitute Passion for Labour. It subsitutes the manure fork for the club.

It is with the manure fork and the Tenebrae harrow that we will go forward into what Amerigo Vespucci called Mundus Novus, into what with more insight St Paul called newness of life and Dante called *Vita Nuova*.

Are you insisting that in any estimation of our human condition we must take account not just of the physical gravity that Newton talked about but of the karmic gravity that Coleridge talked about?

Yes. We boast about our mechanical ability to overcome the gravity of the earth. We have set foot on the moon. But what about what's hanging from our necks?

> Ah! well a-day! what evil looks
> Had I from old and young!

INTRODUCTION

> Instead of the cross, the Albatross
> About my neck was hung.

And in that Albatross is Tiamat, Taurus, Typhon, Leviathan and Draco. In it, adding to its weight, are all the monsters we have slain in our efforts to make the earth safe for civilization.

To emerge from the downward pull of the albatross is altogether more liberating than to emerge from the downward pull of the earth.

And how wonderful it is to listen to Coleridge as he celebrates our psychological, moral emergence:

> Beyond the shadow of the ship
> I watched the water-snakes:
> They moved in tracks of shining white,
> And when they reared, the elfish light
> Fell off in hoary flakes.
>
> Within the shadow of the ship
> I watched their rich attire:
> Blue, glossy green, and velvet black,
> They coiled and swam; and every track
> Was a flash of golden fire.
>
> O happy living things! no tongue
> Their beauty might declare:
> A spring of love gushed from my heart,
> And I blessed them unaware:
> Sure my kind saint took pity on me
> And I blessed them unaware.
>
> The self same moment I could pray;
> And from my neck so free
> The Albatross fell off, and sank
> Like lead into the sea.

This, as Coleridge imagines it, is something that happens to one man, the Ancient Mariner. But can't we imagine, as this book does, that it is something that has happened to us all? In that it has happened to Christ, within the Triduum Sacrum, can't we imagine that it has happened to us all?

The authors of Arthurian romance were right. Much of our inner and therefore of our outer history has turned and continues to turn on a dolorous stroke.

Dolorous stroke or protarchos ate.

And be he bison bull or bull whale, our spear is still embedded in his power to generate.

INTRODUCTION

And for as long as it is embedded in his power to generate it is embedded in our power to generate.

Generating ourselves we unconsciously generate the spear.

The *Pequod* at sea is the Nave at sea, is Esagila at sea, is the pit in Lascaux at sea.

Coleridge and Melville have written the not always subterranean subplot of our long and troubled history from the palaeolithic to the present or, more graphically, from the pit in Lascaux to the quarterdeck of the *Pequod*.

But that isn't the whole story.

Over and above the dolorous stroke depicted in the pit in Lascaux is the dolorous stroke the modern West is philosophically founded on. Concerning this latter, it's as if Newton, Hume and Kant were the Queequeg, the Tashtego and the Daggoo of the modern phase of our voyage. They had already done what Ahab so wanted to do. They had struck through the mask, leaving Coleridge, Arnold and Stevens to suffer the inevitable desolation. It wasn't only they, of course, who suffered. They differ from innumerable others only in that they suffered it publicly in public poems.

Schopenhauer wasn't tempted either to hide from or deny the enormity of what had happened:

Kant has blown the old dogmatic theology to bits and the world stands appalled among the smoking ruins.

Neither was Yeats:

Descartes, Locke and Newton took away the world and gave us its excrement instead.

There is in all of this a kind of Good Friday dereliction.

It's as if we who had hoped for an illumination have found ourselves engulfed in a tenebration.

But what if tenebration were the answer, or a way to the answer?

Let us imagine the hall of the round table in Camelot.

Let us imagine it in Arthur's day and in our day.

In Arthur's day the Grail passed through.

In our day, signifying a deeper call in a time of deeper need, the Tenebrae harrow has passed through.

The question is, will we do what Arthur's knights did, will we follow?

Supposing Newton, Hume and Kant had followed.

However epistemologically bedraggled they looked riding out, can't we imagine them sitting high on their horses, and looking like Magi, riding home?

INTRODUCTION

With what good news?

That the wonder-eye isn't a third eye. That the wonder-eye is a new kind of seeing in the eyes we already have.

Can we say of your book what we can say of the Book of Job, that it attempts to take humanity across a threshold?

No. This book doesn't play at being God. And I seriously hope that it cannot be charged in either content, thrust or tone with anything resembling Luciferian superbia. Such superbia as is for instance implied in Heidegger's description of the poet as a shepherd of being. Just imagine it: Holderlin walking ahead of the evolving universe, walking ahead of it as a pillar of cloud by day, as a pillar of fire by night. In this, as in so much else, Western humanity is walking in the Great Trangression. In this, as in so much else, Western humanity has chosen Psalm eight not Psalm twenty-three as its Magna Carta.

Ecce Ahab

Ahab laying unholy hold of the lightning on the barepoled *Pequod*.

That said, the book seeks to be aware of the evolutionary threshold Jesus crossed when he crossed the Kedron. And here's the rub: it presumes to stay awake where Peter, James and John fell asleep. And God knows, that in itself is a presumption that mightn't be either safe or sane.

Underlying the book, giving it its impetus and shape, is a thesis somewhat as follows: if Jesus has crossed an evolutionary threshold, then there is a sense in which humanity has crossed it, and this implies that to watch with Jesus is to watch with evolving humanity. It implies that to watch with him is to watch with the evolving earth.

In the passional sense, this is a book that would watch. As though they were shepherd's lanterns, it watches with myths, metaphors and mahavakyas. In Tenebrae all our lanterns, inner and outer, are quenched. Quenched we watch, waiting on God. And that is the burden of the song this book would sing.

Not everyone will be happy to hear that the Tenebrae harrow is the Grail of our day.

It is above all in the course of undergoing tenebration that we experience a certain kind of illumination. In particular it mediates an insight into the nature and limits of mind. Striking through the mask is in many ways striking through mind, and the mythic equivalent of this is Narada coming through the pass, is Yaje Woman ascending our river.

INTRODUCTION

And you think of Narada as an epistemological Cortez from the East and you think of Yaje Woman as an epistemological Conquistador from the West?

Yes, we have suffered an epistemological dolorous stroke. Or in terms more consistent with your question, we have for a long time now been enduring an epistemological Year One Reed. But that isn't anything a Christian isn't prepared for. On Golgotha, in the person of Jesus, European philosophy moved house. It moved from metaphysics to metanoesis. And so we can imagine the final philosophical tableau: Jesus looking down into Adam's empty skull, and standing either side of him, dying by reason of his victory, Yaje Woman and King Soma.

So yes, not everyone will be happy to hear that the Tenebrae harrow is the Grail of our day. But how else except in following it can we cope with what we have discovered about ourselves? How else can we cope with Nietzsche's discoveries?

It is because they lie across our introspective path and threaten us therefore in our integrity as persons that these discoveries so challenge us into our next evolutionary transitions. In the case of the first discovery an evolutionary transition as big as Gethsemane. In the case of the second discovery an evolutionary transition as big as Golgotha.

We are talking about our transtorrentem destiny.

To refuse our transtorrentem destiny is to refuse the remedy.

Nietzsche refused the remedy and in this he is in some degree exemplary, in some degree eponymous, to us who have come after him.

It is at our peril that we will leave things there.

It is at our peril that we will turn away from Bright Angel Trail and set our unenlightened sights on the Moon and Mars.

Evolution is with whoever is willing to set foot on the Trail.

Evolution is with whoever is willing to set foot on the Earth.

Evolution is with us crossing the Kedron.

So ride on Isaac, ride on David, ride on Emmanuel.

Emmanuel means God with us.

God is with us in our final evolutionary transitions.

God is with us in our final integration, in our final kenosis.

God is with us in our exodus from metaphysics to metanoesis.

God is with us riding out as scientists and philosophers, riding home as Magi.

It's a harsh book you have written, isn't it? A harsh book mediating a harsh view of life. You say in it that ever since Jesus set foot on it, Bright Angel Trail is aisle. And yet, walking it as it opens out before us in your book, we are much more likely

INTRODUCTION

to meet the Minotaur than the Madonna. Walking it we are much more likely to hear the screaming of archaeornis between canyon rock-walls, than to hear a boy soprano singing Pie Jesu.

However inaccurate his facts, Joseph Campbell makes a point that is worth listening to when he alerts us to

the now well-proven fact that the nervous system was governor, guide and controller of a nomadic hunter foraging for his food and protecting himself and his family from becoming food in a very dangerous world of animals for the first 600,000 years of its development, whereas it has been serving comparatively safe and sane farmers, merchants, professors and their children for scarcely 8000 years. Who will claim to know what sign-stimuli smote our releasing mechanisms when our names were not *homo sapiens* but Pithecanthropus and Plesianthropus or perhaps, even millenniums earlier, Dryopithecus? And who that has knowledge of the numerous, vestigial structures of our anatomy surviving from the days when we were beasts would doubt that in the central nervous system comparable vestiges must remain: images sleeping whose releasers no longer appear in nature – but might occur in art.

In Jung, this becomes something of a philosophy by which to live:

Do we ever understand what we think? We understand only such thinking as is a mere equation and from which nothing comes out but what we have put in. That is the manner of the working of the intellect. But beyond that there is thinking in primordial images – in symbols that are older than historical man; which have been imagined in him from earliest times, and, eternally living, outlasting all generations, still make up the groundwork of the human psyche. It is possible to live the fullest life only when we are in harmony with these symbols; wisdom is a return to them.

D.H. Lawrence was persuaded that in our struggle onwards and upwards into greater consciousness

Our road may have to take a great swerve, that seems a retrogression.

Later he asserts the same idea with but little variation:

Yet, as I say, we must make a great swerve in our onward-going life-course now, to gather up again the savage mysteries. But this does not mean going back on ourselves.

This book does gather up some of the savage mysteries, and it does think in primordial images, not for the heck of it, but because it is a need of the human psyche to do so. The determination of philosophers such as Descartes and Locke to avoid thinking in such images is, almost, a new protarchos ate. However, I do not desire to go past

INTRODUCTION

either man's house in an Anaconda Canoe, nor do I desire to set up a Blue Thunder Tipi in either man's lawn. Also, I don't go all the way with Jung. I don't accept that life in harmony with these images is fullest life. I don't accept that life in harmony with them is wisdom. And that is why in this book the primordial songline grows into the mystical songline, or better, that's why it is subsumed into it. In this last volume Shenona Sagara takes over from Bright Angel.

The illuminations that come with the dark night of the soul aren't mediated by images, savage or civilized.

There is a knowing that isn't mediated by a means of knowing; that isn't obscured or modified by a means of knowing.

There is an unmediated knowing.

That said, I do take your point about the book. And yet, harsh though it is, Golgotha is a Parnassus, and that is good news in the labyrinth, that is good tidings in the canyon.

You are being cryptic.

Going down into our inner hell after his death on a cross, going down into it to harrow it, Jesus didn't seek to do what Orpheus did. Having no lyre but his wounds, he didn't seek to charm the powers. Having come this far by another way, Jesus was more honest than Orpheus. He was more successful.

Are you saying that beauty is ineffective?

No. If we have to have them, our prisons should be as beautiful as cathedrals. That way, when we walk among the mountains, we won't need to feel ashamed.

Your view of Western civilization, your view of it as doomed, how seriously do you take that?

In Nordic mythology, Odin is the great god. One day he conjures a volva, a seeress, and he asks her to foretell the future. This she does, chanting a tremendous, alliterative dirge called Voluspa. In it, in visionary pre-enactment, Odin pre-experiences the cataclysmic end of his world.

This book is a kind of Voluspa. As indeed is a poem in the first volume called 'Missa Tuba Mirum'. It differs from its Nordic original in that it talks not about the end of the world but about the end of a way of being in the world. The hope is that when this happens the raft and the canoe will be waiting for us.

INTRODUCTION

The raft of the Maidu waiting for us in the abyss. And the Anaconda Canoe of the Desana waiting for us at the mouth of primordial river.

This time, seeking integration not repression, we must reach into the canyon. This time, our survival as a species depending on it, we must seek to negotiate the evolutionary channel.

Interesting in this regard is the mesektet boat or night boat of the ancient Egyptian sungod, Atum Re. It was in this boat that he journeyed every night through the underworld. A particularly awful reach of this journey could be negotiated only when the boat had become a serpent. So there, in our own tradition, we have it, a serpent canoe, a cobra canoe. In it, the primeval on our side, we are coming forth by day. And so we see that an old Greek song that began with the words *polla ta deina* has been replaced by an old Egyptian song that ends with the words *pert em hru*. In their original epiphany this is how they look:

So yes. I seriously believe that the evolving earth is with the raft and the canoe in a way that, for the moment, it isn't with Sputnik. Putting it another way: I believe that, for the moment, the evolving earth is with the one who wears the megalonschema more than it is with the one who wears a spacesuit. Implicit in all of this is the literally awful, awe-full question: is there a God who will endure with us and, if neccessary, for us, in the channel?

Seeing how sore amazed Jesus is, and hearing him cry out from the bleak timbers, I believe there is.

Yes, there are mornings, Easter mornings we call them, when the terrible, dead weight of ancient wrong has fallen from us. Our protarchos ate, our act of primal madness, Aeschylus would call it, that ancient wrong.

All through history our house, our house of culture, has been a troubled house. It has been a House of Atreus. No less than Electra was, no less than Orestes was, we are Atreidae. And now, more than ever now, we are doing to Gaia what we did to Tiamat, what we did to Taurus. From Marduk to Ahab, from the Birdman to the Ancient Mariner – what a dreadful cycle! But the cycle was broken in Christ, by Christ, on Calvary. Calvary, that rough little hill, is our Areopagus Rock. And maybe we should excavate a theatre, a Christian amphitheatre, out of that hill, and then we can imagine them, the Easter morning Marys, choephoroi now,

INTRODUCTION

pouring a libation for the damaged Earth, pouring a libation for the damaged sky.

At the heart of your book is Turtle's longing for a world to come ashore on. I cannot quite see how this is relevant to us. Would you enlighten me?

Noah lost the world physically. Over the last three centuries we have lost it, or we have as good as lost it, epistemologically. Let us listen to Newton:

If at any time I speak of light as coloured or endued with colour, I would be understood to speak not philosophically and properly, but grossly and accordingly to such conceptions as vulgar people in seeing all these experiments would be apt to frame. For the rays, to speak properly, are not coloured. In them there is nothing else than a certain power and disposition to stir up a sensation of this or that colour. For as sound in a bell or musical string, or other sounding body, is nothing but the trembling motion, and in the air nothing but that motion propagated from the object, and in the sensorium it is a sense of that motion under the form of sound, so colours in the object are nothing but a disposition to reflect this or that sort of rays more copiously than the rest; in the rays they are nothing but their disposition to propagate this or that motion into the sensorium and in the sensorium they are sensations of these motions under the form of colour.

Before he released the rains and the diluvian waters that would eventually cover the earth and all its high hills fifteen cubits upwards, the Lord god of the Old Testament declared: The end of all flesh is come before me. Here, in this passage by Newton, the end of naïve realism came yet again before us. In the presence of the colourless, cold, inanimate world, Coleridge sank into dejection. Hoping to find solace and meaning in human relationships, Arnold turned away. As though he were *all the king's horses and all the king's men*, Wallace Stevens laboured at putting the subjective and the objective together again. Not overprone to 'bookish theoric', Ahab forged a harpoon and, vengefully in the name of the devil, he baptized it, tempered it, in the savage blood of Queequeg, Tashtego and Daggoo. It is our Excalibur. It is our bleeding lance. It bleeds with the blood of Taurus Dei, Agnus Dei, Albatross Dei and Cetus Dei. Epistemologically in Ahab's hand, it bleeds with the blood of Ropesnake. But Ropesnake is a strange Cheshire cat. Having no substance, he survives our assault. That harpoon wound hanging in the void – that's him – having his last laugh.

In the Great Deep, like Turtle, Ishmael has no world to come ashore on:

And when we consider that other theory of the natural philosophers, that all other earthly hues – every stately or lovely emblazoning – the sweet tinges of

INTRODUCTION

sunset skies and woods; yea, and the gilded velvets of butterflies, and the butterfly cheeks of young girls; all these are but subtile deceits, not actually inherent in substances, but only laid on from without; so that all deified Nature absolutely paints like the harlot, whose allurements cover nothing but the charnel-house within; and when we proceed further, and consider that the mystical cosmetic which produces every one of her hues, the great principle of light, for ever remains white or colourless in itself and if operating without medium on matter, would touch all objects, even tulips and roses, with its own blank tinge – pondering all this, the palsied universe lies before us a leper …

Ishmael is telling Odysseus that the sea isn't winedark, he is telling him that dawn isn't rosy-fingered, he is telling him that instead of delighting in the whiteness of Nausicaa's white arms he should see in it the colourless all-colour of atheism. He is telling him that for all its enchantment and charm Ogygia is a palsied outcrop of a palsied universe. He is telling him that any beach of Ithaca he lands on will be a Dover Beach, a beach in Ulro. And this is where this book begins:

> That it might see us,
> Understand,
> We solved the earth.
>
> That it might see us,
> Show its hand,
> We blitz the rock with metaphors.
> We blitz the land.

Odysseus was able for the Sirens, for the Lotus Eaters, for Polyphemus, for Circe. He was able for the terrors and enchantments of a world that hadn't yet come asunder into the Scylla of appearance and the Charybdis of reality. An able man he was, Odysseus, our ancient Odysseus. But what of our modern Odysseus? Will he be able for what he will discover about himself in the pit in Lascaux? Will he be able for what he will discover about himself on the beach at Punta Alta? Will he be able for the Ulro roar of Dover Beach? Will he be able for the River of the White Hippopotamus? Will he be able for its canyons? Will he be able for nights alone in the heart of darkness?

Will he be able for the epistemological insight that is lying in wait for him in the common etymon of cosmos and cosmetic?

Will he be able for this sentence:

… the sweet tinges of sunset skies and woods; yea, and the gilded velvets of butterflies, and the butterfly cheeks of young girls; all these are but subtile deceits, not actually inherent in substances, but only laid on from without …

INTRODUCTION

Kant argued that space and time are *a priori* forms of our sensibility. As such they are as it were laid on, so that we now talk not of things but of phenomena.

Laid on, projected, superimposed – as when for instance we superimpose a snake onto a rope.

In Sanskrit adhyropa is the word for superimposition and apavada is the word for de-superimposition.

Newton de-superimposed the colour that Homer had superimposed on the sea.

Newton de-superimposed the colour that Homer had superimposed on the dawn.

It might be that Hume's arguments will not induce us to de-superimpose causality and that Kant's arguments will not induce us to de-superimpose space and time, but that isn't crucial to what I wish to say, which is that among Hindus of advaitavedanta persuasion such de-superimposition, relentlessly pursued, is a way of breaking their attachment to the world, or better, is a way of extricating themselves from maya. In other words, where we have tended to regard Newton's apavada as a catastrophe they have happily and enthusiastically integrated a prior and more thoroughgoing version of it into the heart of their spiritual seeking. Indeed, Shankara adopted it as his *via mystica*. Would that we had been so hospitable to our Copernican revolution in philosophy which, as I've elsewhere said, was brought to completion not by Kant but by St John of the Cross, not by Schopenhauer but by Christ undergoing our Good Friday transition from metaphysics to metanoesis.

East and West. Narada and Ishmael.

Narada walking in a red desert with Vishnu. Ishmael walking in a palsied universe with Newton.

In the East, Hindus lost the snake but found the rope. Having found the rope, they saw that the snake isn't other than it.

In the West we have lost both snake and rope and here we are in the metaphysical blank beyond what Ishmael has called the mystical cosmetic.

Little wonder that Turtle yearns for a world to come ashore on.

But who, you might ask, is Turtle?

In the East, Turtle is everyone who has walked with Vishnu. In the West, he is everyone who has walked with Newton, Hume and Kant.

'All visible objects', Ahab declared, 'are but as pasteboard masks.'

This poses a question: what, if anything, is beyond the masks?

Ahab's answer was anguished: 'Sometimes I think there's naught beyond.'

INTRODUCTION

From a poem of hers called 'Sheep in Fog' we know that, if not persistently, then at least on one occasion, Sylvia Plath was a prey to apprehensions not altogether dissimilar to those of the dismasted captain:

> The hills step off into whiteness.
> People or stars
> Regard me sadly, I disappoint them.
>
> The train leaves a line of breath.
> O slow
> Horse the colour of rust.
>
> Hooves, dolorous bells –
> All morning the
> Morning has been blackening,
>
> A flower left out.
> My bones hold a stillness, the far
> Fields melt my heart.
>
> They threaten
> To let me through to a heaven
> Starless and fatherless, a dark water.

In contrast to how things happened for Narada, there is no initiating god who walks with Sylvia. And, whereas Ahab will harpoon his way through, the danger is that, without effort or willingness on her part, Sylvia will slip through – into what? Into the dark water Turtle was so tired of. Into that or worse. Into Ginnungagap, the infinite yawn.

With this poem we are in ghastly trouble. In trouble that ghosts us, ghasts us, nullifies us. It is as if the perceiver and the perceived disappeared together through the grin of the Cheshire cat. This having happened, the grin itself disappears, leaving the naught.

And yet, amazingly, Gautama the Buddha is not perturbed:

I proclaim, friend [he says], that in this fathom-sized, feeling-afflicted ascetic's body dwell the world and the origin of the world and the annulment of the world and the path that leads to the annulment of the world.

Also of course, the author of *The Cloud of Unknowing* has long ago challenged us concerning the naught:

What is he that calleth it naught? Surely it is our outer man and not our inner. Our inner man calleth it All; for by it he is well taught to understand all things bodily and ghostly, without any special beholding to any one thing by itself.

For Eckhart the naught isn't *nihil*:

INTRODUCTION

Everything which has being hangs in the Naught and that same naught is such an incomprehensible aught that all the spirits in heaven and upon earth cannot comprehend it nor sound it.

Let us hear him out on this:

When I say further that 'God is Being' – that is not true. He is quite transcendent. He is a Not-Being above Being.

Mahavakyas Turtle might have brought back from the floorless floor of the dark water.

Mahavakyas coming to us in the seeming void behind what Ahab calls the pasteboard masks, in the seeming *nihil* behind what Ishmael calls the mystical cosmetic.

A good walk it was, our walk with Newton, Hume and Kant.

A blessed walk it will be when in the course of it we integrate our Copernican revolution in epistemology, and this we will do when we walk with Jesus into Tenebrae:

O wretched condition of this life wherein it is so dangerous to live and so difficult to find the truth. That which is most clear and true is to us most obscure and doubtful and we therefore avoid it though it is most necessary for us. That which shines the most and dazzles our eyes, that we embrace and follow after though it is most hurtful to us and makes us stumble at every step. In what fear and danger then must man be living, seeing that the very light of his natural eyes by which he directs his steps is the very first to bewilder and deceive him when he would draw near unto God. If he wishes to be sure of the road he travels on he must close his eyes and walk in the dark if he is to journey in safety from his domestic foes, which are his own senses and faculties.

This is epistemology in the shadow of Good Friday. In it, even Kant's Copernican revolution in philosophy has been called to account by the cry of dereliction. In the fierce light of that cry, it is found wanting in completeness.

If, in your view, the Western adventure ran aground on Dover Beach, and if, again in your view, it is still aground at Key West, how can you continue to hope that we can refloat it at Punta Alta? Wasn't it on an inner, still living Punta Alta that Nietzsche suffered breakdown? And isn't Nietzsche's breakdown a portent of evolutionary breakdown? Can a species as inwardly menaced by all past ages as we are survive?

Let us return to the *Enuma Elish*:

When there was no heaven
no earth, no height, no depth, no name,

INTRODUCTION

> when Apsu was alone,
> he, the sweet water, the first begetter; and Tiamat,
> she, the bitter water, and that
> return to the womb her Mummu,
> when there were no gods—
> When sweet and bitter
> mingled together, no reed was plaited, no rushes
> muddied the water,
> the gods were nameless, natureless, featureless, then
> from Apsu and Tiamat
> in the waters gods were created, in the waters
> silt precipitated,
>
> Lahmu and Lahamu
> were named; they were not yet old ...

Lahmu and Lahamu they are called, these first sediments, these first precipitations of psyche and universe.

Cutting its way down through an accumulation of earth-floors and sea-floors, the Kedron-Colorado has reached and exposed these first sediments, and it was while he knelt between them, archaeornis circling above him, that Jesus endured and survived inward exposure to all past ages. It was while he knelt between them, Neanderthal eating bear-brains in a cave above him, that Jesus endured and survived the great integration.

Where Nietzsche collapsed, Jesus came through. And not only that. It was in Jesus, kneeling between Lahmu and Lahamu, that the evolving earth found the channel. In other words, the next evolutionary transition has already occurred and it is to be sought for not in increased intelligence but in increased integration.

How glad we should be that the soil of Mesopotamia has yielded up its remembrance of Lahmu and Lahamu.

Repeating those names

Lahmu and Lahamu
Lahmu and Lahamu
Lahmu and Lahamu

Repeating them in this way, they sound like a mantra.

Maybe Hindus are right. Maybe the universe is a mantraverse.

Maybe the universe is an aumverse that chants itself as atom and star.

I do not expect, though, that such suppositions will persuade Matthew Arnold to come back to the beach and listen again.

Nor will he, I presume, be induced to concede that the doors of perception can be cleansed:

INTRODUCTION

> The atoms of Democritus
> And Newton's particles of light
> Are sands upon the Red Sea shore,
> Where Israel's tents do shine so bright.

To see them as in any way less radiant, to see them, I was going to say, as anything less than transverberations, would in Blake's sense be a delusion of Ulro.

It is indeed true. We have run aground on an Ulro shore of eye and mind, but there has been an opening:

> Days, weeks passed, and under easy sail, the ivory *Pequod* had slowly swept across four several cruising grounds; that off the Azores; off the Cape de Verdes; on the Plate (so called), being off the mouth of the Rio de la Plata; and the Carrol Ground, an unstaked watery locality, southerly from St Helena.
>
> It was while gliding through these latter waters that one serene and moonlight night, when all the waves rolled by like scrolls of silver; and, by their soft, suffusing seethings, made what seemed a silvery silence not a solitude: on such a silent night a silvery jet was seen far in advance of the white bubbles at the bow. Lit up by the moon, it looked celestial; seemed some plumed and glittering god uprising from the sea.

That vision is the real Golden Fleece. But we haven't brought it home. Not to the modern world. Not yet. On the contrary, we have sought to obliterate it. In our efforts to protect our materialist assumptions and axioms, we've harpooned wonder, we've harpooned vision.

But the vision survives. Listen to Dana, who spent two years before the mast:

> ... one of the finest sights that I have ever seen was an albatross asleep upon the water, during a calm, off Cape Horn, when a heavy sea was running. There being no breeze, the surface of the water was unbroken, but a long heavy swell was rolling, and we saw the fellow, all white, directly ahead of us, asleep upon the waves, with his head under his wing; now rising on the top of the big billows, and then falling slowly until he was lost in the hollow between. He was undisturbed for some time, until the noise of our bows, gradually approaching, roused him, when, lifting his head, he stared upon us for a moment, and then spread his wide wings, and took his flight.

A vision that might shrive the Ancient Mariner, ancient voyaging humanity in us all:

> But do I look very old, so very, very old, Starbuck? I feel deadly faint, bowed, and humped, as though I were Adam, staggering beneath the piled centuries since Paradise.

INTRODUCTION

It's as if we can now again ask and answer the old apocalyptic question. So let us rehearse it:

Watchman, what of the night?

In the polar ocean north of Mundus Novus, drifting in her kayak, Uvavnuk singing her medicine song:

> The great sea has set me in motion,
> Set me adrift,
> Moving me as the weed moves in a river.
> The arch of sky and mightiness of storms
> Have moved the spirit within me,
> Till I am carried away
> Trembling with joy.

Watchman, what of the night?

In the polar ocean south of Mundus Novus an albatross, his head under his wing, riding the waves.

Could it be that we have been vouchsafed such answers only because some lonely souls did sail out to encounter *the terrible scriptures of water and squall*? Could it be that, trusting in Silam Inua as Uvavnuk did, and lying our head by our heart as the albatross did, we can now cross into a new way of being in the world?

In a prelude to its second volume you said of this book that it goes to work at the foundations of Western civilization in the way that a psychoanalyst such as Jung might go to work at the foundations of an individual's psyche. Consistently with this, it isn't passively that you walk the excavated, ancient streets of the Western psyche. Like Cortez in Tenochtitlan, you replace one with another religion. You replace what you would call the futile heroics of Marduk with the dreadful and seemingly inglorious graduations of Jesus in Gethsemane and on Golgotha.

It comes naturally to you as indeed it did to Isaiah to be Cortez in Babylon:
> *Babylon is fallen, is fallen, and all the graven images*
> *of her gods he hath broken into the ground.*

Cortez in Babylon, Cortez in Luxor, Cortez in Ugarit, Knossos, Jerusalem and Athens – if you are yourself a Cortez, there is a chance that that also is who your Christ will be, yet another conquistador, not a healer.

In the orchards outside the walls of Babylon there was a temple called Bit Akitu. As its name suggests, it was in this temple that Babylonians celebrated Akitu, their New Year Festival. An essential rite of that festival was a re-enactment, by recitation mostly, of the origin of all things. For the third time I will quote its opening lines, this time in the original:

INTRODUCTION

Enuma elish la nabu shamamu
Shaplish ammatum shuma la zakrat

When there was no heaven, no earth,
No height, no depth, no name ...

It was into this naught the *Pequod* sailed. And that is why we must concern ourselves with beginnings. The question is, will we do what Babylonians did, will we people the naught with monsters we must do battle with? Will we dive for soil or for sacred seeing as Turtle did? Will we listen as Maoris did till we hear the universe singing the song of its own emergence?

Te Kore
Te Kore-tua-tahi
Te Kore-tua-rua ...

Or will we found our sense of ourselves and world on none of these?
More than anything else, the *Enuma Elish* celebrates Marduk's victory over Tiamat, she being a kind of monstrous condensation of Chaos:

Then they met: Marduk, that cleverest of gods, and Tiamat grappled alone in single fight.
The lord shot his net to entangle Tiamat, and the pursuing, tumid wind, Imhullu, came from behind and beat in her face. When the mouth gaped open to suck him down he drove Imhullu in, so that the mouth would not shut but wind raged through her belly; her carcass blown up, tumescent, she gaped – and now he shot the arrow that split the belly, that pierced the gut and cut the womb.

But supposing there is no chaos, no confusion of elements and energies and no malignant condensation of it called Tiamat or, for that matter, called Moby-Dick. Then indeed are Marduk and Ahab deluded, each of them fighting the particular monster or snake he has projected into the rope.
On this assumption, the second volume opens with an *Enuma Elish* very different from its Babylonian counterpart:

A happening but not by way of occurrence, process or event. A happening out of the Divine Ungrund. A happening in which nothing takes place. Yet now it is: awareness of self and other-than-self, and at the heart of it all a Horsehead Nebula neighing:

Yatra na anyat pasyati, na anyat srinoti, na anyad vijanati, sa bhuma.

It's a song I would sing in the excavated ancient streets of the Western psyche – in streets where, almost without exception, the demiurgic metaphor has found favour.

INTRODUCTION

The demiurgic metaphor is as little applicable to galaxies and stars as it is to dew on the grass on a summer morning.

Since dolphins are neither makers nor builders, it is certain that the demiurgic metaphor is as foreign to them as it is to the universe it is meant to account for.

With Jesus, images of mysterious germination and growing replaced images of building and making:

And he said, So is the kingdom of God, as if a man should cast seed into the ground; and should sleep, and rise night and day, and the seed should spring and grow up, he knoweth not how.

This is as close as we have ever come in the West to what the Chinese mean by *mo wei,* a doctrine which suggests that no one or nothing caused the Universe.

All of this Christians forgot when they came to formulate their creed:

I believe in God, Father almighty, maker of heaven and earth ...

Bit Akitu is the prototype of our Whaleman's Chapel. It is prototype of the *Pequod,* our Esagila at sea.

Marduk's estimation of Tiamat is prototype of Ahab's estimation of Moby-Dick:

All evil, to crazy Ahab, was visibly personified and made practically assailable in Moby-Dick.

Enuma Elish is charter myth to our modern way of being in the world. And, in no matter what modern city it is, our high street is Marduk Street in Babylon. Of our civilization we can surely say, *plus ça change, plus c'est la même chose.*

We need to be healed in our cultural assumptions and axioms. We need to be healed in our myths and in our metaphors. We need to be healed in the way we apprehend things and in the way we relate to things. We need to ask whether things are things in the way that our Indo-European languages think they are.

There are peoples who once a year take their gods down to the sea and wash them.

Better to wash the way we see things.

Better to wash cause and effect out of the way we see things.

The Buddha's Flower Sermon is a Year One Reed that awaits us. It awaits us as Babylonians living long ago in Babylon and Ugarit, as Babylonians living today in Cairo and New York.

And if you think that the Buddha's Flower Sermon is an enormity

INTRODUCTION

you aren't yet able for, then what of the lion-roar, the world-awakening lion-roar, that Christians call the Sermon on the Mount?

Jesus didn't cross the Kedron alone. Our whole religious and cultural inheritance crossed it with him.

It is time to go beachcombing for new and transformed metaphors on the shore of Turiya-Tehom.

Those metaphors will, in Kant's sense, be forms of our sensibility and categories of our understanding. And they will be the *Mayflower* or, better, they will be the Maidu raft that will bring us to a New World.

Are you saying that metaphors will bring us where the original Mayflower *will not? Are you saying that hozhonji songs will bring us where our flying machines will not? Are you saying that it is in the highest degree unfortunate that we have come to rely so much on Promethean* techne *and* mechane*?*

I will answer that indirectly. Our heroes have outgrown the biographies into which we have traditionally fenced them. So, you will not find the old Titan in the place to which Aeschylus led him, nor in the place to which Shelley led him. You will find him in Blue Thunder Tipi. Pitched on its bank, it is mirrored in Medicine River. If he isn't there, seek for him where he sits in the lotus position in Ta'doiko.

Release from the old Enuma Elish *is release from a charter myth, from a foundation myth, from a myth that founds and grounds the psyche. That is serious. It might mean yet another exodus with somewhere to leave but with nowhere to go. This in many ways has been the history of the modern West. It isn't my intention to ascribe either deceit or duplicity to you, but I will ask the question: is all this talk about release from* Enuma Elish *a disguised way of talking about release from the Bible? Is the Bible or the biblical world-view the real target? Are you proposing a post-biblical Christianity?*

There is, I believe, no spiritual tradition that has a privileged or exclusive claim to the Triduum Sacrum. The Triduum Sacrum generates its own holy book. It has been doing so, and not just in Christendom, for millennia and it will continue to do so for as long as human beings are recognizably who they have been and are.

Who or what have we been, who or what are we?

It isn't an opposable thumb or an upright gait or a superior theorizing intelligence or a superior tool-making and tool-using intelligence that distinguishes us as a species. We are distinguished by our capacity, and in

INTRODUCTION

some cases by our willingness, to undergo the Triduum Sacrum. The capacity, which grows and grows, to receive the Gift. It is a capacity to give God a free hand in our final exaltation.

If we were sapient, as we say we are, we would house the Triduum Sacrum in metaphor, in myth, in mahavakya, in ritual and in masonry glorious as anything we see in Bhuvaneshvar or in Gothic France.

That is the wise response to our dis-illusioning walk in the East with Vishnu, to our dis-illusioning walk in the West with Newton, Hume and Kant.

In the way that medieval Europeans had to deal with the Fisher King in his distress, we have to deal with Coleridge in his dejection. It is the task of our age, and it is by our success or failure in this regard that we should be willing to be judged.

To meet the crisis we will need to do what Hindus did: as they moved forward from Veda to Vedanta so must we move forward from Evangel to Evangelanta. I sometimes imagine it: Coleridge answers a knock on his door and there he is, the Ancient Mariner quoting the Kena Upanishad:

There goes neither the eye, nor speech, nor the mind; we know it not; nor do we see how to teach one about it. Different it is from all that is known, and beyond the unknown it also is.

The Ancient Mariner is wiser than his dejected creator: psychopompos to him, he leads him to the door of a Tenebrae Temple.

It sounds intimidatingly alien, doesn't it, that knock on our door?

On the contrary. With the great saying from the Kena Upanishad we are on home ground:

Et facta hora sexta, tenebrae factae sunt per totam terram usque in horam nonam. Et hora nona exclamavit Jesus voce magna, dicens, Eloi, Eloi, lamma sabachthani. Quod est interpretatum: Deus meus, Deus meus, ut quid dereliquisti me?

Given the epistemological crisis that has overtaken us, there is a choice we must make: do we cross the Kedron with Jesus or do we voyage with Ahab through the Sunda Straits?

One thing is certain: sitting in dejection with Coleridge, that won't work. Doing murderous business in great waters, as Melville did, that won't work. Seeking shelter in the charmed circle of conjugal mutuality, as Arnold did, that won't work. To refuse to emerge from somnambulation, as Nietzsche did, that won't work. And since, in Wallace Stevens' Kantian view of it, the objective world is forever hidden, is forever

INTRODUCTION

hooded, we must not expect that we will find final philosophical consolation in the demiurgic singing of his demiurgic Lady. And then there is Sylvia. To die outside the shelter that religion and culture can sometimes give, to die as a flower left out dies, that won't work.

Coleridge, Melville, Arnold, Nietzsche, Stevens and Plath: collectively, they are a native Narada. They have undergone the great dis-illusioning. And this being so, we have to bring mysticism in from the cold.

Taoists say of the sage that he walks behind advancing humanity, picking up whatever great things it discards. Among the great things we in the West have discarded is a ritual called Tenebrae.

So hora nona *is philosophical high noon, is it?*

'I sometimes think there's naught beyond,' Ahab says. It was when Christ looked down into Adam's empty skull – and we must remember that his head when he did so was crowned with the harpoon wound – it was at that moment that nihilism was forever defeated. Since Good Friday, we know there is no *nihil* that supports it.

Our walk in the East with Vishnu and our walk in the West with Newton, Hume and Kant has prepared us for Tenebrae. And here it might be timely to suggest that Good Friday is Tenebrae much more than it is a crucifixion. Indeed, it is quite simple: mystically, Good Friday is Tenebrae.

In a story in this book, we have journeyed from the stable in Bethlehem to an outhouse on an island in the North Atlantic. In it a modern Argonaut called Big Mike has hung up the net of his mind and the net of his heart.

In it we might one day convene a Christian symposium.

In it, indeed, we might one day convene a new Council of Chalcedon.

In what way is his canvas curragh related to the Nave?

How, except in coming to this, can the Nave find the channel?

Must it find the channel for the Beagle*? Must it find it for science?*

It must find it for the evolving earth. Continually, that is, we must find what has been found.

Our mystical songlines aren't Dreamtime songlines. Our walk with Bright Angel and our walk with Vishnu have, neither of them, its source in what Freud has called the pleasure principle. Mostly, they will be trails not taken, won't they?

INTRODUCTION

That might well be so but however deeply buried beneath lesser desires, beneath worldly desires, there is in us a supreme yearning. In our depths we are turiyatropic. And I mean this in exactly the sense in which we say of a sunflower that it is heliotropic.

> Oh how I long to travel back
> And tread again that ancient track!
> That I might once more reach that plain
> Where first I left my glorious train ...

For many of us that ancient track will be rough going. It will bring us across the Torrent into karmic Tsetsekia and Tenebrae. It will involve us in a walk with Vishnu, in a walk with Bright Angel, and, she as it were being the ultimate hierophant, it will involve us in an encounter with the Angel of the Estuary.

In the meantime, how wonderful it is to recall that there have been and are human beings in whom our planet is an evolutionary success. Given the theory of the hundredth monkey, it isn't prematurely that we call it Buddh Gaia.

Not one of our telescopes but is blinded by the glaucoma of scientific seeing. Unable to refract the light of enlightenment, they help us to see but a little, and that the still backward little, of what is astronomically out there.

Will we stay with the little that is still backward? Or will we seek to negotiate the evolutionary channel?

According to Professor Ramsay's calculations quoted by Darwin, that channel is thirteen and three-quarter British miles.

Since Jesus negotiated them, since he negotiated them as Vishvarupa and as Vishvayuga, those miles are aisle. And when it comes to measuring up to what we have been, are, and will be, that aisle defines us.

> But ah! my soul with too much stay
> Is drunk, and staggers in the way.
> Some men a forward motion love,
> But I by backward steps would move
> And when this dust falls to the urn,
> In that state I came, return.

So there they are, thirteen and three-quarter British miles of further evolution opening before us.

The shadow on the rockwall is the shadow of archaeornis.

And the footprints of that early reptile on the Coconino sandstone in the Grand Canyon – they aren't as fixed to their place nor are they as fossilized as they might seem. Alive and well, they continue in the footsteps

INTRODUCTION

of Vishvarupa Jesu crossing the Torrent.
  Already

Lasciate ogni speranza voi ch'entrate …
Abandon hope all ye who enter here …

is beginning to read like

Would I radically misconceive your understanding of Jesus were I to imagine you saying to St Paul

> The Vision of Christ that thou dost see
> Is my Vision's Greatest Enemy?

Yes, you would. To say of Jesus what Jainas might say of him, that he is a Tirthankara, is not to contradict anything that St Paul says of him. A tirthankara is someone who makes or finds or opens the tirtha or ford by which we cross to the farther shore. Jesus found the channel. Christians call it the Triduum Sacrum. By what other *Mayflower*, by what other *Argo*, Nave, *Mayflower*, *Beagle* or *Pequod*, will we reach newness of life in the world we were born into?

I presume that a conclusion such as this emanates from an anthropology of some kind. However, I know of nowhere in your book where that anthropology is consciously and formally articulated.

Does it need to be? And if it were, wouldn't it limit the book's openness to surprise? I am ever mindful of William James' advice: there should be no premature closing of our account with reality. And so, to avoid closure, I will answer your question elliptically.

  It is assumed in this book that we are living through what Germans would call a world-historical crisis. To meet it, I sometimes think that we must endure a negative and a positive diagnosis of who and what we are. The negative diagnosis will suggest to us that we are AIDS virus to the earth. Alternatively, that we are the iceberg into which the earth, voyaging for four thousand six hundred million years, has crashed. In the words of Sir Thomas Browne, the positive diagnosis suggests that: There is surely a piece of divinity in us, something that was before the elements, and owes no homage unto the sun.

INTRODUCTION

Of these two diagnoses, the positive is by far the most difficult, first to take seriously, and then to endure.

In the year A.D. 627 King Edwin of Northumbria held a council of his chief men on the question of his imminent conversion to Christianity. Coifi, the chief priest of the religion they had hitherto professed, spoke disparagingly of the old gods, the old altars, the old rites, and recommended that the King should accept the new teaching. Then someone who was, most likely, an elder and an adviser had this to say:

Your Majesty, when we compare the present life of man on earth with that time of which we have no knowledge, it seems to me like the swift flight of a single sparrow through the banqueting-hall where you are sitting on a winter's day with your thegns and counsellors. In the midst there is a comforting fire to warm the hall; outside, the storms of winter rain or snow are raging. The sparrow flies swiftly in through one door of the hall and out through another. While he is inside, he is safe from the winter storms; but after a few moments of comfort, he vanishes from sight into the wintry world from which he came. Even so, man appears on earth for a little while, but of what went before this life or of what follows, we know nothing. Therefore, if this new teaching has brought any more certain knowledge, it seems only right that we should follow it.

What is so memorable in this story is its picturesque way of telling us that we exist beyond the hall doors of conception and death. Whether our life outside the hall, our life before conception and after death, is as wintry and dark as the story suggests is of course of grave if not grievous concern to us, but first things first.

We aren't only who and what we sociologically are within the hall. We aren't only what we normally say of ourselves in a curriculum vitae that we send to an employer. There are doors at either end of that little list of accomplishments and achievements. It is the journeys and geographies of our lives beyond these doors that the Northumbrian elder, if elder he was, is interested in.

Think in this regard of the journeys and geographies, psychic or otherwise, of the Tibetan Book of the Dead.

Think of the journeys and geographies, psychic or otherwise, of the Egyptian Book of the Dead.

Think of the journeys and geographies of Mesopotamian and Mediterranean *nekuias*.

Think of the journeys and geographies of Orphic eschatological clairvoyance and clairaudience.

Think of the remembered journeys and geographies of Platonic anamnesis.

INTRODUCTION

Think of the journeys and geographies of shamanic initiation.
Think of Dante entering the dark wood.
Think of D.H. Lawrence setting off for God-knows-where in his ship of death.
Add to all of this the awful awareness of immense and difficult and dangerous inwardness that we hear about from the Psalmist:

> I am fearfully and wonderfully made

That we hear about from Wordsworth:

> ... Not chaos, not
> The darkest pit of lowest Erebus,
> Nor aught of blinder vacancy, scooped out
> By help of dreams – can breed such fear and awe
> As fall upon us often when we look
> Into our Minds – into the Mind of man –

That we hear about from so many others, among them Conrad:

The mind of man is capable of anything, because everything is in it, all the past as well as all the future.

And that is only a first inner ordnance survey. But it is enough to be going on with.

What are its implications?

The next and last two steps in evolution – Gethsemane and Golgotha.

And what if any are its socio-political implications?

It implies that, grown wise at last, our statue of Socio-political Liberty will one day be willing to take second place to a statue of Bright Angel.
In other words, freedom from a socio-political ancient regime is of but precarious value until we have crossed the Torrent and integrated our phylogenetic ancient regime.

Your invocation of Bright Angel suggests that we must set foot not just on the earth but in it. It suggests that we must set foot Grand-Canyon-deep in it. But how, without being sore amazed, can we do this? How, without being sorrowful unto death, or frightened unto death, can we do this? How, without being as karmically heavy as Coatlicue is, can we do this?

I can think of no simple answer to that question. Perhaps there is none. I will have to be content therefore with some disparate statements. I will

INTRODUCTION

make them as they come to me.

The Book of Job demands of us, I believe, that we should come to know and acknowledge reality as it is. It demands of us, by way of fulfilling a primary religious duty, that we should come to know and acknowledge it in its unsubduable stupendousness. It is in this sense that the Book of Job is a first attempt to ascend the river. Conrad, who rewrote the book for our time, knows the dangers. Kurtz became a demon of the primeval place. And we might add: whereas Job survived the ascent, survived it, if only barely, in his integrity and sanity, Nietzsche didn't.

Job survived, and now we are heirs to the promise: *For thou shalt be in league with the stones of the field and the beasts of the field shall be at peace with thee.*

It is as heirs to this promise that we will set foot on Bright Angel Trail. It is as heirs to this promise that we will sing his canticle with St Francis.

Still attempting to answer your question, can I remind you that one of the first great pronouncements of the New Testament assures us that with God nothing is impossible. And Kierkegaard insists that until we know this we aren't yet dealing with God.

The third and final statement I would like to make is purely credal: as a Christian, I believe that the earth isn't just the object of God's redemption. At the end below of Bright Angel Trail, I believe, looking up at all its strata, that the earth is consubstantial with Christ in his passion and death and resurrection. Everything will come forth by day. And this puts an end once and for all to the continuing, huge hurt of Manichaean dualism. And in this regard it will surely help us, and even comfort us maybe, to remember the Ramayana, one of the great epics of India. Prominent among the characters who figure in it is Hanuman, the Monkey King. Closer, at least in appearance, to *Australopithecus africanus* than we are, Hanuman gives us hope, for he once opened his vesture and showed that his breast was a shrine to the divine pair, Sita and Rama. It's as if he was agreeing with Sir Thomas Browne when the latter said:

There is surely a piece of divinity in us, something that was before the elements, and that owes no homage unto the sun.

A Christian setting foot on Bright Angel Trail might correspondingly imagine that his or her heart is a shrine to Nuestra Señora de la Soterrana. Apart from the radiance and grace she herself will shed on our path, the child she carries in her arm has long ago harrowed our collective hell.

Evolution from now on is by gracious transmutation, not by the natural selection of favourable mutation.

INTRODUCTION

As well as being its past, alchemy is the future of chemistry.

The north rose window of Notre Dame de Paris, sometimes called the Alchemists' Rose, should be retina and lens of our Hubble eye. The eye altering alters all. The heart altering alters all.

And further: the descent of Agnus Dei as Christians understand it differs quite radically from the descent of Adi Varaha as Hindus understand it. Since Gethsemane, the Trail is aisle. And if we invoke him, Bright Angel, making the abhaya mudra, will descend it with us.

The continuing integration of Bright Angel Trail and the continuing integration of our walk with Vishnu, that rather than our journeys to the Moon and Mars is the evolutionary frontier.

As I know them, the Passion narratives can neither sponsor nor support your belief, almost routine in your work, that Jesus set descending fin-foot on Bright Angel Trail. Where therefore do you locate your authority for saying that he did?

In chapter four of St Paul's Letter to the Ephesians, there is a startling sentence:

When it says 'he went up', it must mean that he had gone down to the deepest levels of the earth.

Jesus didn't go down as a sightseer. He went down passionately, and that means that from within himself he endured a karmic awakening of all that we phylogenically have been and are.

Living in the shadow of the thirteen and three-quarters British miles of karma, living this side of our disillusioning walk with Newton, Hume and Kant, we must rewrite the Passion narratives. Or, if that seems too deliberate, and it is, then we must wait upon what Yeats has called a trembling of the veil.

Within the Passion narratives as they exist are further vast epiphanies of Christ in Gethsemane, are further vast epiphanies, mostly in words spoken, of Christ on Golgotha.

The authority for seeing Christ set foot on Bright Angel Trail is the authority of evoutionary need. Far therefore from having run its course, Christianity is only beginning.

As I see it, evolution by genetic mutation has already given way to evolution by religious or, specifically speaking, by ritual means.

It took sixty million years for eohippus to evolve into horse.

In the course of a passionate night Bright Angel Trail became aisle.

In the course of a dark afternoon we came to see that empirical expe-

INTRODUCTION

rience of God eclipses God, that the subjective-objective divide divides us from God.

Temples in which we ritually inherit the passionate night and the dark afternoon are as inevitable and natural to the earth as the mesas of the Grand Canyon are. It is in them that trilobyte and rattlesnake will find evolutionary fulfilment and evolutionary surcease.

It is no disparagement of Near Eastern auroras already breaking over us to say that the New Testament is still eohippus to the stupendous thing it one day will be.

It's a question I have already asked, but I will ask it again: it is with Darwin's geological hammer not with the golden bough of the priest of Nemi that modern humanity would go forward into the future. Isn't it time that we cut our moorings to ancestral superstition?

Listen to what Ted Hughes has to say:

Stories are old the way human biology is old. No matter how much they have produced in the past in the way of fruitful inspirations, they are never exhausted. The story of Christ, to stick to our example, can never be diminished by the seemingly infinite mass of theological agonizing and insipid homilies which have attempted to translate it into something more manageable. It remains, like any other genuine story, irreducible, a lump of the world, like the body of a newborn child. There is little doubt that, if the world lasts, pretty soon someone will come along and understand the story as if for the first time. He will look back and see two thousand years of somnolent fumbling with the theme. Out of that, and the collision of other things, he will produce, very likely, something totally new and overwhelming, some whole new direction for human life.

That direction has been found, for Brontosaurus as well as for Willie Loman. Can't you see him? Willie walking out of the civilization that has failed him? That thing he has in his hand, that's a manure fork. With it, right there in our town park, he will uncover the Trail. Being the trail to a past that we must integrate, it is also therefore a trail to our present and to our future.

Can't you see him, Willie coming home? That thing he has in his other hand, that's a Tenebrae harrow.

Having the fork and the harrow, *homo faber* has no need for further fabrication. Spiritually speaking, we have no need for further fabrication.

And we didn't steal them, this fork and this harrow.

It is with them that we will integrate Nietzsche's discoveries. And that, quite simply, is to find and navigate the evolutionary channel. In Tsetsekia and in Tenebrae we will navigate it.

INTRODUCTION

Your strictures against Manichaean dualism notwithstanding, it does sometimes seem that your book is a kind of Armageddon between people who wear a ghost-shirt and people who wear a cassock – between, on the one hand, Black Elk praying with his pipe on a peak in Paha Sapa and, on the other hand, Ahab praying with the links of a lightning conductor on a deck of the bare-poled Pequod.

It isn't as simple as that. We need a statue of Bright Angel at the mouth of the Yukon as much as we need one at the mouth of the Hudson. His torch must light the way of people coming east from Asia as it must light the way of people coming west from Europe and Africa.

Coatlicue, the Aztec Earth Mother, serpent-savage in her parts, her jaguar claws cleaned, has reappeared in what we so optimistically called the New World. And here at home in the old world, huger than ever and bellowing and blind, the Minotaur, led by a child, is walking among us.

It is what I have been calling our phylogenetic ancient regime.

It has returned. And it isn't only Nietzsche who has recoiled.

The labyrinth isn't the answer. The old European hero, club in hand or lyre in hand, isn't the answer. Guillotine and Gulag aren't the answer.

We didn't have to wait until Conrad wrote *Heart of Darkness* to know that the ghost-shirt can all too easily become the cassock, or worse.

William Law isn't deceived:

Would you know, Academicus, whence it is that so many false spirits have appeared in the world, who have deceived themselves and others with false fire and false light, laying claim to inspirations, illuminations, and openings of the Divine Life, pretending to do wonders under extraordinary calls from God? It is this: they have turned to God without turning from themselves; would be alive in God before they were dead to their own nature; a thing as impossible in itself as for a grain of wheat to be alive before it dies. Now religion in the hands of self, or corrupt nature, serves only to discover vices of a worse kind than in nature left to itself. Hence are all the disorderly passions of religious men, which burn in a worse flame then passions only employed about worldly matters: pride, self-exaltation, hatred, and persecution, under a cloak of religious zeal, will sanctify actions which nature left to itself would be ashamed to own.

Coatlicue has been unearthed. The Minotaur has returned, Nietzsche hasn't coped with his discoveries. Dostoyevsky's underground man has burrowed his way up into our crystal palace. We have smelled the musks of distant Oregon. Riding into Guernica, Dürer's knight has looked up and seen condors. Psychoanalysing us in a way that Freud didn't or Jung didn't, Lascaux, in its pit, has let us in on a terrible secret.

I know of no other response than to look towards Christ crossing the Kedron.

INTRODUCTION

Now you seem distant and absorbed, unavailable maybe to further conversation.

No, it is not that. Sylvia Plath came to mind, and it occurred to me that the calamity for consciousness and culture depicted in the pit in Lascaux is, for all its enormity, a minor affair compared to the Ginnungagap gaping Sylvia has looked into. Although in another mode, her poem, 'Sheep in Fog', is Nietzsche's second discovery all over again, in Christian terms, formally but not essentially, it is Christ looking down into Adam's empty skull. Sylvia's dereliction and Christ's dereliction differ in this: there was for Christ, right to the end, a God upon whom he called, a God into whose hands he at last commended his spirit, while, for Sylvia, the dark she has come into isn't only starless, it is also fatherless.

'In the age of the world's night', Heidegger says, 'the abyss of the world must be experienced and endured.'

I am reminded of the Buryat version of the diver myth. In this myth, diver-bird must go where Noah's raven and dove cannot go.

In the beginning there was only a dark water and hovering above it, accompanied by swans, loons and other water-birds, was Sombol-Burkan. Longing for a world to come ashore on, he asked the white diver-bird to go down to the floor of the dark water and bring up some soil. Halfway down, diver-bird was challenged by a blood-red crab. 'Where are you going?' crab asked. 'I'm going down to the floor', diver-bird replied. 'I've been in this water forever,' Crab replied. 'There is no floor. So be off with you or I'll shred you with my scissors..' When Sombol-Burkan heard what had happened he gave diver-bird a magic phrase and armed with this he was more than a match for Crab.

> Of what in us is Crab a condensation? Can we overcome it?
> Can we win through to a world?
> Of what in us is Tiamat a condensation? Can we overcome it?
> Can we win through to a world?
> In Friedrich Nietzsche and in Sylvia Plath humanity has once again come to the canyon and the dark water, and what I earlier said of Coleridge I now say, even more insistently, of them. As the distress of the Fisher King was a concern of people in medieval times so in modern times should Friedrich's collapse and Sylvia's trepidation be a concern of ours. We might begin by imagining a fifth Evangelist whose account of the Passion, scripted and scored, will be Maidu raft to us on the dark water, will be Apophis canoe to us in the canyon.

Has it occurred to you that the crab, who challenged diver-bird, might also challenge our Arctic Shaman on his way down to comb our transgressions out of Takanakapsaluk's hair?

INTRODUCTION

No. But it did occur to me that on his way down Ahab looked, and where, but minutes earlier, he had a diabolical harpoon in his hand he now has a comb of walrus ivory in it.

That means that we now have the comb, the manure fork and the harrow.

The hallows we could call them, thinking of their counterparts in the Grail Castle.

Looking at them, it isn't outlandish to hope that our Western psyche can be reconstituted.

That's a tall order.

Nothing less will suffice. So, let us imagine it, and it being an image or scene, let us expect of it what Yeats might expect of it: discontinuing his New Year Liturgy in mid-sentence, the Akitu priest climbs the Ziggurat in Babylon and calls out across all ancient cultures that the old order is over, because now tonight a vicar of Marduk on earth has gone down to the floor of the Abyss, has gone down with a comb not a harpoon, has gone down to comb, and comb out, Tiamat's hair.

These could be the opening lines of a new Enuma Elish.

And so it isn't yet enough to have replaced city wall and labyrinth with Tsetsekia. We must replace Bit Akitu with it. We must replace the Whaleman's Chapel with it. We must replace the *Pequod* with it. In the way that the Kwakiutl welcomed the Great Iakim into their religion, so must we welcome Tiamat into ours. Evolution is with the hospitalities of Kwakiutl firelight, not with lobotomy. And that is why, knowing his own body would be the scabbard, Jesus commanded St Peter to put up his sword.

I'll say it: the human psyche underwent reconstitution in Gethsemane.

To claim Good Friday for philosophy as you have done is somehow scandalous, isn't it? I imagine that Yeats' Magi and indeed Eliot's Magi will either journey past it or go home.

Addressing the epistemological concerns of Romantic poets, literary critics sometimes resort to a distinction, first posited by Yeats, between the mirror and the lamp. The mirror reflects things as they are. Illuminating them, the lamp adds something of its own lustre to them. Within the terms of the analogy, it partially creates what it perceives. So the question is: is the perceiver a mirror or is the perceiver a lamp or is the perceiver something other altogether than either mirror or lamp? It is a vexed question but not one this book is directly concerned with.

INTRODUCTION

In this book the generating or driving distinction is not between the mirror and the lamp but between the mirror and Maag Mahony's shawl. Or rather, it is between the mirror and the lamp on the one hand and Maag's black shawl on the other. From the sixth to the ninth hour, it is cortex and retina to us.

Our mystical songline is in many ways an exodus from the Smoking Mirror to the Tenebrae harrow, and only those who aren't yet caught up in that exodus are likely to be scandalized by an attempt to claim Good Friday for philosophy.

Of all the philosophical words that a person might speak, there is none so momentous as Golgotha.

Imagine it: the nocturnes of Tenebrae being chanted in Plato's Academy.

Imagine them being chanted to an audience consisting of all the characters in his dialogues.

A difficult word it is, this new word that they must learn.

Even for Kant, it would probably mean yet another Copernican Revolution in philosophy.

Yet learn it we must because Yaje Woman ascends our river and Narada walks through the pass at Thermopylae.

Do you therefore look forward to the day when Christians will be as epistemologically hospitable to the empty skull as Zen Buddhists are to the empty enso?

Yes, but we mustn't assume that the enso and the skull are saying the same thing. Epistemologically, they are as little univocal as the Heart Sutra and the Dark Night of the Soul are. Metaphysically, they are as little univocal as Tathata and *en-Sof* are.

Looking back on them now, the Bible readings so regularly conducted on board the Beagle *are sad and quaint. History wasn't on their side. The very voyage itself wasn't on their side. Has it ever occurred to you that you might be a Fitzroy, able in your way to do what you set out to do, but willfully unable for the crates of contrary evidence that are coming aboard? Are you unwilling to endure a change of paradigm, and is this reflected in your book?*

I don't know about being a Fitzroy but, growing up in rural Ireland when I did, I was in a very real sense a European Aborigine and three tall ships did appear off my coast. They were manned by Darwin, Freud and Einstein. And the night I read the geological chapters in *The Origin of Species* I did feel that the ring of Darwin's geological hammer had finally silenced the slow, victorious tolling of the Angelus that I had grown up with. On

INTRODUCTION

calm days we could hear that Angelus as far away as the bogs we cut turf in and when we got down to the lowest spit and started uncovering the ancient fallen tree trunks and their tree stumps, Jackie Buckley who was on the *sleán* would tell us that it was the Flood that had knocked them and because he had over the years observed the direction the tree trunks mostly lay in he would sometimes point a little to the south of Croc An Oir and say, that's where the Flood came from. So yes, although much more unconsciously than Fitzroy, we did live in a biblical world. As for him, so for us, the Flood explained things.

A road of ashes it was, the road that reached away from Jackie Buckley, releasing the fragrance of ancient resins to Einstein, relativizing our absolutes. Fiercely straight, never once anticipating an enantiodromia, it ran through the Future of an Illusion.

But maybe it isn't only Jackie Buckley digging away six-spit deep in an Irish bog who has to outgrow an illusion, who has to endure a change of paradigm.

Early in his career Nietzsche had this to say:

But science, spurred by its powerful illusion, speeds irresistibly towards its limits where its optimism, concealed in the essence of logic, suffers shipwreck. For the periphery of the circle of science has an infinite number of points; and while there is no telling how this circle could ever be surveyed completely, noble and gifted men nevertheless reach, e'er half their time and inevitably, such boundary points on the periphery from which one gazes into what defies illumination.

There is, he maintains, an illusion at work, and with admirable brevity and clarity he tells us what it is:

the unshakeable faith that thought, using the thread of causality, can penetrate the deepest abysses of being

In *The Gay Science* he is scornful:

It is no different with the faith with which so many materialistic natural scientists rest content nowadays, the faith in a world that is supposed to have its equivalent and its measure in human thought and human valuations – a 'world of truth' that can be mastered completely and forever with the aid of our square little reason. What? Do we really want to permit existence to be degraded for us like this – reduced to a mere exercise for a calculator and an indoor diversion for mathematicians? Above all, one should not wish to divest existence of its rich ambiguity: that is a dictate of good taste, gentlemen, the taste of reverence for everything that lies beyond your horizon. That the only justifiable interpretation of the world should be one in which *you* are justified because one can continue to work and do research scientifically in *your* sense (you really mean mechanistically?) – an interpretation that permits counting, calculating, weighing, seeing

INTRODUCTION

and touching, and nothing more – that is a crudity and naïveté, assuming that it is not a mental illness, an idiocy ... assuming that one estimated the value of a piece of music according to how much of it could be counted, calculated, and expressed in formulas: how absurd would such a 'scientific' estimation of music be! What would one have comprehended, understood, grasped of it? Nothing, really nothing of what is 'music' in it!

And it might be that the universe is an oratorio, an Om oratorio in four movements, A, U, M, and the silence that follows. And entering that silence and gazing into what defies illumination, maybe we are on the way back to the Chandogya mahavakya.

As this book understands these things, we are back to Big Mike hanging up the net of his mind and the net of his heart. From within his Tenebrae he called out:

> The fishing is good.
> The fishing is very good.
> The fishing, not fishing at all,
> Is blessedness, is bliss.

A Christianity that is founded on the Triduum Sacrum is invulnerable to scientific discovery.

A Christianity that is founded on the Triduum Sacrum is invulnerable to any of the ways in which the Bible might be found wanting.

A Christianity founded on the Triduum Sacrum can, any day it chooses, walk away from the Bible and stand free of it.

A Christianity founded on the Triduum Sacrum doesn't need to catch up philosophically with Kant or scientifically with Darwin. Rather is it for Darwin and Kant to look down, as Jesus did, into good news in the koshaless skull.

Could it be that the fossilized skull of Toxodon which Darwin rescued for science is portent to science?

Darwin himself tells us how he found it in the Pampas:

Nov. 26th – I set out on my return in a direct line for Monte Video. Having heard of some giants' bones at a neighbouring farmhouse on the Sarandis, a small stream entering the Rio Negro, I rode there accompanied by my host, and purchased for the value of eighteen pence the head of the Toxodon.

A wooden horse outside the gates of Troy.

A fossilized Toxodon outside the gates of our Cerne laboratories.

Seeing him, koshaless and staring, we know that our transtorrentem destiny is upon us.

et egressus est Jesus cum discipulis suis trans torrentem Cedron

INTRODUCTION

We have crossed the Torrent and our planet is an evolutionary success not just from here on but all the way back to its beginnings.

From its beginnings it is Buddh Gaia.

It is on Buddh Gaia that Brontosaurus walks.

And where the Cerne laboratories used to be we will now once again have a Blue Thunder Tipi. Is that it? I am asking this question because you have been accused of myopia to science. How do you respond to the accusation?

It has never occurred to me that those of us who aren't scientists should abdicate to scientists the privilege of talking about the universe. D.H. Lawrence has talked about an immediate anthropology. And maybe there are some highly evolved human beings such as Jacob Boehme and the Buddha who, from within themselves, have access to an immediate cosmology. Without the mediation of myth or math, microscope or telescope, they come to know not only how but why the universe is. Immediately in themselves they know the microcosm and therefore also the macrocosm.

Long before the work of the Copenhagen school of physicists it should have been obvious that the next great task of science is to discover the scientist. Is to explore the explorer. Could it be that having knocked on our cathedral door Yaje Woman will go on to knock on Einstein's?

I sometimes think that the human head, even Albert's brilliant head, could turn out to have been an evolutionary Piltdown hoax unless we integrate Christ's cry of dereliction and, integrating it, see that the Chandogya mahavakya must be our next Galapagos. And so, his re-education in Blue Thunder Tipi complete, and his desire to help us in no way abated, maybe Prometheus will go to Ta'doiko and sit in the lotus position. The lotus position is the perfect scientific posture. In relation not only to ourselves but also to the universe at large, it is the perfect scientific posture.

And in saying this I am not discounting Vishnuanantasayin. I am not discounting revelations in sleep. To sleep in Fern Hill might sometimes be a better way to be an astronomer than to stay awake on Mount Palomar:

> And as I was green and carefree, famous among the barns
> About the happy yard and singing as the farm was home,
>   In the sun that is young once only,
>   Time let me play and be
>   Golden in the mercy of his means,
> And green and golden I was huntsman and herdsman, the calves
> Sang to my horn, the foxes on the hills barked clear and cold,

INTRODUCTION

>   And the sabbath rang slowly
>   In the pebbles of the holy streams.

> All the sun long it was running, it was lovely, the hay
> Fields high as the house, the tunes from the chimneys, it was air
>   And playing, lovely and watery
>   And fire green as grass.
>   And nightly under the simple stars
> As I rode to sleep the owls were bearing the farm away,
> All the moon long I heard, blessed among stables, the nightjars
>   Flying with the ricks, and the horses
>   Flashing into the dark.
>
> And then to awake, and the farm, like a wanderer white
> With the dew, come back, the cock on his shoulder: it was all
>   Shining, it was Adam and maiden,
>   The sky gathered again
>   And the sun grew round that very day.
> So it must have been after the birth of the simple light
> In the first, spinning place, the spellbound horses walking warm
>   Out of the whinnying green stable
>   On to the fields of praise.

What we need is a Mount Palomar that will sometimes sit at the feet of Fern Hill, that will sometimes kneel at the feet of the Hill of the Koshaless Skull.

And this too I would like to say: if it loses its ability to regress to its anantashaya shape and to progress to its lotus shape, our *homo erectus* shape will turn out to be yet another evolutionary dead end.

Crispin is the hero of a poem by Wallace Stevens. Like Kurtz, Crispin sails away from Europe and journeys upriver into a world where green barbarism is, or almost is, paradigm. At home in the crusty town he came from, Crispin would write a couplet yearly to the spring. But now, his old self annulled by a tempest at sea, and his new emergent self enlarged by the thunders of Yucatan, Crispin cannot be content with counterfeit. He loses faith in the old images, the old metaphors, the old tropes. He desires to

>   ... drive away
>   The shadow of his fellows from the skies,
>   And, from their stale intelligence released,
>   To make a new intelligence prevail?

Making a new intelligence prevail can be dangerous. But, given the apocalypse our Titanic intelligence has landed us in, it might now be necessary to let a new or at least another intelligence emerge.

INTRODUCTION

Not far from us here in our own galaxy there is a fully evolved planet. Beings who live on it didn't take the road of science and technology. Millions of years ago, wishing to help them, their Prometheus surrendered to the genius of nature and the Ground out of which it emanated. Over a long geological age, coinciding roughly with our Carboniferous, purely mystical modes of awareness evolved in them. Strange to say, these beings look like crinoids. Every now and then, vast spans of time separating such events, they become aware of a new star in their night sky. All the stars in their night sky are enlightened planets and it is only when a planet becomes enlightened that they become aware of it. Recently, downwards from their morning star, they saw a new star. By what name they call it we don't yet know. But maybe we should call it Buddh Gaia.

What does this imply about the universe as a whole?

It implies that any account of the universe which isn't hagiographical is in arrears of the Truth.

Would you therefore say that Adamnan's Life of St Columba *is truer of the universe than Laplace's* Mecanique Celeste?

After sitting for five or six hours by a waterfall I would.

Talk to me about our next Galapagos.

In the sense of which I mean it here, to go ashore on Galapagos is to go ashore with a new way of understanding ourselves and our new world. Concerned as we are with our efforts to explain things, historians of science must of necessity devote much of their time to the emergence of new explanatory paradigms and in this sense it is likely that there will always be yet another Galapagos ahead of us. Probable it is that staring us in the face right here in our yard are the finches of a new paradigm but, culturally conditioned as we are by modern modes of comprehension, we have for the moment neither the eyes to see them nor the mental disposition to admit them. Its successes notwithstanding, scientific procedure can also be a blindspot big as the eye. So it might be time to explore the explorer.

Before they were called Galapagos, the islands Darwin went ashore on were known as Las Islas Encantadas, the Enchanted Isles. And when, in the seventeenth century, some English adventurers made enquiries concerning them, they were tauntingly told by Spaniards claiming to be in the know that they were 'shadows and noe reall islands'. This estimation of them might have something to do with the mists that so often and so mysteriously veil them, merging them into the general indistinction of their surroundings. Whatever the reason for it, this reply by the Spaniards recalls the general Hindu estimation of things as having no more than the illusory reality of the snake we falsely project into a rope.

And so, the old great question concerning the nature of mind having posed itself yet again, it might well be that Las Islas Encantadas will be our next Galapagos.

What I imagine is this: Darwin who in one incarnation went ashore as El Naturalista seeking knowledge will in a later incarnation go ashore as Narada seeking water for the Lord of the world-illusion.

And that means a Hindu not a Christian Sunday service on board the Beagle, *does it? That means, does it, that where he formerly read the Bible, Captain Fitzroy will now read from the Mardukya Upanishad and its karika?*

The simple and brutal Christian way of putting all this is that Golgotha has always been and always will be our next Galapagos. On Golgotha, in desperate dereliction, we overcome our addiction to consciousness-of.

That's what the empty skull signifies, our broken addiction.

Having overcome the world as addiction on Good Friday we can if we wish walk back in to it as Paradise on Easter morning.

Coming two hundred years after The Lyrical Ballads, *yours is a book in which the ferny glen of Romantic seeking leads back into the Kedron Valley of Christian seeking. It will seem like a falling away, won't it, from the mood of revolutionary resolution and independence the modern world had its origins in?*

There is an Irish poem, pretending to be altogether older than it is, that invites us to listen to the blackbird calling us into nature as well as to the bell calling us to church.

In his early poems, the blackbird's call is Wordsworth's creed:

> One impulse from a vernal wood
> May teach you more of man,
> Of moral evil and of good,
> Than all the sages can.

In a late poem, Emily Brontë walks out of culture into nature:

> I'll walk where my own nature would be leading –
>   It vexes me to choose another guide –
> Where the grey flocks in ferny glens are feeding,
>   Where the wild wind blows on the mountainside.

INTRODUCTION

> What have those lonely mountains worth revealing?
>   More glory and more grief than I can tell,
> The earth that wakes one human heart to feeling
>   Can centre both the worlds of Heaven and Hell.

As we would expect, D.H. Lawrence was splendidly unambiguous:

I always feel as if I stood naked for the fire of Almighty God to go through me – and it's rather an awful feeling. One has to be so terribly religious to be an artist.

Indeed there are two short poems of his that can be read as arguments for Tenebrae.

One is called 'The Hills':

> I lift up mine eyes unto the hills
> and there they are, but no strength comes from
>   them to me.
>
> Only from darkness
> and ceasing to see
> strength comes.

The other is called 'Travel Is Over':

> I have travelled and looked at the world, and loved it.
> Now I don't want to look at the world any more,
> there seems nothing there.
> In not-looking, and in not-seeing
> comes a new strength
> and undeniable new gods share their life with us, when we
>   ease to see.

In a poem of his called 'Sunday Morning', Wallace Stevens decides, however agonistically, to follow the call of the blackbird. The Paradise of this perishable world is what he at once so surely and so ambiguously settles for:

> Supple and turbulent, a ring of men
> Shall chant in orgy on a summer morn
> Their boisterous devotion to the sun,
> Not as a god, but as a god might be,
> Naked among them, like a savage source.
> Their chant shall be a chant of paradise,
> Out of their blood, returning to the sky;
> And in their chant shall enter, voice by voice,
> The windy lake wherein their lord delights,
> The trees like seraphim, and echoing hills,
> That choir among themselves long afterward.

INTRODUCTION

> They shall know well the heavenly fellowship
> Of men that perish and of summer morn.
> And whence they came and whither they shall go
> The dew upon their feet shall manifest.

In the last of his *Four Quartets*, Eliot, reading in Sir Izaak Walton, came to Gidden Hall where in the seventeenth century a watch-bell called an Anglican community to pray:

And there they sometimes betook themselves to meditate, or to pray privately, or to read a part of the New Testament to themselves, or to continue their praying or reading the Psalms; and, in case the Psalms were not always read in the day, then Mr Ferrar and others of the congregation did at night, at the ring of a watch-bell, repair to the church or oratory, and there betake themselves to prayers and lauding God, and reading the Psalms that had not been read in the day, and when these or any part of the congregation grew weary or faint, the watch-bell was rung, sometimes before and sometimes after midnight, and then another part of the family rose and maintained the watch.

Having paid the price for refusing a call to arms, Robert Lowell visits a Quaker graveyard in Nantucket. Aware, as he cannot but be here, of hell-bent energies in man and nature, he leaves the whaleroad for the road to Walsingham:

> There once the penitents took off their shoes
> And then walked barefoot the remaining mile;
> And the small trees, a stream and hedgerows file
> Slowly along the munching English lane,
> Like cows to the old shrine ...

In a poem of his called 'Genesis', it is only in a return to Christianity that Geoffrey Hill can cope with

> The soft-voiced owl, the ferret's smile,
> The hawk's deliberate stoop in air,

It is only from within a religion that confronts this bleeding creation with its bleeding Creator that he can stay hopefully in touch with the one and the other.

In spite of all that is dead and dying about it, Philip Larkin concludes that the church he has visited is serious:

> A serious house on serious earth it is,
> In whose blent air all our compulsions meet,
> Are recognized, and robed as destinies.
> And that much never can be obsolete,
> Since someone will forever be surprising

INTRODUCTION

> A hunger in himself to be more serious,
> And gravitating with it to this ground
> Which, he once heard, was proper to grow wise in,
> If only that so many dead lie round.

As you can see from these excerpts, the blackbird who sings in the vernal wood and in the ferny glen hasn't had things all his own way. If only sometimes in the stunned silence between air-raid sirens, we can still hear the watch-bell in Gidden Hall. And as Hopkins knew:

> I have desired to go
> Where springs not fail,
> To fields where flies no sharp and sided hail
> And a few lilies blow.
>
> And I have asked to be
> Where no storms come,
> Where the green swell is in the havens dumb
> And out of the swing of the sea.

In Yeats's poem 'Byzantium', that sea is gong-tormented, and on a shore of it, on a pavement of the holy city, spirits undergo purification:

> At midnight on the Emperor's pavement flit
> Flames that no faggot feeds, nor steel has lit,
> Nor storm disturbs, flames begotten of flame,
> Where blood-begotten spirits come
> And all complexities of fury leave,
> Dying into a dance,
> An agony of trance,
> An agony of flame that cannot singe a sleeve.

So yes, this book listens to the bell, it listens to the gong. It crosses from the ferny glen to the Kedron Valley. It crosses from the vernal wood to the Garden of Olives. It crosses from Lucy Gray's Lake District dale and vale to the Grand Canyon. And the question it asks or lives is: how adequate to Bright Angel Trail descending and ascending are the literatures of Europe? How adequate is Christianity?

It was in the shock of felt inadequacy that this book had its inception. Having read the geological chapters in *The Origin of Species*, I was the thing itself, the bare forked animal. I was Poor Tom and I was acold. So I cannot much help it if what I have written is a falling away from the mood of revolutionary resolution and independence the modern world had its origins in. Having to go back in order the better to come forward, I had to be content to not participate in modern history. I had to be content to

INTRODUCTION

let modern history pass me by on its way to Finland Station, the Moon and Mars.

> *Binn sin, a luin Doire an Chairn!*
> *ní chuala mé in aird so bhith*
> *ceol ba binne ná do cheol*
> *agus tú fá bhun do nid.*

> *Aoincheol is binne fan mbith,*
> *mairg nach éisteann leis go fóill,*
> *a mhic Calprainn na gclog mbinn,*
> *'s go mbéarthá a-rís ar do nóin.*

It is above all on the way home from Gethsemane and Golgotha, when you yourself are the albatross that has fallen from your neck, that you can sit and listen, outside of history listen, to the blackbird of Derrycairn.

Can the bell be as lyrical as the blackbird?

The bell calls us to radical and total surrender to the Transcendent, it calls us to cross the Kedron into our transtorrentem destiny, and so, however lyrical it might be, it will for most of us throughout most of our lives seem unhearably harsh.

> I fled Him, down the nights and down the days:
> I fled Him, down the arches of the years:
> I fled Him, down the labyrinthine ways
> Of my own mind ...

And yet, as Emerson reminds us, to Brahman belong the wings with which we fly from Brahman.

Speaking generically: as I naturally am, I am an immune system against the Divine. Like a fence-post creosoted against weather and soil I am creosoted against the still-sustaining, still-grounding Ground out of which I emerged. But, at another level of my being, or in another mood of my being, I am a sunflower opened and turning, all day and all night, to the light that never was on sea or land.

The wonder is that the bell can be heard where the blackbird sings.

The wonder is that where the blackbird sings we can hear the sage:

> *Yatra na anyat pasyati, na anyat srinoti, na anyad vijanati, sa bhuma.*

> *Binn sin, a luin*
> *Binn sin, a saoi*

INTRODUCTION

Can I conclude that you have written this book in the belief that Christianity can still ring the bell? Can ring it in a way that modern humanity can hear, even heed?

The builders of Chartres Cathedral lived in a much bigger universe than the one that we live in. Ours is numerically vast. It contains billions of galaxies, all of them subject to laws that can be mathematically formulated. Or so we believe. Theirs was ontologically vast. Cosmologically, it ascended all the way from poverty of being to plenitude of being, from corruption to glory, from misery to jubilation. Spiritually, it ascended from perdition to bliss. The lantern of Ely and the star of Burgos reveal depth dimensions that Mount Palomar is blind to.

The universe is richer than our ways of talking about it. It is richer than the scientific way of talking about it. It is richer than the mythic way of talking about it. It is richer than our most miraculous andantes, than our most mysterious chiaroscuros. And even if they only lighted our way to such acknowledgment, the Ely lantern and the Burgos star would have served us well.

Standing in Chartres, I recall that the people who built it believed that jewels were fragments of celestial or supercelestial light that had fallen into the poverties and hungers and mutabilities of our sublunary world. And when they came to build a house on earth for the Queen of Heaven it was natural, I suppose, and inevitable, that its walls and walks would be a semblance of that light.

A serious house on serious earth it is.

And standing in it, I think I know what Tibetan Buddhists mean when they talk about beings who are jewel born. Standing in it, I believe in angels, beings whose substance is joy, whose minds, mirroring the Divine, are auroras of praise.

Auroras of stone I see in Chartres.

Auroras of wall.

Auroras of soul.

The structure of the atom I see in its rose windows.

In it the blindspot isn't the eye as it was in Democritus. Wholly credible in it are Pascal's night of fire and Suso's noon of heavenly lightnings.

So the answer to your question is yes. This book was written in the belief that Christianity can still ring the bell. More readily than any religion I know, it can integrate Bright Angel Trail as aisle or, better, as ambulatory. It can inherit Golgotha not only as Golgotha, it can inherit it as Hill of the Koshaless Skull. Having Tenebrae, it has a ritual, indeed it has an architectural sacrament that goodshepherds us into and through our

INTRODUCTION

itinerarium transmentem in Deo. And it might be that coming home from the Garden of the Sepulchre on Easter morning a disappointed Christian will find that her rosary has blossomed into five new mystical mysteries:

> Jesus Grand-Canyon-deep in the world's karma
> Jesus on the Hill of the Koshaless Skull
> A'noshma Jesu
> Jesu Anadyomene
> Jivanmukta Messiah preaching his first Evangelanta sermon

Downward from their morning star a new star has appeared. By what name they call it we do not know. We live on it, and we won't be going beyond what is true of it when, sight become vision, we climb Mount Ararat and call it Buddh Gaia.

And so, its subtitle has become the title of your book, has it?

Yes, it was with the glyphs of vision that Turtle came back:

I

Going up that river was like travelling back
to the earliest beginnings of the world ...
JOSEPH CONRAD, *Heart of Darkness*

I

It was the first morning of the world, the Desana say, and there it was, Anaconda Canoe ascending the rainforest river. In it, sitting serenely upright, was Yaje Woman.

Being the Anaconda it was, her canoe was as low as its wake in the water.

With their first eyes, with their eyes of that first morning, the animals of the forest watched her.

She wasn't afraid.

Her way with things was her shape towards things. Like her canoe, she was shaped to the river. She could ascend it, because things that are possible to us only in dream are possible to her when she and we are wide awake.

Rising ahead of her, a waterbird flew between the lianas. Its single screech was a kind of silence.

She wasn't afraid.

Anaconda wouldn't constrict her. Low like his wake in the water, Anaconda would be her canoe.

Coming alongside the House of Waters, the first maloca, she disembarked.

In the house was a man from every tribe.

When they saw her they swooned. It was like drowning. It was what they experienced in the night with their wives.

Outside the house, on the green, Yaje Woman gave birth to a boy child.

Taking leaves from a tooka plant she cleaned herself and she cleaned her child.

On their undersides, the leaves of the tooka plant are blood red.

Who is father of this child? Yaje Woman demanded.

I am, one man said.

I am, said another.

I am, said a third.

The men fought. They killed the child, chopping his umbilical cord into bits. These bits they took home to their tribes and when they planted them they grew into yaje vines, climbing and coiling about the tall forest trees.

And just as in the beginning the child's umbilical cord was chopped so now is the bark of the yaje vine chopped into short lengths, and in boiling they yield a hallucinogenic brew called ayahuasca. They who drink it sacramentally say that it releases them from their bodies and, thus released, they wander in spirit worlds normally closed to us.

That's a story the Desana tell. Entering the rainforest in which they tell it, Darwin soon concluded that appearance isn't always a guide to reality. A fragment of dead twig he picked up turned out to be a living insect. A scorpion he was minutely careful with wasn't in fact a scorpion at all, it was a harmless moth wearing a disguise which proclaimed I am dangerous, I am deadly. What looked like a leaf with holes turned out to be a moth with windowed wings. There was a cosmid moth that looked like a faded flower. There was a moth that had glaring, luminous, false eyes. The heliconian is unpalatable to predators, so other species, themselves palatable, wore the heliconian's warning colours.

These moths are not deliberate deceivers, or it is at least likely that they are not, but however unconscious and unintentional it might be, there is disguise, there is deception and this brings us to the Hindu belief that it isn't only now and then and here and there that we encounter deception. In this very venerable Hindu view of things, the world in its entirety is itself a deception or a mirage and other than heighten our awareness of it and deepen our addiction to it there isn't much else that ayahuasca or soma can do for us.

Christians have a sacramental relationship with the grape vine. Isn't it time that we had an epistemological relationship with the yaje vine? Isn't it time that we so planted a yaje vine that it climbed and wound itself round our grape vine?

What I'm saying is this: isn't it time that Christians asked questions, as fearlessly as Hindus and Buddhists do, about the nature of mind?

And nowhere better to begin than in front of a faded fresco in a thirteenth-century French church. In so far as we can make out, this fresco depicts the temptation of Eve by the Serpent. Astonishingly, it is from an *amanita muscaria* mushroom, tall and stylized, and not from a fruiting broad-leaved tree that the Tempter is addressing the mother of humanity.

This, surely, is a strange and unexpected variation on an old theme. It invites speculation.

Let us suppose that nirvikalpasamadhi is or was our pristine state. Let us then suppose that the Tempter offered us a morsel of hallucinogenic mushroom. We ate it and it gave rise to awareness-of-self and other-than-self. So totally did this new state become second nature to us that we cannot now remember or imagine an alternative and, more often than not, any suggestion that we should overcome it will be met with outraged derision.

But since the suggestion put its foot in our Christian door as long ago as the thirteenth century, maybe we should make the best of a bad job and listen.

Religions tend to agree in at least one thing and that is that something ails humanity. When it comes to saying what it is ails us, however, they differ, in some cases quite radically. Christians say that our troubles have their original and continuing source in disobedience to divine command. Hindus say we are illusioned and the remedy, if only in part therefore, is to undergo a dis-illusioning. If we had the courage to speak for it, we might conclude that this is what the faded fresco is saying. So maybe we should journey towards it.

Moses and Aaron, his brother, led the Children of Israel out of Egypt. Newton and Kant led the peoples of modern Europe out of naïve realism. Since the former story is in many ways an archetype of the latter, we will do well to begin with it. As always, when it has to deal with great events, the Bible is intrepidly eloquent:

A Syrian ready to perish was my father, and he went down into Egypt, and sojourned there with a few, and became there a nation, great, mighty, and populous: and the Egyptians evil entreated us, and afflicted us, and laid upon us hard bondage: and when we cried unto the Lord God of our fathers, the Lord heard our voice, and looked on our affliction, and our labour, and our oppression: and the Lord brought us forth out of Egypt with a mighty hand, and with an outstretched arm, and with great terribleness, and with signs, and with wonders ...

Having walked dryshod through the sea, these descendants of the perishing Syrian came into a great and terrible wilderness in which they now believed that they themselves would perish:

Then came the Children of Israel, even the whole congregation, into the desert of Zin in the first month: and the people abode in Kadesh; and Miriam died there, and was buried there. And there was no water for the congregation: and they gathered themselves together against Moses and against Aaron. And the people chode with Moses, and spake, saying, Would God that we had died when our brethren died before the Lord! And why have ye brought up the congregation of the Lord into this wilderness, that we and our cattle should die there? And wherefore have ye made us to come up out of Egypt, to bring us in unto this evil place? it is no place of seed, or of figs, or of vines, or of pomegranates; neither is there any water to drink. And Moses and Aaron went from the presence of the assembly unto the door of the tabernacle of the congregation, and they fell upon their faces: and the glory of the Lord appeared unto them. And the Lord spake unto Moses, saying, Take the rod, and gather thou the assembly together, thou and Aaron thy brother, and speak ye unto the rock before their eyes; and it shall give forth his water, and thou shalt bring forth to them water out of the rock: so thou shalt give the congregation and their beasts drink. And Moses took the rod from before the Lord, as he commanded him. And Moses and Aaron gathered the congregation together before the rock, and he said unto them, Hear now, ye rebels; must we fetch you water out of this rock? And Moses lifted up his hand, and with his rod he smote the rock twice: and the water came out abundantly, and the congregation drank, and their beasts also.

Thereafter, for forty years, they wandered in the wilderness. Often, enduring longer or shorter periods of near starvation, they succumbed to regressive longings:

We remember the fish, which we did eat in Egypt freely; the cucumbers, and the melons, and the leeks, and the onions, and the garlic: but now our soul is dried away...

As time went by, wandering in the wilderness lapsed into sojourn in the wilderness. A deep and a grumbling vexation settled on the people and again and again it reddened, darkened and reddened, into open scorn. Psalm seventy-eight rehearses the whole story:

He divided the sea, and caused them to pass through; and he made the waters to stand as an heap. In the daytime also he led them with a cloud, and all the night with a light of fire. He clave the rocks in the wilderness, and gave them drink as out of the great depths. He brought streams also out of the rock, and he caused waters to run down like rivers. And they sinned yet more against him by provoking the most High in the wilderness. And they tempted God in their heart by asking for meat for their lust. Yea, they spoke against God; they said, Can God furnish a table in the wilderness? ... Therefore, the Lord heard this, and was wroth: so a fire was kindled against Jacob, and anger also came up against Israel; because they believed not in God, and trusted not his salvation: though he had commanded the clouds from above, and opened the doors of heaven, and had rained down manna upon them to eat, and had given them the corn of heaven. Man did eat angels' food ...

A day came when, genocidally intent, they crossed into Canaan, the Promised Land.

It is a strange and terrible story. Reading it, is easy to see why someone has suggested that we should think of the Bible not as a theology for man, but as an anthropology for God. This isn't, however, immediately relevant to what we are doing here, which is to propose for our consideration the idea that the biblical story might be in some ways an archetype of our own.

It was by way of an epistemological insight that we came into our desert of Zin. Newton was our Moses:

If at any time I speak of light as coloured or as endued with colour, I would be understood to speak not philosophically and properly, but grossly and accordingly to such conceptions as vulgar people in seeing all these experiments would be apt to frame. For the rays, to speak properly, are not coloured. In them there is nothing else than a certain power and disposition to sir up a sensation of this or that colour. For as sound in a bell or musical string, or other sounding body, is nothing but the trembling motion, and in the air nothing but that motion propagated from the object, and in the sensorium it is a sense of that motion under the form of sound, so colours in the object are nothing but a disposition to reflect this or that sort of rays more copiously than the rest, in the rays they are nothing but their disposition to propagate this or that motion into the sensorium and in the sensorium they are sensations of these motions under the form of colour.

In the way that the Children of Israel walked out of Egypt, Newton has walked out of naïve realism, and he isn't perturbed. Never once, it would seem, did he succumb to regressive yearnings, remembering a time when we could say of the sea that it was wine-dark, when we could say of the sea that it was rosy-fingered.

Far otherwise is it with Coleridge:

> O Lady! we receive but what we give,
> And in our life alone does Nature live:
> Ours is her wedding garment, ours her shroud!
>   And would we aught behold, of higher worth,
> Than the inanimate cold world allowed
> To the poor loveless ever-anxious crowd,
>   Ah! From the soul itself must issue forth
> A light, a glory, a fair luminous cloud
>   Enveloping the Earth—
> And from the soul itself must there be sent
> A sweet and potent voice, of its own birth,
> Of all sweet sounds the life and element!

Yes, but what happens when, our genial spirits having failed, we cannot turn Kant's *ding-an-sich* sea into the wine-dark sea we once sailed in?

What happens when, our soul dried away, we cannot weave, out of ourselves weave, a wedding garment for Helvellyn, and it stands there, a *res-extensa* outcrop in a *res-extensa* desert, never to be touched by anything but a dark, *ding-an-sich* dawn?

Coleridge fell into dejection. And in this he was, as far as I know, the first of those who articulated the epistemological suffering of modern humanity in the West.

Like a troubled spirit in a séance, Herman Melville speaks through Ishmael, his medium:

And when we conceive that other theory of the natural philosophers, that all other earthly hues – every stately or lovely emblazoning – the sweet tinges of sunset skies and woods; yea, and the gilded velvets of butterflies, and the butterfly cheeks of young girls; all these are but subtle deceits, not actually inherent in substances, but only laid on from without; so that all deified Nature absolutely paints like the harlot, whose allurements cover nothing but the charnel-house within; and when we proceed further, and consider that the mystical cosmetic, which produces every one of her hues, the great principle of light, forever remains white or colourless in itself, and if operating without medium upon matter, would touch all objects, even tulips and roses, and with its own blank tinge – pondering all this, the palsied universe lies before us a leper ...

It was on Dover Beach that Arnold encountered the naked world, a world stripped of its allurements, a world stripped of its mystical cosmetic:

> The Sea of Faith
> Was once, too, at the full, and round earth's shore
> Lay like the folds of a bright girdle furled.
> But now I only hear
> Its melancholy, long, withdrawing roar,
> Retreating, to the breath
> Of the night-wind, down the vast edges drear
> And naked shingles of the world.
>
> Ah, love, let us be true
> To one another! For the world, which seems
> To lie before us like a land of dreams,
> So various, so beautiful, so new.
> Hath really neither joy, nor love, nor light,
> Nor certitude, nor peace, nor help for pain;
> And we are here as on a darkling plain
> Swept with confused alarms of struggle and flight,
> Where ignorant armies clash by night.

The desert of Zin the Children of Israel came into. The *res extensa* desert or the *ding-an-sich* desert we have come into.

ANACONDA CANOE

Speaking of their desert, the Children of Israel say:

> It is no place of seeds or of figs or of vines,
> or of pomegranates. Neither is there any
> water to drink.

Speaking with Arnold, we say of our desert that it

> Hath really neither joy, nor love, nor light,
> Nor certitude, nor peace, nor help for pain ...

The Children of Israel remember the good things of Egypt:

> We remember the fish which we did eat in
> Egypt freely; the cucumbers, and the melons,
> and the leeks, and the onions, and the garlic.

We remember the images and the metaphors and the pathetic fallacies or should we say the pathetic verities of naïve realism.

> We remember a wine-dark sea.
> The dawn we remember was rosy-fingered.

We remember that when he talked about the process of coming to know, Aquinas could talk of an *adequatio rei ad intellectum*.

But now neither on Dover Beach nor on the beach at Key West – on neither beach when we sing is there an adequation of sea to song:

> It was her voice that made
> The sky acutest at its vanishing.
> She measured to the hour its solitude.
> She was the single artificer of the world
> In which she sang. And when she sang, the sea,
> Whatever self it had, became the self
> That was her song, for she was the maker. Then we,
> As we beheld her striding there alone,
> Knew that there never was a world for her
> Except the one she sang and, singing, made.

No Wallace, the centaur of our *ding-an-sich* self and *ding-an-sich* sea has fallen asunder, and the only cloud there is to guide us by day is a Cloud of Unknowing and the only cloud there is to guide us by night is a Cloud of Forgetting.

Our epistemological desolation continues.

And now, just when we thought things were as bad as they could be, here comes Sylvia.

With Sylvia Plath, we awaken to a new and dreadful apprehension: the world mightn't always ground us, mightn't always be there for us. As we watch them with her, the hills step off into whiteness which, for Ishmael, is the colourless all-colour of atheism. And desolating as it is, that is only a beginning:

> The hills step off into whiteness.
> People or stars
> Regard me sadly, I disappoint them.
>
> The train leaves a line of breath.
> O slow
> Horse the colour of rust.
>
> Hooves, dolorous bells—
> All morning the
> Morning has been blackening,
>
> A flower left out.
> My bones hold a stillness, the far
> Fields melt my heart.
>
> They threaten
> To let me through to a heaven
> Starless and fatherless, a dark water.

It has been a long journey, our journey to Golgotha.

On Golgotha, on Good Friday, the far fields and the near fields, the far mountains and the near mountains, did let Jesus through to a dark water. They let him through into what, at first encounter, may have seemed like a Great Naught behind what Hindus call maya, behind what Ishmael calls the mystical cosmetic.

That's one way of putting it. Alternatively we could say that he underwent the great dis-illusioning. In other words it wasn't so much that the hills let him through as that his psyche opened and there he was in what seemed to be a great no-thing-ness.

This didn't only happen to Jesus. It has happened to innumerable others and it is here that the ropesnake parable and the Narada parable begin to make sense. It is here that we open our door to an interpretation of the Fall that sees the Tempter coiled about an *amanita muscaria* mushroom, the mushroom ancient Hindus call King Soma, the mainstay of the heavens.

On the opposite wall from the faded fresco therefore we should paint its Good Friday correlative:

Christ looking down into Adam's empty skull
   and
Standing on either side of him
Yaje Woman and King Soma

Hindus talk about Mayashakti, a goddess who personifies the source of maya or illusion.

For our purposes we could personify that source as Yajeshakti or Somashakti, and it was in looking down into his own empty skull, it was in continuing to look down into it, that he overcame them, that he overcame the source of maya or illusion within himself.

On the morning of Good Friday Anaconda Canoe ascending our river is ropesnake canoe ascending our river, is a ropesnake epistemology ascending our river, is our exodus from metaphysics to metanoesis ascending our river, is our exodus from evangel to evangelanta ascending our river.

The dis-illusioning that began with Newton completed itself sixteen hundred years earlier on Golgotha.

And so, to return to the faded fresco: the Tempter is King Soma coiled about his own bum trip, and we fell for it.

The great dis-illusioning is not of course the end of the journey.

Hanging there in the seeming Naught, looking down into the emptiness of his own empty skull, Christ cried out in that moment of awful dereliction which, by God's grace, has for so many been a moment of awe-full exaltation.

Exaltation into the Divine Mirum.

Exaltation into that same Mirum appearing to us now as evening and morning a first day.

A Naïve Day.

It was the first morning of the world, the Desana say, and there it was, Anaconda Canoe ascending the rainforest river. In it, sitting serenely upright, was Yaje Woman.

Being the anaconda it was, her canoe was low as its wake in the river.

With their first eyes, with their eyes of that first morning, the animals of the forest watched her ...

II

The Blackfoot Indians lived in Montana. Until white people came, they were in many ways a Pleistocene people living in a Pleistocene land.

Big with big dawns over prairies and mountains, their world had an air of original innocence about it. Even its violence and its terror were innocent, somehow. And it wouldn't surprise you, trailing a fox there, to suddenly look up and see you had tracked it into a living Altamira, a living Lascaux.

A Pleistocene world.

Hungry after hibernation, a bear would emerge from her mountain and hook a salmon from the nearest loud river.

Out of pure crossness, or out of boredom maybe, a cougar would screech in the high pine woods. Above him, precipitously safe on the rock walls, bighorns wouldn't even break off from their grazing to look down on sudden savagery.

Out on the prairies, like outcrops out there, herds of buffalo turn and face into a blizzard. Head fur and shoulder fur icing over, they stand there, like breakers in an inshore ocean, letting it foam over them. Not for them to be concerned about how long this howling all about them will last. The howlings of wolves and the howlings of storms, these also are their lullabies.

Buffalo, particularly the bulls, are tremendous beasts. Naturally huge and high-horned and bearded, they look at you, heads hung heavy and low, out of minds that are inwardly chloroformed and closed down to all dread of the world. Small wonder then that the Blackfoot were reluctant to go out onto the prairies and take them on openly with bows and arrows. It was mostly by guile that they hunted them. They would lure them towards a precipice and stampede them over it into a piskun, or corral, of pine poles at the bottom.

Usually, the luring was done by a medicine man.

Dressed in a buffalo head and buffalo robe, he would walk out into the prairies and approach a herd. In unostentatious, quiet ways he would seek to arouse their curiosity. This done, he would turn and walk slowly away, walking towards the precipice. Knowing, without looking round, that the herd was following him, he would quicken his pace. Slowly, ever so slowly, with no sign of panic he would then break into a run. Suspecting nothing, the buffalo behind him would do likewise. When the buffalo were at full stretch, thundering past, the people, hidden until now behind bushes and rocks, would rise up and make a great clamour. Stampeded in this way over the edge, the buffalo would fall on the rocks below. Almost always their bones or even their backs would be broken, and, there they would remain, immobilized. But if by chance any of them escaped injury they too would be trapped, unable to leap the corral wall. By guile they did it. But a time came when the guile didn't work. Lured to the edge of the precipice, the buffalo would break to left and right, climb down the slow slopes and gambol away.

This had been happening for months. There was famine among the people. Many had died. There was low lamentation in the tipis. One morning, in anguish, a young girl climbed the rock wall and looked out into the prairies. Seeing a herd in the distance she heard herself saying, or she heard some animal depth within herself saying, if only ye would come and tumble over the precipice I would marry one of you. No sooner were the words spoken than, to her amazement, the herd stopped grazing and came thundering towards her. Over the precipice they flowed, an avalanche of food for the people.

The girl was delighted. And coming out of their tipis to see what had happened the people were delighted. In a while there was huge commotion, everyone seeking to secure and take home as much food as he could. In the meanwhile, as from nowhere, a huge bull stood in front of the girl. 'You must come with me and be my bride,' he said. The girl recoiled. 'But you promised,' Bull said. Taking her by the arm, his head hung low, hung horn-high, as they walked, with her desperate heart, he led her away, up the rock wall, into the prairies.

That night when the feasting was at its height her father missed the young girl. He guessed what had happened and at first light, taking his bow and quiver, he went into the prairies seeking her. He came to a buffalo wallow. Not knowing which of several directions he should take, he sat down for a while. A magpie showed up. Very grand he was in his ways. And very busy. Much, much too busy to take any but the most cursory notice of the man. 'What a grand bird you are,' the man ventured. 'Indeed,' said Magpie, interested. 'Indeed.' 'Will you help me?' the man asked. 'I will,' said Magpie, grandly disposing himself to hear what might follow. 'I am sad at heart,' the man said. 'My daughter has been taken from me. A bull buffalo has taken her to be his bride. She is out there somewhere with him. Will you see if you can find her for me? And if you do find her, will you tell her I am waiting for her here at the wallow?'

Delighted, and feeling more important than ever, Magpie flew off.

Such an instinct had he for finding things that it wasn't long at all till he saw her, sitting alone, but not forlorn, in the midst of a great herd. Casually, pretending not to notice her, he alighted beside her. 'Your father is waiting for you at the wallow,' he said.

'Shhhh!' the girl said, pointing to her huge, sleeping husband. 'Tell him to wait,' she whispered. Pleased, very pleased indeed with his increased importance, Magpie flew off. Bull woke up. Stood up. He called for water. Reaching up into his forehead, his bride took down a horn and walked towards the wallow.

'Why did you come?' she asked, approaching her father. 'You will surely be killed out here.' 'I came to take you home,' her father said, jumping to his feet. 'Hurry, let us go now.' 'No, no,' she said. 'Bull is awake and he is waiting, looking out for me even now. If I'm not back soon he will suspect something. He will alert the whole herd and they will come after us and kill us. Wait till some other time,' she said. She filled the horn from the wallow and walked back to the herd. She gave the horn to her husband.

He drank a little. 'Ha!' he roared, his nostrils flaring. He drank again. 'There's someone,' he roared. 'I smell him,' he roared. 'There's no one,' the girl pleaded. He didn't hear her, couldn't hear her, for the rage he was in. For the rage the herd all about her was in. Blind, but not so blind as not to know where the wallow was, the herd turned and faced it. To the girl's consternation, leaving her alone and forlorn, they thundered away. Finding her father they hooked him and trampled him until, indistinguishable it would seem, he was one with the mud.

The girl came. Seeing what had happened, she wailed. 'Aha!' said Bull. 'You are mourning for your father. But we understand you. We understand your grief. For we have grieved for our fathers too. For our fathers and mothers fallen over your precipice. Fathers and mothers and sisters and brothers and daughters and sons. We know your grief. We will give you a chance.' 'What chance is that?' the girl asked. 'If you can bring him to life, we will let you and your father go back to your people.'

'Help me, help me,' the girl pleaded, turning to Magpie. 'Please, will you search the mud and if you find any tiniest morsel of my father bring it to me?' Magpie searched and searched, scratching the mud with his claws, poking it with his bill. In the end he pulled up a fragment of vertebra. He brought it to the girl. Placing it on the good red earth, she covered it with her robe. Sinking into herself until she was almost an invisible voice, she began to sing an old, slow, sacred song.

Having formed a circle, the buffalo were watching. Her song ended, she lifted the robe. Her father was lying there, restored in body but not yet alive. Now again she covered her father with the robe. And, now again, sinking into herself, she sang.

She lifted the robe. To the utter amazement and huge admiration of the buffalo, her father was alive. Magpie was delighted. His head hung low, hung horn-high to his own heart's sorrow, the Great Bull knew he had lost his bride.

'We have seen strange things today,' he said. 'We have seen the people's holy power.'

'And now,' he said, turning to the girl, 'before you and your father go, we will teach you our song and our dance. You must not forget them.'

And the buffalo danced.

Like the shadows of mountains in moonlight they moved. As silently all night and as slowly. And their song was silence. Like shadows in the dreamlit and lamplit caves of the Great Imagination they moved. When daybreak came the caves were gone. Father and daughter walked home to their people. And led by their ailing speared Bull, speared to the heart he was and dying, the herd walked south to their winter grazing grounds. And that's the end of this story. It tells how, once upon a time, wishing for understanding and sympathy between buffalo and people, the buffalo taught the people their buffalo song and dance.

A story told by the Blackfoot Indians.

But it might have been told in Altamira and Lascaux.

Migrating across the steppes of Aurignacian Eurasia, it might have crossed the Bering land bridge and gone south, carried south by its sacred keepers, into the prairies and mountains of Montana. But even if this didn't happen, and it surely didn't happen in the way we have imagined, it would nonetheless be good to know that Europe was once the kind of place in which this kind of story might have been told.

A Pleistocene story about a Pleistocene Europa.

Our first Europa.

Our native Europa.

Our Blackfoot Europa. The Europa of Europe's Serengeti. She climbed a rock wall one morning and, consenting to be bride to the Great

Bull, she called the buffalo. She recoiled of course when the Bull showed up, his head hung low, hung horn-high to her desperate heart. Like our last Europa she recoiled and, given a chance, would have fled, fled, fled, out of Serengeti fled, into strong walled cities fled, into modern Europe fled. But the Bull had taken her by the arm. She walked his way. Three mornings later she came back, she and her father. She had, as a gift from the buffalo, what she and we in the depths of our psyches always have, she had commonage consciousness. But we are children of the last Europa, she who fled.

And we have fled.

Out of Serengeti fled.

Into strong-walled cities fled.

Into modern Europe fled.

And every now and then, in every age, a Theseus or Perseus will go forth to slay the Bull. But the Bull will always stand in our gate. Miraculously destructive now, and dark, he will stand in it. And he will shake the foundations of all our endeavours, for we have sought to exclude him, building so many and such strong cities against him. Cities there are of course which from the beginning have welcomed and included him. Bhuvaneshvar and Khajuraho have done so. Here he lies down on the sacred yard. He is garlanded with flowers. He is serene. He looks towards the womb chamber of the temple. He is called Nandin.

Our Pleistocene Europa.

Our Blackfoot Bridge for three nights to the Great Bull.

Our Lady of Commonage Consciousness.

On the third morning she came home, she and her father, she and her Perseus, he no longer a bull slayer, not now a dragon slayer, ready to hang up his bow.

Our Aurignacian Europa.

Our Aurignacian Andromeda.

Our Aurignacian Ariadne.

Under her robe of commonage consciousness, wombed by it, wombed by her song of commonage consciousness, our Perseus was reborn. It's the song I listen for in Montana. It's the song I listen for in Altamira and Lascaux. In the eighteen-sixties I think it was. In or about the time when the first white pioneers into Montana would have heard our Blackfoot story. In or about that time in the highlands of southern France, in a grotto outside her village, Bernadette Soubirous had eighteen visions of Mary, the Mother of Jesus. For many Christians, Mary isn't only the mother of Jesus. She is also Mother of God. She is Queen of Heaven. And since she appeared there, millions of pilgrims have come to her grotto. They walk in candlelit processions, singing her hymn.

A couple of years before the apparitions, when Lourdes was still a quiet, out of the way place, a French prehistorian came here. Investigating the grotto, he uncovered evidence of Pleistocene living in it. Was there, I sometimes wonder, an Aurignacian Bernadette Soubirous? Following a dream trail away from her people, did she come here and hear our Aurignacian Ariadne singing alone in her grotto, singing her song of commonage consciousness? Following a dream trail away from her people, did she come here and see her, Our Lady of Commonage Consciousness. And what did she look like? And what was her song like? And what did she say?

And when she sang, did the animals of our lost Serengeti come and lie with her here on her holy mountain? We don't know. We can only hope that, surviving somewhere, her singing still is.

In medieval times pilgrims came from far and wide to Chartres Cathedral. And it was little to be wondered at that they did. For the cathedral, it was claimed, housed a famous relic, the tunic Mary wore the night she gave birth to Jesus in a stable in Bethlehem. One night a great fire or Destroying Angel swept through the town, engulfing everything, even the cathedral. The townspeople were in despair. There was no arguing with the ashes of their earthly and heavenly ambitions. The Queen of Heaven had withdrawn her favour from them. A few days later, however, there was joy in the smouldering town. It had just been discovered that, miraculously preserved by Our Lady herself, the tunic had survived unharmed in the cathedral crypt.

In Chartres no one saw ashes or smelt old smoke that day. Walking in procession behind their miraculous relic, they saw a new town and overlooking it from its hill a new and glorious house on earth for Our Lady Queen of Heaven.

And what of the robe our adolescent, Aurignacian girl covered her father with? Covered all dragon slayers with.

Covered Theseus with. Covered Perseus with.

Covered Kadmus with. Covered St George with.

Covered Siegfried with. Covered Beowulf with.

What of that robe? And what of her song? Has her song survived? Head hung low, hung horn-high to our desperate hearts, the returned Bull tells us it has, it has, it has.

Our Buffalo Song. Our Buffalo Dance.

The Dance of Commonage Consciousness.

TURTLE WAS GONE A LONG TIME

III

Among the Inuit she is mother of sea beasts. She has many names. Takanakapsaluk is a name many people know her by. Her story is brutal and short. She was the one who wouldn't marry. Her father was angry at this. And one day he rowed her out into the ocean mists and threw her overboard. Surfacing, she reached for the boat and held on. Her father chopped her fingers off. She sank through the twilights and nights of the ocean down to its dreaming floor. These being marvellous times, times when the world dreamed not only by night but also by day, her chopped-off fingers, floating away on the ocean, underwent a most wonderful transformation. They turned into sea beasts. Into walruses, seals, dolphins, porpoises, whales.

Whale songs in the oceans and the wide, wild wailings of seals in remote coves caused amazements of shining that night in the stars. In those days no one who looked into nature saw laws of nature. All animal and human eyes that looked and all the things they looked at were a common miraculousness, a common dream.

In those days the sun sank below the southern horizon. For a long lone time it was night. It was the same night all day and all night. And a child asked his father why this was so. Far away in the south, he said, there has been a blizzard. There's a man in front of his igloo shovelling snow. He is shovelling it higher and higher, scattering it far and wide. That's why the sun cannot show through. But don't be afraid. One day the man will have done his work. The sun will come back. Caribou will come back. Geese will come back. Bears will come inland off the sea ice and the flowers of the tundra will open. Dreamtime. Strangetime. The sun gone below the horizon of the world. Consciousness gone below the horizon of the night psyche. Strange things happen in dreamtime. Becoming a seal, an Inuit shaman dives to the floor of the ocean and touches it with his paddles. That's why there is healing in his hands. Touching you with those hands it is with the depths of your psyche he is touching you. When he sings for you, touching you with this songs, it is with seal voice and whale voice he is singing. In all the far depths and far coves of your psyche he is singing with seal voice and whale voice and wolf voice for you and you are healed because once again you are whole. And how wonderful it is to walk out of an igloo into a northern morning. *Sila ersinarsinivdluge*, he calls after you walking away. *Sila ersinarsinivdluge*. Dot be afraid of the universe.

ANACONDA CANOE

Great initiations come to the shaman. Dream initiations initiate him, or her. She is ovum again. She is seed again. She is sown in the depths of the common psyche. Immense dyings happen and immense growings. Immense, immense dyings. And immense growings.

And how awful it is being it. Being an ovum fertilized with immense dying. Being an ovum to growings and dyings. And the shaman must be ovum. Out of his dying he grows. Out of his having given everything up he is given his life as a healer among his people. From all his immense dyings the shaman comes home to his igloo singing. And out of the great universal psyche helping animals come to him. Spirits come. And he has a drum to call them. And in dreamtime now, in his igloo, the shaman drums and while he drums the great universal psyche is inwardly and outwardly open to all that it is, to whale and bear and wolf and mountain and star.

And all our walls, walls inside and walls outside, are walls of fear and with seal voice and whale voice and swan voice the shaman sings to them and they go down and the man inside us stops his shovelling and caribou calve on the tundra and in the swamps, on tussocks and islands, geese sit on their hot eggs.

Her father had hopes for her, that she would grow up a good woman, that she would be wife to a respected, good man and that she would be mother to brave and happy children. But no, she wouldn't, never, never. She wouldn't marry. Her father was very angry. Saying it was fishing they were going, he rowed her out into the ocean one morning and out there, out of sight of land, he threw her overboard. Surfacing, she reached for the boat and held on. He chopped her fingers off. She sank to the floor of the ocean and her fingers, floating away, carried far away by the currents, turned into dolphins and porpoises and walruses and seals and whales.

And that is how Takanakapsaluk, she who wouldn't be mother, became mother of sea beasts. Mother to whale song and seal's wail. She lives, shamans say, in a house on the floor of the ocean. And in front of her house, they say, in a pool there, watched over by her, are the beasts she is mother to. When people are good, when they walk in the way of the great world, then those beasts are free to come and go. Then walruses and porpoises and dolphins and seals and whales are free to rise to the surface where the people hunt them. When people are bad, when they ignore or live contrary to the great way, then a wall of anger, her anger, grows about her house and pool, shutting herself and all sea beasts in. In the world above, hunters wait all day every day at their seal holes, but nothing shows and the people go hungry. Only the shaman knows what has happened.

And only he can do anything about it. People come to him in his hut one night. Quietly, one by one, they come, coming down the dark passage into the light. They take off their outer polar-bear skins. They sit in seal skins. And they wait, watching him, but not over-curiously. The shaman is dressed in his sacred robe. He is in the shadows, singing and drumming. His robe is outlandish and strange. It's as if he was wearing his nature inside out. Dressed in it, he is dressed in his helping dreams and in his helping visions. For that robe has been dyed in the depths of his psyche. It has been soaked and dyed in an inner source of revelation and dreamvision. And whenever he moves, convulsed from within by what he is seeing, his robe rattles, for onto it and into it he has sown all his helping spirits and animals.

He sits in the shadows, singing and drumming.

The people sing for him, sending him on his way.

In a trance, leaving his body, the shaman calls from near at hand. In a while again he calls from farther away. From farther and farther away each time he calls. They can hardly hear him so far away is his voice. Then he is gone. And while he is gone the people will sing. It is a way well known to him, this way going down the shaman is on. Perils and perditions innumerable open before him. Provoked by his very presence here, the one great anger becomes many angers and a shaman is powerful only when, opposed by them, he can appease them or subdue them or pass through them.

Through a rock that opens and closes crushingly he must pass. He comes to mountains that have no way round them. He must climb them and the only way to do this is by a ladder the mountains themselves let down. It's a ladder whose rungs are knives and, bewilderingly, the knives hold themselves now on their flat sides, now on edge. He comes to a great river. It can only be crossed on a sword bridge. Half way there, a storm blows, and below him now is a river of fire voracious for him. Having failed to turn him back, or destroy him, with fire and flood, the anger becomes insidious. A seal woman stands at the door. Opening her bodice, she invites him in. On the far side of a stream is a man like himself, dressed like himself, a wounded shaman. He calls for help. But if, on this road of deceptions, the wayfarer who has come through the clashing rocks and climbed the ladder of knives, if he now accepts the invitation to love or if he now responds to a call for help, he will be destroyed. The impulse to a night of love he must resist. The impulse to compassion he must resist. All allurings and lurings he must resist. Never, never, for no matter what reason, must he turn aside. Trodden since time began, it is a well known way.

ANACONDA CANOE

A way which at any moment can cease from before our feet, can turn about, open its mouth and swallow us down into the final terror, the terror of having no terror at all to be terrified of. A dangerous way. Helped by his helping spirits, however, the shaman overcomes all obstacles and he comes at last to the wall of anger that has grown about Takanakapsaluk and her beasts. Even outside the wall he can hear from within the dreaming and heavy breathing of dolphins and porpoises and seals and walruses and whales. With whale voice and seal voice he sings to the wall. With wolf voice, howling forlornly and alone, he sings. The wall opens. The shaman goes through. He crosses a yard, opens her door and sees her, Our mother of sea beasts, Takanakapsaluk. She is sitting there sullen and speechless, her hair all crawling and angry, infested with lice, with the sins of a people who no longer walk in the great way. Taking a comb of walrus ivory, the shaman combs her hair, combing its infestations and its anger our of it, combing it into a wonder of fallings, falling lovely and rich around her seal's shoulders.

Takanakapsaluk is appeased. The wall of her anger disappears. And knowing that the beasts are already rising, the shaman leaves. In his snow hut on the winter tundra, his people are singing for him. In a silence between songs they hear him, calling from far, far away. The next time he calls, he is nearer at hand. With immense convulsions, he re-enters his body. He comes out of the shadows. His people about him, not curiously looking, give thanks.

Outside in the night the hunters have called their dogs. They have harnessed them to their sleds and are setting out. Before the moon coming up will be set the famine will be over.

An Inuit story.

A story for us.

For I imagine a grotto or cave on the floor of *anima mundi* and in it, shut in by a wall of anger, Our Mother of Archetypes. We've been living contrary to the great way. Her hair is infested. And for centuries now no great caves or cathedrals or temples have risen from the depths. No Altamira, Lascaux, or Niaux. No Stonehenge, Bhuvaneshvar or Borobudur.

And we are hungry.

We are shelterless.

We have no snowhut in our tundra, none we can go to at night to sing for our shaman going down. No going down to harrow hell. No going down to bring Eurydice back.

No going down to talk to Tiresias.

No Jesus going down.

TURTLE WAS GONE A LONG TIME

No Orpheus going down.
No Odysseus going down.
No Inanna going down.

No. But here is a snowhut on the winter tundra and in it, his people sitting there singing for him, an Inuit shaman going down by another way to another depth, going down to a depth below all old-world depths, going down dangerously by a dangerous way to the rich roots of a rich universe, going down to comb Takanakapsaluk's hair.

An Inuit shaman going down to comb the hair of her who is

> Sealwoman
> Walruswoman
> Whalewoman
> Mother of Seabeasts
> Mother of Archetypes

We have walked contrary to the Great Way. We have too totally followed Thubalcain. Thubalcain forged the first hammer and said to the great world I will shape you to suit us. The ancestors of dolphins and whales slipped over the side of their foothold and committing themselves to great nature said to it, shape us to suit you.

And wouldn't it be good if, going down, our shaman took our Thubalcain hammer with him and, like a seed, sowed it for three days and three nights in the depths of the universe. Returned to us, it would have the genius of that universe in it and again maybe, within a few centuries, we would have wonders like the rose windows of Chartres and the sun wheels of Konarak. Mountains and outcrops aren't inconveniences of dead matter. They are profundities of hibernating nature. And when, once again, we are in the grain of the great world they will work with us for us. And the aisles of our Chartres and the terraces of our Borobudurs will be Bright Angel Trails, Dark Mara Trails, tracks in the Great Journey.

Architecturally and ritually, we will know that there is a great journey and like the ancestors of dolphins and whales, there will always be those who will slip over the side of their rock of faith and surrender to the abyss of faith.

But nothing of all this can happen until we have found a shaman who, protected by the world, will go down into the depths of the world and, coming to the wall of anger, will wail at it with seal voice and whale voice and wolf voice.

And when the wall opens our shaman will go through and taking a comb of walrus ivory he will comb

ANACONDA CANOE

> Whalewoman's hair
> Sealwoman's hair
> Walruswoman's hair

combing our killing cosmologies and our killing creation stories out of it, combing our scripts for history and the universe out of it, combing our reductionisms and dualisms and humanisms out of it, combing all imaginations that aren't out of the Great Imagination out of it, combing all ways that aren't out of the Great Way out of it. Our shaman in a cave in a depth of the world's psyche, combing Takanakapsaluk's hair, combing the dark of it down over her sealwoman's shoulders. When she is appeased, he will leave, knowing that already, excitedly in a Palaeolithic cave, a child has looked up and called out, Look Papa, Bulls!

Could it be? we wonder. Could it be that our hungry times are at an end?

Whale songs are rising. Archetypes are rising. Caves are rising. And it must be that now at last we are ready for them, for, following a fox here and a dog there, we are walking into them.

Seeking their dog in a wood one day, four young boys walked into Lascaux.

Taking shelter from a shower one day, three brothers noticed an opening in the side of a hill and entering it, exploring it, they found themselves being stared at by a Pleistocene wizard. Or sorcerer. Sorcerer he is called. The sorcerer of Les Trois Frères. He has grown into what he is wearing. It is likely that in his mind he is what he is wearing: big, branching antlers, wolf's ears, a lion's beard, bear's paws and a horse's tail.

A terrifying apparition. Antlered and strange, he stares back at us from the hidden recesses of our psyches. A warning. An opening into terror underground.

And wouldn't it be a most awful tragedy if, in our search for psychic wholeness, we ended here in a state of bewildered, frightened, blind archetypal possession?

And, surely, that possibility should give us pause. A story from the rainforest which I tried to tell ran aground, coming towards us, on Golgotha. And that was by no means a calamity. That was good. And it might be that here now, in this inmost cavern of a Pleistocene cave, our Inuit story will lose its nerve. It might be that here, in this inner yawning, we will give up. Confronted in our own inner underground by this antlered strange staring, we might back away and refuse all further growing into psychic wholeness.

So maybe, before we back away or walk on, we should sit here and say it:

If the opening we are, and are in, is wide enough to let in the light it is wide enough to let in the dark, if it is wide enough to let in heaven it is wide enough to let in hell, if it is wide enough to let in great healing it is wide enough to let in great illness, if it is wide enough to let in sanity it is wide enough to let in insanity, if it is wide enough to let in God it is wide enough to let in Satan Sabbaoth.

Where we are now none of all of this is a long way off. Our trail has led us into an inner yearning in which we are confronted by an antlered, strange staring.

We must seek to understand that staring. Karmically, in the course of our spiritual growing, phylogeny in us comes flush with ontogeny in us. And looking at the antlered, bearded, horse-tailed Sorcerer, it would appear that in him ontogeny is trapped in phylogeny. He didn't walk on. He stayed with the glamour and power of it all. Being Vishvarupa became for him the end of the journey, not just a terrifying stage of it. He didn't walk into Gethsemane and sweat it all away. And now, for the moment, he is trapped, terrified of himself and of us who have happened upon him. Bright Angel Trail and all other trails going down are dangerous and serious. And knowing this, maybe, now again, we can return to our snowhut on the tundra.

We live in hungry times. Like the little man in the story we've been shovelling so skyscrapingly high and wide that we've eclipsed the divine light in the world.

In the depths of the great psyche, in her grotto there, Takanakapsaluk is angry. Her hair is lousy with our wrongdoings. A wall of anger has grown about her and her sea beasts. Call them sea beasts. Or call them the seed imaginings out of which the universe happens. All closed down in the crypt of her anger. Nothing, no vision we might live by in harmony with all things, comes to the surface.

There is famine. And so tonight, in ones and twos, we come to sit with our shaman in his igloo. He sits behind us in the shadows. We drum for him and we sing for him.

Our shaman going down. For our sakes going down. God speed you Shaman.

IV

There was famine among the Lakota Sioux. One morning two of their bravest hunters went out into the prairies. They climbed a low hill. Their eyes were horizon-wide with hunger, but they saw nothing, no shimmer of pronghorn, no herd of buffalo, bull-led, grazing. It was strange. As if, dream drawn there, the herds were in an enchantment beyond the horizon. Even their most powerful shaman, fasting and singing and drumming, couldn't break the enchantment. If that's what it was. Whatever it was, the hunters didn't brood overmuch about it that morning.

They saw her coming. A woman in shining buckskin. A woman surely.

And yet for one strange moment there was something very big, something very brown and four-footed about her gait. She was beautiful. She approached them. Seeing her near at hand one of the hunters had instinctive thoughts about her. She called him to her. She surrounded them both with a mist. When the mist dispersed, the hunter was a small heap of bare bones and worms at her feet. Addressing the other hunter, she told him to go back to his people and tell them to prepare for her coming. Unaware of his hunger now and running for all he was worth, the hunter was soon among his people. Uncexemoniously, unannounced, he stood before Chief Standing Hollow Horn in his tipi. He told him his story.

Chief Standing Hollow Horn sent a crier among the people. By nightfall they had built a great lodge. Three mornings later she came. She was ordinary. And yet, as she approached him in the great lodge, Chief Standing Hollow Horn knew that even good thoughts about her would be dangerous. She brought their religion to the Sioux. It amounted to living in such a way that the herds could come back. In particular, it meant that where recently they had fallen into the habit of saying 'us' and 'them' they now once again would learn to say 'we'.

Out on the prairies four evenings later, going away, she rolled a first time on the ground and she was a red buffalo. She rose up a beautiful woman and walked away. She rolled a second time on the ground and she was a black buffalo. She rose up a beautiful woman and walked away. Rolling a third time she was a brown buffalo. She rose up a beautiful woman and walked away. She rolled a fourth time on the ground and she was a white buffalo calf. She got up. She walked away. Then suddenly, growing fainter, she was out of sight. White Buffalo Calf Woman is the name the Sioux have known her by ever since.

TURTLE WAS GONE A LONG TIME

>   She, Ordinary Woman
>   Buffalo Calf Woman

Did she walk the prairies of Aurignacian Europe? Did she bring their religion to a forgotten Aurignacian people? If we peeled away the Europe of Jesus and Europa's Europe, would we sense her presence? I imagine we would. I imagine a tribe of Aurignacian hunters. They call themselves the Goose People. Goose was the first shaman. And engraved outside on the hide of every tipi are her wholly enclosing wild wings. At night, in dreams, she flies with her people to the summer breeding grounds, and the winter feeding grounds, of vision. And they have a cave, these people. So they are strong. They aren't shut out by their mountain. Often, having waned with the moon, they will sit six caverns deep in it. They will sit six caverns deep in a seeing that isn't inflamed by seeking or hunting eyesight.

>   That's how they see
>   That's how they know
>   That's how they hunt.

Their mountain does their deepest thinking and their deepest dreaming with them. With its bare cave walls it imagines herds of wild horses and auroch and bison out there on the prairies for them. Walls of their mountain are walls of the one, universal imagining. And we only exist in reality because we exist antecedently as mirage.

Mountain mirages of the one great mind become realities of the one great way. In the night, when their shaman talked, he would say, the mirage that I am goes before the reality that I am. The reality that I am is a continuous realizing of the continuously imagined mirage that I am. Drumming all night deep in the mountain this old shaman would pray:

>   Mirage us, Mountain
>   Mirage us magnificently
>   Mirage wild horses and bison
>   Mirage huge herds of auroch
>   Mirage huge herds of deer
>   Mirage us, Mountain
>   Mirage us magnificently
>   Do but mirage us
>   Magnificently, Mountain
>   And we shall be magnificent.

And so he would sit six caverns deep with his people. Six caverns deep in their great imagining mountain. There was one last cavern only he would enter. Protected by his humility he would keep walking. Even when the mountain roared at him showing its stalagmite and stalactite teeth to him he kept walking. His humility had no grovelling or fawning in it. It had eagle wings in it. And ocean floor fins in it. But wherever he went, with wings or with fins, his going was always a going with the one great way. Protected by his humility he could walk unharmed in all the mountain's chewings. He would sit in the last earth dark. Softly, only once, he would call on his drum, calling for whatever it was the first dark was imagining, or mirageing, into the one universal way. Protected by the eagle wings and the ocean floor fins of his humility he always came back. Old as the rain, coming and going like the rain, his songs, like the rocks, had lichens on them. Had owl calls in them. Don't think about the universe, he would say. Waned like the moon, dark like the moon, go into its caves and, being nothing, being the nothing you were before you existed, be one great imagining with it.

But people aren't always able for the Great Way. Even an Aurignacian people who live from the imagining dark of their cave and their mountain aren't always able. And so it was. Goose was old. In their dreams Goose could no longer fly with them to the summer breeding grounds and the winter feeding grounds of vision.

A hill there was. I don't know what its name was in Aurignacian Europe. In Christian Europe it is called the Hill of Chartres.

This was the hill two hunters climbed on a cold Aurignacian morning. Looking for herds of wild horses and bison and auroch and mammoth they were.

They saw her coming
SHE
A Wonder Woman

But was she? What was she? Why so high-shouldered? And why, fleetingly, for a strange moment did she walk with a four-footed gait?

SHE
White Buffalo Calf Woman
Good thoughts about her and bad thoughts about her are dangerous.
Under Europa's Europe are her footprints.
Under Europa's Europe are her human footprints coming.
Under Europa's Europe are her buffalo footprints going away.

V

The Ojibway live in the country of the Great Lakes in North America. Traditionally, before white people came, their way of life demanded that among them in every generation there would be great warriors and great hunters. Men stalwart in muscle and stalwart in extrovert mind. Men as little shy of their splendour and wonder as rattlesnakes and bull bison are.

There are always those, however, who do not fall in with the revered norms of their people. And so it was that among them there was a man who lived and walked by another way. An easy-going, mild man. When he looked at a bear he didn't only see it as meat for his family. When he looked at a tree he didn't only see timber. When he looked at a person he didn't only see a life story or a life.

Often in the woods he would withdraw from his hunting and sit in silence and for hours maybe mind in him wouldn't be his mind, it would be the mind of the wood and he wouldn't see the trees as he saw them, he would see and experience them as they saw and experienced themselves.

Coming home empty-handed one evening, his wife, who was hungry and had waited all day, quarrelled with him. She pointed to four hungry children. Hanging up his bow and his quiver of arrows he asked them not to be angry with him. He sat down and talked to them. Ye believe, I know, there is something wrong with me or odd about me. And maybe there is. My bow and arrows and my meat axe don't grow as naturally and as unconsciously out of my mind as his talons and bill grow out of an eagle's mind. In the woods sometimes I am an eagle who lays down his talons and his bill. I retire from hunting and I sit in the silence. I did that today. And so tonight ye have no food. And we are a family without glory among the people, or power. I don't cross the pain thresholds and the terror thresholds that the great hunters and warriors cross. They cross them extravagantly, spectacularly, and obviously, for all to see. And they have therefore the prestige and the power and the glamour that can only be found on the far side of those thresholds. That is one of nature's ways. In forests far to the south of us there are animals called jaguars and pumas. They are strong. And they are ferocious. And they are that way because one of their ancestors, driven with hunger, feeling the hunger of her cubs, went into and crossed some enormous terror thresholds and triumphed, bringing down and killing an animal far bigger and more dangerous than herself. Ever since, jaguars are mighty lords. They call them night suns, so ferociously do they roar and glow in their endless, wet forests. Lords, because they crossed a threshold others have recoiled from. Ours, I suppose, in some ways anyway, is a terror threshold world. And we are a terror threshold people.

Spectacularly, and extravagantly, and obviously for all to see, that's what we are. But we also have a limit. It is Thunderbird. Wakinyan Tanka. Great Thunderbird of the West. Anyone who has caught sight of her has been turned back to front for very dread. But maybe someday, someone seeking light and life will cross into her terrors too and come back, his face as it should be, where it should be, his mind all right.

That's our way. Our Ojibway way. But it isn't my way.

His oldest son hadn't listened, for he had already sworn to himself that when he grew up things would be different. He wouldn't, like his father, come empty-handed home from the hunt. And he would win honour and glory for his family. He would be a night sun. If he had to, hunting in them, he would light up all dark, Ojibway woods with his ferocity.

In a few years, as of tribal wont, he was ready for his vision quest. This was sacred and very serious. For now, for the first time in his life, he would be taken out beyond the known rivers and woods and left there alone, inwardly and outwardly exposed to the full tremendousness of the world. And how tremendous it was out there. Tremendous in a big brown bear standing on his hind legs, immobile and almost invisible, eating berries. Tremendous in a rattlesnake suddenly awake and alarmed on the other side of a log you must now, irreversibly, step over. Tremendous in bison, thirty of them, bulls, cows and calves, shoulders and muzzles shagged with ice, standing there, facing into a blizzard, letting it flow over them like another night of dreamless, calm sleep.

But that is easier said than done.

Yet, having that star blanket to wrap himself in, he had all the goodwill of all the good powers in the world that were pleased, in the past as now, to favour and bless his people. A white blanket with an eight-pointed blue star radiating outwards in eight red and blue amazements of fire and light to a sober blue border.

> Blue Star
> Bright Star
> Star of red and blue amazement

Seeing that star on the side of a dark and lonely hill, the powers would come to him. Good and evil powers would come to him. Would come to this star, his star, come down to earth. His grandmother had begun making that blanket for him the day he was born. And three days before he had set out on his quest, while he was still in the sweat lodge being purified and prayed for by the sacred elders, she had offered three of her very old and very gnarled finger joints to the sun for him, asking that he might walk safely and successfully out there, even if every bone in his body was a roost all night every night for Thunderbird and his Terrors.

For the first three days and nights nothing remarkable or strange happened. Although he did wonder about the wet otter he saw. It hadn't rained and there was no water, living or stagnant, that he was aware of near by. On the fourth morning, weary and bored, he climbed into a great oak. He sat in the crotch of it. Or rather he sat on the deep bed of twigs that had accumulated there, for centuries maybe. He was hardly settled, his arms about his knees and his head resting on them, when he knew he was trapped. Even if he wanted to now he couldn't get down. He was an acorn. He was growing. Not upwards and outwards into a great oak, but downwards and inwards into his nothingness. This was a terror he hadn't expected or predicted. The terror of growing downwards and inwards into the void. He knew he must become void. But everything in him resisted it and fought it. All the terrors and the horrors happened. In the end, in eternity, he consented. He went the way of his growing. He went the way of his own dissolution. Hearing dissolved. Seeing dissolved. Thinking dissolved. Dreaming dissolved. Every last sense of himself as a personal identity dissolved. The whole process of dissolution itself dissolved. And the nothingness he had become was altogether too rich to be bliss. Add bliss to it and you would only be impoverishing it.

All this he saw in an instant. In his instant of nothingness.

And now, out of that nothingness, upwards and outwards, there was again a growing. It was back into his personal identity he was growing. He was who he was again.

Or was he? Was he who the wood was? He climbed down from the oak. He inhaled the earth-brown air and walked away, yet not away, for with every step he took he knew that, from now on, all walking away would turn out in the end to be a walking back towards. He knew. Or maybe it was the wood that knew. In the wood, walking in it as he was, he was walking in a knowing that was altogether other than anything he himself or the wood itself had ever learned. He hadn't learned to listen to a wood like a hungry hunter. He hadn't learned to set wild fire to an impulse to revenge as a warrior would. In the oak today he had learned that he wouldn't walk back from his vision quest with the walk of an Ojibway warrior or with the walk of an Ojibway hunter. The oak or something in the oak had abducted him, had ravished him down into his own nothingness.

In that ravishing he had lost what he had come to find before he had found it. He walked in the red twilight under maples. Their millionfold murmurings and their millionfold occlusions of sunlight didn't fascinate him now. He picked up one of last year's leaves and looked at it, nostalgically, for he couldn't promise himself that he would ever again return to his old allegiance to things minutely observed. Something had happened. He had been waylaid. Carried totally off course. In his mother's womb he grew into something. In the oak's womb he grew into nothing. There were two germinations in the one acorn he had become. A germination of all that it was downwards into the void and a germination of all that it was upwards into self-awareness in a world. In his instant of nothingness he knew, or returned from that instant of nothingness he knew, that until both germinations have happened no human life is whole. He looked at the leaf he was carrying. Even visually it was different from how it would have appeared had he seen it the day before. It was healed of what his eyesight would have done to it had he looked at it. He was looking at it but not through a wound in his seeing, that wound in all our seeing that has the subjective on one side and the objective on the other. That wound was gone from his seeing. The leaf was a pure appearing.

'Was it Thunderbird?' his father asked him when he came home two days too soon.

'It wasn't,' the boy said.

'Was it the fasting?'

'No.'

'What terror was it then?'

'It wasn't the terror.'

'Or the loneliness?' the father asked.

'No.'

The father smiled. 'Like me,' he said looking at his son.

'How like you?'

'You've come home empty-handed from your hunt.'

'I have,' said the boy. 'And it will take me all my life maybe to explain to myself and to you and to the people what that means. What it means to have come home empty-handed.'

'So you won't become a great warrior?' his mother asked.

'No.'

'Or a great hunter?'

'No. Four days ago I went out to hunt. I became the hunted.'

'What hunted you?'

'The seed I became captured me.'

Fearing that their son had lost his wits they asked him no more questions. The boy took off his star blanket and handed it to his grandmother. Taking it in her mutilated, unhealed hands she asked him had it helped him. It helped me, he said. Of course it helped me. But there is a dark it didn't follow me into or light my way in.

With a useless husband and now useless oldest son, the mother, ageing herself, hadn't much to look forward to. And because she had such a bleak picture of their future so deeply rooted in her mind and eyes and heart, it was only after months that she could admit it: It is true, she said, not once since that day he came home empty-handed have we wanted for anything.

The boy grew into a man. He left his family and erected his own tipi. On its outside, sprung from the earth as it were, he painted a great oak, the boughs of it reaching all the way round to the door flap. He painted an exact replica of it inside.

It was strange to sit in that tipi with him. Strange in the firelight. Firelight playing on his face one night, the oak overarching, seeming to listen, he told his eldest son a story. Once upon a time there was a poor family. The father was a dreamer. He never came gloriously home from a war or gloriously, roaring, home from a hunt. His family had nothing to be proud of. In a hidden depth of his heart his oldest son was hurt by this and in the woods one day, sitting alone, he swore that when he grew up things would be different. Either as mighty warrior or a mighty hunter he would win glory and honour and respect for his family. He could hardly wait for the day of his vision quest. For the first three days and three nights of that quest nothing much happened. It might be that an otter that walked past had something to communicate. It was strange that the otter was wet for it hadn't rained and there wasn't any water, running or stagnant, anywhere nearby.

By the morning of the fourth day the boy was weak from his fasting. He was cross too, for another night was over and he hadn't dreamed. Weak as he was, he emerged from his vision pit and went off aimlessly wandering. In a clearing, suddenly overshadowed as if by a cloud, the boy looked up. He saw a Sky Being descending. Tall and beautiful, all tassels and plumes, he walked towards the boy. 'We must wrestle, you and me,' he said. Finding strength from he knew not where within him, the boy accepted. They wrestled for hours. Then the Sky Being broke off. 'Tomorrow again,' he said. And he reascended. On the following morning when the boy came into the clearing the Sky Being was waiting. They wrestled all day, the boy once again finding strength from somewhere below his weakness and his hunger. In the evening the Sky Being broke off. 'If you win tomorrow,' he said, 'your victory will be a source and seed of great blessing for your people.' The sun wasn't yet up when the boy was in the clearing. The Sky Being was there before him.

Again today, all day, they wrestled. From below his hunger and weakness, the strength of all rivers and mountains and thunders and oaks rose up in the boy. The whole earth was in him, he felt. It was wrestling with heaven. In the evening, overcome and dying, the Sky Being broke off. 'I will tell you what to do,' he said. 'Clean a patch of ground and dig a trench in it. Bury me and cover me over with the crumbled red clay. Go home to your father and tell him what happened. Come back, both of ye, every few days to this place and keep the soil clear of weeds.' The boy did as he was told. The third time they came, they saw something new in the world, thirty or forty shoots of it growing green and strong, beautiful tall corn, all tassels and plumes, growing all summer long out of the red earth. 'That's how corn came into the world,' the father concluded. 'That's my story.'

'Your story?' the boy asked.

'The story I wanted to tell you.'

'Did you, when you were young, go on a vision quest?'

'I did.'

'What happened?'

'Instead of gaining what I hadn't, I lost what I had. I came home empty-handed.'

'Did you go out again?' the boy asked.

'I did. The following year.'

'What happened?'

'I've told you. There is one thing you won't understand though, not now, tonight. I was altogether an older man, I was many, many times older the first time I went out than I was going out a year later.'

'When will I understand it?'

'When your oak overarches you. When you germinate downwards into the void. When you germinate downwards into your nothingness.'

'What then?'

'In times of great want, when a great transition is called for, the heavens and the earth must wrestle with each other. And the person chosen or doomed to wrestle with the heavens must first become nothing.'

'Then what?'

'Corn. We will call it corn. That's as good a name as any for the wonder that happens.'

VI

It is interesting to recall how the mesas and eminences within the Grand Canyon have been named: Shiva Temple, Buddha Temple, Deva Temple, Brahma Temple, Zoroaster Temple, Wotan's Throne, Vishnu Temple, Solomon's Temple, Castor Temple, Pollux Temple, Diana Temple, Vesta Temple.

Apart from a Semitic slip of the tongue, it seems like yet another act of Indo-European aggrandizement.

There are questions to be asked. In virtue of what in him or about him, in virtue of what done by him or won by him, is a mesa named for Castor, is a mesa named for Pollux? In virtue of what in him or about him, in virtue of what done by him, said by him, thought by him, is a mesa named for Zoroaster, is a mesa named for Wotan? Is it in virtue of her virginity that a mesa has been named for Vesta? Is it in virtue of having turned a hunter into a stag who was devoured by his own hounds that a mesa has been named for Diana? And why Diana? Why not Artemis?

All over again, this is Kurtz ascending the river. We ascend it on our terms, not in its terms. We ascend it in a steamboat not in Anaconda Canoe.

And why was no mesa named for Coatlicue, the Earth Mother as Aztecs knew her?

And why were no mesas named for the twins of the Navajo, they who set out to find their divine Father, they who on their way were given instruction and help by Spider Woman?

And why was no side-canyon, why was no cliff, why was no creek named for Old Man Coyote? Surely, no matter what sea-floor we are walking on or walking under in the canyon, it will be good for us to remember his advice:

Now, if you are overcome, you may go to sleep and get power. Something will come to you in your dream, and that will help you. Whatever those animals who appear to you in your sleep tell you to do, you must obey them, be guided by them. If you want help, are alone and travelling, and cry aloud for aid, your prayer will be answered – perhaps by the eagles, or by the buffalo, or by the bears. Whatever animal answers your prayer you must listen.

It could be that the reptile who left his footprints on the Coconino sandstone will answer your prayer.

It could be that the amphibian who left her footprints on the Supai Formation will answer your prayer.

It could be a fossilized trilobite in Bright Angel shale who will answer your prayer.

It could be that Anaconda will answer your prayer.

Neither inwardly nor outwardly is nature so hostile as we sometimes fear it might be. If fairy stories say sooth, then the wolf is as true to her nature when she is helping us as she is when she is regurgitating gobbets of us for her cubs. Let us listen to a medicine man of the Kwakiutl:

I was out paddling for seals one day. My helmsman was Leelameedenole. He was a brave man. Nothing ever frightened him, neither gales nor vicious animals, dangerous fish, or the sea-monsters we frequently see when hunting at night. That is why we have to have courageous fellows for our steersmen. I was paddling along at Axolis, when I saw a wolf sitting on a rock. With both his paws he was scratching the sides of his mouth. He whined as we approached and was not afraid of us; not even when I got out of my small travelling canoe and went to where he sat. He whined and I noticed that his mouth was bleeding. I looked in and saw a deer bone stuck crosswise between his teeth on both sides, very firmly. He was evidently expecting me to do something; either to kill him or to help him out of his trouble. So I said to him: 'Friend, you are in trouble and I am going to cure you, like a great shaman – for which I expect you to reward me with the power to get easily everything I want, the way you do. Now you just sit still here while I fix up something to help me get rid of that bone.' I went inland and picked up some twigs from a cedar tree which I twisted into a string, and when I returned the wolf was still sitting there on the rock with his mouth open. I took hold of the back of his head and put the string, thin end, into his mouth, tied it to the middle of the bone and pulled. Out came the bone. The wolf only sat staring at me. 'Friend.' I said, 'Your trouble is ended. Now don't forget to reward me for what I have just done for you.'

When I had said that the wolf turned around to the right and trotted off – not fast. And he had gone only a little way when he stopped, turned his muzzle to me and howled – just once. He howled and went into the woods. I stepped into my small canoe and paddled away with my steersman. Neither of us spoke of the wolf. We paddled and anchored in a cove where no wind ever blows. Lying down in our small canoe, our eyes immediately closed in sleep, for we had risen before daybreak and were very tired. And I dreamed that night of a man who came and spoke to me, saying, 'Why did you stop here, Friend? This island is full of seals. I am Harpooner-Body on whom you took pity today, and I am now rewarding you for your kindness, friend. From now on there will be nothing you want that you will not obtain. But for the next four years you must not sleep with your wife.' I woke and called to my steersman. He rose and pulled up the anchor. We went ashore, where I washed in the sea and stepped back into the canoe, eager to see whether, as Harpooner-body had said in my dream, there were actually a lot of seals on the rocks of the island. For I did not believe in dreams, or in shamans, or in any of the beliefs of my people; but only in my own mind. We paddled out before dawn, and approached the rocky, treeless shore which I saw was covered with seals, all tight asleep. I took my yew-wood seal club, stepped ashore and clubbed four big ones, while the rest tumbled off into the water. I put the four aboard, and we travelled home.

So now there was at least one thing in which I believed, namely the truth of Harpooner-Body's words, delivered to me in dream. And from that time on it was easy for me when out hunting to get seals and every other kind of game.

Two years later, in the summer of 1871, I went to Victoria with my three nephews, my wife, and their wives and children. Returning home in our large travelling canoe, we came to Rock Bay, on the north side of Seymour Narrows, and went ashore there. Stepping out of the canoe, my eldest nephew saw four nice boxes on the beach, full of very nice clothing, two bags of flour and all kinds of food. We could see no one around who might own those things and so we carried them aboard and moved on. When we came to Beaver Cove, a northeast wind sprang up and we stayed there for six days. It was then ten days after we had found the box and my whole company was now sick. In the morning we set off. It was calm. And when we arrived at Axolis we unloaded our cargo – all of us sick with the great smallpox, which we contracted when we picked up the boxes. We all lay in bed in our tent. I saw that our bodies had swelled and were a dark red. I did not realize that the others were dead, but presently thought that I was dead. I was sleeping, but then woke because of all the wolves that were coming, whining and howling. Two were licking my body, vomiting up foam, trying hard to put it all over me, and they were rough when they turned me over. I could feel myself getting stronger, both in body and in mind. The two kept licking and after they had licked off all that they had vomited, they vomited again, and when, again, they had licked this off, I saw that they had taken off all the scabs and sores. And it was only then that I realized that I was lying there among the dead.

Evening fell and the two wolves rested. I must have become afraid, being the only one alive there, for I crawled away to the shelter of a thick spruce, where I lay all night. With no bedding and only the shirt I had on, I was cold. The two wolves approached and lay down on each side of me, and when morning came, they got up and again they licked me all over, vomiting up white foam and licking it off. I was getting stronger, and when strong enough to stand, I realized that one of those two wolves was the one from whose mouth I had taken the bone. All the others had remained in attendance too. And now I was quite well. I lay down and there came to me the figure that had told me in my dream that his name was Harpooner-Body. He sat down seaward of me and nudged me with his nose until I responded by lying on my back, whereupon he vomited foam and pressed his nose against the lower end of my sternum. He was vomiting magic power into me, and when he had finished he sat back. I became sleepy and dreamed of the wolf that was still sitting at my side. In the dream he became a man who laughed and said, 'Now, friend, take care of this shaman power that has gone into you. From now on you will cure the sick, you will catch the souls of the sick, and you will be able to throw sickness into anyone in your tribe who you wish should die. They will all now be afraid of you.' That is what he said to me in my dream.

I woke and was trembling, and my mind since then has been different. All the wolves had left me, and I was now a shaman. I walked the way to Fern Point, where I remained alone for a long time in one of the seven abandoned houses there. On the way I met a man whom I told of the deaths of my whole crew, and he left me in fear and hurried home. I was not depressed, but just kept singing my sacred songs, evening after evening, the four songs of the wolf. For I was just like someone drunk, completely happy all the time. And I stayed there, at Fern Point, for more than the period of one moon.

A passing canoe-man heard my song and he spoke of it to all the people at Teeguxtee. They immediately decided to invite the new shaman whose song had been heard to come and cure their sick chief ...

This isn't our Western way. Biblically encouraged, we attempt to rule over and subdue.

How different the attitude of an Athabascan hunter:

We know what the animals do, what are the needs of the beavers, the bear, the salmon, and other creatures, because long ago men married them and acquired this knowledge from their animal wives. Today the priests say we lie, but we know better. The white man has been only a short time in this country and knows very little about the animals. We have been here thousands of years and were taught long ago by the animals themselves.

It could be a voice out of Pleistocene Europe. A voice out of Altamira, out of Lascaux. But we will have none of it. It being our manifest destiny to do so, we will name the mesas of the Grand Canyon. One we will call Castor. One we will call Pollux. One we will call Zoroaster.

But how appropriate is it to re-institute the religion of Zoroaster in the Grand Canyon? How appropriate or helpful is it to echo and re-echo the Zend-Asvesta off the rockwalls of the inner gorge?

'Mistah Kurtz – he dead.'

How different things would be if the Book of Job had been our *Mayflower*.

How different things would be if, instead of the Bozeman Trail, Bright Angel Trail had been the manifest destiny of people coming east across the Bering Straits, of people coming west across the Atlantic.

As it is, we have substituted a change of address for evolution.

And it is bad for us and it is bad for the earth that we and the earth are going separate ways.

It matters little whether the Bozeman Trail has Oregon in mind or the moon in mind.

Evolution doesn't have Willie Loman land in mind.

But the trail remains and it has, surprisingly, been given a good name.

It is the Gethsemane Angel, not Liberty in our limited sense, who is holding the torch for the evolving earth.

It is holding it for the trilobite who left his shape but not his seeking in palaeozoic shale.

It is holding it for the amphibian who left her footprints in the Coconino sandstone.

It is holding it for a child asleep in a Navajo cradle.

> I have made a cradle board for you, my child,
> May you grow to a great old age.
> Of the sun's rays I have made the back,
> Of black clouds I have made the blanket,
> Of rainbow have I made the bow,
> Of sunbeams have I made the side-loops,
> Of lightnings have I made the lacings,
> Of river mirrorings have I made the footboard,
> Of dawn have I made the covering,
> Of Earth's welcome for you have I made the bed.

Old Man's advice we have. The song and the dance of commonage consciousness we have. Fire sent down not fire stolen we have. A habit of saying 'we' where once we said 'us and them' we have. A cradle we have. A religion for the Grand Canyon we have.

We have a chance.

2

Trying to find the channel ...
JOSEPH CONRAD, *Heart of Darkness*

I

In the Basilica de San Vicente in Ávila there is an icon of the Virgin and Child which is called *Nuestra Senora de la Soterrana* – Our Lady of the Underworld.

Looking at her, I feel I'm a revenant from the ancient Mediterranean world, and I ask, who is she? Is it by misadventure, as it was with Persephone, that she finds herself here? Has she eaten the food of the dead? If she has, can she never return? As corn? As Kore?

But no. She is not Persephone. Nor is she Ereshkigal. She is who and what Christians who praise her and pray to her say she is:

> *Salve Mater Salvatoris!*
> *Vas electum! Vas honoris!*
> *Vas coelestis Gratiae!*
> *Ab aeterno Vas provisum!*
> *Manu sapientiae!*
>
> Mother of our Saviour, hail!
> Chosen vessel! Sacred Grail!
> Font of celestial grace!
> From eternity forethought!
> By the hand of Wisdom wrought!
> Precious, faultless Vase!

She is *aula regalis*, royal court or hall.
She is *eligenda via coeli*, chosen path of heaven.
She is:

> *Imperatrix supernorum!*
> *Superatrix infernorum!*
>
> Empress of the highest
> Mistress over the lowest

She is *stella maris*, star of the sea
She is who and what her Loreto litany says she is:

> Holy Mary, pray for us
> Holy Mother of God, pray for us
> Holy virgin of virgins, pray for us
> Mother of Christ, pray for us
> Mother of divine grace, pray for us

Mother most pure, pray for us
Mother most chaste, pray for us
Mother inviolate, pray for us
Mother undefiled, pray for us
Mother most loveable, pray for us
Mother of good counsel, pray for us
Mother of our creator, pray for us
Mother of our saviour, pray for us
Virgin most prudent, pray for us
Virgin most venerable, pray for us
Virgin most renowned, pray for us
Virgin most powerful, pray for us
Virgin most merciful, pray for us
Virgin most faithful, pray for us
Mirror of justice, pray for us
Seat of wisdom, pray for us
Cause of our joy, pray for us
Spiritual vessel, pray for us
Vessel of honour, pray for us
Singular vessel of devotion, pray for us
Mystical rose, pray for us
Tower of David, pray for us
Tower of ivory, pray for us
Ark of the covenant, pray for us
Gate of heaven, pray for us
Morning star, pray for us
Health of the sick, pray for us
Refuge of sinners, pray for us
Comfort of the afflicted, pray for us
Help of Christians, pray for us
Queen of angels, pray for us
Queen of patriarchs, pray for us
Queen of prophets, pray for us
Queen of apostles, pray for us
Queen of martyrs, pray for us
Queen of confessors, pray for us
Queen of virgins, pray for us
Queen of all saints, pray for us
Queen conceived without original sin, pray for us
Queen assumed into heaven, pray for us
Queen of the most holy rosary, pray for us
Queen of peace, pray for us.

ANACONDA CANOE

In St John's apocalyptic vision of her, gravity has given way to grace:

And there appeared a great wonder in heaven, a woman clothed with the sun, and the moon under her feet, and upon her head a crown of twelve stars.

In Yeats's vision of her, no less apocalyptic than St John's, she is fierce:

> The Roman Empire stood appalled,
> It dropped the reins of peace and war,
> When that fierce Virgin and her Star
> Out of the fabulous darkness called.

Thirteen centuries later Dante prayed to her:

> *Vergine Madre, figlia del tuo figlio,*
> *Umile ed alta piu che creatura*
> *Termine fisso d'eterno consiglio,*
> *Tu sei colei che l'umana natura*
> *Nobilitasti si, che il suo fattore*
> *Non disdegno di farsi sua fattura ...*
> *La tua benignita nor pur soccorre*
> *A chi dimanda, ma molte fiate*
> *Liberamente al dimandar precorre.*
> *In te misericordia, in te pictate,*
> *In te magnificenza, in te s'aduna*
> *Quantunque in creaturae di bontate.*

Petrarch prayed to her:

> *Vergine bella, che di sol vestita,*
> *Coronata di stelle, al sommo sole*
> *Piacesti si che'n te sua luce ascose;*
> *Amor mi spinge a dir di te parole;*
> *Ma non so' ncominciar senza tu aita,*
> *E di colui ch'amando in te si pose.*
> *Invoco lei che ben sempra rispose*
> *Chi la chiamo con fede.*
> *Vergine, s'a mercede*
> *Miseria estrema dell umane cose*
> *Giammai ti volse, al mio prego t'inchina!*
> *Soccorri alla mia guerra,*
> *Bench'i sia terra, e tu del ciel regina!*

Troubadours, almost, of the Queen of Heaven. Troubadours, not bhaktas. In the Hindu tradition, a bhakta is someone who has a passionate, a yearningly rapturous, devotion to a goddess or a God.

TURTLE WAS GONE A LONG TIME

Mahadeviyakka was a bhakta of the god Shiva. We might even think of her as Shiva's Shulamite. Indeed we might think of her songs to and about Shiva as a kind of Song of Songs:

> Four parts of the day
> I grieve for you.
> Four parts of the night
> I'm mad for you.
>
> I lie lost
> Sick for you, night and day,
> O Lord white as jasmine
>
> Since your love
> Was planted
> I've forgotten hunger,
> Thirst and sleep.

★ ★ ★

> If sparks fly
> I shall think my thirst and hunger quelled.
>
> If the skies tear down
> I shall think them pouring for my bath.
>
> If a hillside slide on me
> I shall think it a flower for my hair.
>
> O Lord white as jasmine,
> If my head falls from my shoulders
> I shall think it your offering.

★ ★ ★

> Locks of shining red hair
> A crown of diamonds
> Small beautiful teeth
> And eyes in a laughing face
> That light up fourteen worlds –
> I saw his glory
> And seeing, I quell today
> The famine in my eyes.
>
> I saw the haughty Master
> For whom men, all men,
> Are but women, wives.
>
> I saw the Great One

ANACONDA CANOE

Who plays at love
With Shakti,
Original to the world

I saw his stance
And began to live.

★ ★ ★

O mother I burned
In a flameless fire

O mother I suffered
A bloodless wound

Mother I tossed
without a pleasure

Loving my Lord white as jasmine
I wandered through unlikely worlds.

★ ★ ★

For hunger
There is the town's rice in the begging bowl.

For thirst
There are tanks, streams, wells.

For sleep
There are the ruins of temples.

For soul's company
I have you, O Lord,
White as jasmine.

★ ★ ★

Every tree
In the forest was the All-Giving Tree,
Every bush
The life-giving herb
Every stone the Philosopher's Stone
All land a pilgrim's holy place
All the water nectar against age
Every beast the golden deer
Every pebble I stumble on
The wishing crystal:
Walking round the jasmine Lord's
Favourite hill

TURTLE WAS GONE A LONG TIME

I happened
On the Plantain Grove.

★ ★ ★

You can confiscate
Money in hand;
Can you confiscate
The body's glory?

Or peel away every strip
You wear,
But can you peel
The Nothing, the Nakedness
That covers and veils?

To the shameless girl
Wearing the White Jasmine Lord's
Light of morning
You fool,
Where's the need for cover and jewel?

Mahadeviyakka and the Shulamite.

It wouldn't seem odd to hear Mahadeviyakka singing a song the Shulamite sang:

> I am the rose of Sharon
> And the lily of the valleys
>
> I am the lily among thorns
> So is my love among the daughters
>
> As an apple tree
> Among the trees of the wood
> So is my beloved among the sons.
>
> I sat down under his shadow
> With great delight
> And his fruit was sweet to my taste.
>
> He brought me
> To the banqueting house
> And his banner over me was love.
>
> Stay me with flagons
> Comfort me with apples
> For I am sick of love.

ANACONDA CANOE

The evidence of the Christian centuries would sometimes suggest that the biblical Song of Songs is a Magna Carta permitting, and indeed promoting, a kind of Christian bhakti yoga, a yoga of passionate devotion. Bride mysticism we call it, for, as Eckhart tells us, the soul at its core is female. In this regard however the gospels aren't encouraging.

Mary Magdalene wiped the feet of Christ in her hair but when, on the morning of his resurrection, she yielded to a very human kind of acknowledging impulse, he recoiled, saying, do not touch me. It's as if, as a means of communication between the human and the divine, the sense of touch was at that moment proscribed. It's as if the God were saying: from now on there can only be worship from the far side of an unbridgeable ontological gulf and that without hope of a final embrace.

In India it is not so. Nights there are in Vrindavan when Krishna, the Blue God, will take up his flute and play and, awakened by that heavenly music, the Gopis, the wives of the cowherds, will leave their beds and swoon towards him, each of them into the ecstasies and raptures of the divine embrace, and this is possible because, being the Blue Wonder that he is, Krishna multiplies himself, so that, on any one night, there are as many Krishnas as there are Gopis who come.

Krishna has a favourite Gopi. She is called Radha. And Radhabhava, the state of being Radha in the enrapturing embrace of her favouring God, is the supreme goal that many Hindus, passionately yearning, have imagined for themselves.

Among Christians, officially at least, the ontological gulf between creature and creator remains. And yet Mary Magdalene did wipe the feet of Christ in her hair. And it might be that Mary Magdalene is the first of many Christian Gopis, the first of many Christian bhaktas, the exemplar and archetype in our tradition of bhakti yoga. It is not, is it, outrageous to suggest that she is our Radha? And it might be that there is more to her than meets our biblical eye. Could it be that she is Sophia Prunikos, incarnate as a harlot in the city? Could it be that she is the suffering Shekinah who has wandered downwards into the unremembering dark worlds?

> O mother I burned
> In a flameless flame
>
> O mother I suffered
> A bloodless wound
>
> Mother I tossed
> Without a pleasure

TURTLE WAS GONE A LONG TIME

> Loving my Lord white as jasmine
> I wandered through unlikely worlds.

From the far side of the gulf it will come, the Lord's Day, a day of anger, a day of wrath.

So Christians say. And so we sing:

> *Dies irae, dies illa,*
> *Solvet seclum in favilla,*
> *Teste David cum Sibylla.*
>
> *Quantus tremor est futurus,*
> *Quando judex est venturus,*
> *Cuncta stricte discussurus!*
>
> *Tuba mirum spargens sonum*
> *Per sepulchra regionem*
> *Coget omnes ante thronum*

In Sir Walter Scott's translation:

> That day of wrath, that dreadful day
> When heaven and earth shall pass away,
> What power shall be the sinner's stay
> How shall he meet that dreadful day.
>
> When shrivelling like a parched scroll
> The flaming heavens together roll;
> When louder yet and yet more dread
> Swells the high trump that wakes the dead.

Tuba Mirum. The last trump.

Wouldn't it be a wonder if on Doomsday that *Tuba Mirum* sounded not like the trumpet of judgment calling us to account but like the flute of Krishna calling us, each of us, as Radha was called, into the blue swoonings of the divine embrace?

Let us listen to Marguerite Porete. She is talking to us about the final stages of the soul's journey into what we might call Radhabhava or, in biblical terms, Shulamabhava:

Love: Being completely free and in command on her sea of peace, the soul is nonetheless drowned and loses herself through God, with him and in him. She loses her identity, as does the water from a river – like the Ouse or the Meuse – when it flows into the sea. It has done its work and can relax in the arms of the sea, and the same is true of the soul.

Her work is over and she can lose herself in what she has totally become: Love. Love is the Bridegroom of her happiness enveloping her wholly in his love and making her part of that which is. This is a wonder to her and she has become a wonder. Love is her only delight and pleasure.

The soul has now no name but Union in Love ... she is then ready for the next stage.

* * *

Reason: Can there be a next stage after this?
Love: Yes, once she has become totally free, she then falls into a trance of nothingness, and this is the next highest stage. Then she lives no longer in the life of grace, nor in the life of the spirit, but in the glorious life of divinity. God has conferred this special favour on her, and nothing except his goodness can now touch her ... what it means is being in God without being oneself ... she hears what she cannot hear, exists where she cannot be, feels what she cannot feel. She holds on to this: he is with me, there is nothing I shall fear.

>   Radhabhava.
>   Shulamabhava.
>   He brought me to the banqueting house
>   And my soul 'is drunk on the wine it cannot drink'.

So, in spite of a reverent restraint in our tradition, maybe we can think of the Song of Songs as a mystical Magna Carta of Christian bhaktas.

Talking from experience, Ruysbroeck assures us that there is a night of spiritual espousals, as does of course St Teresa of Ávila.

And it is this same Teresa who would sometimes kneel in prayer before an icon of the Virgin and Child which is called *Nuestra Senora de la Soterrana* – Our Lady of the Underworld.

Given the difficulty we have with our humanity, the underworld we will at our peril forget is the one described by D.H. Lawrence:

The abyss, like the underworld, is full of malefic powers injurious to man.

For the abyss, like the underworld, represents the superseded powers of creation. The old nature of man must yield and give way to a new nature. In yielding, it passes away down into Hades, and there lives on, undying and malefic, superseded, yet malevolent-potent in the underworld.

This very profound truth was embodied in all the old religions, and lies at the root of the worship of the underworld powers. The worship of the underworld powers, the *chthonioi,* was perhaps the very basis of the most ancient Greek religion. When man has neither the strength to subdue his underworld powers – which are really the ancient powers of his old superseded self; nor the wit to placate them with sacrifice and the burnt holocaust; then they come back at him, and destroy him again.

Hence every new conquest of life means a 'Harrowing of Hell'.

Like a Persephone of our time, albeit a Persephone with an almost shocking difference in temperament and destiny, Nietzsche discovered that this underworld of lost, or past, biological ages was still at work in his highly civilized self:

I have discovered for myself that the old human and animal world, indeed the entire prehistory and past of all sentient being, works on, loves on, hates on, thinks on in me.

Cro-Magnon life thinking in me. Simian life thinking in me. Dinosauric life thinking in me. Trilobite life thinking in me. Fossilized algal life of the Gunflint cherts thinking in me.

At any time a most awful discovery. Calamitously awful when we have concluded that Christ in Gethsemane is an unenlightened irrelevance.

Nietzsche's discovery is of course the psychological correlative of Darwin's discovery on Galapagos. And now that we have made these discoveries, it could be that the safety and continuance of the human species will depend on whether we rediscover Gethsemane and Golgotha.

Traditionally, it was said of Jesus that he harrowed hell. It would be truer to say that he was harrowed. Sore amazed in Gethsemane, the hell of superseded life in him, in us, was harrowed, not just for our sake, but for the sake of all that has lived, is alive now, or will live, out of and with this evolving earth.

And so it is that where Christ was harrowed our Lady is Queen.

And there appeared a great wonder in heaven, a woman clothed with the sun, and the moon under her feet and upon her head a crown of twelve stars.

The great wonder in heaven is also a great wonder in the underworld.

In the underworld she is:

        Mirror of justice
        Seat of wisdom
        Cause of our joy
        Spiritual vessel
        Vessel of honour
        Singular vessel of devotion
        Mystical rose
        Tower of David
        Tower of ivory
        House of gold
        Ark of the covenant
        Gate of heaven
        Morning star

She who is all of these is also, still being all of them,

> Nuestra Senora de la Soterrana

The first salutation of a new litany in her honour might be

> Bhakta's delight

As bhakta's delight she is companion to us in our underworld journey.
   As bhakta's delight she is guide to us in our underworld journey.
   As bhakta's delight she is guru to us in our underworld journey.
   As bhakta's delight we invoke her protection and good counsel in our underworld journey towards the light.
   Julian of Norwich comforted us, saying,

> All shall be well
> And all shall be well
> And all manner of thing shall be well

   Since Nuestra Senora is Queen in it, our underworld might one day be our Vrindavan.
   In the meantime, invoking her help and the help of Bright Angel, we might come through where Kurtz failed.
   Ascending the primeval river not by steamboat but by canoe, coming down in other words from Psalm eight to Psalm twenty-three, we might come forth by day.

II

It was, we presume, in a trance of prophetic vision that Isaiah speaks of what will happen to Idumea:

… the cormorant and the bittern shall possess it; the owl also and the raven shall dwell in it; and he [God] shall stretch out upon it the line of confusion, and the stones of emptiness … and thorns shall come up in her palaces, nettles and brambles in the fortresses thereof; and it shall be an habitation of dragons, and a court for owls. The wild beasts of the desert shall meet with the wild beasts of the island, and the satyr shall cry to her fellow; the screech owl shall rest there, and find for herself a place of rest. There shall the great owl make her nest, and lay, and hatch, and gather under her shadow: there shall the vultures also be gathered, every one with her mate.

   Having humanity as a whole in mind, Freud hoped that where the id is, ego shall be. Having Idumeans in mind, Isaiah foresaw that where the ego is the id shall be, and this we remember is precisely what happened to Nebuchadnezzar:

The same hour was the thing fulfilled upon Nebuchadnezzar: and he was driven from men, and did eat grass as oxen, and his body was wet with the dew of heaven, till his hairs were grown like eagle's feathers, and his nails like bird's claws.

It wouldn't surprise us to see him looking back at us, in sorrow and in terror, from a still undiscovered cave-wall in Les Trois Frères.

Altogether more awful is what happened to Lucifer:

How art thou fallen from heaven, O Lucifer, son of the morning!
How art thou cut down to the ground which didst weaken the nations!
For thou hast said in thine heart, I will ascend into heaven. I will exalt my throne above the stars of God: I will sit also upon the mount of the congregation, in the sides of the north: I will ascend above the heights of the clouds: I will be like the most High: yet thou shalt be brought down to hell, to the sides of the pit.

In Kurtz, as Conrad conceived him, there is something of both Nebuchadnezzar and Lucifer:

You should have heard him say, 'My Ivory'. Oh yes, I heard him. 'My Intended, my ivory, my station, my river, my –' everything belonging to him. It made me hold my breath in expectation of hearing the wilderness burst into a prodigious peal of laughter that would shake the fixed stars in their places. Everything belonged to him – but there was a trifle. The thing was to know what he belonged to, how many powers of darkness claimed them for their own. That was the reflection that made you creepy all over. It was impossible – it was not good for one either – trying to imagine. He had taken a high seat among the devils of the land – I mean literally ... how can you imagine what particular region of the first ages a man's untrammelled feet may take him into by way of solitude.

Nowadays, however, we are faced not just with the collapse of civilization, or with the collapse of the collective psyche. Instead of talking about gaining the moon we should be talking about losing the earth and therefore also ourselves. It is, consequently, time to accept that it is with, not away from, the earth that we will evolve. And this means that we will look, not to Theseus setting out from Troezen to Athens, but to Jesus setting foot on Bright Angel Trail. It is within the Triduum Sacrum that we will find the way to a new culture.

There is of course no good reason why a new culture should be a new civilization. Culture and civilization are not synonymous. It isn't more and more streets that make the essential difference. What we exiguously need are rituals in which we and the earth can continue to evolve. Having these, the Sugers and the Sinans will follow. Having these, trees will dream the dream with us. Having these, stone will work with us.

But, at no time more than when we set foot on Bright Angel Trail, should we remember Idumea, should we remember Nebuchadnezzar, should we remember Lucifer, son of the morning.

Yet again our attempt to come through might end in a whisper:
'The horror! The horror!'

III

Of all the facts of our existence there is perhaps none more astounding than the fact that experience of self and other-than-self is so soluble in dreamless sleep. Salt is soluble in water. Yet, having been dissolved, it nonetheless suffuses the water and, if present in sufficient quantity, is perceptible to the sense of taste. Experience of self and other-than-self doesn't, however, survive its dissolution, however momentary or prolonged that dissolution might be. During dreamless sleep it is simply not there. And in that blankness no lamenting its loss, no yearning for its restoration. That something so fundamental to what we are should be so soluble, so vanishable is, when you come to think of it, little short of alarming. And it is, I sometimes think, not a little strange that no European philosopher has tangled with this wonder. For wonder it is. And it is in wonder, Aristotle assures us, that philosophical enquiry begins.

Of all the precipices we approach in the course of our lives there are few so precipitous perhaps as the one we approach and walk over, into a total forgetting of ourselves and our surroundings, every night.

How can it be, from the point of my own consciousness, that I am so soluble? Seeing, with all its glories and horrors, soluble. Hearing soluble. Touch, taste and smell soluble. All the scenery, and soundery of dreaming and waking soluble. All superficial and deep thinking soluble. Awareness-of in all its moods and modes soluble. Can anything so soluble as consciousness-of be a sure foundation? If consciousness-of is my only foundation, I am, as it were, a kind of Columbus who sets out to cross the Atlantic in a ship built of all too soluble salt.

And yet it is in and through consciousness-of that I am a person. Where no consciousness-of is, there is surely no person. So the person I am is soluble. My total solubility in dreamless sleep is inevitable and essential in what I am. Can it be that the only inevitable thing about me is the fact that I am not inevitable? One degree below freezing-point and there is a person, one degree above it and there isn't. One degree below freezing point and there is a dream that there is a person, one degree above it and there is the void of dreamless sleep with no dream crystallizing in it.

Am I only a dream that I am? Shakespeare wondered. And at one stage, if only provisionally, and for the dramatic time being, he concluded.

> We are such stuff as dreams are made on
> And our little life is rounded with a sleep.

And having dreamed that he was a butterfly, Chuang Tzu turned the tables on his dream, wondering, wide awake, whether he wasn't in fact a butterfly that had been dreaming all its life that it was a human being.

Does it really matter though? For the fact is that butterfly and human being are both of them soluble in dreamless sleep.

And maybe Advaitavedantins and Buddhists are right. Maybe mind is a kosha. Instead of being the window that we think it is, maybe mind is the blind.

Not a conclusion, this, that the humanist West would be delighted to open its gates to.

But there is some kind of haunting or knocking on our Iron Curtain. There are strange intuitions that would come in. And what if our cultural autoimmune system entered into collusion with these intuitions? What then? A nihilist Armageddon of all that we cherish? I don't think so. No. In Ireland is told a legend called The Children of Lír. It is the story of Lír's three daughters. Lír's second wife, their step mother, bewitched them, turning them into swans. Their doom was that they would live for three hundred years in Lake Derravaragh, for three hundred years in the tempestuous sea of Moyle between Ireland and Scotland, and three hundred years in the Western ocean. Only when they heard the sound of the first Christian bell out of Ireland coming to them there on the waves, would they be able at last to swim ashore and be persons again.

Are we all Jivanmuktas, only we don't know it? And if we are, what prevents us from knowing it? Is each of us his own, her own, wicked stepmother? Have we bewitched ourselves? Shaking off the spell, will we ever walk ashore into Nirvikalpasamadhi, and be the Jivanmuktas we natively are? Yes, the sages of the East would say, but only after enormous effort. Whole lifetimes of effort maybe. For the spell is profound, consisting, as it does, of kosha after kosha after kosha after kosha.

So there is good news for us Children of Lír, for us children of our own or of some great mayin's enchantment.

But in case we are tempted to rush prematurely into the streets and noise this news abroad over loudly, it would perhaps be no harm at all, having heard it, to sit for a while and reflect. For when we have seen what this news implies it is likely that it will scandalize us. And someone whose perspective on things is Nietzschean would think it a sign of healthy instincts in a person to be scandalized.

For Plato body is the soul's tomb. Among other things this implies, in Hindu terms, that body is a kosha or covering cutting the soul off from remembrance and vision of its transcendent gloriousness. For Plato and his followers this wasn't at all a shocking belief and the reason why it wasn't was that, for them, soul is the source and locus of consciousness, is the centre and source of personal identity. Body is a negative accretion. An acquired impediment to vision. A cataract. An eclipse. Although less than gracious and generous towards body, this belief didn't therefore threaten people in their centre of existential self-esteem. The Hindu doctrine of kosha does. For, according to Advaitavedantins at least, it isn't only body that is kosha. In our modern sense of it, psyche also is kosha. Released from the eclipse of the body and back in its seventh heaven it is kosha. And the heavenly vision by which it is beatified is kosha.

As mental activity mind is kosha. Consciousness-of is kosha. Awareness of self and other-than-self is kosha. Self-experience is kosha. In the very centre, and however deep it is, in the deepest depth of my psychological inwardness, I am kosha. Anything of which I can say I am it, that's me, that I am, is kosha.

In saying all this I don't of course wish to be understood as implying that everything I've called a kosha is a separate layer in an onion of koshas. I only wish to suggest that in the deepest core of my being, as self being, I am kosha. All I-amness is kosha. And however multifarious in its aspects this great covering might be, it doesn't eclipse or occlude an inner third eye or an inner soul seeing. Seeing implies duality. Duality is maya. Soul-seeing or eye-seeing, which our koshas covered, would itself be a kosha.

Beyond the multifarious eclipse that I am is the Divine-Without-Form-and-Void, one only without a second. A Divine Mirum so vast and marvellous that it could never be only a divine nature or a God.

There is nothing that isn't this Divine Mirum and if we are under the illusion that we are outside it, it is within it that we are outside it.

And how immense is the journey we must undertake, how immense is the journey that must overtake us, swallowing us into its terrors and chasms if we are ever again to set foot in the house we never left.

A lot of koshas to let fall as the Children of Lír let fall their swan forms.

A lot of enchantment to let fall on the way to self-loss in Brahmanirvana.

When will we hear it?
Coming to us across the waves of Derravaragh, when will we hear it?
Coming to us across the waves of Sea of Moyle, when will we hear it?
Coming to us across the waves of the Western ocean, when will we hear it?

>   Aum
>   Aum
>   Aum

The Aum of the Mandukya Upanishad

>   Waking
>   Dreaming
>   Dreamless Sleep
>   The Fourth, Turiya.

Silent O Moyle be the roar of thy waters.

IV

It is St John of the Cross who says it:

O wretched condition of this life wherein it is so dangerous to live and so difficult to find the truth. That which is most clear and true is to us most obscure and doubtful and we therefore avoid it though it is most necessary for us. That which shines the most and dazzles our eyes, that we embrace and follow after though it is most hurtful to us and makes us stumble at every step. In what fear and danger then must man be living seeing that the very light of his natural eyes by which he directs his steps is the very first to bewilder and deceive him when he would draw near unto God. If he wishes to be sure of the road he travels on he must close his eyes and walk in the dark if he is to journey in safety from his domestic foes which are his own senses and faculties.

Mystics aren't popular. And reading a passage like this it is easy to see why. Their diagnosis of what ails us is so offensive to our empirical self-esteem that we naturally, almost by reflex, shut them out.

As timbers are creosoted against fungus and woodworm and wet and damp so are we creosoted against what the mystics say.

There is a difference though. The timbers are creosoted from outside in. We are creosoted from inside out. In the timbers, in other words, the creosote isn't the native sap. In us it is. And this, as St John of the Cross indicates, is a source of wretchedness in us.

The timbers are creosoted against disease. We are creosoted against ultimate health. Natively and naturally in our very constitutions, from the moment of conception and beyond, we are creosoted against it.

Medical practitioners tell us that we have an autoimmune system against illness. Mystics tell us that we have an even more fundamental autoimmune system against health.

There is suffering in the world. And the religions of the world, each in its own way, have attempted to deal with the suffering, seeking to alleviate it, eliminate it or soothe it.

Also there have been and are systems of secular ideas which have had their origins in a response to suffering. In a response particularly to human suffering. Recently in the West we've had Marxism and psychoanalysis.

But the value of any attempt to deal with suffering will depend in the long run on whether it correctly diagnoses its source.

If someone who is suffering from AIDS goes to see a doctor and the doctor tells him that he has acne or chickenpox or smallpox or an allergy to milk products then it is likely that the remedy he will propose won't be effective.

There is a seeing which isn't by means of eyesight or by means of mind sight. A seeing which isn't eclipsed by eyesight or mind sight. A seeing which is mystical. And maybe it is only in this seeing that the primordial first cause of suffering is known.

The Desana Indians live in the tropical rainforest that smothers the headwaters of the Amazon. The yaje vine grows here. When its bark is chopped into small lengths and boiled for a long time it yields a juice which, when drunk, gives rise to altered states of consciousness. In most people, more often that not, it gives rise to amazing visions, hallucinations if you like. Sacramentally, this vine is to the Desana what peyote is to the Huichol Indians, what soma is or was to Hindus.

Let us now suppose that our own central nervous systems are vines of a kind. Are yaje vines. In us, naturally and natively, they give rise to all actual and all possible states of dreaming and waking. All such states are states of hallucination. If for the moment we think again of the biblical story of Adam and Eve in the Garden of Eden. In this garden was the tree of knowledge of Good and Evil. Coiled about it was a serpent. But supposing that it was a serpent only in appearance, that it was in fact a yaje vine. Adam and Eve ate of its fruit or drank of its juice or whatever. It gave rise in them to states of dreaming and waking awareness. Forgetting that their first Eden was a state beyond duality they allowed this dense eclipse of illusory awareness of illusory objects to establish itself centrally.

In and through this dense eclipse they became empirical persons. It is in and through it that we, their descendants, are persons.

> Yaje vine is within
> Land of cocaine is within
> Peyote bush is within

And we are junkies. We are junkies to the eclipse that we are. And that's our trouble. To come down from this yaje vine high that we are, that is the whole purpose and point of mystical living.

There are those of course who think that mystical living has to do with swooning intensities of feeling and vision. A kind of ultimate high, in other words. On the contrary, it is a total coming down from the high we already are, the purely illusory high in and through which we are persons.

We are junkies to the high that we are and that's why the thought of coming down is so unthinkable.

Cold turkey when we are attempting to break our addiction to heroin is one thing. Cold turkey when we are attempting to break our addiction to our inner yaje vine, to our inner prenatal peyote bush, that is another thing altogether. And many indeed are they who have borne witness to the horror of it. They have also, however, borne witness to the bliss of what Sufis call *fana* and *baqa*.

V

Speaking of a certain St Bartholomew in his *Mystical Theology*, Dionysius the Areopagite has this to say:

Me thinks he has shown by these his words how marvellously he has understood that the good cause of all things is eloquent yet speaks few words, or rather none; possessing neither speech nor understanding because it exceeds all things in a super essential manner and is revealed in its naked truth to those alone who pass right through the opposition of fair and foul and pass beyond the topmost altitudes of the holy ascent and leave behind them all divine enlightenment and voices and heavenly utterances and plunge into the darkness where truly dwells, as saith the Scripture, that One which is beyond all things.

Beyond Mount Sinai and Mount Olympus. Beyond the highest ascent of Moses and highest ascent of Diotima. Beyond the Mi'raj of Muhammad and beyond the Mi'raj of Black Elk.

A dark into which we won't come by ascending, into which we won't come by descending.

In the darkness of Good Friday on Golgotha we know that all our Diotima and Jonah journeys are journeys within an eclipse, are journeys within a mirage of great heights and great depths, are journeys within a mirage of our own projection.

Hindus talk of *viksepashakti*, this power to project that is in us all. The power by which we project a snake into a rope, by which we project a multitudinous, vast world onto the Divine Without Form and Void.

We live in the eclipse we project. In it are holy heights and sacred deeps, Buraqs and Leviathans. In it are heavens and hells unendurable to anyone who isn't pure spirit. A heaven whose joy is endurable only by beings who are as metaphysically tough as angels. A hell whose despair is so deep that it is endurable only to beings as spiritually tough as demons are.

It is one thing to say that all that is, is by way of projection, that all that is, is Maya, is eclipse. It would be altogether evil and criminal, however, to deduce from this that everything is insignificant.

Walking to work on a summer's morning I will often find a slug crossing the road. As most people would, I lift it, feeling it shrinking in my hand, and I leave it in the deep wet grass where the rising sun won't desiccate it. Always when I do this I'm aware that the hand that saves the slug is a hand that has murder in it.

This is the moral anguish of being human. And in Gethsemane, in every height and depth of his being, Jesus became that anguish. This to him was the cup of trembling, this to him was the wine of astonishment. Even the rocks and the olive trees reddened with this anguish. It will not do to walk past the slug saying that like myself it is illusory. It will not do to walk past Gethsemane saying that like myself it is a mirage.

In the presence of suffering we have no choice but to disembark from our ropesnake canoe. Here the claims of morality take precedence over claims of epistemology. Here, at no matter what cost in contradiction, we cannot but be naive realists. Here we should be willing to admit that it isn't in a ropesnake canoe that we will either find or navigate the channel.

VI

'For the Jews require a sign,' St Paul said, 'and Greeks seek after wisdom.'

A sign of God's providence in their lives, a sign of his particular favour and loving kindness towards them, a sign that he would see them through to a glorious end on his Holy Mountain, that is what Jews sought. In every age and in every generation they sought it.

The burning bush was a sign. Although it burned it wasn't consumed, no branch of it or twig of it breaking off and turning to ashes. It survived its own burning unburnt. And leaving the sheep he was shepherding, Moses turned aside to see it and a voice called to him out of it:

I have surely seen the affliction of my people which are in Egypt and I have heard their cry by reason of their taskmasters and I know their sorrows. And I am come down to deliver them out of the land of the Egyptians and to bring them up out of that land unto a good land and a large, unto a land flowing with milk and honey.

The opening of the Red Sea and the Children of Israel walking dry shod through it was a sign. Their God was with them. Their God would see them through. Their God was their Good Shepherd.

The pillar of fire by night and of cloud by day that went before them in the wilderness, that was a sign.

And in every age it delighted Jews to remember the signs and the wonders and the miracles which their God, their Good Shepherd, had wrought among them:

For ask now of the days that are past which were before thee since the day that God created man upon the earth and ask from the one side of heaven to the other, whether there hath been any such thing as this great thing is, or hath been heard like it? Did ever people hear the voice of God speaking out of the midst of the fire as thou hast heard and live? Or hath God assayed to go and take him a nation from the midst of another nation by temptations, by signs and by wonders and by war and by a mighty hand and by a stretched out arm and by great terrors according to all that the Lord your God did for you in Egypt before your eyes.

And the Children of Israel settled in Canaan. And prophets were born to them and through them yet again wonders unheard of, and signs.

And Jesus came. And touching the hem of his garment a woman was healed of an issue of blood. A man of signs he was, of miracles, of wonders.

But Jesus was angry at this endless seeking after signs among his people: 'An evil and adulterous generation seeketh after a sign; and there shalt no sign be given to it but the sign of the prophet Jonas.'

What is this sign? Mystically, what is it? His God demanded of Jonah that he go to Niniveh and prophesy against it. Zealously tribal in outlook, Jonah refused. He fled. He came to Joppa, to the wharves there. Finding a shipmaster who was overseeing the final preparations for a voyage, Jonah asked him what city he was bound for. For Tarshish, the shipmaster said. Jonah requested passage and was given it. He paid the fare and went on board, going down into the hold hoping that there, in the dark below the waterline, he would be hidden from and have respite from the awful demand of his God; that he should, by forewarning them, avert a hated people from the disaster they were walking into.

It was good to be outward bound, all sails full in a following wind, all currents and tides favouring. It was good to have dropped below the horizon. But the sailors didn't sing to the ship's good sailing. Rather did they seem unnerved. A sense they had of a bad omen on board. And that sense deepened when the darkness came, when a tempest engulfed them. Many tempests below many horizons they had seen, but the like of this one, no, this was an opening into abysses they had never imagined. It must be something or someone on board was cause. They cast lots to determine.

Unmistakably, it was him, the one who was in the hold, hiding there, below the waterline.

Jonah was thrown overboard and, swallowing him, Leviathan turned flukes and sounded with him, yawning him out into the void below the roots of the mountains.

The weeds of the Great Deep were wrapped about Jonah's head. Jonah cried to the Lord his God. Coming to him again, Leviathan swallowed him, rose with him and yawned him out on dry land. That, briefly, is Jonah's story.

And what does it signify?

Of what is it a sign?

Of the signless, of our journey into self-loss in the signless, a Mahayana Buddhist would say.

It is a sign, St John of the Cross would say, of the passive dark of the soul, that most awful phase of the mystical journey when, inwardly and outwardly, our rock of faith has vanished leaving us lost and bewildered, with nothing to reach for in the abyss that was before world was or psyche was.

Within and without are one psyche. Not so much one psyche as one awareness-of, in many moods and modes. It is over the sides of this awareness-of we are thrown. And now, as Tauler says, everything depends on a fathomless sinking in a fathomless nothingness. And how incomprehensible it is and how marvellous, that this fathomless nothingness should now become a fathomless nothingness of faith, an abyss of faith, a void of faith, a divine abyss of faith, a divine void of faith. We begin to have faith in the nothingness. The weeds of the Great Deep are wrapped about our minds. That means that now the lobes of our minds are as dark awake as they are in dreamless sleep. They are willingly dark, willingly without awareness-of. And now we know, but it isn't we who know it and it isn't with our minds that we know it, there is nonetheless a knowing that all our knowings were an eclipse and that all our desires were the desires of a film projector for the illusions it had itself projected.

How strange! Thrown over the sides of our psyches. Thrown over the sides of dreaming and waking awareness-of into safety, total safety.

How strange! It is they who are still in the ship, they who have sextant and astrolabe and sounding lead and compass and charts, who have clear and calm nights to sail in and known stars to navigate by, they who are on perfect course for haven and home, how strange! It is they who are lost. Lost reaching home. At home lost.

Jesus said it. And in this incarnation now or in a subsequent one a time will come for us all when sextant and astrolabe and compass will say it; the faithful, unfailing north star will say it:

> No sign is given you but the sign of Jonah.

VII

Now, tonight, there are people who have fallen into the hells within themselves. Or, as the Tibetan Book of the Dead would have it: there are people who, now, tonight, are engulfed and swallowed by the hells they themselves have projected. It is out of ourselves our hells are.

There were nights ten years ago and recently again when I felt I was myself in hell. Blinded by natural eyesight, unaware of where I was walking I walked into it. I would like to talk about that walking even though in doing so I am drawing attention to myself. But it isn't in so far as I am in any way unique or singular that I would talk. No. It is out of the common journey I would talk. The journey we don't always walk in, for, more often than not, it walks us.

I will make it short.

In my early thirties I yielded to a longing for silence and solitude, so I came to Connemara and here to my great delight I found both.

For the first three years I went every day into the woods and the mountains. In fantasy, of course, I had taken my life like a rag in my hands and had squeezed my education and my conditioning out. Out of pure seeing in me, out of pure sensations of hearing and seeing and touch and taste and smell, mind would grow again in me. Mind in me would be sensuous seeing in me, would be fingertips touching toadstools or oakbark in me.

There were times when the fences between me and my surroundings were gone down. The river by night and the woods and the mountains by day, these, as they sensuously were, these did my thinking for me. And their thinking wasn't other than their mode of being sensuously manifest. Mind was manifestation of itself in sensousness.

Somedays, for hours on end, I would sit on a rock under Simon's Falls in the Owenglin river. Sitting there with my eyes closed, I would get to know the falls in hearing experience, every sound of it, big and small, near and far. Then I would open my eyes and experience these same Falls as a seeing. Always I was struck by how stupendously different from each other are the Falls we hear and the Falls we see.

By such means I came to have a naked awareness of the miracle that is hearing, of the miracle that is seeing.

I was happy. I was growing. And now, as it had never been, all my growing was a growing in pure wonder.

As time went on I went less and less often into the mountains. Although I didn't realize it at the time, I was responding now to an opposite need, a need for introversion, a need to go deeper than senses could go or mind could go, a need to go into and be in the mysterious dark behind them.

This need took over. And now every day it was into the dark woods I would go. I had found a great beech. I would climb up into it and sit quite comfortably in its twig-strewn crotch. It was dark here. It was the kind of dark a seed would germinate in. To be in that dark was to be a seed.

Always, once I was settled down in that dark, I would do the same thing. Imaginatively, I would journey down through the kainozoic, the mesozoic and the archaeozoic into the dark which I imagined existed before biological evolution began.

It wasn't a going down whole and entire into the dark. As I descended I let go of all the biological structures and functions my phylum had acquired in the kainozoic, all it had acquired in the mesozoic and all it had acquired in the archaeozoic. In the dark I was biologically nothing. And that's how I would remain for hours. It would often be night when I would return into my biological identity and walk home.

This went on every day for four months. I began to feel desolate. And I sometimes wondered; what if one day on my way back into my biological identity the door is closed against me?

It happened one day in the mountains. Or something like it happened. As if I was a system of sandbags against the void, all that I biologically was was swept away. I was in the dark, inwardly and outwardly ruined, and I had an agonized sense that the world we are aware of in dreaming and waking is a vast deception. Not just an illusion. A deception.

Back in my room that night and every night for months and months I was, I suppose, in hell. Better have horrors and terrors all about you than nothingness.

I had squeezed my mind out, or so I thought. But I hadn't squeezed my psyche out. I hadn't squeezed its neuroses, its potential psychoses and bad karma out.

I remembered the blacksmith at home, how he would take the red hot iron shoe and lay it to the hoof of the horse, burning a shallow bed or mould for itself in it. That's how my neuroses were laid, burningly, to the quick of my soul. There were nights when, literally, I felt that my room was thick with moral pollution. And it was out of me that the pollution was rising, like smoke and smoulderings from the hoof of the horse.

One night I felt I wouldn't be there in the morning. Like a saucepan of water left on a blazing fire I would have evaporated, body and soul. As the Psalm would have it, Deep in me called unto Deep. And, simultaneously with this calling I prayed for one particular favour: let me be the only victim God, let me be the only victim God, let me be the only victim God.

In the small hours, exhausted, I would go to bed hoping that I would be pliant enough and compliant enough to assume the shape and walk the way of whatever nightmare might nightmare me. One night, I said, I have no way out. But immediately I had said it I found myself saying, having no way out is the only way.

It was like being Egypt being me. The twelve plagues were laid, huge and red hot, to my soul. And the plagues were all that was wrong with me. Hell didn't have to go elsewhere for plagues. It had more than it needed waiting ready to hand right there in my psyche.

The red wind of karma it is called in the Tibetan Book of the Dead. And that karma isn't only individual, it is also phylogenetic. The earth's karma and the psyche's karma are one and the same. The Grand Canyon is within as well as without. Within and without is the same inheritance. And that's why hell can be Grand-Canyon-deep in us.

We could talk about hell all night. We could seek to itemize and name its terrors and torments, its assaults and engulfings, but that wouldn't get us very far.

There is one further thing I would like to say though, and here again I am talking personally.

From the very beginning I felt there was Divine Love in what was happening to me. Even in the plagues, or behind them somewhere, there was love. As if hell has divine compassion and comfort and kindness in it. As if hell is the heaven we aren't yet able for.

To be in heaven and not be able for it because of selfhood and self-will, that is hell.

All I have to do is set foot in heaven and selfhood in me will turn it into a hell.

Hell has heaven in it. And heaven will, in the end, have the upper hand, for selfhood and self-will are sheddable.

Only selfhood burns in hell, Jacob Boehme says.

And that is good news, particularly in Christendom. Dante would have written a very different poem had he been so fortunate as to have someone like Jacob Boehme for guide.

VIII

And it came to pass in those days that Jesus came from Nazareth of Galilee and was baptised of John in Jordan. And straightway coming up out of the water he saw the heavens opened and the Spirit like a dove descending upon him. And there came a voice from heaven saying, Thou art my beloved son in whom I am well pleased. And immediately the Spirit driveth him into the wilderness. And he was there in the wilderness forty days tempted of Satan and was with the wild beasts and the angels ministered unto him.

Seeking to understand what happened to him here, I sometimes imagine it was into the arid immensities of Arizona Jesus was driven, across them to the edge of the Grand Canyon and down into it, down into all the ages of the earth's history, down into all its karma, down into long nights alone in the cockatrice's den.

Here, phylogenetically, that is karmically, he was with beasts. Here there were sudden and bewildering openings into hitherto hidden inwardness. Here there were awakenings he had never walked in. Here angles ministered unto him. Here, when the karma of the one Grand Canyon within and without was a Marasena assaulting him, there was also, risen from the muladhara depths of nature, a Mucalinda who protected him.

This was the hidden opening the spirit drove him towards in the wilderness. This is the Bright Angel Trail going down which Eagle, Ox, Lion or Man hasn't talked about. This is the hidden Grand Canyon in Gethsemane.

Behold now Behemoth, a voice said to him in that Canyon.

Behold your karma.

TURTLE WAS GONE A LONG TIME

Behold Leviathan. She carries us down.
He was gone for forty days, or was it for forty years.
Behold the lily of the field, he said, walking among us again.
And we did behold.

But we also couldn't but behold him. And beholding him we knew that, somewhere out of sight and out of mind, he had been sore broken in the place of dragons and covered in the shadow of death.

And Jesus returned in the power of the Spirit into Galilee, and there went out a fame of him through all the region round about. And he taught in their synagogues, being glorified of all. And he came to Nazareth, where he had been brought up: and, as his custom was, he went into the synagogue on the sabbath day and stood up for to read. And there was delivered unto him the book of the prophet Esaias. And when he had opened the book, he found the place where it was written, The Spirit of the Lord is upon me, because he hath anointed me to preach the gospel to the poor; he hath sent me to heal the brokenhearted, to preach deliverance to the captives, and recovering of sight to the blind, to set at liberty them that are bruised. To preach the acceptable year of the Lord.

Seeking, I look into nature here in Connemara, but I don't see laws of nature, I see surprises of nature, miracles of nature.

On an evening in January the temperature drops to freezing-point and atmospheric moisture turns into snowflakes, each one a miracle of form, each one different from all the others.

In September, fully grown, a caterpillar climbs a tree. It spins a cocoon, attaching it to the trunk. The colour pattern of the cocoon perfectly matches the colour pattern of the trunk. Not even a hungry blackbird or thrush will detect it. Inside, the caterpillar is undergoing a very strange process. It is broken down or should we say it is cannibalized by an intuition of something new, a new growing, within itself. The caterpillar isn't architect or clerk of works or general overseer of this growing. It doesn't in any way seek to engineer it or direct it. The growing is its own wisdom and on a fine day in June a butterfly opens and closes its wings on a rose-covered cottage wall.

There is a freezing-point in nature. And there is a miracling-point.

And it isn't that this miracling-point is here but not there, is at this depth but not at that depth. In every depth of it and at every point of it nature is miracling-point.

Where the raindrop becomes a snowflake, where the miracling is, and it is everywhere all about us, that's where Jesus came from.

And miracles happened in his presence. He didn't perform them. Miracles aren't performed. They happen. A woman needed only to touch the hem of his garment, and that but passingly, for her to rise up and walk away, healed of an old affliction.

Seeking to understand you I am Jesus. But maybe such a quest should begin only at the end of a long, long, Lent, only after I've fasted for years from all biblical and Christian beliefs about you.

It might be that every couple of thousand years or so there are events on earth which throw the heavens and the hells open, which throw open all the realms and hierarchies of being and non-being.

The life of Jesus they say was such an event.

From the night of his birth until after his ascension all the gates and all the doors into all the levels of reality were open.

Talking to us about the night of his birth, St Luke has this to say:

And there were in the same country shepherds abiding in the field, keeping watch over their flock by night. And, lo, the angel of the Lord came upon them, and the glory of the Lord shone round about them: and they were sore afraid. And the angel said unto them, fear not: for, behold, I bring you good tidings of great joy, which shall be to all people. For unto you is born this day in the city of David a Saviour, which is Christ the Lord. And this shall be a sign unto you; Ye shall find the babe wrapped in swaddling clothes, lying in a manger. And suddenly there was with the angel a multitude of the heavenly host praising God and saying, Glory to God in the highest, and on earth peace, good will toward men.

Again at his baptism the heavens opened and on Good Friday night, gone down into the underworld, it is told of Jesus that he or someone called out: 'Lift up your heads, O ye gates, and be ye lift up, ye everlasting doors and the King of Glory shall come in.'

Even after his ascension all doors and gates to all realms were open. On the day we call Pentecost fire came down from heaven, cloven tongues of it, and rested upon his first disciples.

From all of this we can I think conclude about Jesus that in him every level of inwardness was open to all the others. In his psyche there was no closed door, no shut gate. No pearls secreted about neuroses cutting them off. No repressions. No imperious voice imperiously saying, 'Thus far shalt thou come and no farther and here shall thy proud waves be stayed.' In his psyche there were in fact no levels. It was all a stupendous oneness of crypt and choir.

As above so below. As within so without.

Doors open within, doors open without. No gates and doors within, no gates and doors without.

And so we come back to what must surely have been the critical turning-point in his life:

TURTLE WAS GONE A LONG TIME

And it came to pass in those days, that Jesus came from Nazareth of Galilee, and was baptised of John in Jordan. And straightway coming up out of the water, he saw the heavens opened, and the Spirit like a dove descending upon him: And there came a voice from heaven, saying, Thou art my beloved Son, in whom I am well pleased. And immediately the Spirit driveth him into the wilderness. And he was there in the wilderness forty days, tempted of Satan; and was with wild beasts; and angels ministered unto him.

And Grand-Canyon-deep in the wilderness Jesus was contemporary with all that was kainozoic, mesozoic and archaeozoic in his psyche.

And Jesus was sore amazed.

And he was alone, sweating the red terror of a red Triassic dream.

And Bright Angel ministered unto him, saying, Fear not.

And Jesus cried, 'Fearfulness and trembling are come upon me and horror hath overwhelmed me.' And Bright Angel said, 'Fear not, fear not.'

And Jesus cried, 'I am sore broken in this place of dragons.' And Bright Angel said, 'Fear not, fear not.'

And yet again Jesus cried, inwardly, I am come before myself, I am come before a King of Terrors.

And Bright Angel said, Fear not.

And Bright Angel said, As without so within. Ordovician without Ordovician within. Punta Alta without Punta Alta within. Galapagos without Galapagos within.

That night and following it for thirty-nine nights more Jesus was Grand-Canyon-deep in the world's karma.

Jesus endured.

Jesus survived.

On all our behalf something vast was accomplished.

Bright Angel Trail became aisle.

And for Jesus, as for us all, there yet remained the Dark of Good Friday on Golgotha:

Yatra na anyat pasyati, na anyat srinoti, naanyad vijanati, sa bhuma.

Nada nada nada nada nada y en el monte nada.

Oh dichosa ventura.

IX

Tadeen Hanrahan is a bachelor living on his own. The house he lives in doesn't give him much shelter. On a winter's day you'd see his few cows standing with their backsides to his gable end and you'd know that they were warmer outside than Tadeen was inside.

Tadeen heard that my father and mother weren't well, so one night on his way to the village he called in to see them. I showed him up into their room and I left him with them. Back in the kitchen, I could hear Tadeen asking them how they were. Not too bad, they said, not dying anyway. That satisfied Tadeen. So he changed the subject and started telling them all the local news, most of it bad news.

My father noticed that Tadeen had cotton wool in his right ear. 'Is the ear bad, Tadeen?' he asked. ''Tis,' Tadeen said, 'for the last four months. Desperate pain in it sometimes and I'm deaf in it now. But I don't mind being deaf in it, for, as I often say to myself, isn't it enough of the world's misery I'm hearing with the one ear.'

Does it happen to us all? Are we all Tadeens, recoiling from our own and the world's enormity? It wouldn't be wholly unfair to his way of seeing things to suggest that Blake thought so:

The visions of Eternity, by reason of narrowed perceptions
Are become weak visions of Time and Space fixed into furrows of death
Till deep dissimulation is the only defence an honest man has left.

And in one of his major poems, Wordsworth sees our early growing as a process of visionary degradation and loss:

>   Our birth is but a sleep and a forgetting:
>   The Soul that rises with us, our life's Star,
>   Hath had elsewhere its setting,
>   And cometh from afar:
>   Not in entire forgetfulness,
>   And not in utter nakedness,
>   But trailing clouds of glory do we come
>   From God, who is our home.
>   Heaven lies about us in our infancy!
>   Shades of the prison-house begin to close
>   Upon the growing boy,
>   But he

> Beholds the light and whence it flows,
>   He sees it in his joy;
> The Youth who daily farther from the east
>   Must travel, still is Nature's Priest
>   And by the vision splendid
>   Is on his way attended;
> At length the Man perceives it die away,
> And fade into the light of common day.

Marvellous neo-Platonic statements, these, of our condition. And it almost hurts me to find that I have reservations about them. But I do have reservations. Or enquiries anyway.

I want to enquire about the nature of the afar we come from. Is there only one afar? Or are there several? Are there afars that are nearer and afars that are farther away? Is there an afar that is always afar? An afar so serene that there is no escaping from it even in ecstasy. Neither ecstasy, rapture or swooning is a way into it, or a way out of it, or a way to be in it.

There is, isn't there, a Great Afar. The Great Afar within every heart. The Afar that persons can't be persons in, that souls can't be souls in, that angels can't be angels in, that gods can't be gods in. Thinking of it even the greatest gods bless themselves in countless Good Fridays. But all the depredations and sufferings and derelictions and anguish of all our Good Fridays are useless, unable altogether to soothe the altogether deeper pain of having awoken to a sense of our otherness than and from the Great Afar.

The Great Afar isn't other than anything. There is no otherness in it. All otherness than it and all distance from it is in us. And once it is awake there is no pain like the pain of otherness. Offer us then the darkness and anguish of a thousand Good Fridays to drink and that pain won't be soothed or scared. It is nearness itself, the Great Afar. But how far away from it we are. How far away from it is the bliss of heaven, is the perdition of hell. It is there within our hearts.

There is a Great Afar. Within all the hearts of all that is it is. And there is a great round of existence in which all the heavens, earths and hells and all that is in them are caught up. This is the round of transmigrations and our coming from afar as Wordsworth sees and celebrates it is a coming from somewhere within it. A rising or falling or a moving to and fro of one experience of self and circumstances to another experience of self and circumstances.

And it isn't, always, trailing clouds of glory that we come. We come seeking refuge, I'm sure of it, sometimes.

If we surprise a spider out in the open it will freeze. And our conception, I often think, is a kind of freezing. A folding up, a closing down, a shying away from the splendours and wonders and terrors and horrors of the antarabhava, that state of states we find ourselves in between death and rebirth. So that the ear that closed down in Tadeen Hanrahan was itself in origin and function a device for shutting out and closing down. Hearing is a device for enabling us not to hear what we aren't yet ready to hear. We have taken refuge in hearing small things smally to ensure that we don't for the moment have to hear big things bigly.

There is a sense, I often think, in which it wouldn't be altogether crazy to suggest that it is we ourselves who are the causes of our own minds and our own bodies. It is we ourselves who project them, as octopuses project their inkclouds. The difference between us and the octopuses is that, obviously for the lifetime, we become what we project. We are a taking refuge, a hiding out, a freezing as spiders freeze and for the same reasons. We become the eclipse with which we would eclipse the stupendous. And so the weary wheel goes round and round. And within it always, in all the heights of all its heavens and in all the pits of all its hells, is the Great Afar.

Descriptively, no word will ever be spoken about the Great Afar. We can talk only about our journey towards it. We can talk about samadhis, paravrittis, samapattis, satoris. We can talk about dark hideous nights of the spirit. About all of this and more we can talk. It is good that we talk. Good that there are Buddha voices, Shankara voices, Niffari voices, Eckhart voices in the world.

And when we have stumbled into this journey or been swallowed by it, it will be good to know that all the karma, archaeozoic, mesozoic and kainozoic, of our inner psychic canyons won't only be our Marasena assaulting us, it will also, collectively, be our Mucalinda protecting us. And this will be so because always, externally, is the Great Afar.

X

Darwin came ashore on an outer, Nietzsche on an inner, Punta Alta.

Unlike Job in his first encounter with the unsubduable enormities of psyche, savannah and sea, Darwin at Punta Alta is above all else a scientist, and this means that he must not for the moment invest the facts in his own emotional response to them. Aware that they are indeed extraordinary, he names the animals whose fossilized remains he uncovers:

First, parts of three heads and other bones of the Megatherium, the huge dimensions of which are expressed by its name. Secondly, the Megalonyx, a great allied animal. Thirdly, the Scelidotherium, also an allied animal, of which I obtained a nearly perfect skeleton. It must have been as large as a rhinoceros: in the structure of its head it comes, according to Mr Owen, nearest to the Cape Anteater, but in some other respects it approaches to the armadillos. Fourthly, the Mylodon Darwinii, a closely related genus of little inferior size. Fifthly, another gigantic edental quadruped. Sixthly, a large animal, with an osseous coat in compartments, very like that of an armadillo. Seventhly, an extinct kind of horse, to which I shall have again to refer. Eightly, a tooth of a Pachydermatous animal, probably the same with the Macrauchenia, a huge beast with a long neck like a camel, which I shall also refer to again. Lastly, the Toxodon, perhaps one of the strangest animals ever discovered: in size it equalled an elephant or megatherium, but the structure of its teeth, as Mr Owen states, proves indisputably that it was intimately related to the Gnawers, the order which, at the present day, includes most of the smallest quadrupeds: in many details it is allied to the Pachydermata: judging from the position of its eyes, ears, and nostrils, it was probably aquatic, like the Dugong and Manatee, to which it is also allied ...

The remains of these nine great quadrupeds, and many detached bones were found embedded on the beach, within the space of about 200 yards square.

How different, in Spenser's *The Faerie Queene,* is the response of Sir Guyon to what he saw at sea:

> Most ugly shapes, and horrible aspects,
> Such as Dame Nature selfe mote feare to see,
> Or shame, that ever should so fowle defects
> From her most cunning hand escaped bee;
> All dreadfull pourtraicts of deformitee:
> Spring-headed *Hydraes,* and sea-shouldring Whales,
> Great whirlpooles, which all fishes make to flee,
> Bright Scolopendraes, arm'd with silver scales,
> Mighty *Monoceroses,* with immeasured tayles.
>
> The dreadfull Fish, that hath deserv'd the name
> Of Death, and like him lookes in dreadfull hew.
> The griesly Wasserman, that makes his game
> The flying ships with swiftnesse to pursew,
> The horrible Sea-satyre, that doth shew
> His fearefull face in time of greatest storme,
> Huge *Ziffius,* whom Mariners eschew
> No lesse, then rockes, (as travellers informe,)
> And greedy *Rosmarines* with visages deforme.

ANACONDA CANOE

> All these, and thousand thousands many more,
> And more deformed Monsters thousand fold,
> With dreadfull noise, and hollow rombling rore,
> Came rushing in the fomy waves enrold,
> Which seem'd to fly for feare, them to behold:
> Ne wonder, if these did the knight appall;
> For all that here on earth we dreadfull hold,
> Be but as bugs to fearen babes withall,
> Compared to the creatures in the seas entrall.

Having seen a squid that rose from it, it is not imperturbably that Ishmael is aware of the seas entrall:

Almost forgetting for the moment all thoughts of Moby-Dick, we now gazed at the most wondrous phenomenon which the secret seas have hitherto revealed to mankind. A vast pulpy mass, furlongs in length and breadth, of a glancing cream-colour, lay floating on the water, innumerable long arms radiating from its centre, and curling and twisting like a nest of anacondas, as if blindly to clutch at any helpless object within reach. No perceptible face or form did it have; no conceivable token of either sensation or instinct; but undulated there on the billows, an unearthly, formless, chance-like apparition of life.

Had it been Tennyson who saw it, he might well have concluded that it was the Kraken, and that Doomsday therefore was at hand:

> Below the thunders of the upper deep;
> Far, far beneath in the abysmal sea,
> His ancient, dreamless, uninvaded sleep
> The Kraken sleepeth: faintest sunlights flee
> About his shadowy sides: above him swell
> Huge sponges of millennial growth and height;
> And far away into the sickly light,
> From many a wondrous grot and secret cell
> Unnumbered and enormous polypi
> Winnow with giant arms the slumbering green.
> There hath be lain for ages and will lie
> Battering upon huge seaworms in his sleep,
> Until the latter fire shall heat the deep;
> Then once by man and angels to be seen,
> In roaring he shall rise and on the surface die.

Ishmael knows what Tennyson knows:

> There rolls the deep where grew the tree.
> O earth, what changes hast thou seen!

> There where the long street roars, hath been
> The stillness of the central sea.

But Ishmael's *In Memoriam* differs from Tennyson's. Remembering the antechronical Leviathans that have come to light from the earth's entrall beneath our cities and farms and parks, he isn't merely sad as Tennyson is, he is horror-struck:

Detached broken fossils of pre-adamite whales, fragments of their bones and skeletons, have within thirty years past, at various intervals, been found at the base of the Alps, in Lombardy, in France, in England, in Scotland, and in the states of Louisiana, Mississippi, and Alabama. Among the more curious of such remains is part of a skull, which in the year 1779 was disinterred in the Rue Dauphine in Paris, a short street opening almost directly upon the palace of the Tuileries; and bones disinterred in excavating the great docks of Antwerp, in Napoleon's time. Cuvier pronounced these fragments to have belonged to some utterly unknown Leviathanic species.

But by far the most wonderful of all cetacean relics was the almost complete vast skeleton of an extinct monster, found in the year 1842, on the plantation of Judge Creagh, in Alabama. The awe-stricken credulous slaves in the vicinity took it for the bones of one of the fallen angels. The Alabama doctors declared it a huge reptile, and bestowed upon it the name of Basilosaurus. But some specimen bones of it being taken across the sea to Owen, the English Anatomist, it turned out that this alleged reptile was a whale, though of a departed species ... so Owen rechristened the monster Zeuglodon; and in his paper read before the London Geological Society, pronounced it, in substance, one of the most extraordinary creatures which the mutations of the globe have blotted out of existence.

The Minotaur under Knossos, under Cretan civilization wherever it reached. Zeuglodon, or a cousin of his, under Paris. Toxodon under Buenos Ayres and Monte Video. Punta Alta under every Old World and New World plaza and park. And everything that geologists discovered without, Nietzsche discovered as samskarahs or karmic formations within:

I have discovered for myself that the old human and animal world, indeed the entire prehistory and past of all sentient being, works on, loves on, hates on, thinks on in me.

And neither in Tsetsekia nor in Carnival do we welcome what is under our cities into our cities. We welcome neither Zeuglodon nor the Kraken as the Kwakiutl, although terrified of him, welcome the Great Iakim:

> The Great Iakim will rise from below;
> He makes the sea boil, the Great Iakim,
> And we are afraid.

An enacted Tsetsekia in which we welcome the Great Iakim. An enacted Enuma Elish in which we slay Tiamat.

Thinking of it as a Tsetsekia that spontaneously enacted itself and hoping that it will help you or even heal you, I will tell you a dream, Friedrich: I am walking down Charing Cross Road in London. I turn into Old Compton Street and I've only walked but a little way when I see it, there on the other side, a striptease club I used to frequent when I was a younger man. When at last the traffic stalls, I cross over and go in. And I am charmed. Gone are all the pornographic enticements, all the luridly illuminated chiaroscuros of stairwell and wall, and in their place there is a great open room and it is filled with a lovely light, the kind of eternal light that ancient Egyptians hoped they would come forth into.

On the floor, stretching away to the far high-windowed wall, there is rack after rack of summer clothes. They are marvellously bright. Wear them down a coalmine or in hell and they will not darken or stain. Coming to see that they are unisexual, I stand there a long while becalmed in silent wonder. I leave. Walking down Old Compton Street, I am aware that I have a four-pronged manure-fork in my hand. On the prongs there are scales of dried cow dung. I turn into Wardour Street. But it could be into Marduk Street in Babylon or into the Way of the Dead in Teotihuacan or into Rue Dauphine in Paris that I have turned. I am in an eighteenth-century park. As I walk in it, manure fork in hand, I'm alarmed to see that it has become a savannah. I do not see them but I think there are hominids in the bushes. Maybe Lucy is watching me. Continuing to walk, I come upon a patch of ground that is different in colour and texture from its surroundings. Using the manure fork, I begin to dig. I uncover three granite steps. I stand on the lowest of them.

I am looking down into what I can only think of as an oceanarium. It is agelessly far away – beneath its nearness to me, it is agelessly far away in space and time. On the far granite embankment of it there is a man. Coming forward to the brink, he bends deeply, reaching his hands down into the water. More by mimed suggestion than by actual effort on his part, something is rising. Even before it breaks the surface, I can see that it is an immense iron grid. Up and up it comes tilting inwards, as if on hinges, into the embankment I am standing on. Now again I am looking down into the water. Up from the depths something tremendous, green and blue, breaking to turquoise, is rising. Even while it is still immersed I can see that it is a tangle of living immensities – immense not so much in physical size as in luminous, pleromic aliveness, and draped across them all, undulating in and out of manifestation, is a snake or a snake-form whose beginning and end I cannot see. Seeing no strangeness, none at all, in the ascription, I call him a dogfish and yet if ever the infinite richness of things could openly declare itself from a finite form, this thing surely, this undulating thing that I am looking at, this surely is it.

Now I am where the man was and could I but look down on myself from the lowest of the three granite steps I also would be as infinitely far away and far below as he seemed to be.

An otter comes towards me. Fearing that he will bite my small toe, I recoil. Without consciously thinking about it, I am aware of the corral snake who bit the small toe of a boy in a forest between Mexico and Guatemala.

I am sitting on the water. Behind me, his mouth wide open and watering, there is a mesozoic reptile. His gape increasing to canyon size, he plunges towards me, but at the last moment, for a reason I don't yet understand, he veers away to the right of me. The next time he comes, starting from the same place, he veers to the left of me. And now I know. Or I think I know. These first lunges are rehearsals, a whetting of his appetite.

Sitting there, looking straight ahead, I can nonetheless see what he is up to behind me.

The better to launch himself at me, he is thrashing the water with his hugely fluked tail.

Furiously, all agape, he comes. I am resigned, but only because there is nothing I can do.

I am in the jaws of the canyon. But I'm not crushed. And I'm not swallowed. And now I see why. Instantly transformed, this Kraken or Great Iakim or Tiamat or Shalyat has become a harmelss, shy little animal, swimming away, and going about its foraging business. I wake up.

Lying there, I dared to hope that we can come ashore at Punta Alta. I dared to hope, lying there, that we can come through the canyon, that we can ascend the river.

Having Nietzsche in mind and having Kurtz in mind, having the quite terrible fate of the one in mind and the quite terrible fate of the other in mind, I will put it this way:

> Entrall of the psyche
> Entrall of the city
>
> The savannah's entrall
> The sea's entrall
>
> They are one entrall.

But, where Dante saw,

    Abandon hope all who enter here

we see

XI

Geologically, Uluru is a sandstone outcrop in the Australian outback. Spiritually, it is an outcrop of aboriginal dreaming. Just as the Theban hills in Egypt are alive with the archetypal wonder of the past, so is Uluru alive with the archetypal wonder of the future.

Digging like Howard Carter through the accumulated rubble of my mind, I might one day discover and uncover sixteen stone steps going down. Like necropolis seals my eyes might break and I might see.

But how do I approach Uluru? How do I relax and allow the bedrock of my mind to outcrop so hugely? How do I find a way back beyond all the lobotomies of my civilized growing?

A lobe of aboriginal mind outcropping there in the outback.

The lobotomized lobe. The lobe to which our kind of consciousness is Gorgon. The lobe which the builders of culture in Europe rejected. The lobe that dreams archetypally.

A Tutankamen's tomb which, opened up by Howard Carter, has shown us the splendour of our archetypal past. An Uluru which, opening up to a shaman in trance, will show us the splendour and wonder of our archetypal future.

It is only through its archetypes that psyche can be manifest and real to itself. Without them it languishes. And a languishing psyche can all too easily become a scorpion's tail of venom and despair. Not that a flourishing psyche is necessarily harmless. From within us also when it flourishes nature is glorious in mambas and primroses.

And archetypes aren't windows or doorways into the bliss of Brahmanirvana. Neither will they light our way there. Like everything else that is psychic, conscious and subconscious, they are condensations of the eclipse that we naturally are. And yet to have walked away from Uluru, or, not being jivanmuktas, to pretend that we can walk away from it, is a great misfortune.

There are kinds of archetypal possession which are neither pleasant nor blessed. Much of the havoc and many of the bewildering contradictions in our human relationships have their profligate origins here. Within us, a Hebrew psalmist might say, is a place of dragons, and in it, when we come seeking wholeness, we can be sore broken. And yet, in the long run, it is surely a good thing to run the risk, under grace, of more and more growing from within our own depths.

It only the whole psyche that is wise. But we shouldn't be too excited at the prospect of achieving such wisdom. For even when it is wise the whole psyche is such only within blind limits. The wisdom of the whole psyche is the wisdom of an eclipse that doesn't know itself to be an eclipse. The wisdom of the whole psyche isn't prajnaparamita. Prajnaparamita isn't the wisdom of anyone or anything. It is the Divine Ground that eternally is before a sense of self and other-than-self arose so strangely within it.

Yet, even though it isn't prajnaparamita, the wisdom of the whole psyche is nonetheless greatly to be desired. It is good that there should be Theban hills and Ulurus on the road home.

There is a stage in the mystical journey when all strong rocks are broken, all on which the spirit might rest. Like the raven that Noah released we have nowhere now for the sole of our foot. We are niralamba, a fathomless sinking in a fathomless nothingness. But until that day comes it is good that we have in our outback a rock of the ages, a rock as old and as strong and as wise as Uluru.

It is always Dreamtime, always Altjeringa, in this rock, and looking into it now after our lobotomized millennia we see that the Tutankhamen's tomb of our archetypal past has become the rainbow snake cave of our archetypal future.

If the outcrop from which its stones were quarried hadn't already dreamed it, then no amount of work by how many soever workmen could have raised a cathedral like Chartres.

The Dreamtime dream of Chartres was in the workmen's hands, it was in their hammers and chisels. And we will build such a building again only when our hammers and chisels have been soaked for centuries in the dreaming of Uluru.

And Uluru is dreaming again. All the outcrops in all our outbacks are dreaming.

As I climb it even with the soles of my feet I'm aware of Altjeringa imaginings on the sides and summit of Derrada Hill.

What has been can be again. Closing our Gorgon eyes we can see, if we will, the dreams that the outcrops about us are dreaming.

What has been can be again. Uluru, the primary lobe of our dreaming, can be. Bhuvaneshvars can be. Cathedrals more glorious that Chartres can be. Buddh Gayas can be. Will be. Because now after two thousand years of thinking objectively about the universe we are ready, defeated at last, to begin dreaming and thinking subjectively with it. We are ready at last to dream and to think with that great universe out of which, each a wonder, mamba and primrose have arisen.

What has been can be again. Bhuvaneshvars will be. And in them, in their crypts, in their choirs, in their garbhagrihas, in stairs ascending and descending, in those Bhuvaneshvars which the outcrops around us even now are dreaming, in them, because of grace abounding, it will be safe and sane to celebrate the liturgy of human wholeness.

From all eternity there is One Only Without a Second. Its isness is neither is nor not is. Within it, for reasons we cannot divine, there occurred a dividing, there occurred in time a sense of self and other-than-self, and within every sense of self, particularly in higher selves, there occurred a primary repression.

There's a primary dividing. There's a primary repression. Overcoming them both is a dangerous undertaking. We call it the mystical journey.

Overcoming the primary repression is, usually, a side-effect of the samadhi in which the primary dividing is closed.

So what we now need is an outcrop which will dream itself, dreaming itself in our hammers and chisels, into a Buddh Gaya which, within itself somehow, is also a Bhuvaneshvar.

From all eternity is The-Divine-Without-Form-and-Void. It isn't other than we are. Yet we have constituted ourselves in a kind of dream otherness from it. In nirvikapsamadhi we wake up from our otherness.

For many of us that awakening is incarnations away.

In the meanwhile we are persons. We are infinitely serious. In any one life we can live conventionally and uneventfully, or we can go mad. We can ascend into heaven or go down into hell. And what a crying shame it would be not to be compassionate. Compassionate with souls in hell and with angels in heaven, with starving outcasts in Calcutta and with well-fed tycoons in Fifth Avenue. Out of the deep below passion in the heart, compassionate with insect and sage.

There is One Only Without a Second and within it, in that peace beyond bliss of never having left it, are the real dream woes of our dream otherness from it.

Be our Bhuvaneshvar, Uluru. Be our Buddh Gaya. Awaken us from the raptures of heaven and the fireless perditions of hell.

Be our House of many dragon caves. Be our Chartres in which all our crypts have arisen into the purifications and illuminations of its choir. Be our House of many samadhis. Be our House of many Mucalindas.

XII

The better to learn his lesson, Job had gone about the world and seen its wonders. He had meditated on canyon floors and kept vigil on Vulture Peaks. In Africa a tribe of Bushmen had trance-danced about him all night and healed him of an eye illness. Having spent three years with a Buryat shaman in Siberia he was ready at last to sing himself into a trance and ride the drumbeat into wisdoms and worlds which our dreaming and waking have eclipsed. The old questions no longer plagued him. And having opened his door to him, the old King of Terrors no longer tormented him. Behemoth, Leviathan and Ostrich weren't powers external to his psyche and therefore excluded. And so it was that in a temple of Shiva in India, reverently standing before the Great God, he had said:

> Shivo' ham
> Brairavo' ham

In a temple of Kali standing before her in her form of Durga he said:

> Sa' ham

The praying of India helped him. In temples of Shiva, sure at last of the blessings of that God, he took a chance, running the stupendous risk of letting the depths of his nature happen to him. In a temple of Kali, touching her tusks and her skulls and her swords, he confronted all that was sexually awful in his image of woman. The destroyed Tiamats, Leviathans, Pythons and Rahabs of his own culture lived again. In the silence of a dark night, meditating alone in his Marabar cave, he heard her, Tiamat singing the slow, low whale song she sang in the beginning. That song was in the beginning, and any Babylon, Uruk or Jerusalem that had built walls against it wouldn't flourish, not psychically, not spiritually, not mystically. All walls of all such cities would always end up as wailing walls.

The praying of India helped him. In the Garbhagrihas of his temples, Shiva helped him. Present in her dreadful icons, Kali helped him.

And then there was Vishnu. Vishnu as Matsya, a fish. Vishnu as

Kurma, a turtle. Vishnu as Varaha, a boar. Vishnu as Narasimha, a man-lion.

Vishnu was Omniform. He was Visvarupa. In Vishnu's divine presence, overshadowed and cared for by the holy auspices of one of his temples, Job found the courage to let his nature happen to him. Job came through. Job came home and, religiously and culturally ever since, the Middle East is more hospitable to more of what we are. It is more hospitable to more of what is.

XIII

I know so little about you. I know what your name was. It was Tjentmutengebtiu. You were a priestess in ancient Egypt and when you died traditional funerary rites were performed on your behalf. That's all I know about you, Tjentmutengebtiu. And yet I feel an affinity with you, for I have seen a photograph of your religiously decorated coffin, of your innermost, mummiform body case of cartonnage, to be precise.

It isn't necessary for our present purposes to talk in any great detail about the kinds and types of coffin the ancient Egyptians buried their dead in. We only need to know that many of them were decorated. To put it this way might, however, give a false impression. Aesthetic considerations of course there are but it wasn't solely with an aesthetic end in view that they were decorated. These coffins were sacraments. Pictorially, they were ritual enactments or pre-enactments of the dead person's long night journey to the Field of Reeds.

To be buried in such a coffin was to be buried in a womb boat or cocoon boat that knew the way. It was to be buried in a sacrament that would talk for you, would answer all dreadful questions at all dreadful portals for you. It was to be buried in an amulet that had already hallucinated and completed your journey for you. It was to be buried in a pictorially all powerful *Fare thee well*.

How wonderful it was that your people had a boat for you, moored and waiting for you when you needed it, Tjentmutengebtiu. How wonderful it was that your people had, as it were, a shaman's shawl for you. Dressed in that shawl you could walk among the growling enormities of the underworld and arrive unharmed home.

In Europe, nowadays, we have no such shawl.

And yet sometimes, walking to work maybe, I will put my hand in my trousers pocket and find my rosary beads in it. And how strange that is.

TURTLE WAS GONE A LONG TIME

The hand that was once a fin, was once a foot, is now a fistful of mysteries. The joyful and sorrowful and glorious mysteries of the Christian story.

A Christian hand. The hand of a man who, as a child, was baptized into the Christian story.

And yet it might be an ancient Egyptian hand. The hand of an Egyptian priestess. Your hand, Tjentmutengebtiu.

Your priestly handful of mysteries in ancient Egypt.

My gardener's handful of mysteries in modern Europe.

The joyful and sorrowful and glorious mysteries of Isis and Jesus.

Maybe one day in the Field of Reeds we will shake hands, me and you, Tjentmutengebtiu.

Maybe one day, meeting each other, we will shake joyful, sorrowful and glorious hands there.

Only I don't know.

For our Christian handful they say is dying.

And so it was that, last April, finding a blackbird's nest in an unpruned apple tree, I dropped my rosary beads in it.

Hoping that nature would hatch out a new clutch of archetypes for us I was.

A new clutch of shruti and smriti.

New mahavakyas.

A vision by which we might live and be healed in our brave new world of neuroses and nebulae.

With this new vision stitched and embroidered and dyed into it, we might, even here in Europe, have a shaman's shawl.

Who knows! Even here in Europe we might once again have a mesektet boat moored to our dreaming.

It was in that boat, standing undisturbed astern, that the Sun God journeyed every night through the underworld.

You had a boat, Tjentmutengebtiu. Old in night knowings and knowing the way, it was come, coming low, for to carry you home.

And you had a shawl.

Your coffin was shaman's shawl to you. It was Sun God's boat to you.

An illusion which, ideally, should have no future, Freud would call it.

An opium, Marx would call it. An opium no one will need or be addicted to once the industrial workers of Europe have taken the universe in hand.

Yes. Indeed.

Once we have taken the Horsehead Nebula in hand and have haltered it with our manifesto then, of course, obligingly, the universe will walk our way down the road we have scripted for it and never, never, never will a galaxy we have haltered unhorse us, as Lucifer was unhorsed, into modern Moscow or New York.

Don't heed us, Tjentmutengebtiu.

We are caterpillars who don't believe in butterflies.

Don't heed us.

Go down into your cocoon and lie, totally surrendered, as though dead, in it.

Let it row you into the night of disintegrations and awakenings.

Let it take you home, holy and whole, to the Field of Reeds.

In a dream I go to you there. I drop my rosary beads into your hand.

Into its instant transformation into a blackbird's nest in an apple tree.

In April, advent to apple blossom time, it isn't only swallows will fly back to us.

Tjentmutengebtiu, holy and whole, at home at last, going down a small path to a well in the paradise of her Lord Osiris.

There are mysteries we dare not speak of. We who are still in the flesh we dare not speak of them. But we have seen your sun wings, Tjentmutengebtiu. We have seen them showing and growing from within your chrysalis. And we wonder what that might mean. Does it mean that in the depths of our souls we are all one wingspan with the sun? Does it mean that in the depths of our souls we are all one wingspan with all the high heavens that have always, unknown to us, overlighted us from within?

We dare not say, we who are still in the flesh. We dare not, we who are still this side of Good Friday.

This side of Good Friday we pray:

May Isis and Nephthys and Neith and Selkis walk with us wherever it is souls walk after death.

May the Djed Pillar stand with us.

May Horus and Thoth rain blessings upon us.

Aware in our need of our oneness with them, may we pray with all ancient and all modern peoples.

In whatever form it might choose, ancient Egyptian and Christian, may the Paraclete come.

May Good Friday find us.

On our way into it, may Isis, Nephthys, Neith and Selkis sing to us:

Yatra na anyat pasyati na anyat srinoti, na anyad vijanati, sa bhuma.

On Easter Sunday morning we will see that the here and now is also home. Behind the veil of our terror of it, we will see it is home. Behind the veil of our self seeking it is samadhi.

And so, it is good to see you, Tjentmutengebtiu. It is good to see you going down a small path to a well in this paradise all about us.

> God be praised.
> Going to that well and coming from it.
> God be praised.

And may we be as out of your way awake and working, God, as we are in dreamless sleep.

May we be as out of your way awake and working, God, as we are in dreamless sleep.

May we be as out of your way awake and working, God, as we are in dreamless sleep.

Coming and going from your well we will, God. We will consider the lilies of the field, how they grow.

XIV

It is years ago now, fourteen or fifteen years ago I suppose, since I saw a film called *Elvira Madigan*. It was a love story.

The man was middle-aged and married. An aristocrat, he was an officer in the army. The woman was young. She was very beautiful and she earned a living as a rope-walker in a travelling circus.

They fell in love and in the innocence of their longing for each other they eloped, walking off into the world.

And the world they walked in was a wonder of summer meadows and trees and birds singing in the trees and butterflies that wouldn't be caged, not even for moment, by the happy hands of two people in love.

Settled, respectable society might well disapprove of what they had done, but the world, it would seem, was with them. As if in every open primrose nature was saying, I am always an accomplice with those who, seeing me, see wonder.

Round the corner, however, not waiting, just there, was that other more familiar world, the world of brutal necessities and contingencies. Now and then, ominously, it put in an appearance.

Being a deserter from the army, the man would be in trouble if he were recognized. This meant that they couldn't be in open, undisguised contact with people. It also meant that he couldn't look for work.

For a while yet, however, there were other meadows to chase other butterflies in and there were other woods to be man and woman in. Hardly at all did they need to speak to each other of their love. Above them in a trembling of leaf light or all about them in the humming summer grasses nature did their fondest talking for them.

A man and a woman had fallen in love. And in order that their love for each other might flourish they broke free from the common world.

And yet, however often they cupped their hands upon them, playing in the meadows, the butterflies they chased had so far eluded them.

Also now it began to appear that the life they had hoped for would, that too, elude them.

Separated for so long from the small salvations of the settled world, Elvira's health gave way. A fortune-teller she consulted told her the future was black.

In the days and nights that followed things went from bad to worse.

One day, knowing what would happen, inviting it to happen, Elvira got up from where they were sitting in utter hopelessness under a tree. She walked into the sunlit meadows and yet once again, she tried, as she so often had, to cup her sunlit hands on a sunlit butterfly. Just as it was about to happen, a shot rang out and the closing hands closed no further. Another shot rang out. And that was it. They had lived, but not outlived, their dream of love in a lovely but cruel world.

There is a scene in this film that I often remember. In a wood I think it is. Elvira and the man she's in love with are sitting there talking. Looking at her the man knows, he need only look at her to know, why he loves her. Then, in an idle moment, he wonders about her love for him. What, he wonders, does she see in him? He asks her. 'Until I met you,' she said, 'I only had courage to walk on the rope. You gave me courage to walk on the ground.'

In our century man has walked on the moon. Setting foot on it, Neal Armstrong said, it's a small step for me but it's a giant leap for humanity.

It might well be. But I'm not so sure. For I sometimes think that we've walked on the moon only because, like Elvira Madigan, we haven't the courage, not yet, nor the grace, to walk this great and sacred earth.

Bacon distinguishes between what he calls movement local and movement essential.

Movement local is ordinary physical movement from one place to another, from the Earth to the Moon, from Mars to the heart of the last megagalaxy. It also includes, I suppose, all those movements, through promotion, from being for instance a roughneck on a tramp steamer to being admiral of a nation's fleet.

Movement essential always involves a transformation. As in the transformation of a caterpillar into a butterfly. As in the transformation of a human being into a Bodhisattva.

Movement local will often have its excitements and delights as when we who live in northern Europe move to the south and the sun in summer. It is often a good and a necessary thing to get up and go. To another culture. Or, now that we are able, to another planet. But it would be a shame, surely, were we to use all our movements local or our need for them as an excuse for not standing still, sitting down like a caterpillar where we are, facing the dangers and strangeness of movement essential.

It's as if I can hear Lao Tze calling us down from the dizzy heights of our Nicene creeds and Chalcedonian definitions, calling us down from the side-effects in intergalactic fantasy of Einstein's famous formula, calling us down from any heights into which our Ascension Thursdays can take us, Lao Tze calling us to come down and set foot for the first time on the earth we were born into.

Whose will it be, that sacred foot that will first set foot on our sacred earth? To set foot on the earth. And to walk in it. To walk out into its lonely and wild places with a barefoot heart and a barefoot mind. To honour it by being barefoot. By being without shoes of any kind. Shoes cobbled in Chalcedon. Shoes cobbled in Zurich.

Elvira in a travelling circus. Elvira walking a tightrope. A symbol, she, of who and what we are and want to be. And yet if we plait every spinal cord that has been, is, and will be, into a rope and if we string that rope between the galaxies and walk them all in the way that we now pretend to walk the earth, then at the end of all our walking we will still not know anything of any importance about the universe.

Well might Lao Tze have said:

> Without leaving his door
> The sage knows everything under heaven.
> Without looking out of his window
> He knows all the ways of heaven.
> For the further one travels
> Away from Tao, away from
> The Unity into the Multiplicity
> The less one knows.
> Therefore the sage arrives
> Without going
> Sees all without looking
> Does nothing, yet achieves everything.

Zen Buddhists are fond of dividing the mystical journey into three phases: first there is a mountain, then there is no mountain, then again there is a mountain.

We are and we will be Elvira Madigans walking our highly strung, highly hallucinating spinal cords, we are and we will be Elvira Madigans walking our land of cocaine highs until we come down and die not only to life but also to death, not only to the here and now but also to the hereafter. We must come down from our highs and die to being and non-being. We must, in short, die to all experience of self and other-than-self.

Out of the Divine-without-form-and-void the mountain reappears.

Its peaks are paramitas. Paramitas too are its Olduvais and Grand Canyons.

In every Olduvai and in every Grand Canyon are Eloras and Ajantas.

And because we are out of Nirvana and ready for it, we are ready for the earth. We are ready for ourselves and for others and for all things. We are ready at last for the universe. And our movements local within it won't be the movements of fugitives from it.

So come down, Elvira. Come down and walk down into our Olduvais with us. Come down and walk down our Bright Angel trails into our canyons with us.

Who knows! When the sun shines there may be butterflies.

And maybe, Elvira, you'll catch one, closing your hands at last on your own transformation.

Closing your hands at last on a willingness to walk the precipitous earth. Precipitous in canyons within and without.

Precipitous in lion mouths within and without. Precipitous in Heavens within and without. In Hells within and without. Precipitous asleep. Precipitous awake.

It is above all in our willingness to surrender to Gravity that Grace can be effective in us.

Bright Angel Trail going down into and under the roots of Medulla and mountain is our way to the Moon.

Bright Angel Trail going down into and under the roots of Medulla and mountain is our way to the Stars.

Bright Angel Trail going down into and under the roots of Medulla and mountain is our way to the Earth.

Bright Angel Trail going down into and under the roots of Medulla and mountain is the Christmas Night of Ascension Thursday.

Breathe warmth on our homecoming, Wolf. Breathe warmth on our homecoming, Stegosaurus.

Sing a First Noel, Archaeornis.

Until we met you, Lao Tze, we only had courage for the rope. You gave us courage for the snake in the rope.

The snake isn't other than the rope.

Earth isn't other than Tao.

Precipices in Tao don't hurt.

The fortune-teller you went to has thrown the cards again for you, Elvira.

It's a New Day, they say.

Every day from now on is Taoday, they say.

Settle down with the man you love, they say.

> *Sila ersinarsinsinivdluge.*
> Do not be afraid of the universe.

XV

Black Elk's vision, both as vision and healing ritual, was the great religious event of the last century. The great religious event of this century is a series of four etchings by Picasso called *The Blind Minotaur*. Quite simply, they are a witness to profound redemption, and not only that. Since art is sometimes sacramental, they sacramentally enact or pre-enact that redemption. Redemption in the profoundest of interior places. Root redemption. Looking at them, we know that our inner collective hell has been harrowed.

One year, everywhere in the ancient world, the corn was rich, to admiration, and to wonder, particularly in old women and old men who had never seen the like. They didn't at first know why. Sun and rain, seed sowing and soil were much as they always had been. Unless it was that all sowing this year was a sacrament of Demeter's first sowing. Unless it was that all growing this year was a sacrament of Persephone's first growing. Could it be that anyone who sowed this year was Triptolemus walking between the Corn Mother and the Corn Maiden? The first bread they made that year they didn't themselves eat. Walking to Eleusis they offered it to Mother and Maiden, giving thanks. And their flocks flourished, and the work of their hands, and they wondered.

> Adonis, the Python Priestess at Delphi said,
> There is a new Adonis, and he is risen.

And then they heard it. At Delphi, beside an opening in the ground there, they heard it, the piping.

Sinking into trance, then into vision, Pythonessa saw him:

Far away and far below in the last and deepest cavern of his labyrinth, the Minotaur playing the pipes of Pan.

It was music more plaintive than Pan himself had ever played, even when he played the world's first love song to Syrinx.

Blind from such long engulfment in darkness, Minotaur was playing the eclogues of the Underworld.

In all the underworlds of all ancient peoples they were heard and, hearing them, there was no Eurydice but knew that now again she had a chance. The power that restrained her was broken. But no. Even before the end of the first slow air, the Power that restrained her was itself redeemed.

That's why, eating bread made from it, people believed that Demeter herself sowed the corn that year, that Persephone reaped it. And that's why, that year, there was such skill in the carpenter's hands, such consent in the wood that he carved.

Generations would live and die before it was known that the piping was heard, heard first by Hades himself, on the night of Good Friday.

Our religion, our culture, not yet ready for him, the Minotaur didn't emerge till our day.

But there he is now, coming among us, a little girl with flowers in her arm, or a dove in her arm, leading him. Immense he is. But however vast it is, his brutality isn't brutal.

And she, the child, how frail she is. And yet, how intent she is, how sure. Surer than Orpheus she is. Surer than Orpheus leading Eurydice. She, her face so familiar, remembered from somewhere, the repressed in us all towering big and blind above her.

One thing, though, we don't yet know. Where did the Pan pipes come from?

Some say Pasiphae. Pasiphae was the Minotaur's mother. She was a Queen. Supported from below by a bodice, her breasts, not always for mothering, were always bare. No.

She didn't mother her bull-chested, bull-shouldered, bull-headed baby, and an old, old nurse was heard to predict that no good, and much trouble, would come from this, because Pasiphae rejecting the Minotaur was humanity rejecting itself. And some there are who say that Pasiphae's despair at the prodigy that emerged, half crying, half bellowing, from her womb wasn't complete. The birth of her son was also in some sense the birth of a vision. Vision of a day when, as a consequence of some immense passion, we would be altogether more able for altogether more of what we are, and that's why she asked Daedalus, who designed and excavated it, to hang the Pan pipe on the last wall of the last cavern in the labyrinth.

And the girl who so surely leads the Prodigy civilization isn't able for? Who is she?

However familiar her face might be, is she the Beatrice of the repressed? Is she the Beatrice who leads from the labyrinth into the light of day? Is she the Beatrice whom Dante, blinded by vision, couldn't see or meet? Couldn't acknowledge or know?

Able, at her age, for fairy story and myth, she is able to be mythic mother to the Minotaur.

Openly acknowledging him as her son, she walks with him, towering so hugely above her, into our civilized world, into our religion, into our temple.

Mother more able for more of what we are she is, this little child.

Whoever she is, she is walking among us now, leading the rejected son past the accepted son, adolescent now, and altogether too tenderly nurtured in civilized sentiment to be able for what he is seeing. Expecting perhaps to see Venus rising from the sea, he walked out of his walled city and came shorewards. But now this. In him, yet again, the old encounter of civilization and savagery. And yet, may grace abound to him, he hasn't turned away, or, like the sailors, sailed away. It is back into our frightened past that they are sailing. They are indeed our Cretan past. The boy is our Periclean future. He might even be the future Christianity will only be able for when it crosses the Kedron with its Founder. The boy is brave. He is inwardly brave. Although terrible beyond all expectation the thing he has seen, he is a Theseus who will not resort to dagger or sword.

The new Theseus.
The new Ariadne?

Is that who she is?

Whoever she is, she has come. And her coming and her son coming with her mean that now at last our yearnings for

Vita Nuova

are a little less fantastical.

XVI

On a Greek amphora of the sixth century BC there is a scene with satyrs. We might think of them as a thiasos of satyrs, and however unpriestly they might look, it wouldn't perhaps be altogether injurious to the sacred to suggest that their work is liturgical. For the moment, they are votaries of Dionysus. Two of them, their horsetails and their phalloi fiercely pertinent, are picking and bringing the clusters of grapes to where a third, no less fiercely endowed than they, is standing in a basket treading them. The basket is resting on a low platform or table that is tilted slightly towards one end. Channelled down the slope of this platform, the juice pours into a waiting container. Suggesting not refinement of culture but a heightened kind of savagery, a fourth satyr, more elementally animal than animals themselves are, is playing the double pipes. Given the occasion, the music is surely in the Phrygian mode, likely to arouse, not allay, passions. Intent and absorbed, his back to the others, a fifth satyr is pouring the divinely anarchic, sanguine sap into an urn in which presumably it will ferment and mature.

Viniculture, wine-making, music, the handiwork of potter and willow-weaver – well indeed might the scene suggest the appropriation of culture by savagery. Something like it occurred in Europe in our century. In our case though, the savagery that captured our mills and our minds, our facts and our figures, our hammers and our sickles, the steam that lifted lid of a cast iron-kettle and $E = mc^2$ – the savagery that captured us wasn't Satyric. It was *nacht-und-nebel* savagery. Savagery of a uniquely diabolical kind.

And it poses a terrible question: did the Greek satyr we sent to hell on the morning of Christ's nativity return as the Christian devil? In other words: to suppress an instinct or a dark energy is not to get rid of it, it is to negatively transform it, and lay ourselves open to unconscious possession by it.

Suppress the satyr and soon, as well as being savage, he will be malign.

Are we able for the moral demands of Christianity? Can we eat and drink one day from the Gundestrup cauldron, and then, at the end of an overnight exodus, eat and drink the next day from the Ardagh chalice?

How morally healthy are the moral demands of Christianity? Can we leave the theranthropic Gods of Egypt, ibis-headed Thoth, falcon-headed Horus, cow-headed Hathor – can we leave them firmly believing that with Yahweh's help we will never again even so much as dream of a golden calf? Can we by simply suppressing Egypt in us walk morally forward into the Holy Land?

Montaigne was clear-eyed:

They want to get out of themselves and escape from the man. That is madness: instead of changing into angels, they change into beasts; instead of raising themselves they lower themselves.

Pascal echoed him:

Man is neither angel nor brute, and the unfortunate thing is that he who would act the angel acts the brute.

And William Law was under one less illusion than many a religious zealot:

Now religion in the hands of self, on corrupt nature, serves only to discover vices of a worse kind than in nature left to itself. Hence are all the disorderly passions of religious men, which burn in a worse flame than passions only employed about worldly matters: pride, self-exaltation, hatred and persecution, under a cloak of religious zeal, will sanctify actions which nature left to itself would be ashamed to own.

Milton had a morality for the morning of Christ's nativity. But so had Blake. Milton would widen the gulf between heaven and hell. Blake would marry them.

Even with grace abounding, maybe Blake's is the only morality we are able for.

To suppress the Gundestrup cauldron is, very likely, to turn it into a witch's cauldron.

To suppress the amphora is, very likely, to turn it into the chalice in a black mass.

Would we be running a risk morally altogether too great were we to invite the satyrs to join us treading our grapes, making our wine?

To begin with we could do it in a morality play. Or, dare we aspire to it, in a miracle play.

Christian now, having Christ's passion for theme, a chorus of satyrs all over again.

Chorus of Bethlehem angels. Chorus of Gethsemane satyrs.

Antiphonally they sing on Holy Thursday.

Antiphonally they sing on Good Friday.

On Easter morning, singing not antiphonally but in unison, satyrs and angels sing the same hosannas.

He is risen!

Dionysia has grown into Christysia
And we have it. A theatre, stone cut, cut into the side of Golgotha.
And do come. Come Aeschylus, come Euripides, come Sophocles. Bring all the tragic heroines and heroes with ye. Bring Orestes, bring Electra, Phaedra, Antigone, Oedipus, Hippolytus, Medea, all of them, bring them all with ye. And you, Shakespeare, and you, Schiller, and you, Racine. Led by Melpomene through Colonus, led by her past Areopagus Rock, come with Lear, Ophelia, Phèdre, Faust, Die Jungfrau and Maria, come with them all, because we have it.

> We have the theatre
> We have the chorus
> We have the passion
>
> The hero's tomb we have
> We have the miracle play
> It is called
> *The Marriage of Heaven and Hell*

XVII

The day he crosses the threshold of a monastery on Mount Athos, a prospective monk is, more than likely, already aware that the life he is committing himself to will, if it is to complete itself, proceed through three formally distinct yet essentially continuous stages. First, for a period of one to three years, he will be a *rasophore,* a wearer of the rason, the tunic which signifies that he is a postulant, still on probation. Then, usually for a few years, he will be a *stavrophore,* a wearer of the wooden crucifix or cross. Alternatively, he will at this stage be called a *microschemos,* a wearer of the micron schema or little habit. Finally, he becomes a *megaloschemos,* a wearer of the megalon schema, the great and angelical habit. Suggesting the seriousness of the monk's vocation, the front of this great habit is centrally emblazoned with the Golgotha cross and skull and laterally with the instruments of Christ's passion, also with symbolic Christian monograms. Pictorially, this habit is a kind of Christian Book of the Dead. It signifies the monk's willingness to die to this world. More positively, it signifies his willingness, in an identification of himself with Christ in Gethsemane and on Golgotha, to die out of time into eternity.

To Theseus and his Athenian contemporaries, Mount Athos, by whatever name they knew it, would have suggested a savage, dragonish world far to the north of civilization. It was into that world the *Argo* sailed. Even if you were Theseus or Hercules or Orpheus, you only had to ascend any one of its rivers to find yourself, possibly defeated, in the heart of our European darkness. Medea lived here. It was therefore not just a savage world. It was a spooky world. It was the fee, fi, fo, fum world of our earliest nightmares. All of the most awful things that happen in fairy stories happen here. Wasn't it from here that Abaris, a shaman, flew southwards on an arrow into what we thought of as our enlightenment? Herodotus knew that a people called the Getae lived here. They worshipped or had magical dealings with a god or aboriginal shaman called Salmoxis:

> The belief of these people in their immortality takes the following form: they never really die, but every man, when he takes leave of this present life, goes to join Salmoxis, a divine being who is also called by some of them Gebeleizis. Every five years they choose one of their number by lot and send him to Salmoxis as a messenger, with instructions to ask him for whatever they may happen to want. To effect the dispatch, some of them with javelins in their hands arrange themselves in a suitable position, while others take hold of the messenger by his hands and feet, and swing him up into the air in such a way as to make him fall on the upturned points of the javelins. If the man is killed they take it as a sign that Salmoxis is in a favourable mood; if he escapes, they put it down to his own bad character, tell him what they think of him, and send another messenger instead. The instructions are of course given to the messenger while he is still alive. This same tribe of Thracians will, during a thunderstorm, shoot arrows up into the sky and utter threats against the lord of the lightning and the thunder, because they recognize no god but their own.

It was in this world, more real than imagined in his day, that Euripides spent the last years of his life.

Into it, to tutor Alexander, Aristotle came. Into it, centuries later, a Christian who would one day be called Peter the Athonite came.

As we would expect, Peter's biography underwent a transfiguration into hagiography, but that surely is in accord not just with human desire. It is in accord also, altogether more deeply, with the pristine, wild world he settled in.

This is Peter's story: when he was still a very young man, Peter vowed that he would become a monk. Within a few years, however, he had joined the Byzantine army and was fighting Arabs in Syria.

He was captured and imprisoned and this misfortune he ascribed to the fact that he hadn't kept his vow. He prayed to St Nicholas, a saint so renowned for miracles and wonders that even Arabs would sometimes intercede with him. When, in a way that was indeed wonderful, Peter was released, he sailed to Rome and there a few years later he was ordained by no less a spiritual dignitary than the Pope himself. He took ship for the Levant. On the way, he dreamed that he saw St Nicholas and the Virgin talking together. Turning to him, the Virgin told him that Athos was in her gift and that for the rest of his life he would live there under her protection. A few days later the ship was sailing past Athos but now again a wonder occurred:

Though the wind still blew and the sails billowed, the ship suddenly stopped. The sailors were at a loss and asked each other: 'What is this sign, this new wonder that in an open expanse of sea and with a favourable wind the ship is not moving?' Anxious to put their minds at rest, the saint told them: 'Children, if you wish to know the meaning of this, tell me the name of this place.' They replied: 'It is the Holy Mountain, venerable father, which from ancient times has borne the name of Athos.' Then he said to them: 'Perhaps this sign has occurred on my account. Unless you abandon me here you will not be able to proceed.' Sadly the sailors lowered the sails and approached the shore, and with tears and lamentations left him there. He climbed up a difficult path and, after resting in a cool and level place, he began to explore his new retreat. Passing through streams and valleys and over hills, he came to a dark cave. It was surrounded by thick vegetation and so many animals that they outnumbered the stars in the heavens or the grains of sand in the sea. It was also infested by a host of demons who raised up so many trials against the holy man that no tongue could recount or even credit them.

Alone in a savage land, in a cave alone there, Peter prayed.

The Cyclops who came, the one-eyed fee, fi, fo, fum Polyphemus who came, was Satan.

Where Hercules with his club would have failed, and where Orpheus with his lyre would have failed, Peter by his praying came through.

Peter, the great Argonaut, like Job, came into the savage, yawning places of inwardness and outwardness, but he didn't become a Mistah Kurtz.

The Book of Job is our journey up the river.

It is our journey up the Danube and the Lena.

It is our journey up the Amazon.

It is our journey up the Colorado.

Inwardly and outwardly, Peter ascended the river and the megalon schema is the golden fleece he won for us, and on Athos to this day it is given to anyone who, in sacramental identification with Jesus, is willing to cross the Kedron and undergo our transtorrentem evolution.

Coming forth by day, we will see that our last account of the universe will be, no, not a biography – being true to the wonder we are walking abroad in, it will be a hagiography.

XVIII

Let us look again at the first of Nietzsche's two discoveries:

I have discovered for myself that the old human and animal world, indeed the entire prehistory and past of all sentient being, works on, loves on, hates on, thinks on in me.

The trilobite of Bright Angel shale thinks in him. The amphibian who left her footprints in the Supai Formation thinks in him. The reptile who left his footprints in Coconino sandstone thinks in him.

It's a terrible discovery, isn't it? The hands with which we play the Kreutzer Sonata are morphologically homologous to the fins of the shark. The hands with which we sculpt the St Peter's Pieta are structurally analogous to the feet of the hyena.

The fins and the feet recrudesced in Nebuchadnezzar:

The same hour was the thing fulfilled upon Nebuchadnezzar: and he was driven from men, and did eat grass as oxen, and his body was wet with the dew of heaven, till his hairs were grown like eagle's feathers, and his nails like bird's claws.

The fact that we live this side of Darwin on the beach at Punta Alta and Nietzsche on a beach under his own pons does not mean that we know ourselves more deeply and therefore more apprehensively than Job did, or than Jonah did. It does not mean that we now have reason to be more alarmed at ourselves or more afraid of ourselves than Nebuchadnezzar was or than Oedipus Tyrannus was.

Living this side of Darwin and Nietzsche does, however, mean that we now understand ourselves somewhat differently. Or should we say it means that we now understand something of what we are somewhat differently. Where formerly we might have ascribed the cause of our House of Atreus actions to Fate, to an Alastor, to possession by an evil spirit, or to some other supernatural agency acting upon us from without, we now tend to look to inner archaic life which, in the interests of civilization, we've attempted to suppress.

> More real in image than in fact
> The pool that nature looks in overflows;
> Under the moon's fourth shoulder nature grows
> But, among spoors still intact,
> The spoor of her latent beast

> Is found
> On Pasiphae's calving ground.
>
> Our climb to clear air was ascetic, was ashen;
> But since Nature's more backward than we had supposed,
> Since it clings to itself with such nuclear compassion,
> It is Heaven's fifth column itself has composed
> The scene where its will survives in cold blood:
> On Europa's grave the Bullgod chews the cud.

The answer to this is not to build an impounding labyrinth, as Cretans did, under civilization. And it is inordinately not helpful that Theseus should go down, sword in hand, into that labyrinth.

The Tsetsekia of the Kwakiutl is altogether better. In Tsetsekia, Pasiphae's calving ground becomes holy ground, open ground, ground ceremonially open to all whatsoever is in the sea's, is in the mind's, entrall.

The greatest of all Tsetsekias enacted itself in Jesus. At the end below of Bright Angel Trail he ran the risk of being another Nebuchadnezzar or, even more terribly, he ran the risk of being another Aztec Earth Mother.

Sometime after Cortez and his men conquered Mexico, a statue of the Aztec Earth Mother along with much other religious rubble was buried beneath the new vehemently European, vehemently Christian order. Towards the end of the eighteenth century, purely by chance, a group of workmen unearthed it. So horrified were they by the dumb yet elementally eloquent power of it that, as soon as they conveniently could, they reburied it. Word got out of course and now again it underwent exhumation. Or should we say resurrection. To look at it is not to see a representation of the Earth Mother, it is to see the Earth Mother herself. Here a representation has been taken over by that which it was intended to represent. How, a Jew who had come through the sea and the desert with Moses might ask, how can we look at her and live?

At the end below of Bright Angel Trail, Jesus looked in a mirroring pool and somehow, seeing her, he lived.

In that hitherto unimaginable integration of phylogenetic inwardness, we acquired evolutionary legitimacy. And not only that. In it and through it the evolving earth itself found the way through, it found the channel.

Good News, that, for Nebuchadnezzar. Good News, that, for Nietzsche.

Good News, that, for any Gilgamesh, Kadmus, Minos, Quetzalcoatl, Aeneas or Ishmael who would ascend the river and dig or plow, with Palamabron's plow, the *sulcus primogenius* of a new city, and civilization.

XIX

Ishmael had come up on deck, but it hadn't worked, he hadn't come up out of the dream. The cassock he was wearing, yet wasn't wearing, it was real, it was more real as miasma than the cassock the mincer would wear as he sliced them out, Bible leaves they called them, Bible leaves of whale blubber.

'Bible leaves! Bible leaves! Thin as Bible leaves!' the mates called, and the mincer supplied them, tumbling them down into a tub.

Two hours later, the *Pequod* moving under indolent sail in the Japanese cruising-ground, Ishmael was still wondering whether it would ever fall from him. From where would the prayer come? From what heights or depths would it come? And what kind of prayer would it be, the prayer that would cause the cassock to fall from him?

Like the cassock Queequeg wore or like the cassock the mincer wore, his cassock was made from the pelt of the sperm whale's penis. In the dream it was a suffocating fit for him. It was out of an intense orgasm of suffocation, a sperm-whale's orgasm of suffocation, crushing his chest, crushing his mind, that he awoke.

He couldn't be sure that he hadn't died.

He couldn't be sure that he wasn't dead.

He crossed and sat, forward from the windlass, with Bulkington.

The moon was already well up when Bulkington spoke.

I know a man it happened to, he said.

What happened to him?

I don't know what it was but whatever it was it has happened to you.

Did it kill him?

I only know that the first island with a Christian steeple in it that we came to, he jumped ship.

'I had always hoped that somewhere deep within me I wasn't on this voyage,' Ishmael said. 'But now I know.'

Bulkington's way of not asking him about what it was he knew was itself a question hanging imperatively in the air.

Ishmael responded: you mightn't see it, with your physical eyes you mightn't see it, but I'm wearing the cassock.

Do you know anyone on this ship who isn't? Bulkington asked. Do you know anyone on or off this ship who isn't?

Ishmael refused the invitation, if that's what it was, to a more general conversation, and when he at last felt that he could graciously do so, he got up and, as amiably disposed as he could make himself out to be, he walked away.

Halfway down the stairs he saw what he had so often seen, and almost as often avoided, the lonely, open sea of his soul in Bulkington's eyes. He turned and came back up.

Again, there was Bulkington's way of being silent.

Ishmael took refuge in talk: even if there is none of us but wears it, the cassock does not distinguish us, or define us, not in the way that having a rumen distinguishes ruminants, not in the way that having cleft hooves distinguishes ungulates.

Bulkington didn't need to let Ishmael know that he could match him in learning, but the word 'ungulate' as, on a previous occasion, the word 'cetaceous', did provoke him.

Do you remember the day we first sat together, there by the starboard gangway, splicing ropes? Assuming that I didn't already know of them and their work, you talked to me about a famous palaeontologist in London called Owen and an even more famous one in Paris called Cuvier. In lingering but defeated disbelief, you told me that they had named animals Adam didn't name and he didn't name them, you went on to tell me, because they didn't walk before him, and they didn't walk before him because by the time he, a newcomer, had shown up they and their world were long ago extinct. What I particularly remember from that day was your need to talk, your need to confront both yourself and me with the actual world we were living in. Like God guiding Job into the presence of Leviathan, you guided me into the presence of Zeuglodon. In his presence you were yourself man enough to let Saturn's grey chaos roll over you. You said: if there was a world before Adam maybe there will be a world after him. The evidence of the rocks suggests we will have our day. Only our day. Up from beneath a fashionable street in Paris comes the news that we and the whales we hurt are ephemeral. The next day you did what all of us on the most awful of whaleships did, you drank Ahab's grog, committing yourself thereby, come what might, to strike through the mask.

I remind you of all of this because I wish, for a reason not very laudable, to tell you that one night, a long time ago now in London, I went to hear Professor Owen. It was, I don't suppose I need to tell you, the night Zeuglodon came back from what you call his pre-adamite world and walked before us, for, like *cetaceae*, he was a land animal before he was a sea animal.

Something also there is I'd like to tell you. The day we sat together splicing rope, you must surely remember it, I was comforted by you that day. In the way that, through Isaiah, the biblical God would have comforted his people, I was comforted.

Comfort ye, comfort ye my people, saith your God. Speak ye comfortably to Jerusalem, and cry unto her ...

There was comfort in knowing that someone else was as anguished as I was, anguished not just by what had come to light, anguished in his efforts to remain somehow significant in a universe that doesn't have us either particularly or paradigmatically in mind.

So why, a carpet-bag slung over your shoulder, did you walk a gangway into a whaleship?

Having walked with Job and come home with no vision I could lay my head on, I felt, against all odds, that I might be saved, that I might be plucked out, if I fled with Jonah.

Pious man that he was, Jonah didn't deliberately strike through the mask. A whale, or something that left a wake as wide as a whale's, carried him through it. So why, while it was still possible, didn't you jump ship?

You know the Latin word for ship, don't you? For all its madness, the *Pequod* is my nave. For all its madness, I'll stay, still hoping, with Western civilization. Also, there is a kind of purification in facing what is inwardly and outwardly terrible. Without the terrible I'd wilt. In the presence of the terrible I know I'm a living soul. In the presence of the terrible I know it's from God not from godlessness that I'm fleeing. To flee from him, into a whaleship if necessary, is the only good way to go towards the God I believe in. To put myself in the way of disaster, final disaster, disaster you wouldn't recover from, that's the only way I can pray. It's simple, a world the terrible is gone from is a world that God is gone from.

Will you ever be ready to come into the New Testament?

The saddest sentence ever written is in the New Testament:

And I saw a new heaven and a new earth: for the first heaven and the first earth were passed away; and there was no more sea.

For me, no more sea means no more soul.

In my case, it means the cassock.

And the Bible leaves of whale blubber, they aren't blank. Even as they fall down into the tub, the aren't blank, they are Magna Cartas.

Guaranteeing us what right?

The right to rule over the earth and subdue it that God gave to Adam.

ANACONDA CANOE

After the Flood he gave it more elaborately to Noah:

And God blessed Noah and his sons, and said unto them, Be fruitful, and multiply and replenish the earth. And the fear of you and the dread of you shall be upon every beast of the earth, and upon all the fishes of the sea: into your hand are they delivered. Every moving thing that liveth shall be meat for you: even as the green herb I give you all things.

That's the cassock we are wearing. That's the Queequeg tattoo we are inwardly and outwardly tattooed with. And the man who put those words into the mouth of his God, he was tattooed. In him, and with him, our civilization became a whale ship. You remember it, don't you, the pulpit in the Whaleman's Chapel in New Bedford? It was deliberately designed to look like the prow of a whale ship, the prow of our civilization. It is on that prow that we are now sitting, you and me, and the task we have set ourselves is to strike through the mask. We, in other words, intend to harpoon the six days of creation.

So why haven't you instigated a mutiny?

Better by far that I would never delude myself into thinking that I could be Cortez to my own culture, or to my own religion. I know of no new face of God that I could install on the old summits of the old pyramids. And that reminds me. I once overheard you saying that this whaleship was, still is I suppose, your Yale and your Harvard. I know what you mean. The doomsday glare of the tryworks is a good place to test your reactions as you watch Aeschylus leading humanity forward to Oreopagus Rock, as you watch Sophocles leading humanity forward to Colonus. I put it this way, because it is not unreasonable to hope that where one comes others will one day follow. The failure was of course that on neither of these journeys did we come through the labyrinth under our civilization. And that's what this whaleship sometimes feels like. It feels like the labyrinth come overground.

But Theseus taking a dagger to the Minotaur and Ahab launching a harpoon at the world-illusion, surely these are in no way comparable? In possible, awful consequence, surely they aren't comparable?

Ahab is searching for ground he can trust, for ground that isn't yet another deception, and that surely is a quest that has been and will be common to people in all ages. It is the misdirected, vengeful intensity of his quest that might yet bring us into perdition. This much however we must grant him: in him and through him we will yet again come to know those extreme limits which, as human beings, we may not overpass. So even if this voyage ends in disaster, we will not have come this far in vain. A civilization in which an Ahab hasn't yet shown up is a civilization that doesn't know itself. In no matter what civilization, it is only when someone gets it grandly wrong that we can begin to see how we might get it right.

So you're staying?

Yes, I'm staying. Tomorrow I'm aloft, on the main masthead.

If you see sight of him will you call?

I'll call.

Having clarified things for himself and for someone else, Bulkington was ready for what he once referred to as the cyclically recurring Mesopotamian fight for order and civilization. Lingering yet awhile on deck, Ishmael wasn't sure he was able for a Book of Revelation, written on Bible leaves of Zeuglodon blubber, which was opening itself before him, almost nightly now, in sleep. Descending the stairs to his bunk below waterline, he longed for the tidiness of an earlier vision:

And I saw a new heaven and a new earth: for the first heaven and the first earth were passed away; and there was no more sea.

They were, just then, sailing into the Sea of Typhoons.

XX

In a savage land at the far end of the last known sea, Jason swore by all the Gods that, no matter what, he would be faithful to Medea, a nature enchantress and moon-witch who, in return, promised that she would help him to find and bring home the Golden Fleece. Ten years later, a humanly justifying excuse having presented itself, Jason was unfaithful. But however altered, at one level, circumstances might be, a vow to the Gods cannot be revoked. Forever afterwards, even if those gods had in the meantime been overthrown, the demands of the vow must be met. Gods come and go. *Dike* always is, and the Gods are no less subject to it than humans are. So Jason had done huge wrong. It was the kind of wrong that threatened the established order at its foundations. He had no choice but to be what, by his act, he had already become, a wanderer, an outcast, people everywhere only wanting to see the back of him.

One day, skirting Mount Pelion, Jason took heart. He climbed to where Chiron lived. Chiron was a centaur, half man, half horse. The world even then was only barely able for a being as real as he was. A time would come when, in the interests of beings of lesser reality, he must fade back into the Imagination out of which Mountains and Minotaurs and Typhons and Pythons had emerged. Indeed, a time had already come when, with his club, Herakles was reducing the world to suitable, safe size and when, with his lyre, Orpheus was bewitching it, cheating it, stealing its savagery. The first great age of the earth was giving way to an age of heroes, and Jason, himself a hero, had until recently assumed that this was good. It was on this assumption that he had set sail for shores unknown in the *Argo*. Now, however, having lived so long outside civilization, he wasn't so sure. Certainly it would not now occur to him to say that the earth was a better place for having no Nemean lion in it, for having neither Hydra nor Echidna nor Ketos in it.

As he climbed, Jason wondered whether Chiron mightn't be a sole survivor from that much-murdered, first world.

Coming to his cave door, Chiron didn't back away when he saw who it was. Even if it meant moral condemnation, or worse, he would and did welcome his foster child, his pupil in arts and wisdom, of so many years ago.

Chiron took getting used to. And yet, seeing him, as much from memory as in immediate sensation, Jason knew how wrong it would be to regard him as a being of two halves, horse from his hips back, human from his hips up. A hybrid he was not. Indeed, no one else he knew was so single in his nature as Chiron was. His appearance notwithstanding, there was in Chiron no no-man's-land between hoof and heart, hip and head. Chiron was consummate in the way that the very wild mountain he lived on was.

It was evening before they came round to what, from the beginning, they wanted to talk about.

I already know a version of your story, Chiron said.

But you would like to hear it from me?

I'd like to know if it is a story that will be told in time to come?

Because of what, in it, will a story be told in time to come?

How can we say? Until we have heard it how can we say? And even when we have heard it, it is difficult to say. What we do know, however, is that once we have heard it we cannot forget it. And not only that. At the first opportunity, we will find ourselves telling it. A story is great when, as we tell it, it tells us. It is great when we emerge from this telling with a deeper and a surer sense of ourselves. There is a sense in which our stories create us. Or, if you believe that a God created us, then you might say that our stories take over from where he left off – calling us into richer, greater life, they continue his work, and when they do this they aren't only great stories, they are sacred stories. Have you become a great story? Have you, in spite of the moral contagion that infests you, become a sacred story? Have you, instead of bringing home a myth, become a myth that will deepen itself and deepen us every time it is told? I ask you these questions because, having captained the *Argo,* you are, whatever else besides, a hero.

Ask anyone nowadays about the voyage of the *Argo,* ask Nauplios who sailed with us, and he will, more than likely, tell you the tale told. He will tell you that Pelias, half-brother to Aeson the rightful heir, had usurped the throne of Magnesia. Warned by an oracle that one of them would successfully challenge him, he saw to it that all of his near relatives were murdered, all except Aeson whom he imprisoned. What Pelias didn't know at the end of this bloody purge was that the one who would indeed mount the challenge was alive and well, and not only that, he was protected by the presumption that he had no connection with the royal family. This is how it had come about: Aeson, the rightful heir, had married Polymele. Knowing what was in store for him, Polymele gave out that a son she gave birth to was still-born and she called the few distant kinswomen who were still alive to mourn. Disguising his cries with their wailing, they smuggled him out of the city and gave him to Chiron, a centaur who lived on Mount Pelion, to rear him. For a reason we cannot divine, Chiron changed his name from Diomedes to Jason, which means healer.

As we would expect, Jason flourished under Chiron's instruction and a day came when, spear in hand, he took his leave and came down intending, come what might, to enter the city. Crossing the river in the plain below, he left one of his sandals in the mud. That day, as it chanced, Pelias was on his royal rounds and when he saw the stranger his heart sank within him, for, recently again, he had gone to consult the oracle at Delphi and it had warned him to expect trouble from a man wearing one sandal. No matter how ominous the situation, Pelias wasn't the kind of man who would walk away.

Who are you? he demanded of the stranger.

You may call me Diomedes or you may call me Jason. I'm the son of Aeson.

If you were king and someone challenged your right to the throne, what would you do? Pelias asked.

Knowing that he wouldn't return from so dangerous a journey, I would send him to Clochis to bring home the Golden Fleece, Jason replied.

Unknowingly, in his reply, Jason had sealed his own fate. For there was indeed such a Golden Fleece. It is a well-known story. Athamas was Jason's great grandfather. He and his wife Nephele had two children, Phrixos and Helle. A year or so after Nephele had died, Athamas married Ino. A cruel and selfish woman, Ino would have Phrixos and Helle, who were now her step-children, out of the way. To this end, she persauded Athamas that the only way to avert famine in the land was to sacrifice them, both of them, on the same altar, to Zeus. Aware of the dreadful thing that was happening, Zeus turned the altar into a golden ram who carried them eastwards around mount Pelion and out over the sea. Falling momentarily asleep, Helle fell off and drowned in a reach of sea-water that would ever afterwards bear her name, the Hellespont. Phrixos fared better. Reaching an unknown world at the end of an unknown sea, the ram came down. Disburdened, he lay down offering his neck in surrogate sacrifice. Reluctantly, as though it were himself he was sacrificing – reluctantly, at first, but then reverently and with determination, Phrixos took the proffered knife. He hung the Golden Fleece of the Golden Ram, or should we say, he hung the Golden Fleece of his own Golden Self, on an oak tree. And there, at the end of the world, it would forever remain were it not that Jason had unconsciously committed himself to voyage in the wake of the ram's self-sacrifice ...

Realizing at this point that the story he had set out to tell was telling itself in a way he hadn't foreseen, Jason broke off.

You didn't do what the ram did, did you? Chiron asked. You didn't, when you came to the end of the world, offer your throat to the road-opening knife, did you? There was a Bosphorus you didn't go through, wasn't there?

Jason knew, now for the first time, that it wasn't only in breaking his vow to the gods that he had failed. There was a frontier he hadn't crossed. There was a boon he hadn't come home with.

Is it so, Jason asked, that every time I tell the story of the voyage, it will accuse me of some new failure?

It isn't always by success that we succeed. Now more than ever should you be willing to be an Argonaut. Now more than ever should you be will to go where the story takes you.

A Herakles or an Orpheus who has what it takes to board the *Argo* might have what it takes to board the story. What use of the heroism of the Argonauts, what use the club and the lyre, at the frontier we have now come to?

With that question the age we live in has come to an end.

Which age do you mean? The age that is now emerging from our victories over all that is terrible and primal?

However long that age, however glorious its achievements, the question on which it will founder has already been asked. A question that has been asked is a question that someone somewhere will live. It is a question that someone somewhere, in conscious self-sacrifice, will be lived by. In him, whoever he is, humanity will come to, and come through, its final Bosphorus. A Bosphorus between an old and a new way of being in the primal world.

Will it always be primal, the world?

Chiron came to all fours. With frightful but gentle ease, he turned Jason onto his back. Laying a hoof on his heart the centaur said, You've come home with a boon. You've come home with a question.

XXI

Human inwardness isn't as terrifying as we sometimes fear it might be. In particular, it isn't as hopelessly terrifying as we might conclude reading some stanzas by D.H. Lawrence:

> There is the other universe, of the heart of man
> that we know nothing of, that we dare not explore.
> A strange grey distance separates
> our pale mind still from the pulsing continent
> of the heart of man.
>
> Fore-runners have barely landed on the shore
> and no man knows, no woman knows
> the mystery of the interior
> when darker still than Congo or Amazon
> flow the heart's rivers of fulness, desire and distress.

This suggests that anyone who journeys inwards is in danger of becoming another Kurtz who with his last breath will be heard to whisper, 'The horror! The horror!'

The Chandogya Upanishad tells us, however, that we have reason to be altogether more hopeful:

[The teacher speaks:] 'Now, in this city of Brahman there is a dwelling-place, a tiny lotus-flower; within that there is a tiny space. What is within that is what you should seek: that is what you should really want to understand.'

If his pupils should say to him: 'Granted that there is a dwelling place, a tiny lotus-flower, within the city of Brahman and that within that there is a tiny space, what, then, is to be found there that we should seek out and really want to understand?'

Then he should say: 'As wide as this space around us, so wide is the space within the heart. In it both sky and earth are concentrated, both fire and wind, both sun and moon, lightning and the stars, what a man possesses here on earth and what he does not possess: everything is concentrated in this tiny space within the heart.'

If they should say to him: 'If all this is concentrated within the city of Brahman — all beings and all desires — what is left of it all when old age overtakes it and it falls apart?'

Then should he say: 'It does not grow old with the body's ageing nor is it slain when the body is slain. This is the true city of Brahman; in it are concentrated all desires. This is the Self, exempt from evil, untouched by age or death or sorrow, untouched by hunger or thirst; this is the Self whose desire is the real, whose will is the real.'

Julian of Norwich has something quite similar to say. As we would expect, of course, where the Upanishadic sage talks about the city of Brahman, Julian talks about the city of Christ or, to be more precise, she talks about the soul as a worshipped city at the heart of which Christ dwells:

And than our lord opened my ghostly eye and shewid me my soule in midds of my herte. I saw the soule so large as it were an endles world and as it were a blissfull kyngdom; and be the conditions I saw therin I understode that it is a worshipful syte [city]. In the midds of that syte sitts our lord Iesus, God and man, a faire person and of large stature, heyest bishopp, solemnest kinge, worshipfulliest lord; and I saw him clad solemnly and worshiply. He sitteth in the soule even ryte in peace and rest. And the Godhede ruleth and gemeth hevyn and erth and all that is; sovereyn myte, sovereyn wisedom, and sovereyn goodness. The place that Jesus takith in our soule, he shall never removen it without end as to my syte; for in us is his homeliest home and his endless woyng.

For Teresa of Ávila, the soul is no less a wonder than the jewel at the heart of the lotus that Tibetan Buddhists would chant themselves, sing themselves, hymn themselves into:

> *Om mani padme hum*
> *Om mani padme hum*
> *Om mani padme hum*
>
> Homage to the jewel at the heart of the lotus
> Homage to the jewel at the heart of the lotus
> Homage to the jewel at the heart of the lotus

TURTLE WAS GONE A LONG TIME

Here is what Teresa says:

I begin to think of the soul as if it were a castle made of a single diamond or of very clear crystal, in which there are many rooms, just as in heaven there are many mansions. Now if we think carefully over this, sisters, the soul of the righteous man is nothing but a paradise in which, as God tells us, he takes his delight.

Here again the soul is a kind of manipura, a jewel city which, ascending from below, is the third chakra. But soul is a marvel, a mirum, altogether more tremendous than any or all of the chakras. In the presence of soul, our chakras, all seven of them, are enraptured into a black-shawled, weeping awareness of their own poverties. Like withered gardens of Adonis are the withered glories they hold in their hands.

The truth is the soul cannot be described. We can only describe our own reactions to it. It is those reactions we are trying to imagine when we call it a manipura.

Yeats wrote a poem called 'A Dialogue of Self and Soul'. But how, in the presence of soul, could self have remained so composed, so sober, so dish-water dull, so fecund-ditch dull? The evidence suggests that while he was writing this poem Yeats was nowhere near, let alone in the presence of, his own soul. Had he been in the presence of his own soul, he couldn't but have yearned, in grief and delight, for the purifying fires of Manipura.

> At midnight on the Emperor's pavement flit
> Flames that no faggot feeds nor steel has lit,
> Nor storm disturbs, flames begotten of flame,
> Where blood-begotten spirits come
> And all complexities of fury leave,
> Dying into a dance,
> An agony of trance,
> An agony of flame that cannot singe a sleeve.

Had he been in the presence of his own soul, he couldn't but have sung as the Shulamite sang, she singing in the streets of Manipura, she singing of her shepherd in the hills:

> I AM the rose of Sharon, *and* the lily of the valleys.
> As the lily among thorns, so *is* my love among the daughters.
> As the apple tree among the trees of the wood,
> So *is* my beloved among the sons.
> I sat down under his shadow with great delight,
> And his fruit *was* sweet to my taste.
> He brought me to the banqueting house,

and his banner over me *was* love.
Stay me with flagons, comfort me with apples:
For I *am* sick with love.

Had Yeats been in the presence of his own soul in which God wonyth, he'd have sung, as Marguerite Porete sang, of being drunk on the wine he couldn't drink.

So, to return to where we started, to the suggestion that human inwardness isn't as hopelessly terrifying as we sometimes imagine it might be.

D.H. Lawrence is probably right when he asserts that only very few of us have come ashore on deep, phylogenetic inwardness.

Jesus did. And, as we would expect, the manner of his doing so is endlessly instructive:

Then cometh Jesus with them unto a place called Gethsemane, and saith unto his disciples, Sit ye here, while I go and pray yonder. And he took with him Peter and the two sons of Zebedee, and began to be sorrowful and very heavy. Then saith he unto them, My soul is exceeding sorrowful, even unto death: tarry ye here, and watch with me. And he went a little further, and fell on his face, and prayed, saying, O my Father, if it be possible, let this cup pass from me: nevertheless not as I will, but as thou *wilt*. And he cometh unto the disciples, and findeth them asleep, and saith unto Peter, What, could ye not watch with me one hour? Watch and pray, that ye enter not into temptation: the spirit indeed is willing, but the flesh is weak. He went away again the second time, and prayed, saying, O my Father, if this cup may not pass away from me, except I drink it, thy will be done. And he came and found them asleep again: for their eyes were heavy. And he left them, and went away again, and prayed the third time, saying the same words. Then cometh he to his disciples, and saith unto them, Sleep on now, and take your rest: behold the hour is at hand.

When Jesus went forward alone, a first time, to pray, he descended into the Cainozoic.

When he went forward alone, a second time, to pray, he descended into the Mesozoic.

When he went forward alone, a third time, to pray, he descended into the Palaeozoic.

It was here, on this inner shore, that we began to acquire the right to call ourselves *homo sapiens sapiens*.

Nietzsche came ashore here. Nietzsche was bright, he was also tragically unwise, and it is little to be wondered at therefore that he didn't come through.

Here where he foundered, here where humanity also might founder, there should be a warning sign:

If you do not know what the Psalmist knew, don't come ashore here. But what, we might ask, did the Psalmist know? This he knew:

If I ascend up into heaven, thou *art* there: if I make my bed in hell, behold, thou *art there*.

If I take the wings of the morning, *and* dwell in the uttermost parts of the sea; even there shall thy hand lead me, and thy right hand shall hold me.

If I say, Surely the darkness shall cover me; even the night shall be light about me.

Yea, the darkness hideth not from thee; but the light shineth as the day: the darkness and the light are both alike *to thee*.

For thou hast possessed me in my reins: thou has covered me in my mother's womb.

I will praise thee; for I am fearfully *and* wonderfully made: marvellous *are* thy works: and *that* my soul knoweth right well.

Let us say it as simply as Sir Thomas Browne has said it:

There is all Africa and her prodigies in us. There is surely a piece of divinity in us, some thing that was before the elements, and owes no homage unto the sun.

When we know, and in utter humility accept, that Divine Ground grounds us, when we know, and in utter humility accept, that Divine Ground grounds us in all the heights and depths of our being, when we know, and in utter humility accept, and in utter surrender acknowledge, that Divine Ground grounds us in all our inner heavens and hells, then we are ready, praying as Christ prayed, to go ashore, then we are ready, praying as Christ prayed, to ascend the river.

Gethsemane and Golgotha aren't starting-points for the ascent. Morally and epistemologically, they are the ascent.

God opened a ghostly eye in Julian. And think of St Teresa of Ávila's astonishment when, quite unexpectedly, God opened the eyes of her soul.

Buddhists talk of a wisdom eye. They call it the *prajnacaksus*. The author of *Theologia Germanica* distinguishes between the eye with which we look into time and the eye with which we look into Eternity. Blake alerts us to his liberation from the purely corporeal:

I question not my corporeal or vegetative eye any more than I would question a window concerning a sight. I look thro' it and not with it.

Could it be that it is only when we look at it with a vegetative eye that human inwardness will appear to be as primevally dark as it did to D.H. Lawrence?

Our deepest inwardness isn't psyche, it is soul.

Divine Ground ground, psyche, grounds soul.

And there is no river, inner or outer, that isn't also in some sense a sushumna.

There is no pool, inner or outer, that isn't also a chakra, a Linn Feic.

And anyone who loses heart seeing Kurtz in his clearing will regain heart seeing St Kieran in his *cluain*. We can ascend the river, and as we ascend it we will at times be aware that in a cultural sense

it is much more difficult and delicate to be true to an unborn future, than to an accomplished past.

Having ascended the river, having ascended it as Christ not as Kurtz ascended it, we can build the new holy city. We can build Manipura.

Entering it, we might pray as Yeats prayed:

> O sages standing in God's holy fire
> As in the gold mosaic of a wall
> Come from the holy fire, perne in a gyre,
> And be the singing-masters of my soul.

Leaving it, passing onwards, we might pray his dying prayer with D.H. Lawrence:

> Give me the moon at my feet
> Put my feet upon the crescent, like a Lord!
> O let my ankles be bathed in moonlight, that I may go
> Sure and moon-shod, cool and bright-footed
> towards my goal.

XXII

In Conrad's *Heart of Darkness*, Marlow the narrator tells us of his efforts to ascend the primeval river, in this case the Congo, but in a century when lights went out all over Europe it could of course be the Thames, the Tiber, the Shannon, the Rhine or the Seine:

Going up that river was like travelling back to the earliest beginnings of the world, when vegetation rioted on the earth and the big trees were kings. An empty stream, a great silence, an impenetrable forest. The air was warm, thick, heavy, sluggish. There was no joy in the brilliance of sunshine. The long stretches of the waterway ran on, deserted, into the gloom of overshadowed distances. On silvery sandbanks hippos and alligators sunned themselves side by side. The broadening waters flowed through a mob of wooded islands; you lost your way on that river as you would in a desert, and butted all day long against shoals, trying to find the channel ...

Karmically, it is an underworld river. Ancient Egyptians knew of it. They called it the River of the White Hippopotamus. Thinking of it, there are two questions we ask: must we ascend it? and can we ascend it?

In answer to the first question it seems to me that it is emerging *with* not *from* our phylogenetic past that we will come forth by day. And it is in this light that we can see how astoundingly different Jesus in Gethsemane is from anything the ancient world had hitherto imagined or thought possible. Jesus didn't harrow hell. Rather was it that our collective hell was harrowed in him.

In the sense of having faced our darkest possibilities and in the sense of having dealt with them by inwardly integrating all the ages of earth and psyche, Jesus ascended the river. And it wasn't only Kurtz, the light-bringer regressed to all-fours, that he rescued. Watching with Jesus in Gethsemane, we come to know that neither Lucifer nor Nebuchadnezzar is the final verdict on our humanity. It isn't inevitable that the whispered, last words of deinanthropus should be 'The horror! The horror!'

How sad that Promethean humanity should think that it can ascend the primeval river by steamboat. The Dessana ascend it, not by slaying all that is inwardly and outwardly primeval, but by enlisting its help. Hence their canoe. Hence Anaconda Canoe.

It was ancient Egyptian belief that the sun went down every evening into the Western Mountain. To reach the eastern horizon it must journey through the underworld. A fearful journey it was. Reaches of it could only be navigated when the night barque of the god became a serpent. Became in our sense a Cobra Canoe.

Did his night in Gethsemane picture itself in Jesus? Did it dream itself, hallucinate itself, in him? Did he see himself ascending the river in a Cobra Canoe? Did he see himself entering a canyon where, on an exposed shoal of Silurian sea-sand, the white hippopotamus had left a mirroring footprint? Did the rockwalls, high as the Jurassic and higher – did they echo and re-echo his thoughts? Did they tell him he must drink the karma of the mirrored ages?

Here it was that the evolving Earth found the channel.

XXIII

On the floor of the Grand Canyon, looking up and looking down, we remind ourselves that by present reckoning the earth is four thousand six hundred million years old. This more or less is the lapse of time that Darwin and others of his generation struggled to come to terms with. In the *Origin of Species* we read:

A man must for years examine for himself great piles of superimposed strata, and watch the sea at work grinding down old rocks and making fresh sediment, before he can hope to comprehend anything of the lapse of time ... He who most closely studies the action of the sea on our shores, will, I believe, be most deeply impressed with the slowness with which rocky coasts are worn away. The observations on this head by Hugh Miller, and by that excellent observer Mr. Smith of Jordan Hill, are most impressive. With the mind thus impressed, let anyone examine beds of conglomerate many thousand feet in thickness, which, though probably formed at a quicker rate than many other deposits, yet, from being formed of worn and rounded pebbles, each of which bears the stamp of time, are good to show how slowly the mass has been accumulated. Let him remember Lyell's profound remark, that the thickness and extent of sedimentary formations are the result and measure of the degradation which the earth's crust has elsewhere suffered. And what an amount of degradation is implied by the sedimentary deposits of many countries! Professor Ramsay has given me the maximum thickness, in most cases from actual measurement, in a few cases from estimate, of each formation in different parts of Great Britain; and this is the result:

	Feet
Pelaezoic strata (not including igneous beds)	57,154
Secondary strata	13,190
Tertiary	2,240

— making altogether 72,584 feet; that is, very nearly thirteen and three quarters British miles.

How, reading it at the foot of these thirteen and three-quarters British miles, does the Book of Genesis read? How, when Stegosaurus rolls the scree of a Silurian sea-floor down around it, does the contract the Abraham and his God entered into read?

How, reading them at the foot of these thirteen and three-quarters British miles, do the major texts of European literature read? How, the shadow of ichthyosaurus falling upon it from on high, does Dante's *Vita Nuova* read?

How, reading them at the foot of the thirteen and three-quarters British miles, do the major works of European philosophy read? How, the shadow of Zeuglodon falling upon it, does Plato's *Timaeus* read?

It was here, at the foot of these thirteen and three-quarters British miles of canyon sediments, that Saturn's grey chaos rolled over Ishmael. Here, seeing the extinction of Zeuglodon, he saw the extinction of humanity. And in this moment of seeing he was in a sense our new Deucalion.

Two questions pose themselves. How, starting from here, can this new Deucalion find the channel? How, starting from here, can this new Deucalion open or find the trail to civilization and culture?

Certain it is that the trail that Theseus opened between Troezen and Athens – that most certainly isn't the trail we seek. Nor is it likely, this side of the voyage of the *Beagle,* that Athens is the kind of city that we will ever again build for ourselves.

How pitiful in this regard is Shelley's belief that the best we can hope for is a repetition, albeit on a higher, purer octave, of Greek achievement:

> The world's great age begins anew,
>   The golden years return,
> The earth doth like a snake renew
>   Her winter weeds outworn:
> Heaven smiles, and faiths and empires gleam
> Like wrecks of a dissolving dream.
>
> A brighter Hellas rears its mountains
>   From waves serener far;
> A new Peneus rolls his fountains
>   Against the morning star.
> Where fairer Tempe's bloom, there sleep
> Young Cyclads on a sunnier deep.
>
> A loftier Argo cleaves the main,
>   Fraught with a later prize;
> Another Orpheus sings again,
>   And loves, and weeps, and dies.
> A new Ulysses leaves once more
> Calypso for his native shore.
>
> O! Write no more the tale of Troy,
>   If earth Death's scroll must be!
> Nor mix with Laian rage the joy
>   Which dawns upon the free:
> Although a subtler Sphinx renew
> Riddles of death Thebes never knew

ANACONDA CANOE

Another Athens shall arise
    And to remoter time
Bequeath, like sunset to the skies,
    The splendour of its prime;
And leave, if naught so bright may live,
All earth can take, or Heaven can give.

Saturn and Love their long repose
    Shall burst, more bright and good
Than all who fell, than One who rose,
    Than many unsubdued:
Not gold, not blood their altar dowers,
But votive tears and symbol flowers.

Oh cease! must hate and death return?
    Cease! must men kill and die?
Cease! drain not to its dregs the urn
    Of bitter prophecy.
The world is weary of the past,
Oh, might it die or rest at last!

    A shadow, thirteen and three-quarters miles high, has fallen across your altar dowers and symbol flowers, Percy. And since, as Nietzsche discovered, the most archaic past still thinks in us and dreams in us – this being so, it isn't wise to believe that we can, in the course of a few revolutionary years, walk forever away from Laian rage, from oppression, murder, hate and death. Echoing from the rockwalls of the inner gorge in the Grand Canyon, your Helladic Marseillaise sounds premature. As indeed does your rejection of Christ in Gethsemane, Christ on Golgotha, Christ in the Garden of the Sepulchre.

    It was in Jesus that we negotiated the thirteen-and three-quarter-mile trail to civilization and culture. What other than news of this channel, this trail, can any new *Argo,* any new Nave, any new *Beagle* bring home? Having the future of evolution in mind Galapagos looks to Golgotha-Borobudur.

    Having *vita nuova* in mind, Galapagos looks to Gethsemane, Golgotha-Borobudur and the Garden of the Sepulchre.

    Since Jesus walked them, the thirteen and three-quarters miles have been aisle. In the Tenebrae Temple they are ambulatory, the channel the evolving earth has been seeking.

    Having found that channel, our planet is an evolutionary success.

3

Walkabout

Veni Creator Spiritus
Veni Creator Spiritus
Veni Creator Spiritus

A dream: I am standing on a bank of the Shannon estuary. There is a woman beside me. She isn't only a person, however. She is also, somehow, a cosmology. She opens out a map of the locality. The map is green and new, yet it only knows about old things. It has no knowledge at all that the modern world with its modern way of seeing things and doing things has happened. The newest things it has knowledge of are two medieval towers. Even they have an immemorial look about them. Indeed, reflecting on them, it occurs to me that I can see them at all only because, for the moment, I am looking at things through Hindu eyes. Towers they are that have never once condescended to history. Rising like mahavakyas above treetops of a primeval forest, they are, I think, an invitation to come home from history. Folding her map, the woman tells me about a very strange animal that lives hereabouts. It eats itself, leaving nothing of itself, not even a morsel, behind. I am standing on a washed, shingle shore. It is here that the river is losing its identity in the ocean. And here I see it, the strange animal. Or rather I don't see it, for it has already eaten itself. I see its empty shell. An outgrowth of the bedrock under the shingle, it is hurtful in its stoniness. On its inside, patchily, it is red and raw. Looking at it, I know it has eaten itself only recently. I am frightened. I wake up.

A dream which, in part, could be a commentary on a verse of the Mundaka Upanishad:

> *Yatha nadyah syandamanah samudre*
> *Astam qacchanti namarupe vihaya,*
> *tatha vidvan namarupad vimuktah*
> *paratporam pupusam upaiti divyam.*
>
> As rivers, leaving name and form behind them,
> Flow into their home in the ocean
> So does the Knower, from name and form released,
> Go to that Divine Person who is beyond the beyond.

The Ganges losing its identity in an eastern ocean.

Ganga Sagara

The Shannon losing its identity in a Western ocean.

Sionna Sagara

Is that who the woman with the map was? Was she Sionna? Was she Sionna Sagara? Or, calling her by her more ancient name, was she Shenona Sagara?

    Can we, with Joyce, think of her as Anna Shenona?

    Can we think of her as Anna Shenona Plurabelle?

    Was she also the very strange animal?

    I imagine her final prayer, and it isn't to a mad father that she prays it:

> Between me and Thee, there is an 'I am' that torments me. Ah! through Thy 'I am' take away my 'I am' from between us both.

I imagine her final song, and it isn't to a mad father that she sings it:

> Vivo sin vivir en mí,
> Y de tal manera espero,
> Que muero porque no muero.
>
> En mí yo no vivo ya,
> Y sin Dios vivir no puedo;
> Pues sin él y sin mí quedo
> Este vivir, qué será?
> Mil muertes se me hará,
> Pues mi misma vida espero
> Muriendo porque no muero
>
> I live without inhabiting
> Myself – in such a wise that I
> Am dying that I do not die.
>
> With myself I do not dwell
> Since without God I cannot live.
> Reft of myself and God as well,
> What serves this life (I cannot tell),
> Except a thousand deaths to give?
> Since waiting here for life I lie
> And die because I do not die.

    'God expects but one thing of you,' Eckhart says, 'and that is that you should empty yourself in so far as you are a created human being so that God can be God in you.'

The empty skull at the foot of the cross.

    The empty shell on a shingle shore at Shenona Sagara.

    Christ looking down into the empty skull.

    Shenona Sagara looking down into the empty shell.

    Skull and Shell.

Unutterably other than the nihil of the nihilist is the nothingness they portend. Listen to Suso:

When the soul, forgetting itself, dwells in that radiant darkness, it loses all its faculties and all its qualities, as St Bernard has said. And this more or less completely, according to whether the soul — whether in the body or out of the body — is more or less united to God. This forgetfulness of self is, in a measure, a transformation in God; who then becomes, in a certain manner, all things for the soul, as Scripture saith. In this rapture the soul disappears, but not yet entirely. It acquires, it is true, certain qualities of Divinity, but does not naturally become divine ... to speak in the common language, the soul is rapt by the divine power of resplendent being above its natural faculties into the nakedness of the Nothing.

Listen to Eckhart:

Comes then the soul into the unclouded light of God. It is transported so far from creaturehood into nothingness that, of its own powers, it can never return to its agents or its former creaturehood. Once there, God shelters the soul's nothingness with his uncreated essence, safeguarding its creaturely existence. The soul has dared to become nothing and cannot pass from its own being into nothingness and back again, losing its own identity in the process, except God safeguard it.

Shenona Sagara and Bright Angel
Bright Angel and Shenona Sagara

Emanation of the canyon
Emanation of the estuary

Sefirah of the canyon
Sefirah of the estuary

Angel of the canyon
Angel of the estuary

Taking over from Virgil and Beatrice, they guide us to Ground more glorious than Paradise:

When the good and faithful servant enters into the joy of his Lord, he is inebriated by the riches of the house of God; for he feels, in an ineffable degree, that which is felt by an inebriated man. He forgets himself, he is no longer conscious of selfhood; he disappears and loses himself in God, and becomes one spirit with him, as the drop of water which is drowned in a great quantity of wine. For even as such a drop disappears, taking the colour and the taste of the wine, so it is with those who are in full possession of blessedness.

Before he retired from view, Old Man, the creator of all things, assured us that wild and savage nature can be on our side. Anaconda can be on our side. But that isn't all. There aren't only savage emanations. Among us here-below there are heavenly emanations. Perfect in their kind, they are therefore glorious. And when we need him, the Angel of the Canyon will be on our side. And when we need her, as we do now, the Angel of the Estuary will be on our side.

Yet again, this dream having dreamed itself, I found myself thinking of something I had often thought about.

I had often imagined a Christian exodus. A liturgical exodus. An exodus in which, crossing the Kedron with Jesus, Christians would cross over from ritual re-enactment of the Last Supper to ritual re-enactment of Tenebrae.

Pascal draws our attention to the 'difference between a book accepted by a people and a book that creates a people'.

As I imagined it, Tenebrae could create a people. Or in the case of Christians, it could recreate them.

Already, for years now, I had the groundplan of a Tenebrae Temple and I often thought that one day I would go to the centre of Ireland and plant it there.

Had that time arrived, I wondered?

I was living in Kildare.

Walking every step of the way, giving myself a chance to get used to the idea, I went to see Bridie Prendergast in Coolcarrigan. Bridie worked in the big house and Patsy, her husband, worked in the garden. They lived in a flat upstairs in one of the outbuildings.

A good woman and a grand woman, as well able for fun as philosophy, Bridie wasn't to be trifled with. In her there was a low, smouldering ferocity. To my cost I had learned how easy it was to set fire to that ferocity. We had taken each other's measure.

Over coffee, I talked to her about the groundplan. What I said I don't well remember. So frightened was I by what I was doing, it is likely that I wasn't as forthcoming as I otherwise might have been. Indeed, it is probable that much of what I said was by way of being a protective diversion.

> ... but man, proud man,
> Dressed in a little brief authority,
> Most ignorant of what he's most assured,
> His glassy essence like an angry ape
> Plays such fantastic tricks before high heaven
> As make the angels weep.

The angry ape wasn't far to seek in me, yet here I was proposing something fantastic.

I was conscious of Shelley's warning:

> O, thou, who plumed with strong desire,
>   Wouldst float above the earth, beware!
> A Shadow tracks thy flight of fire –
>   Night is coming!

Desperately also, I was aware of the old Kabballistic assurance that an impulse from below evokes a corresponding impulse from above.

> *Itharuta dil-tata*
> Impulse from below

In the century of *Mein Kampf*, indeed in any century, impulses that are in any way out of the ordinary need discerning. That's why, not a little like the Ancient Mariner, I'd have talked to anyone who would have listened to me. I was talking to Bridie. Opening the groundplan, I laid it on the table before her. It's what I'm up to, Bridie. It's the groundplan of a new temple and I thought that I'd go tomorrow to the centre of Ireland and plant it there.

In a poem called 'The Second Coming', Yeats is of the opinion that the old centre cannot hold:

> Turning and turning in the widening gyre
> The falcon cannot hear the falconer;
> Things fall apart; the centre cannot hold;
> Mere anarchy is loosed upon the world,
> The blood-dimmed tide is loosed, and everywhere
> The ceremony of innocence is drowned;
> The best lack all conviction, while the worst
> Are full of passionate intensity.

As I understood it, or intended it, planting the groundplan in the centre of Ireland was a way of beseeching the earth and the heavens to help humanity. It was a way of praying for a centre that would reconfigure us philosophically in relation to all things.

I gave her an opportunity to respond.

Daggers in her eyes, I felt she was stalking me.

Having nowhere to run to, I stood my ground, taking refuge in talk.

Uisnech was the old centre.

What I have here is, if you like, the groundplan of a new Uisnech.

At the heart of the old Uisnech there was a stone called *Aill na Mireann*, the Stone of Divisions. The divisions were the centre itself and round about it the four provinces of Ireland.

At the heart of this groundplan also there is an *Aill* and round about it are its four architectural emanations or, in geological terms, its four foothills.

I am frightened to say it, but maybe you have already guessed, it is the groundplan of a new temple, a temple that attempts to give architectural, good-shepherding shape to the mystical journey. In Christian terms, it attempts to give architectural, good-shepherding shape to the Triduum Sacrum.

In geological terms it is in sequence: it is Bright Angel Trail descending which is the Gethsemane experience; it is Tenebrae which is Good Friday, the dark night of the senses and soul; it is Bright Angel Trail ascending which is Easter, the fana and baqa that Sufis talk about, or as Eckhart has it:

... comes then the soul into the unclouded light of God.

In ancient Egyptian terms, it gives architectural, good-shepherding shape to the journey they called Coming Forth by Day.

Now again I gave Bridie an opportunity to say something.

Cigarette in hand, she said nothing. Fixed by her gaze, I felt like the Peer Gynt onion. She was peeling me with her eyes. What, I wondered, would she find at the core? An emptiness? A little rottenness?

I know what it is, Bridie, I know what you're up to. You are giving me enough rope to hang myself with, aren't you? And it is indeed likely that in all of this I am walking where angels fear to tread but coming through your door I didn't call up the stairs and say, Here Comes Everyman.

Today, walking here, I emerged from Everyman. Like a hermit crab emerging from her shell I emerged from Him. I'm attempting to stand alone.

Luxuriously, yesterday, I might have wallowed in the feeling that there is a Dream that dreams us.

The Dream that dreams us might well have been my moral alibi. More seriously perhaps, it might have been my existential alibi.

An individual standing before God today, I permit myself no such luxury.

Centred in selfhood, I am assuming full moral responsibility for what I am, even for what I unconsciously am, and for what I'm up to.

It's a paradox, isn't it? Spiritually we must get rid of the self, morally we must assume it, it being the condition and ground of moral action in the world. And yet, that isn't, I suppose, the whole story. At a certain stage in the spiritual journey, even when we aren't being consciously moral, everything we do is none the less morally beautiful.

We are living, at that stage, not from selfhood in us, but from Divine Ground in us.

Anyway, Bridie, that's not all. There is still more hanging rope to come.

It sometimes happens that an Australian Aborigine, working in Melbourne or Perth, will suddenly down tools, walk to the edge of the city, drop his industrial clothes and go walkabout in a world that originally was, and probably still is, cosmologically responsive to our cosmological dreams.

It is much like Adam's dream: he awoke and there she was, real as the trees, real as the grazing animals, Eve, the woman he had dreamed of, still walking towards him.

Wherever and whenever there is such responsiveness, that is, or then is, what Australian Aborigines call the Dreamtime.

In the original Dreamtime, when only a featureless waste existed, beings such as Karora, Kunapipi and Indjuwanydjuwa emerged and, going walkabout, they only had to dream of something – a river, a forest, a range of mountains – and there it was, and there it still is, the world they dreamed, the world we live in.

I sometimes feel there is something in it.

There are Inuit who most certainly feel there is something in it:

In the very earliest times, when both people and animals lived on earth, a person could become an animal if he wanted to, and an animal could become a human being. Sometimes they were people and sometimes animals and there was no difference. All spoke the same language. That was the time when words were like magic. The human mind had mysterious powers. A word spoken by chance might have strange consequences. It would suddenly come alive and what people wanted to happen could happen – all you had to do was say it. Nobody can explain this: that's the way it was.

Is there any possibility that the way it was is the way it still is? Do we only have to down tools, walk to the edge of our cities and go walkabout in order to see and know that the way it was is the way it still is?

Dreamtime always is.

I therefore thought that, going to the centre of Ireland, I would go walkabout, if only for a prayerful hour or two. As I see it, that walkabout would be an act of faith that the way now is the way it was when, in the beginning, Kunapipi, Karora and Indjuwanydjuwa set out on their wanderings.

Am I mad, Bridie?

Do it, she said.

Stubbing out her cigarette, she said it again.

The third time she said it she was excited.

When Patsy came in we talked about sport. The last clean thing left in the world, he said.

There is a little chapel in the grounds of Coolcarrigan. Of cut stone with a little round tower, it would remind you, if you didn't look too closely at it, of medieval Ireland. Being a building of recent times, it was of course totally cleansed of unconscious haunting. Nowhere in it or on it or in its trim surroundings was there any suggestion that it had ever dreamed a dreadful dream of centaurs, owls, cockatrices or dragons. It didn't gargoyle God or gargoyle the devil or gargoyle the rain. There was no remembrance in its stones that the outcrop from which they were quarried had dreamed a great dream with the great world. There was no suggestion, not even in its portals and thresholds, of something tremendous and dangerous. Never at night would it become the Chapel Perilous of a Gawain or Parsifal who had set out seeking further rumours of some far mystery. No. Neat as a syllogism, it suggested that 'the real is rational and only the rational is real'.

I turned off the avenue onto the path that would bring me to it. I was thinking of nothing in particular. It was like sleeping on a problem I couldn't solve.

Out of Asia, following a cow, Kadmus came. Whenever the cow would lie down, there he would build his city.

The cow going with him meant that the earth was going with him. It meant that, compliant and co-operating, his unconscious was going with him. He wouldn't therefore be destroyed.

I crossed the little bridge over the moat. The double wooden door was closed, but unlocked. Expecting it to creak or groan on its hinges, I opened it and went in.

Not knowing at all what I would do, I went to the baptismal font and lowered my head down into its emptiness.

It was into total *kenosis* I was lowering it.

Like Adam's skull, like the skull at the foot of the cross on Golgotha, I would be for as long as the baptism lasted

> Blank as a piece of uncarved wood
> Yet receptive as a hollow in the hills.

That is Lao Tzu's way of putting it.

Crossing the threshold, coming out, I reassumed the carved contours of being a distinct individual.

Walking home to Tommy's and Charlotte's house, I thought of a poem by Rilke:

> Sometimes a man stands up during supper
> and walks outdoors, and keeps on walking
> because of a church that stands somewhere in the East.
>
> And his children say blessings on him as if he were dead.
> And another man who remains inside his own house
> dies there, inside the dishes and in the glasses,
> so that his children have to go far out into the world
> toward that same church, which he forgot.

Church in the East. Church in the West. Church wherever we are. Church that gives architectural shape to our longing for home. Church that gives shape to the Triduum Sacrum. Church that goodshepherds us into and through the canyons and voids of the mystical journey.

What a blessing it is, I thought, that Jesus stood up after supper and walked out. Until he did walk out, those canyons and voids were excluded. Biblically, we had set bars and doors against them, saying

> Thus far shall ye come and no farther.

In Jesus, having crossed the Kedron, all of the bulwarks were washed away, and now, knowing the blessings that awaits us in them, canyon and ginnungagap, Gethsemane and Tenebrae, are religiously incorporated in our Temple.

How wonderful, I thought. Jesus didn't only go out to bring in the lost sheep of Israel. He crossed the Kedron so that everything our biblical bulwarks kept out might come back in. In him abyss and beast came in. In him Tiamat and Tehom came in. Only he was hurt. For years it was a marvellous world. To walk in it was to walk in Paradise. Then, the calamity. In the person of John of Patmos we regressed to the old bad habits. These, overnight, had become canonical. The epidemic was accepted and welcomed as norm, and now again we sang the old psalm:

> For God *is* my King of old,
> working salvation in the midst of the earth.
>
> Thou didst divide the sea by thy strength:
> Thou brakest the heads of the dragons in the waters.

> Thou brakest the heads of leviathan in pieces,
> And gavest him *to be* meat to the people inhabiting the wilderness.

In Gethsemane, St Peter drew his sword. Consenting to be sheath to all such dragon-slayer's swords, Jesus commanded him to put it up.
Christianity took it down.
With it, it having become a *malleus maleficarum*, we broke heads.
As though Christ hadn't crossed the Kedron we pray:

> Awake, awake, put on strength, O arm of the Lord:
> Awake, as in the ancient days, in the generations of old.
> *Art* thou not it that hath cut Rahab,
> *And* wounded the dragon?

I had often imagined it: the raven that Noah sent out coming back in our day. Abyss-black above us he calls out:

> Ginnungagap is God
> Tehom is Turiya

Noah didn't need to build an ark. He needed only to read the Mandukya Upanishad.

In my room that evening I leafed through Kierkegaard's *Journals,* lingering on passages I had long ago underlined:

The highest of all is not to understand the highest but to act upon it.

God creates everything out of nothing – and everything which God is to use he first reduces to nothing.

During the first period of a man's life the greatest danger is not to take the risk. When once the risk has been really taken the greatest danger is to risk too much. By not risking at first, one turns aside and serves trivialities; in the second case, by risking too much, one turns aside to the fantastic and perhaps to presumption.

That is called risking; and without risk faith is an impossibility. To be related to spirit is to undergo a test.

There is a God; his will is made known to me in Holy Scripture and in my conscience. This God wishes to intervene in the world. But how is he to do so except with the help of, *i.e.* per man? Now one can say, we can all say: yes, that is of course what he does, but not per me: no one of us wishes to be that individual; for if God is to intervene in the world it must be through the individual.

Fundamentally a reformation which did away with the Bible would now be just as valid as Luther's doing away with the Pope.

Christendom has long been in need of a hero who, in fear and trembling before God, had the courage to forbid people to read the Bible. That is something quite as necessary as preaching against Christianity.

Post-biblical Christianity! I had often attempted to imagine it.

A Christianity that had crossed over, as in an exodus, from Evangel to Evangelanta.

A Christianity whose sacred texts are the writings of its own mystics. Upanishads we might call them.

A Christianity whose prototypical temple gives architectural shape to the Triduum Sacrum.

A Christianity whose religious and cultural creative ritual is Tenebrae.

A Christianity whose defining sacramentum is the Tenebrae harrow.

It is an awful question: just as there were Jews who followed Jesus out of traditional Judaism, are there Christians who might now be ready to follow him out of traditional Christianity? Could traditional Christianity permit and bless such a development within it? If not, it would perhaps be better that it didn't happen at all. Another sect would mean more sectarianism. Setting fire to religious passions, it might even give rise to a thirty years' war.

Out of Gethsemane the command comes to us: put up your sword.

I yearned for biblical permission and precedent for what I was doing. There was none that I could think of. And yet it was as if the die was already cast. I could only do it and run the risk of God's displeasure.

Knowing what I wanted I opened the Bible and read:

> Except the Lord build the house,
> They labour in vain that build it.
> Except the Lord keep the city
> The watchman waketh *but* in vain.
>
> *It is* vain for you to rise up early,
> To sit up late ...

I went to bed and next morning, not so early, I took a lift with Tommy as far as Barberstown Cross. Hitching from there I got a lift to Maynooth.

Called after the old Celtic god Nuadhu, the placename suggested Dreamtime Ireland. And already in a reawakened depth of my mind, I was walking, not in Ireland, but in *Iath nAnann*, in the country of the goddess Anu or Danu.

Iath nAnann is as much a state of mind as it is a country and to get my bearings in it I rehearsed the few facts, if facts they are, that I knew.

No one knows for sure where the Indo-European homeland was. A common conclusion from the available evidence is south Russia. A case has been made for Anatolia. Certain it is, however, that wherever it was, there was movement of people together with their language, religion, gods and culture, out of that homeland. Eastward, that movement reached the Bay of Bengal. Westward, it reached Galway Bay. On its way west the goddess Danu gave her name to the rivers Don and Danube, and in the south-west of Ireland there are two beautiful hills that are called Da Chich Danann, the two breasts of Danu. Locally, nowadays, they are known as the Paps.

Danu is also known at the eastern extremity of the Indo-European expansion. There is a hymn to her in the Rig Veda.

As I might think of the bare facts about Christ in the Christian creed, so did I think of these few facts about Danu. Reciting them was a kind of credence.

Belonging as she does to both, Danu, I thought, might one day sponsor a meeting of East and West.

Under her auspices, *Sionna Sagara* and *Ganga Sagara* might someday sing the same Gayatri:

> From darkness lead me to light,
> From ignorance lead me to wisdom,
> From non-being lead me to being.

Under her auspices Christians might come to see that the Triduum Sacrum is their mystical Magna Carta.

Under her auspices, the Mandukya Upanishad might come west and the Tenebrae harrow go east.

Under her auspices we might yet discover that our God is not a jealous God, allowing no other Goddess or God to be worshipped beside him.

Suddenly, crossing the road, I was aware of my need for a Goddess whose bhakta I could be.

How dangerous would it be to be bhakta to Macha, the Celtic Horse-Goddess?

How outlandish in a Christian country would it be to be a bhakta to Danu? To be her bhakta even when, in a dream of her, she shows you that the stream between her breasts is as deep as the Colorado?

The earth's deepest songline and the Christian songline are one and the same, and although he staggered and fell into a Deep below all depths as he did so, Jesus did walk it. In him, as he walked it, all the old seafloors of the one psyche, the Earth's and ours, were harrowed, and now there is none of us but can be a bhakta to Buddh Gaia.

Thinking of the mountain ash that grows from a heather-red rockwall between Danu's breasts, I thought of Nietzsche and Pascal, the two strange geniuses in whom the Gethsemane experience in its modern form erupted among us. I thought of Pascal's terror of interstellar outwardness and of Nietzsche's terror of archaic inwardness.

Where, if outwardness and inwardness are so terrifying, can we find rest?

Pascal was enraptured into safety. In this incarnation, in so far as we know, Nietzsche wasn't. Indeed, arrogantly making use of Zarathustra as his ventriloquist's dummy, he ran the risk of becoming our Nebuchadnezzar.

Like no one else we have record of, Nebuchadnezzar was engulfed by the archaic in us:

The same hour was the thing fulfilled upon Nebuchadnezzar; and he was driven from men, and did eat grass as oxen, and his body was wet with the dew of heaven, till his hairs were grown like eagle's feathers, and his nails like bird's claws.

But the mountain ash between Danu's breasts! Not terrified like Pascal of outwardness, not terrified like Nietzsche of inwardness, still young, still slender, showing no sign of how voluptuous it one day will be, it is pure existential trust, pure existential credence, in how things are.

Growing from a heather-red rockwall between Buddh Gaia's breasts, it is, I sometimes think, wiser than I am. It is, I sometimes think, Buddh Gaia's bhakta.

An image it is of what each of us might one day become.

But then, as Rilke reminds us, we are adventured more than trees are, more than animals are.

Adventured for better, and also, sometimes very obviously, for worse.

I had walked through a Christian town that has an Iath nAnann name.

It was still an Iath nAnann songline I was walking.

It was with no little sense of relief that I felt, walking through Kilcock, that I had walked out of Danu's Dreamtime. It was only briefly, if at all, that I was able for it. Not that I was particularly able for modern Ireland either. Its demands, however, were more familiar. To walk in it I didn't feel that I must, in reverence, put off my shoes from off my feet as

Moses had to do when he would stand in the presence of the burning bush.

Ever since, years ago, I bought a second-hand copy of the King James Bible I knew the story by heart. I had often thought of it, illegitimately of course, as a story from the Hebrew Dreamtime. Falling back from such a position, I would then think of it as a story from a time when historical fact easily and regularly fused with what Coleridge called the esemplastic power, not just the esemplastic power of the primary human imagination, but the esemplastic power also of the primary Earth.

A difficult one, that, for a modern European to swallow:

> The esemplastic power of the primary Earth.

An Australian Aborigine would have no trouble with it.

Watching his wand turn into a snake, maybe Moses also would have no trouble with it.

That his contemporaries could not accept it is what troubled Blake:

The tree which moves some to tears of joy is in the eyes of others only a Green thing that stands in the way. Some see Nature all ridicule and deformity and by these I shall not regulate my proportions; and some scarce see nature at all. But to the Eyes of the Man of Imagination, Nature is Imagination itself. As a man is, so he sees. As the Eye is formed, so are its powers. You certainly mistake when you say that the Visions of Fancy are not to be found in This World. To me This World is all one continued Vision of Fancy or Imagination.

Now again, this time with less embarrassment, maybe we should ask an Inuit shaman to open that door for us.

Door into the primary mind, door into the primary world:

In the very earliest time, when both people and animals lived on earth, a person could become an animal if he wanted to and an animal could become a human being. Sometimes they were people and sometimes animals and there was no difference. All spoke the same language. That was the time when words were like magic. The human mind had mysterious powers. A word spoken by chance might have strange consequences. It would suddenly come alive and what people wanted to happen could happen – all you had to do was say it. Nobody can explain this: that's the way it was.

Dreamtime.
   Inuit Dreamtime.
   Hebrew Dreamtime.
   Universal Dreamtime.
   Dreamtime of the primary mind in rock and star.

Time when a wand turned into a snake.
Time when a bush burned and wasn't consumed:

Now Moses kept the flock of Jethro his father in law, the priest of Midian: and he led the flock to the backside of the desert, and came to the mountain of God, *even* to Horeb. And the angel of the Lord appeared unto him in a flame of fire out of the midst of a bush: and he looked, and behold, the bush *was* not consumed. And Moses said, I will now turn aside and see this great sight, why the bush is not burnt. And when the Lord saw that he turned aside to see, God called unto him out of the midst of the bush, and said, Moses, Moses. And he said, Here *am* I. And he said, Draw not nigh hither: put off thy shoes from off thy feet, for the place whereon thou standest is holy ground. Moreover he said, I *am* the God of thy father, the God of Abraham, the God of Isaac, and the God of Jacob. And Moses hid his face for he was afraid to look upon God. And the Lord said, I have surely seen the affliction of my people which are in Egypt, and have heard their cry by reason of their taskmasters; for I know their sorrows; and I am come down to deliver them out of the hand of the Egyptians, and to bring them up out of that land unto a good land and a large, unto a land flowing with milk and honey.

Although God himself chose Moses to lead the exodus, Moses demurred:

And Moses answered and said, But, behold, they will not believe me, nor hearken unto my voice: for they will say: The Lord hath not appeared unto thee. And the Lord said unto him, What *is* that in thine hand? And he said, A rod. And he said, cast it on the ground. And he cast it on the ground, and it became a serpent; and Moses fled from before it. And the Lord said unto Moses, Put forth thine hand, and take it by the tail. And he put forth his hand, and caught it, and it became a rod in his hand.

Moses set out. In an inn on the way God sought to kill him, but he did eventually lead the Children of Israel out of bondage, leading them dry-shod through the sea into the desert of Zin:

Then came the children of Israel, *even* the whole congregation, into the desert of Zin in the first month: and the people abode in Kadesh: and Miriam died there, and was buried there. And there was no water for the congregation: and they gathered themselves together against Moses and against Aaron. And the people chode with Moses, and spake, saying, Would God that we had died when our brethren died before the Lord! And why have ye brought up the congregation of the Lord into this wilderness, that we and our cattle should die there? And wherefore have ye made us to come up out of Egypt, to bring in unto this evil place? It *is* no place of seed, or of figs, or of vines, or of pomegranates; neither is there any water to drink. And Moses and Aaron went from the presence of the assembly unto the door of the tabernacle of the congregation, and they fell upon their faces; and the glory of the Lord appeared unto them. And the Lord spoke unto Moses saying, Take the rod and gather thou the assembly together, thou, and Aaron thy brother, and speak ye unto the rock before their eyes; and it shall give forth his water, and thou shall bring forth unto them water out of the rock: so thou shall give the congregation and their beasts drink. And Moses took the rod from before the Lord, as he commanded him. And Moses and Aaron gathered the congregation together before the rock and he said unto them, Hear now, ye rebels: must we fetch you water out of this rock? And Moses lifted up his hand, and with his rod he smote the rock twice: and the water came out abundantly, and the congregation drank, and their beasts *also*.

An exodus which, down the generations, Jews have looked back at in admiration and amazement:

For ask now of the days that are past, which were before thee, since the day that God erected man upon the earth, and *ask* from the one side of heaven unto the other, whether there hath been *any such thing* as this great thing *is,* or hath been heard like it? Did ever people hear the voice of God speaking out of the midst of the fire, as thou hast heard, and live? Or hath God assayed to go *and* take him a nation from the midst of *another* nation, by temptations, by signs, and by wonders, and by war, and by a mighty hand, and by a stretched out arm, and by great terrors, according to all that the Lord your God did for you in Egypt before your eyes?

In the context of what I was up to, it was somehow important to retell this story. As important as it is for Aborigines to rehearse and remember the Dreamtime wanderings of the Altjeringa Mitjina.

To me, on the way to the centre, it posed a question:

Could this exodus be precedent to another exodus? Not an exodus from Christianity to something beyond it, but an exodus within Christianity. An exodus, bringing the Evangel with us, from Evangel to Evangelanta. An exodus from ritual re-enactment of the Last Supper to ritual re-enactment of Tenebrae.

Not only is this a question to which I have no answer, it is a question I'm not able to ask.

Likely it is that only Christ can ask it and answer it. From the heart of the Triduum Sacrum ask it and answer it.

In the meantime:

> Give us this day our daily bread
> Forgive us our trespasses
> Lead us not into temptation
> Deliver us from evil
>
> Amen

ANACONDA CANOE

Why did the Lord, his God, seek to kill Moses?
The Bible doesn't pretend to know:

And Moses went and returned to Jethro his father in law, and said unto him, Let me go, I pray thee, and return unto my brethern which *are* in Egypt, and see whether they be yet alive. And Jethro said to Moses, Go in peace ... And Moses took his wife and his sons, and set them upon an ass, and he returned to the land of Egypt: and Moses took the rod of God in his hand ... And it came to pass by the way in the inn, that the Lord met him and sought to kill him.

I thought of a poem by Rilke:

> I can tell by the way the trees beat, after
> so many dull days, on my worried windowpanes
> that a storm is coming.
> And I hear the far-off fields say things
> I can't bear without a friend,
> I can't love without a sister.
>
> The storm, the shifter of shapes, drives on
> across the woods and across time,
> and the world looks as if it had no age:
> the landscape, like a line in a psalm book,
> is seriousness and weight and eternity.
>
> What we choose to fight is so tiny!
> What fights with us is so great!
> If only we would let ourselves be dominated
> as things do by some immense storm,
> we would become strong too, and not need names.
>
> When we win it's with small things,
> and the triumph itself makes us small.
> What is extraordinary and eternal
> does not *want* to be bent by us.
> I mean the Angel who appeared
> to the wrestlers of the Old Testament:
> when the wrestlers' sinews
> grew long like metal strings
> he felt them under his fingers
> like chords of deep music.
>
> Whoever was beaten by this Angel
> (who often simply declined the fight)
> went away proud and strengthened
> and great from that harsh hand,

> That kneaded him as if to change his shape.
> Winning does not tempt that man
> This is how he grows: by being defeated, decisively,
> By constantly greater beings.

Without intending it or anticipating it, I had for almost an hour now been on a biblical walkabout. The truth is that for all my difficulties with them, some of these old narratives are my songlines. The Book of Job, the Book of Daniel, the Book of Jonah – these are songlines of my first world. I return to them as often as an Australian Aborigine returns to his.

Even now standing on the road outside Kilcock, I couldn't go on until I had remembered the story of Jacob fighting at the Jabbok:

And he rose up that night, and took his two wives, and his two womenservants, and his eleven sons, and passed over the ford Jabbok. And he took them, and sent them over the brook and sent over that he had. And Jacob was left alone; and there wrestled a man with him until the breaking of the day. And when he saw that he prevailed not against him, he touched the hollow of his thigh; and the hollow of Jacob's thigh was out of joint as he wrestled with him. And he said, Let me go for the day breaketh. And he said, I will not let thee go, except thou bless me. And he said unto him, What *is* thy name? And he said, Jacob. And he said, Thy name shall be called no more Jacob, but Israel: for as a prince hast thou power with God, and with men, and hast prevailed. And Jacob asked *him*, and said, Tell *me*, I pray thee, thy name. And he said, Wherefore *is* it *that* thou dost ask after my name? And he blessed him there. And Jacob called the name of the place Peniel: for I have seen God face to face and my life is preserved. And as he passed over Penuel the sun rose upon him, and he halted upon his thigh.

Such a simple sentence:

And there wrestled a man with him until the breaking of the day.

Wounded but blessed, Jacob limped forward into the sunrise. Is it only in and through such a fight, fought in some one individual, that humanity can go forward into its future?

Is it only in and through such a fight, fought at a ford, that humanity can go forward into its past and thence into its present and its future?

Crossing the Jabbok.

Crossing the Kedron.

Having crossed the Kedron into Gethsemane, Jesus fought phylogeny in himself. Or rather, seeking full, conscious integration in him, phylogeny fought him. He too was wounded. He too won a blessing. And now, because of that particular fight at that particular ford, Bright Angel

Trail is a songline. Songline descending, songline ascending. Songline on which we can sing ourselves into our past, our present and our future. Songline on which Pascal is at peace with interstellar outwardness, on which Nietzsche is at peace with archaic inwardness.

What other Good News than this do we need to hear in our time? News the dove brings back:

> Bright Angel Trail is the Earth's songline.
> Being the Earth's songline it is our songline.

News the raven brings back:

> Tehom is Turiya

News that would have heartened and delighted Job when Hell was naked before him, when the Abyss, and the Angel of the Abyss, had no covering.

News that would have heartened and delighted Jonah when, having turned flukes and sounded, the Great Fish yawned him out into the void below the universe.

Hurt though he is at the end of yet another terrible century, there is perhaps a Suffering Servant who, on all our behalf, is limping like Jacob into the sunrise.

I Daniel was grieved in my spirit in the midst of *my* body and the visions of my head troubled me.

And I Daniel fainted and was sick *certain* days: afterward I rose up and did the king's business; and I was astonished at the vision, but none understood *it*.

Therefore I was left alone and saw this great vision, and there remained no strength in me: for my comeliness was turned in me into corruption, and I retained no strength.

> Winning does not tempt that man.
> This is how he grows: by being defeated, decisively,
> by constantly greater beings.

Among us, Job's journey to Behemoth and Leviathan is a songline.

Among us, Jonah's journey to the Great Deep that Hebrews called Tehom is a songline.

Songlines to Beast and Abyss.

Among us, since Jesus crossed the Kedron, Bright Angel Trail is a songline that wanders not across the Earth, but down into it, down therefore into ourselves, all the way down until, in Tenebrae below beast and abyss, we hear the first sound out of Divine Ground:

TURTLE WAS GONE A LONG TIME

Om

There is evening and morning a first Mandukya Day.

Half-heartedly, standing on the side of the road outside Kilcock, I hitched a white truck. I was surprised when it showed signs of slowing down. It turned out to be a mobile unit of the national radio.

The driver was a very open, welcoming man, a natural talker. In his bearing, as he drove and talked, there was no hint of any misgiving about the value and meaning of life.

A wonder it is to me, whenever I encounter it, that such confidence can exist this side of re-immersion in Divine Ground.

As we experience it, our isness is ex-isness, it is isness out of and outside of, and as such you would expect that it will sometimes succumb to fear and trembling, if not indeed to nightsweats and waking perturbation.

There was no evidence that any of this was true of the man beside me.

Coming as we did from counties that were often in spectacular opposition, we talked about football.

As we talked, I didn't know that a few years later I would be back in this truck, in the inner hermetic broadcasting chamber of it, telling a story that I'd heard from Martin Halloran.

Walking to the pub we were one winter's night when he asked me to shorten the road.

What do you mean, Martin, shorten the road?

I mean shorten the road. A story shortens a road, don't it. Tell me a story.

No story comes to mind, Martin.

One comes to my mind, he said, half shouting and off he went:

In the last century, out in harvest time it was, there was a journeyman carpenter walking the roads of Donegal. That was no strange thing in them days. In them days the roads of Ireland was thronged with all kinds and classes and manner of people.

'Twas the bad times that was in it that had them walking, searching for work, searching for a night's shelter. There was journeymen carpenters, journeymen weavers, journeymen tailors, journeymen tinsmiths, journeymen pipers, journeymen singers and storytellers. And beggars. Droves of them. But the man I'm talking about was no beggar, even though the times been bad, him too, the poor bastard, he was badly cladded and badly shod. It was evening time and getting dark when he came to a mighty gate with a gate-lodge inside it. In he went and up the avenue and as luck would have it, just as he was nearing the yard gate, who did he meet coming out but a man who was someway important. Good evening, your honour, the journeyman said. Have you work, maybe, for the likes of me? I'm a carpenter and I have my own tools.

The journeyman was a good ways down the avenue, walking away into the night, when he heard someone calling.

Yes, it turned out, there was some work he could do, a week's work making troughs for pigs, and things like that.

In the evenings, having nothing else to do, the journeyman fell to carving a sow and her *bonavs* out of a section of tree trunk that he found in the woodshed. The day after it was finished the big man himself, a lord he was, he came that way. He saw the carving and, God knows, 'twas no surprise, he was dumbfounded. That lord you can be sure was a travelled man, but the like of this that was there before now, no, the like of that he had never seen. A sow and her *bonavs*. A sow giving suck to her nine *bonavs* and no tit for him, the little runt himself, standing there squealing. 'Twas a wonder, surely.

The lord offered the journeyman a house on the grounds and a good wage.

Thanking you kindly, the journeyman said, I've made the troughs for the pigs and now I'll be on my way.

Badly cladded and shod as he was, he slung his toolbag over his shoulder and walked off into the world.

That's my story, Martin said, and it has me puzzled.

Why didn't he stay, John? According to your way of thinking, why didn't he stay?

Don't know, Martin.

Nor do I. But anyway that's my story and it shortened the road for us, didn't it. And stories shortened the road for the Goban Saor and his son. Did you read about the Goban Saor and his son in your school book, John? Anything anywhere in Ireland that you couldn't imagine how it could have been built, you don't even need to ask, for you can be sure 'twas them that built it. 'Tis said they built Toombeola Abbey. In the evening there wasn't sight or light of it. In the morning when the people opened their doors, there it was, corbelled and coped, no one having to put so much as a hand to it.

Do you think could it be, John?

I'll answer that by telling you a story, Martin. In the Dingle peninsula, on a summer's evening about thirty years ago, there were two men talking together on the side of the road. One of them was Mike File, Peig's son. The other was a visitor, from Cork I think. It was a calm evening, calm on land and calm on sea. The only sound to be heard was the sound of a stream coming down Sliabh an Iolair. The visitor drew Mike's attention to it. Mike listened for a long while and then, opening his eyes, he said: *Tá sé ag glaoch orainn isteach sa tsíoraíocht as a bhfuil sé féin ag teacht* – it is calling us into the eternity out of which it is itself flowing.

There are evenings like that here in Connemara, Martin, and when I look at the mountains and listen to the streams I'm inclined to think that instead of being the exception, miracles are the rule. So yes, Maurteen, it could have happened. And not only that, it could happen now. God only knows what we might see when tomorrow morning, or any morning, we open our doors and look out.

> Heartily know,
> when the half-gods go
> The gods arrive.

Why didn't he stay, John? Martin asked on the way home.

The journeyman carpenter is it?

Yes. Why didn't he stay?

The question I'd like to ask is, who was he?

Who was he? Martin repeated, surprised by the question.

Yes. Who was he?

The effects of drink still strong upon me, I allowed myself to imagine that he might be Vishvakarman in human disguise. Was he Vishvakarman, Martin?

Who!

Vishvakarman, the divine architect of the Gods. The Samildanach they called him in ancient Ireland. Master that he is in all arts and in all crafts, there is nothing he can't turn his hand to. He showed up in Tara once, and if it happens that he is walking the roads again, in disguise it must be, then surely the *side*-mounds of Ireland are open again and a time of great wonder is upon us. The sow and her *bonavs* are but a first intimation.

No, Martin, no, he couldn't stay. His tool bag slung over his shoulder, he has to keep walking. Walking the roads of Ireland until ...

Until Ireland, if only for a night, is Fodhla. Until Ireland, if only for a night, is Inis Fáil. Until living, if only for a night, in Fodhla, we imagine the wonder and then, coming out of disguise, he will build it. We will open our doors in the morning and there, like Toombeola Abbey, it will be. And standing in it we will say, how dreadful is this place. Surely it is none other but the House of God and the Gate of Heaven.

Would you say tis true, Martin? Would you say the *side*-mounds of Ireland are open?

I never heard that they were closed.

Could it be, Martin, that the way to the Otherworld Well is open?

Again you will probably say that you didn't know it was ever closed, but, as I sometimes see it, Martin, St Patrick came to Ireland and within a few centuries the wound in Christ's side was the only well we would acknowledge.

Strange isn't it, Martin, that a spear-wound was our well, is still our well.

Strange isn't it, Martin, that we sought and found shelter in a spear-wound. In a spear-wound and four spike-wounds.

> Deep in thy wounds, Lord,
> Hide and shelter me;
> So shall I never, never
> Part from Thee.

Is there any explanation at all for the fact that we crossed over so easily from well to wound?

A most marvellous well it was, this Otherworld Well. It had many names. Nectan's Well. Connla's Well. The Well of Segais. Hazel trees grew over it. Nuts fell into it from these trees. Every seventh year some of them were carried downstream into the rivers of Ireland and this was not to be wondered at, because whenever they might be said to have their physical source, it was in this Otherworld Well that they had their eternal source. You can see, can't you Martin, why Mike File said of the stream coming down Sliabh an Fhiolair,

Tá sé ag glaoch orainn isteach sa tsíoraíocht as a bhfuil sé féin ag teacht.

Anyway, Martin, anyone who found one of those Otherworld nuts and drank the imbas in it became a great poet and a great seer. And how, unless you were a great seer, seeing into the life of things, could you be a great poet?

> From well to wound.
> From wound to well.

There is a biblical way of understanding Jesus. Maybe there is also an ancient Irish way of understanding him: the way to the Otherworld Well was closed. Attempting to open it, Jesus fought the jealous, possessive dragon. He was deeply wounded. We've been so mesmerized by the wounds we have almost forgotten the well.

The Great World is calling us, Martin.

> *Tá sé ag glaoch orainn.*

We only have to open our doors in the morning and there it is. The world we are in is the Great World.

Tá sé ag glaoch orainn.

It is into one and the same Great World that Christ and the blackbird of Derrycairn are calling us.

Hear Christ and you hear the blackbird. Hear the blackbird and you hear Christ.

Binn sin, a luin Doire an Chairn!
   ní chuala mé in aird so bhith
ceol ba binne ná do cheol
   agus tú fá bhun do nid.

Aoincheol is binne fan mbith,
   mairg nach éisteann leis go fóill,
a mhic Calprainn na gclog mbinn,
   's go mbéarthá a-rís ar do nóin.

'Tis a strange world, Martin.

'Tis like going out to your stable in the morning. You pull back the bolt, you lift the latch, you open the door and out walks horse. As on every other morning for the past twenty years, you are doing it again this morning, you pull back the bolt, you lift the latch, you open the door and out walks a lion or out walks an altogether different Jesus than the one we've been used to.

Will I tell you a story, Martin?

Thinking he was rescued from what he was having to endure, Martin leapt at the offer.

May Christ and his blessed Mother bless you, John. Do John. Shorten the road, tell me a story.

I'm sorry, Martin, but it's more of the same. I'm a little like the Ancient Mariner tonight. I feel I've killed something. Killed or hurt the biblical understanding of Christ. Killed or hurt the Christian story. And that's why I've fixed my glittering eye on you.

On Ascension Thursday Jesus and the Apostles were standing around on the top of a hill. No one was expecting anything in particular until, suddenly, as if he was a plumed dandelion seed, Jesus was rising into the sky. Rising and rising away from the earth until he was received into a cloud. And that was the last that his disciples saw of him. Jesus, so the story went, had ascended into heaven. But I often wonder, Martin. And I'm often puzzled. The way you are puzzled about the journeyman carpenter.

I sometimes think that the cloud into which Jesus was received was a very dark cloud indeed. And at the heart of it, in the deepest dark of it, was the Great Fish that had swallowed Jonah. Swallowing Christ, it carried him down, down, down, and yawned him out ino the void below the roots of the universe, below the roots of the psyche. But this is only a way of talking, Martin. There was no actual whale in the cloud, no actual swallowing, sounding or yawning out. All of this imagery is just an attempt to imagine what is imageless. It is trying to put pictures and processes where no pictures or processes are. As an experience, it is like waking up in dreamless sleep and finding that dreaming and waking have walked out on you.

This experience need only last an instant. Afterwards, forever, we know that, conscious and unconscious, psyche is the blind not the window.

'Tis a long road that has no turning, Martin. And the turning I'm talking about, the turning that engulfed Christ in the cloud, that is the most awful turning anyone will ever walk into.

In it we see that heaven isn't the end of the journey.

In it we see that heaven is but an interlude.

In it our rock of faith becomes an abyss of faith, a Tehom of faith, a Turiya of faith.

In it, as St John of the Cross says, we lay the foundations of our love on what we cannot see or feel and that is not altogether unlike what Hindus call *adarshana* yoga and *asparasa* yoga, the yoga in which there is nothing to see, nothing to be in touch with.

Fénelon has said:

God felt, God tasted, and enjoyed, is indeed God but God with those gifts that flatter the soul. God in darkness, privation, forsakenness and insensibility is so much God, that is as it were God bare and alone.

There they are, the Good Friday Gifts of the Holy Ghost: darkness, privation, forsakenness and insensibility.

Good Friday yoga is the yoga of those deprivations.

A wonder it is that Christianity has made such deprivation, such dereliction, religiously respectable.

Flagons and apples
and
Tenebrae

The Garden of spices
and
The Hill of the Koshaless Skull

The cry of dereliction
and
Oh Dichosa Ventura

Reality is bigger than our biblical map.
We need to open the stable door.

There is Holy Thursday in the Garden of Olives, Good Friday on Calvary and Easter morning in the Garden of the Sepulchre.

There is Holy Thursday in Gethsemane, Good Friday on Golgotha and Easter morning on the shore of Turiya-Tehom.

It was down into this second cycle that Jesus was carried on Ascension Thursday. It was in this second cycle that Christianity crossed over from Evangel to Evangelanta.

Out of the first cycle Christianity can grow.
Out of the second cycle also it can grow.

In these two cycles, Christianity has the richest possible beginnings from which to grow.

Carried down into the second cycle, Jesus stood Grand-Canyon-deep in the world's karma: that is Gethsemane. He came to the Hill of the Koshaless Skull: this is Golgotha. He came ashore from Turiya-Tehom: that is Easter.

Metamorphosis in insects isn't moored to a holy book. Likewise Christianity: having its origins in the Triduum Sacrum, Christianity isn't moored to the myths, cosmologies, philosophies and ethnic histories of the ancient Eastern Mediterranean and its hinterlands.

Rather is it the case that holy books will grow from the Triduum Sacrum, as in a sense the writings of the Christian mystics have grown from it, and what else but Upanishads and Gitas are these writings?

Upanishads and Gitas called: *Mystical Theology, The Sermons of Eckhart, The Sermons of Tauler, The Life of the Servant, The Mirror of Simple Souls, The Sparkling Stone, Theologia Germanica, The Cloud of Unknowing, The Scale of Perfection, Revelations of Divine Love, Itinerarium Mentis in Deo, Treatise on Purgatory, Dark Night of the Soul, Ascent of Mount Carmel, Spiritual Canticle, Interior Castle, Life of St Teresa, Self Abandonment to Divine Providence* ...

Put them within a single cover and there you have it:

The Risen Bible

The Triduum Sacrum has generated its own Holy Book. But the Triduum Sacrum cannot and will not be bound by the book it has generated.

ANACONDA CANOE

A ritual we have and a book

Tenebrae
and
The Risen Bible

Could it be that the Holy Source that gave them to us will give us a third thing: a temple that will give architectural shape to Tenebrae?

That's it Martin. I don't know if it shortened or lengthened our road. Or obliterated our road. I've kept it to myself for a long time but tonight, you perhaps being a victim of it, I let it out. And there is one more thing I would like to say: I sometimes think that the veil of our traditional understanding and experience of Jesus has been rent.

Jesus walks through

And looking at him we know that the second coming isn't a new coming. Rather is it a deeper understanding of the first coming. In particular, it is a deeper understanding of what it is to cross the Kedron.
   One last thing, Martin.
   If St Macdara was still alive, I would row myself over to his island tomorrow and ask him to shrive me.
   Of what? you might ask. Of having altered a sacred story to suit my own needs.

On our way west from Kilcock, as luck or chance would have it, the driver fell silent for a while. That suited me because I didn't want to cross the Boyne and not have time to think about it.
   In ancient times in Ireland it wasn't only the rainwater and the springwater of its catchment area that flowed into the Boyne. The mind of a people also flowed into it and it pooled in Linn Feic where Eo Fis, the Salmon of Wisdom, lived.
   Again now, I needed the Inuit to take me across the threshold back into Iath nAnann:

In the very earliest time when both people and animals lived on earth, a person could become an animal if he wanted to and an animal could become a human being. Sometimes they were people and sometimes animals and there was no difference. All spoke the same language.

   Depending on his needs or desires at any one time, Eo Fis could be a salmon in Linn Feic, the foal foaled last night in your stable, or the stranger with little to say sitting at your fireside. He could, you might say, slip in and out of forms as we in our day slip in and out of moods. In his case a change of mood did very often mean a change of form. Sometimes, changing shape in the middle of a sentence, he'd trot away leaving you to interpret his fox barks not far from your house later that night.

Mostly, though, he is content to be a salmon in Linn Feic. Some nights he swims upstream to the other worldwell the Boyne has its source in. Resting in the shadows of the hazel that overgrows the well, he is indeed the seer that his name suggests he is. Beyond being a seer Eo Fis has never ventured. Never once has it occurred to him that he might be blinded by his salmon brightness. He doesn't know that vision veils. And never has Linn Feic, overhung by an ordinary cloud, been his Cloud of Unknowing.

Immersed in Linn Feic.

Immersed in maya.

Eo Fis will leave Linn Feic when with Vishnu's good guidance and grace, he undergoes his Narada initiation.

To be baptized not into but out of our Dreamtime pool in our Dreamtime Boyne.

How diluvian it is, this initiation out of immersion onto high ground.

Christians call it Golgotha, that high ground.

It's a terrible thought – Eo Fis, our old salmon god, on Golgotha.

On Golgotha, looking down into his own empty skull, he will hear the strange question:

Did you bring the water?

Golgotha in Iath nAnann.

Golgotha between the breasts – but no, we will say it as people living locally could say it – Golgotha between the Paps of Danu.

An Iath nAnann of Dreamtime songline.

An Iath nAnann of mystical songline.

Imagine them: the as-yet-unheard-of Upanishads and Gitas we will one day sing on our mystical songlines.

To imagine a future for ourselves in a particular Dreamtime is to imagine it also in the universal Dreamtime. And the universal Dreamtime is as much the time we live in now as the very earliest time the Inuit talk about.

That was the time when words were like magic. The human mind had mysterious powers. A word spoken by chance might have strange consequences. It would suddenly come alive and what people wanted to happen could happen – all you had to do was say it. Nobody can explain this. That's the way it was.

I think of Arthur's time when mirabilia were the forms of a people's sensibility and the categories of their understanding.

So as they stood speakynge, in com a squyre that seyde unto the kynge,

'Sir, I brynge unto you mervaylous tydynges.'

'What be they?' seyde the kynge.

'Sir, there ys here bynethe at the ryver a grete stone whych I saw fleete abovyn the watir, and therein I saw stykynge a swerde.'

Than the kynge seyde, 'I woll se that mervayle.'

Again, not being much able for Ireland's Dreamtime, I was glad to come back into the modern world. As I anticipated, we soon crosssed the Boyne. Looking at it, I had second thoughts. I wasn't at all sure that I was glad to be back. Here, along this recently engineered reach of it, it looked so mongrel, so like a very bad cross between a creek and a canal. And it surely didn't have its source in an otherworld well. Surely no one would now expect to find nuts of otherworld wisdom floating upon it. Unlike the stream tumbling down Sliabh an Fhiolair, it had lost the power to call us into the strangeness and unexpectedness of things, into the eternity out of which, long ago, it had flowed. And yet, time was when Boyne was Boann. And Boann, a willowy lady, she was a goddess. She had paramours. She was *noi-chruthach*: when you looked at her she appeared to you, sometimes successively, sometimes simultaneously, in nine different shapes.

I imagined her, Boann noi-chruthach, dancing the dance of her shapes.

I imagined her, Boann noi-chruthach, dancing the dance of her disguises and guises.

When, I wondered, looking at her, would modern physics catch up with ancient intuition.

I initiated a conversation about football with the driver and for the next hour or so, agreeing and disagreeing, we replayed three famous games between Kerry and Dublin, our respective counties.

Leaving home that morning, I had no precise picture of where I would start walking. Since the centre I had in mind was spiritual not geographical, I was happy to leave things to chance.

On the side of the road on our right I saw a sign pointing to Clonmacnoise. On our left, a couple of miles farther on, there was another sign pointing to it. I asked the driver to let me out.

It was like disembarking from the Ark before the dove had returned and announced dry land.

A first eruption of terror that was, because that's not how things were objectively. Objectively it was high summer. There were hayfields on either side of the little winding road I had taken. I only had to look at any one of them and sight in me wasn't only vision, it was visionary. This wasn't due to any sudden recovery of paradisal powers in me. Even if it was a pool that mirrored them, it too would be visionary.

I thought of the Zen Master who painted things not as he saw and experienced them but as they saw and experienced themselves.

And was it the same master or another who, retiring to sleep at night, would say, now I'll let the trees do my thinking for me. What a heresy my Western head is, I thought, continuing round the next turn of the road. Not just a heresy of false beliefs but, altogether more serious, a heresy of little capacities. The little capacities of mind and eye with which I see a tree hurt the tree, as indeed I am myself hurt when someone looks at me with diminishing or reductive intentions.

It wasn't working.

Talking like this to myself was an attempt to walk away from the terror I was feeling. Not for the first time since I thought about this journey, it occurred to me that I might fall ill with Daniel's sickness. I wasn't, like Daniel, carrying a vision, but I was doing something I wasn't able for.

I, Daniel, was grieved in my spirit in the midst of *my* body, and the visions of my head troubled me.

And I, Daniel, fainted and was sick *certain* days; afterwards I rose up and did the king's business: and I was astonished at the vision but none understood it.

Therefore, I was left alone and saw this great vision and there remained no strength in me: for my comeliness was turned in me into corruption, and I retained no strength.

It was like being calved or foaled by one world into another. All the protective colouration that camouflaged me in the first world gave me an outlandish visibility in the second. I could only hope with Hölderlin

>... where there is danger, there grows
>Also what saves.

I could only hope with Rilke that when we venture or are ventured beyond the common protections of nature and culture we aren't necessarily, in that situation, walking into the jaws of perdition. Depending on our disposition, it can happen that our unshieldedness will shield us. Or, as Rilke himself puts it: in the end it is on our unshieldedness that we depend.

As Shakespeare imagined him, his unshieldedness didn't shield King Lear. Gone out beyond the protections, when the welkin cracked his mind cracked.

ANACONDA CANOE

Did St Patrick have intimations that he too might crack? Is that why he fashioned his famous breastplate?

> For my shield this day I call
> Heaven's might
> Sun's brightness
> Moon's whiteness
> Fire's glory
> Lightning's swiftness
> Wind's wildness
> Ocean's depth
> Earth's solidity
> Rock's immobility.

It reminded me of the cradle a Navajo father made for his child:

> I have made a cradleboard for you, my child,
> May you grow to a great old age.
> Of the sun's rays I made the back,
> Of black clouds I have made the blanket,
> Of rainbow I have made the bow,
> Of sunbeams have I made the side-loops,
> Of lightnings have I made the lacings,
> Of light on high horizons have I made the footboard,
> Of dawn have I made the covering,
> Of earth's welcome for you have I made the bed.

I remembered Uvavnuk's song:

> The great sea has set me I motion,
> Set me adrift,
> Moving me as the weed moves in a river.
> The arch of sky and mightiness of storms
> Have moved the spirit within me,
> Till I am carried away
> Trembling with joy.

The cradle, the song and the groundplan of a temple.

Could it be true, I wondered? Could it be that there is a dream that dreams us?

Was I being dreamed?

It was as if, carrying the cradle, the song and the groundplan, I was carrying the intuitions or elements or seeds of a culture.

I was wide awake. Still coping with latent terror, I was walking, not somnambulating, into a village called Bun na hAbhann. Then it happened.

Quietly, without my willing it, my mind was in seance with its racial past, and I heard it.

The shamanic drumbeat of shamanic Eurasia

The drum was called

> Seal Sounds
> or
> Otter Sounds
> or
> Waterbird Sounds

I was walking in the world of the diver myth, world in which, in the beginning, a seal or an otter or a waterbird dived to the floor of the abyss and returned with soil to make a world.

Finding myself passing a church, I turned and went in. How glad I was that neither sight nor sound of the drum died out as I crossed the threshold.

A soft drumming it is, this original Eurasian drumming. Soft as the footfalls of a lynx.

Sitting there listening to it, I imagined otter going down, otter collecting, otter ascending.

I imagined him, human for the moment, coming into the church, walking up the aisle and offering his little fistful of soil, his little fistful of universal potencies, to God.

An otter again, he trots down the aisle and out the door. And that was it. The drumming had stopped. The seance was over.

No magic that I was aware of in my words, no mysterious powers that I was aware of in my mind, I sat there in what Heidegger has called the age of the world's night and prayed that there would once again be ground that would ground us.

Opening the Bible I had brought I read:

And the flood was forty days upon the earth; and the waters increased, and bore up the ark, and it was lift up above the earth. And the waters prevailed, and were increased greatly upon the earth; and the ark went upon the face of the waters. And the waters prevailed exceedingly upon the earth; and all the high hills, that *were* under the whole heaven, were covered. Fifteen cubits upwards did the waters prevail; and the mountains were covered ... and it came to pass at the end of forty days, that Noah opened the window of the ark which he had made: and he sent forth a raven, which went forth to and fro, until the waters were dried up from off the earth. Also he sent forth a dove from him, to see if the waters were abated from off the face of the ground: but the dove found no rest for the sole of her foot, and she returned unto him into the ark, for the waters *were* on the face of the whole earth: then he put forth his hand, and took her, and pulled her in unto him into the ark. And he stayed other seven days; and again he sent forth the dove out of the ark; and the dove came in to him in the evening; and, lo, in her mouth *was* an olive leaf pluckt off: so Noah knew that the waters were abated from off the earth.

A fistful of universal potencies from the floor of the abyss, a little fistful, not more, and now again a world to go walkabout in. And the Christian God isn't a jealous God. He isn't biblically jealous. A Eurasian story of origins is welcome to cross his threshold and live in his presence. And welcome also, surely, is the Mandukya Upanishad.

Prometheus unbound.

God biblically unbound.

But there they are, the stupendous biblical songlines. The songlines of Noah, Job, Jonah, and Jesus. The songlines I became heir to in my baptism.

Noah, Job, Jonah and Jesus: in one form or another, each of them encountered beast and abyss.

Beast as social degradation and chaos in Noah's case. Beast as beast in Job's case. Beast as nightsea journey in Jonah's case. Beast as phylogeny coming flush with ontogeny in the case of Jesus.

In them, finally, abyss experienced as Tehom became abyss experienced as Turiya.

Sitting there, in that church in Bun na hAbhann, the questions that posed themselves to me were simple: what other songlines than theirs am I, a Christian, able to walk? What other songlines than theirs do I, a Christian, need to walk?

Job, it seemed to me, was the Indjuwanydjuwa of the Christian tradition and Jonah its Kunapipi.

Noah, Job, Jonah and Jesus: in the end, in Jesus, these four songlines became one, a single trail, Bright Angel Trail descending and ascending.

How, I wondered sitting there, could I inherit this news? How, short of an inner exodus, liturgical and doctrinal, could Christianity inherit it?

Bring in the drum, I thought.

Bring in the drum that keeps a seal's breathing-hole open into Tehom.

Bring in the Upanishad which tells us: it being Turiya, Tehom is shantam, shivam, advaitam – utterly tranquil, peaceful-blissful, beyond duality.

Bring in the drum, bring in the trail, bring in Tehom, because these and more we will bring in the day we bring in the Triduum Sacrum.

Tehom
om
om
om

Om, the Mandukya Upanishad tells us, has four padas or quarters:

> Vaishvanara – waking awareness
> Taijasa – dreaming awareness
> Susupta – dreamless sleep
> Turiya – Divine Ground

When, God being gracious, the Red Sea of waking, dreaming and dreamless sleep opens, then, by God's grace, and by God's grace alone, we go through.

Bringing in the Mandukya Upanishad won't be easy. In it the sages of India have crossed over from talk about the world to talk about experience. What, other than our experience of it as a world, is the world? It is the question Berkeley asked and Kant asked. In this crossing over, Berkeley and Kant will be our Moses and our Aaron.

And Jesus returned in the power of the Spirit into Galilee: And there went out a fame of him through all the region round about. And he taught in their synagogues, being glorified by all. And he came to Nazareth, where he had been brought up: and, as his custom was, he went into the synagogue on the sabbath day, and stood up for to read. And there was delivered unto him the book of the prophet Esaias. And when he had opened the book, he found the place where it was written, the Spirit of the Lord *is* upon me, because he hath anointed me to preach the gospel to the poor; he hath sent me to heal the broken-hearted, to preach deliverance to the captives, and recovering of sight to the blind, to set at liberty them that are bruised.

To set at liberty them that are philosophically bruised.

To set at liberty them that are epistemologically bruised by their hard Egyptian bondage, hard biblical bondage, hard Christian bondage, to naïve realism.

The good news is that a Moses and an Aaron have gone down into Christendom and called upon us to come forth.

Lazarus, come forth.

Come forth so far as to hear a Hindu parable: In India, long ago, there lived a man whose name was Narada. Narada was a hermit. He practised the most fearful austerities. Sometimes, on a blazing hot day, he would light four fires and sit between them. He regularly denied himself both sleep and food. Throughout it all, and it lasted for many incarnations, Narada remained the kindliest of men. No one went unhelped from his door. One day it was Vishnu, the great god himself, who was standing at his door. So impressed by Narada's sanctity was Vishnu that he had come down to grant him the boon of his choice.

That I should know the secret of your Maya, that, said Narada, is the boon I desire.

Hesitating, Vishnu smiled. A mysterious smile it was, having in it something that communicated a sense of possible calamity.

Narada insisted.

Then, said Vishnu graciously, let us walk.

To begin with, as Narada would have expected, it was a pleasant walk along forest paths that he so well knew. Then, to his surprise, they emerged from the forest into a blazing red desert. Two hours into it, Vishnu complained of thirst and fatigue. Less than an hour later he sat in the fragmented shade of a fragmented rock and, in a hoarse whisper, said, 'I can go no further.' Recovering his breath, but only a little, he continued, 'At the end of the desert, two hours away, there is a village. Toughened as you are by the fierceness of your austerities, you will reach it and still have strength enough left to bring me back some water.'

Narada set out. None of the many ferocities he had to endure defeated him. Coming into the lovely green village, he knocked on the first door. A charming young woman opened it and, looking at her, Narada, the old ascetic, was spellbound, and quite forgot what he had come for. He went in and sat down, joining the family at their evening meal. It was as if he had always belonged to the household and had, just now, come in from the rice fields and taken his customary place in it. The next morning, he went with them to the rice fields. He worked all day. And that was but the first of many such days. Having no remembrance of any other life than the one he was now living, Narada one day asked the father of the household for the hand of the young woman, his daughter, in marriage. In time three children were born to them and when the old man died, Narada, by his bequest, became head of the household.

One year the monsoon season broke furiously. For weeks, it continued furiously. There were those who talked about the end of all things. Hearing the river burst its banks one night, Narada, together with his wife and children, went out into the chaos of waters. Wading to higher ground, first one child, then another, and then the third, was swept away. From a long way off his wife wailed and he himself, the first out, the first to have been overwhelmed, he was going down in what he was sure was the final engulfing when, suddenly, there was silence, and light, and intense desert heat, and behind him he heard a voice he recognized, 'Did you bring the water? You've been gone for almost a half an hour.'

Narada's story.

The story of our exodus from philosophical hard bondage. Telling it to myself as I did, in a church, I had assumed moral responsibility for inviting it across the Christian threshold. Sitting there, I imagined a Bible in which the story of Narada had replaced the story of Noah. For, philosophically understood, who else but Narada is Noah.

The story of Narada is the story of Noah come to full philosophical or if you like Upanishadic maturity. Instead of thinking of the great journey as a journey in four stages called Noah, Job, Jonah and Jesus, we can now think of it as a journey whose stages are Narada, Job, Jonah and Jesus. The stage that Narada gives his name to is the great disillusioning. Until this moment, I will have assumed, almost instinctively, that psyche is the window. Now I know that it is the blind. Now I know that just as there is healing of the psyche, so also is there healing from it.

Avarana and *Kosha* are words Narada will bring with him into our world.

Viksepashakti and *avaranashakti* are words he will bring.

Adhyaropa also, and *apavada*.

Words as holy as *hosannah*. Words coming into our religion.

It isn't of course the case that once we have experienced the great disillusioning we then walk away from it into the next stage. All subsequent stages are, among other things, a deepening experience of it. A deepening understanding and integration of it. Gradually, over years, the calamity comes to be seen and welcomed as a blessing.

With the Psalmist, Job might have said

Blessed be the name of the Lord, for he hath shewed me his marvellous kindness in a strong city.

Sitting in one or another of the gates of this, his strong city, at evening, Job would be wise. His wisdom, though, in spite of all the respect it was accorded, was of the cautionary kind you might find in Proverbs:

Drink waters out of thine own cistern, and running waters out of thine own well.

Go to the ant, thou sluggard: consider her ways and be wise.

When pride cometh, then cometh shame: but with the lowly is wisdom.

As a jewel of gold in a swine's snout, so is a fair woman which is without discretion.

The name of the Lord is a strong tower: the righteous runneth into it, and is safe.

Boast not thyself of to morrow; for thou knowest not what a day may bring forth.

Although not without premonitory rumblings, dark Enkidu energies erupted in Job one night. Circling his city, they blew their savage ram's horns.

Within and without, Job's world collapsed.

Not in his house, not in his family, not in his city, not in his culture, not in his religion — in nothing that previously sheltered him did Job find shelter now.

Sitting on the dungheap of his former wisdom he cried:

Am I a sea or a whale, that thou settest a watch over me? When I say my bed shall comfort me, my couch shall ease my complaint: then thou scarest me with dreams, and terrifiest me through visions: so that my soul chooseth strangling and death rather than my life.

Wherefore then hast thou brought me forth out of the womb? Oh that I had given up the ghost, and no eye had seen me! I should have been as though I had not been; I should have been carried from the womb to the grave.

I have said to corruption, thou art my father: to the worm, thou art my mother and my sister.

When I looked for good, then evil came unto me: and when I waited for light, there came darkness.

I am a brother to dragons and a companion to owls.

Job was a wholly unsheltered man.

Not a single savannah bush stood between him and the terrors of inwardness.

Not a single savannah bush stood between him and the terrors of outwardness.

Wholly unsheltered. And wholly undefended.

Neither nature nor culture offered him a breastplate against the rush and charge of Enkidu from within.

Neither nature nor culture offered him a bullfighter's cape with which to divert the rush and charge of behemoth from without.

God spoke to Job out of a whirlwind.

And in Job, with God's harsh help, humanity opened its eyes wider than it had ever opened them before.

Job opened his eyes wide towards inwardness.

Job opened his eyes wide towards outwardness.

In that was healing.

The healing was temporary. A respite in a continuing big journey.

Chosen by God to do God's business, which meant he must walk against the grain of culture and conscience, Jonah fled not into safety but into the maw of a waiting whale. Turning flukes, the whale sounded and yawned him out into the Great Deep below the roots of universe and psyche. It was as if the Red Sea of all actual and possible worlds had opened and Jonah had walked dryshod through into no-thing-ness. Or better, it was as if the Red Sea of experience of self and other-than-self had opened and Jonah had walked dryshod through into the possibility of final and blessed liberation. He wasn't able for it. All his karmic energies activated, all of them hallucinating themselves all around him, he had, by reason of inclination well-nigh inevitable, crossed into the *chonyid bardo*. Emerging thence into the *sidpa bardo*, there awakened in him an intense, even fierce, longing to return to the world. He did return. But climbing the path to his house he knew that he had for the moment missed a stupendous opportunity.

Then cometh Jesus with them unto a place called Gethsemane, and saith unto the disciples, Sit ye here while I go and pray yonder. And he took with him Peter and the two sons of Zebedee, and began to be sorrowful and very heavy. Then saith he unto them, My soul is exceeding sorrowful, even unto death: tarry ye here and watch with me. And he went a little further, and fell on his face, and prayed, saying, O my father, if it be possible, let this cup pass from me, nevertheless not as I will, but as thou wilt. And he cometh unto the disciples and findeth them asleep, and saith unto Peter, What, could ye not watch with me one hour? Watch and pray, that ye enter not into temptation: the spirit indeed *is* willing but the flesh is weak. He went away again the second time, and prayed, saying, O my Father, if this cup may not pass away from me, except I drink it, thy will be done. And he came and found them asleep again: for their eyes were heavy. And he left them, and went away again, and prayed the third time, saying the same words. Then cometh he to his disciples, and saith unto them, sleep on now, and take *your* rest: behold the hour is at hand ...

when he must set foot on Bright Angel Trail, must consent to climb down, or be engulfed down, through all the old sea-floors, down into the fire-floor where Bright Angel is waiting.

'This is the cup,' Bright Angel says, pointing to a mirroring rockpool. 'It mirrors the karma of the ages, the rock walls of karmic sediment you have come down through. It is the cup that will not pass.'

Consenting, Jesus knelt at the edge of the rockpool. He cupped his hands down into it. Raising them, he waited till the water in them settled, till it mirrored the ages. Then he drank it.

Not since the formation of our galaxy had so important an event occurred.

On the day following, climbing it in mystical stages, Jesus climbed the

Hill of the Koshaless Skull. When, enabled by grace, he at last looked down into the emptiness of that skull, it was accomplished: *Oh dichosa ventura*.

Our Christian songline.

Although reaches of it are named Narada, Job, Jonah and Jesus, it is nonetheless a single songline.

It isn't of course a prescribed way. The mystical journey isn't an inevitable sequence of inevitable experiences. And yet there are many who, like Narada, undergo a profound disillusioning. Here we awaken to the unreality of what we normally experience as reality. It is like waking up from waking. There are those who, like Job, open their eyes wide, unselectively wide, to inwardness and outwardness, to unintegrated Enkidu energies within, to energies without that never submissively signed their names to our Psalm-eight or second-stasimon sense of ourselves. There are those who, like Jonah, discover that the ground of their being is abyssal. They discover that the Divine Ground that grounds them is, as it were, a Divine Ungrund. There are those who, like Jesus, look down into the emptiness of the empty skull. How wonderful it is to think of Australian Aborigines walking the songlines of Jarapiri, the Great Snake, of Kolakola, the Red Kangaroo, of Mamu-boijunda, the Great Spider who barked in the dawn lights, of Indjuwanydjuwa who, his wandering over, turned to stone.

How wonderful it also is to think of those Christians who walked the Christian songline.

Think of Catherine of Siena:

I have chosen suffering for my only consolation and I will gladly bear this and all other torments in the name of the Saviour for as long as it shall please his Majesty.

Think of Marguerite Porete. Think of her in that wonderful, awe-full moment when her soul

> falls from love to nothingness.

Think of Catherine of Genoa:

This form of purgation, which I see in the souls in purgatory, I feel in my own mind. In the last two years I have felt it most; every day I feel and see it more clearly. I see my soul within this body as in a purgatory, formed as is the true purgatory and like it, but so measured that the body can bear with it and not die; little by little it grows until the body will die. I see my spirit estranged from all things, even things spiritual, which can feed it, such as gaiety, delight and consolation, and without the power so to enjoy anything, spiritual or temporal, by will or mind or memory, as to let me say that one thing contents me more than another. Inwardly I find myself, as it were, besieged. All things by which spiritual or bodily life is refreshed have, little by little, been taken from my inner self, which knows, now they are gone, that they are fed and comforted. But so hateful and abhorrent are these things, as they are known to the spirit, that they all go, never to return. This is because of the spirit's instinct to rid itself of whatever hinders its perfection; so ruthless is it that to fulfil its purpose it would all but cast itself into hell.

Think of Dame Julian of Norwich. One night she dreamed that the Fiend, coming with the stink and fire of hell, took her by the throat:

And in the slepe, at the begynnyng, methowte the fend set him in my throte, puttand forth a visage ful nere my face like a yong man; and it was longe and wonder lene; I saw never none such. The color was rede like the tilestone whan it is new brent, with black spots therin like black steknes, fouler than the tilestone. His here was rode as rust, evisid aforn, with syde lokks hongyng on the thounys. He grynnid on me with a shrewd semelant, shewing white teeth; and so mekil methowte it the more oggley. Body ne hands had he none shaply, but with his pawes he held me in the throte and would have stranglid me, but he myte not. This oggley shewing was made slepyng, and so was non other. And in all this time I trostid to be savid and kepid be the mercy of God. And our curtes lord gave me grace to waken, and one this had I my lif. The persons that were with me beheld me and wet my temples, and my herte began to comforten. And anon a lyte smoke came in the dore with a grete hete and a foule stinke. I said: 'Benedicite domine! It is all on fire that is here!' and I wened it had ben a bodily fire that shuld a brent us al to dede. I askid hem that wer with me if thei felt ony stynke. Thei seyd nay, thei felt none. I said 'Blissid be God!' for that wist I wele it was the fend that was comen to tempest me. And anon I toke to that our Lord had shewid me on the same day, with all the feith of holy church, for I beheld it is bothen one, and fled therto as to my comforte. And anone all vanishid away, and I was browte to gret rest and peas withouten sekenes of body or drede of conscience.

Think of Teresa of Ávila:

I saw an angel close by me on my left side, in bodily form. This I am not accustomed to see unless very rarely. Though I have visions of angels frequently, yet I can see them only by an intellectual vision, such as I have spoken of before. It was the Lord's will that in this vision I should see an angel in this wise. He was not large, but small of stature, and most beautiful – his face burning, as if he were one of the highest angels, who seem to be all of fire: they must be those whom we call cherubim ... I saw in his hand a long spear of gold, and at the iron's point there seemed to be a little fire. He appeared to me to be thrusting it at times into my heart, and to pierce my very entrails. When he drew it out he seemed to draw them out also and to leave me all on fire with a great love of God. The pain was so great that it made me moan, and yet so surpassing was the sweetness of this excessive pain that I could not wish to be rid of it. The soul is satisfied now with nothing less than God. The pain is not bodily, but spiritual, though the body has its share in it, even a large one. It is a caressing of love so sweet which now takes place between the soul and God that I pray God of his goodness to make him experience it who may think that I am lying.

Of themselves, these last two testimonies serve to demonstrate that when we open the door wide enough to let in God we are opening it wide enough to let in the Great Adversary; when we open it wide enough to let in heaven we are opening it wide enough to let in hell; when we open it wide enough to let in the light we are opening it wide enough to let in the dark; when we open it wide enough to let in the Great Sanity we are opening it wide enough to let in the great insanity.
 The Christian songline walks us into and through enormities.
 It might be to Jonah that Tauler is talking:

The great wastes to be found in the divine ground have neither image nor form nor condition, for they are neither here nor there. They are like unto a fathomless Abyss, bottomless and floating in itself. Even as water ebbs and flows, up and down, now sinking into a hollow, so that it looks as if there were no water there, and then again in a little while rushing forth as if it would engulf everything, so does it come to pass in this Abyss. This, truly, is much more God's Dwelling place than heaven or man. A man who verily desires to enter will surely find God here, and himself simply in God: for God never separates himself from this ground. God will be present with him, and he will find and enjoy Eternity here. There is no past nor present here, and no created light can reach unto or shine into this divine Ground: for here only is the dwelling place of God and his sanctuary. Now this Divine Abyss can be fathomed by no creatures; it can be filled by none, and it satisfies none, God only can fill it in his infinity. For this Abyss belongs only to the Divine Abyss, of which it is written: Abyssus abyssum invocat. He who is truly conscious of the ground, which shone into the powers of his soul, and lighted and inclined its lowest and highest powers to turn to their pure Source and true Origin, must diligently examine himself and remain alone, listening to the voice which cries in the wilderness of this ground. This ground is so desert and bare that no thought has ever entered there. None of all the thoughts of man which, with the help of reason, have been devoted to meditation or the Holy Trinity (and some men have occupied themselves much with these thoughts) have ever entered this ground. For it is so close and yet so far off, and so far beyond all things, that it has neither time nor place. It is a simple and unchanging condition. A man who really and truly enters, feels as though he had been here throughout eternity, and as though he were one there-with.

Of it, with the Mandukya Upanishad, he might have said: it is *shantam, sivam, advaitam* – utterly tranquil, peaceful-blissful, beyond duality.

Through Fénelon, centuries later, the answering echo of Christ's cry of dereliction came back to us:

God felt, God tasted, and enjoyed, is indeed God, but God with those gifts that flatter the soul. God in darkness, in privation, in forsakenness, in insensibility, is so much God that it is as it were God bare and alone.

An exodus from Chalcedon to the Kedron.

An exodus from Chalcedon to the Cry of dereliction.

An exodus from credal Christianity to Triduum Sacrum Christianity.

An exodus from a Christianity chiefly concerned to establish who Jesus was to a Christianity chiefly concerned to establish what he undertook and underwent from the moment he turned to cross the Kedron.

An exodus from a Christianity founded or refounded on belief to a Christianity founded on ineluctable experience.

Being as much a fact of human nature as metamorphosis is a fact of insect nature, the Triduum Sacrum requires of us only a simple, if also vulnerable, willingness to listen to those who have been through it.

It is only when we have reached the bottom of the abyss of our nothingness, and when we are firmly fixed there, that we are able, to use the words of Holy Scriptures, to walk in God's sight in justice and truth.

How precious is this state of nothingness! We have of necessity to reach it before God can fill us; for our soul needs to be interiorly empty before God can fill it with his own unique Spirit. As long as these crucifying operations last, everything – spirit, memory and will – exists in a terrifying void, in sheer nothingness. Let us cherish this mighty void, since God deigns to fill it; let us cherish this nothingness, since God's infinity is to be discovered in it.

This nought may better be felt than seen; for it is full blind and full dark to them that have but a little while looked thereupon. Nevertheless (if I shall trulier say) a soul is more blinded in feeling of it for abundance of ghostly light.

What is he that calleth it nought? Surely it is our outer man and not our inner. Our inner man calleth it All; for by it he is well taught to understand all things bodily and ghostly, without any special beholding to any one thing by itself.

Comes then the soul into the unclouded light of God. It is transported so far from creaturehood into nothingness that of its own powers it can never return to its faculties or its former creaturehood. Once there, God shelters the soul's nothingness with his uncreated essence, safeguarding its creaturely existence. The soul has dared to become nothing, and cannot pass from its own being into nothingness and back again, losing its own identity in the process, except God safeguarded it.

ANACONDA CANOE

Songs of the Christian songline.
 Songs whose refrain should be

> *Oh dichosa ventura*

Even when we are sore amazed in Gethsemane or are derelict on Golgotha, their refrain should be

> *Oh dichosa ventura*

And when the songs of our songline are Tenebrae nocturnes our antiphon, fifteen times repeated, will be

> *Oh noche, que guiaste,*
> *Oh noche amable mas que el alborada ...*

Each time we extinguish a Tenebrae harrow candle we will sing it:

> *Oh noche, que guiaste,*
> *Oh noche amable mas que el alborada ...*

When the last candle is entombed and the sanctuary is in darkness we will sing it:

> *Oh noche, que guiaste,*
> *Oh noche amable mas que el alborada ...*

How astonishing! Knowing them to be blessings, Christianity has opened its sanctuary door to darkness, Night, no-thing-ness and the abyss.
 No-thing-ness is not *nihil*. No-thing-ness is the Rich Nought. The abyss isn't tohu-wavohu. Tohu-wovohu is the snake we've projected into the rope.
 How astonishing! Our rock of faith has become

> An abyss of faith
> A Tehom of faith
> A Turiya of faith

It's as if Noah's ark turned flukes and sounded and yawned him out into Tehom, into Turiya. Imagine it, Moses de Leon calling out to Noah:

When God gave the Torah to Israel, He opened the seven heavens to them, and they saw that nothing was there in reality but His Glory; He opened the seven worlds to them, and they saw that nothing was there but His Glory; He opened the seven abysses before their eyes, and they saw that nothing was there but His Glory.

The only existence the abyss has is an abyss of faith, Tehom of faith, Turiya of faith.

And darkness, privation, forsakenness and insensibility to God's presence are Golgotha gifts of the Holy Ghost.

> In the darkness of Good Friday, God.
> In deprivation of all consolation temporal and spiritual, God.
> In Godforsakenness, God.
> In insensibility to God, God.

On Golgotha, on Good Friday, it is with my abandonment by God that I worship God.

Crossing the Kedron with Jesus, entering his temple with Jesus, the seeking soul lays 'the foundation of its love and delight on what it neither sees nor feels, on what it cannot see or feel – namely, on God, incomprehensible and supreme'.

As if, singing itself, a Chandogya mahavakya were to go before us into Tenebrae:

> *Yatra na anyat pasyati, na anyat srinoti, na anyad vijanati, sa bhuma.*

As if, singing itself, a Sufi prayer were to go before us into Tenebrae:

> Between me and Thee there is an 'I am' that torments me. Ah!
> Through Thy 'I am' take away my 'I am' from between us both.

As if, singing itself, a Christian mahavakya were to go before us into Tenebrae, where

… the spirit beholds a Darkness into which it cannot enter with its reason. And there it feels itself dead and lost to itself and one with God without difference and without distinction. And when it feels itself one with God, then God himself is its peace and its enjoyment and its rest. And this is an unfathomable abyss wherein man must die to himself in blessedness, and must live again in virtues whenever love and its stirring demand it.

Eckhart says as much:

So long as the soul beholds forms, even though she behold an angel, or herself as something formed: so long is there imperfection in her. Yes, indeed, should she even behold God, in so far as he is with form and number in the Trinity: so long is there imperfection in her. Only when all that is formed is cast off from the soul, and she sees the Eternal One alone, then the pure essence of the soul feels the naked, unformed essence of the divine Unity – more, still a Beyond-Being. O wonder of wonders, what a noble endurance is that where the essence of the soul suffers no suggestion or shadow of difference even in thought or in name. There she entrusts herself alone to the One, free from all multiplicity and difference, in which all limitation and quality is lost and is one. This One makes us blessed.

Suso stops short of claiming that the union of the soul with God is 'with difference and without distinction':

When the soul, forgetting itself, dwells in that radiant darkness it loses all its faculties and all its qualities, as St. Bernard has said. And this more or less completely, according to whether the soul — be it in the body or out of the body — is more or less united to God. This forgetfulness of self is, in a measure, a transformation in God; who then becomes, in a certain manner, all things for the soul, as Scripture saith. In this rapture the soul disappears, but not yet entirely. It acquires, it is true, certain qualities of Divinity, but does not naturally become divine ... to speak in the common language, the soul is rapt by the divine power of resplendent Being above its natural faculties into the nakedness of the Nothing.

Songline of joyful, sorrowful and glorious mysteries. But it isn't only in its glorious mysteries that it is glorious. Even in Gethsemane, in its sorrow unto death there, it is glorious. Glorious also it is in its cry of Good-Friday dereliction.

Glorious when, leaving our hermitage, it leads us into and through a great disillusioning.

Glorious when, our Psalm-eight sense of ourselves in ruins, we open our eyes wide, unselectively wide, to unsubduable inwardness and to unsubduable outwardness, to our night psyches and behemoth.

Glorious when, seeking refuge there, our ship-wake to Tarshish becomes a whale-wake to Tehom.

Glorious when, attempting to integrate ancient life in us, our Kedron becomes our Colorado.

Glorious when, in Tenebrae, it sings to us from the Koshaless Skull:

God in darkness, privation, forsakenness and insensibility is so much God that it is, as it were, God bare and alone.

The Christian songline: given the miracles and calamities of illumination and grace that can occur, the only safe way to walk it is in a continuing assimilation of our life to the life of Christ. Or saying the same thing in another way: it is only in a continuing, life-long baptism of our life into the life of Christ that it is safe to walk it.

Songs of our Christian songline.

Suites of songs. Itineraria of songs.

An itinerarium of Eckhart songs.

An itinerarium of St John of the Cross songs.

An itinerarium of Marguerite Porete songs:

The soul becomes herself by becoming nothing, and once she has gone out of herself and become nothing, she has true knowledge of the gifts of God through the miracle of his gift to her, which she receives in faith.

Now the soul sees what God is; that he Is, that all things come from him and that she herself is nothing, being not what he is. So she feels amazing humility at the thought of the infinite goodness of God giving her nothingness free will. She sees herself as nothing but wickedness, and yet with this wonderful gift of free will this giving of being to what had none out of the pure goodness of God. Then such divine goodness is poured into the soul, in a ravishing flash of divine light, that she suddenly sees that she must remove this great gift of free will from anything that is not God, and never again place it where he is not.

The soul is now nothing, seeing her nothingness by the divine light that is in her; yet she knows everything, since the depth of her knowledge of her nothingness is such that it has no beginning and no end and cannot be measured. It is an immeasurable depth, but without being able to plumb this depth, she finds herself in it, which is something no one can do who has not reached this stage. The more she sees of herself, the more she realizes she cannot see the true extent of her wickedness. She sees herself naked in the darkest dungeon of sin. So she sees herself without the use of her sight; this is the utmost depth to which humility can attain, where there is no room for pride, since this total darkness shows her herself with total clarity.

So the soul has fallen from the state of love to the state of nothingness.

When these souls have come to love God as he is, they are made conscious of their own nothingness – being nothing, having nothing, either from themselves, their fellow-Christians, or even from God himself. The soul is then so small she cannot see herself; all created things are so far from her she cannot feel them; God is so infinitely greater she cannot grasp him. Through this nothingness, she has the sureness of knowing nothing, being able to do nothing by herself, and willing nothing. And this nothingness brings her everything, which otherwise she would not have.

She is afloat on a sea of peace, drifting without any impulse from inside herself or any breeze from outside, because she is in full command and beyond interference or care. If she did anything through her outer senses, this would remain outside her, and if God did anything in her, this would be him working in her for his own purpose and so also outside her. What she does no more burdens her than what she does not do; she has no more being in herself, having given it all freely without asking 'why'.

Being completely free, and in command of her sea of peace, the soul is nonetheless drowned and loses herself through God, with him and in him. She loses her identity, as does the water from a river – like the Ouse or the Meuse – when it flows into the sea. It has done its work and can relax in the arms of the sea, and the same is true of the soul. Her work is over and she can lose herself in what she has totally become: Love. Love is the bridegroom of her happiness, enveloping her wholly in his love and making her part of that which is. This is a wonder to her and she has become a wonder. Love is her only delight and pleasure.

The soul has now no name but Union-in-Love. Yes, once she has become totally free, she then falls into a trance of nothingness, and this is the next highest stage. Then she lives no longer in the life of grace, nor in the life of the spirit, but in the glorious life of divinity. God has conferred this special favour on her, and nothing except his goodness can now touch her.

What it means is being in God without being oneself, since to be in God is being.

Songs of our Christian songline.
    Song, or songs, of the blackbird of Derrycairn.

> *Binn sin, a luin Doire an Chairn!*
> *ní chuala mé in aird so bhith*
> *ceol ba binne ná do cheol*
> *agus tú fá bhun do nid.*
>
> *Aoincheol is binne fan mbith,*
> *mairg nach éisteann leis go fóill,*
> *a mhic Calprainn na gclog mbinn,*
> *'s go mbéarthá a-rís ar do nóin.*

Stanzas from an Irish poem in which Oisín, a survivor from pagan times, asks Patrick, bringer of Christianity to Ireland, to listen to nature as well as to Christ, to listen to the blackbird of Derrycairn as well as to St Paul.

Of course! we say. Of course! Silence your Christian bell for a while and listen to the blackbird. Particularly when it is the blackbird of Derrycairn that sings, silence your bell.

There comes a day, however, when we might ask that blackbird, or another blackbird singing across the river from us, to shut up.

Day of calamity.

Day when the veil of our psyche is rent. As on Good Friday the veil in the temple was rent, so is it rent, and we, however briefly, are in Tenebrae.

Or, putting it less violently; day when the Red Sea of our psyche opens and we walk through into Tehom, which we can't yet think of as Turiya.

On that day, however beautiful his song, the blackbird of Derrycairn has nothing to say to us.

Our song out of ourselves that day is

> *Abyssus Abyssum invocat*

> Abyss calling unto Abyss
> Deep calling unto Deep
> Tehom calling unto Tehom

Plunged in the silence that was before the world was, heeding the silence that was before the world was, we ask the blackbird to shut up.

Our Psalm-eight, or second-stasimon, sense of ourselves is lamentable. It is hurtful to ourselves and hurtful to nature. It is surely true, however, that there are in human beings gulfs of possibility which, from within their own natures, aren't available to animal or plant. Or to angels either, if Pico della Mirandola is right:

O supreme generosity of God the Father, O highest and most marvellous felicity of man! To him is granted to have whatever he chooses, to be whatever he wills. Beasts as soon as they are born (so says Lucilius) bring with them from their mother's womb all they will ever possess. Spiritual beings, either from the beginning or soon thereafter, become what they are to be for ever and ever. Or man when he came into life the Father conferred the seeds of all kinds and the germs of every way of life. Whatever seeds each man cultivates will grow to maturity and bear in him their own fruit. If they be vegetative, he will be like a plant. If sensitive, he will become brutish. If rational, he will grow into a heavenly being. If intellectual, he will be an angel and the son of God. And if, happy in the lot of no created thing, he withdraws into the centre of his own unity, his spirit, made one with God, in the solitary darkness of God, who is set above all things, shall surpass them all.

Rilke believed that nature has ventured and adventured human beings more than it has ventured and adventured animals and plants.

Some there are who go with the venture. So far forward or so far out do they venture and adventure themselves that, in the end, their unshieldedness is what they depend upon.

The hope is that

> where the danger is, there grows
> also what saves.

Jesus went with the venture.

As Narada he ventured himself. As Job he ventured himself. As Jonah he ventured himself. He ventured himself to the floor of the Grand Canyon. He ventured himself into the darkness of Good Friday on Golgotha.

Having ventured himself, he has more to say to us than animal or plant has. He has more to say to us than the blackbird of Derrycairn has.

Nature isn't enough.

ANACONDA CANOE

St Patrick's Deer's Cry isn't enough:

> For my shield this day I call:
> Heaven's might
> Sun's brightness
> Moon's whiteness
> Fire's glory
> Lightning's swiftness
> Wind's wildness
> Ocean's depth
> Earth's solidity
> Rock's immobility

Wonderful though it is, the Navajo cradle isn't enough:

> I have made a cradleboard for you, my child,
> May you grow to a great old age.
> Of the sun's rays I made the back,
> Of black clouds I have made the blanket,
> Of rainbow I have made the bow,
> Of sunbeams have I made the side-loops,
> Of lightning have I made the lacings,
> Of river mirrorings have I made the footboard,
> Of dawn have I made the covering,
> Of earth's welcome for you have I made the bed.

Uvavnuk's song, or the way of being in the world that it sings, isn't enough:

> The great sea has set me in motion,
> set me adrift,
> moving me as the weed moves in a river
> The arch of sky and mightiness of storms
> Have moved the spirit within me
> Till I am carried away
> Trembling with joy.

The deer's cry and the cradle.
The blackbird's song and Uvavnuk's song.
In the way that seals need breathing-holes in the icecap, so do we need breathing-holes in nature. We need to breathe transcendentally.

> The woods are lovely dark and deep,
> But I have promises to keep,
> And miles to go before I sleep,
> And miles to go before I sleep.

'Sleep on now, and take your rest. Behold, the hour is at hand', when, like Narada going with the venture, we go forth.

How shattering it is to hear the forgotten yet familiar voice:

> Did you bring the water?

Sitting there we ask: throughout how many incarnations have I been gone? Into how many worlds have I wandered? How often have I gone down into the hell worlds? How often have I ascended into the heaven worlds? How many times have I been a husband? How many times have I been a mother? How many times an animal? How many times a plant?

> You've been gone for almost a half an hour.
> Did you bring the water?

Short of a great disillusioning, will we ever remember the errand we are actually on?

Or, more momentously: short of a great disillusioning, will we ever remember the errand or journey we ought to be on?

Sitting in that church in Bun na hAbhann, I had myself almost forgotten the errand I was on.

Thinking of the groundplan I had brought as an attempt to give architectural shape to the mystical journey, I walked up the road looking for a wild field that I might plant it in. All time is Dreamtime, I thought. So, to walk these ordinary roads on this ordinary day could in itself be a dreamtime walking. A walking as spontaneously creative as the walking of Kolakola, the Red Kangaroo.

> I, Kolakola, am hurrying on without delay;
> From my hollow I am hurrying on without delay.
> I, the young kangaroo, am journeying
> A far journey without a halt;
> Leaving behind a thin trail I am journeying
> On a far journey without a halt.

Kolakola, the Red Kangaroo, and Jarapiri, the Great Snake.

> Jarapiri's ribs move him along,
> He leaves a meandering track.
> Jarapiri's ribs move him along
> He leaves a meandering track.
>
> Great Snake, Jarapiri, singular being,
> Wander Walbiri earth
> Great Snake, Jarapiri, give name

ANACONDA CANOE

> To all Walbiri plants.
> Great Snake, Jarapiri, wind source
> With rain on your forked tongue
>
> Jarapiri's ribs move him along,
> He leaves a meandering track.
> Jarapiri's ribs move him along,
> He leaves a meandering track.

White man got no dreaming, Australian Aborigines say. Yet here I was, my mind marinated since birth in white culture, marinated over many incarnations maybe in white culture, and here I was pretending to walk in the universal Dreamtime.

D.H. Lawrence believed that even if we could we shouldn't return to the resinous ages; that, even if we could, we shouldn't cluster at the tribal drum, the rainmaker's drum, the drum of the ancestral shaman, any more. And in East Africa one night, reacting violently, Jung broke up a native dance. On the point of joining it, he recognized the threat that was in it to the integrity of his white psyche.

'Whom the Gods wish to destroy they first make mad.'

Since I left Kildare that morning, that saying had been with me. With me because of a sense I had of having crossed or trespassed a limit.

Cross that limit a person might, but not with impunity.

On his way down to Egypt to do God's business, God sought to kill Moses.

No one needed to come from over the horizon to tell me that I wasn't Moses. I knew who I was, a small farmer's son from north Kerry, so what was I doing walking these roads looking for a Dreamtime field in which I would ask the Dreamtime earth to give architectural shape to the Christian Songline, to the mystical journey? Not for the first time in my life I was aware that just as a lung can collapse so can a psyche.

Twenty years earlier I had written about a situation similar to the one I felt I was now in:

> In a land
> Where the lightning
> And thunder are one,
> The woodpigeons flew
> Through the wounds
> Of the hunter,
> And then, like our echoes,
> The hills threw us back.

I sat on the side of the road and asked, have I crossed a limit, God?
Actaeon crossed a limit unconsciously. Had I crossed one consciously?
No psalm that I knew had the words that I needed.
I made do with

> lead me in a plain path because of mine enemies

Any enemies I might have had at that moment were, more than likely, impulses and energies from within myself.

Only all too well was I aware that, even if it were available to me, I wouldn't feel secure in St Patrick's breastplate. Having Actaeon as stag to his own hounds in mind, I knew the deer's cry wasn't enough. I needed more than nature's protections.

Invoking its protections, I sank into my baptism. I sank into a divinely sponsored, sacramentally conferred openness to the Transcendent.

In my baptism, the initiative was with God, not with me. In it, the initiative was with Artemis, not with Actaeon. In this we see nature responding to grace, not nature setting off for the heights on its own.

How easy it is on that ascent to set off avalanches:

> O, Thou, who plumed with stong desire
>   Wouldst float above the earth, beware!
> A Shadow tracks thy flight of fire –
>   Night is coming!

How, I would ask St Patrick, how ever did you come to imagine that the ocean floor could protect you during your encounter with Tehom? Did you imagine that it could guide you into and through Tehom?

There comes of course a time when, as the Book of Job assures us,

> thou shalt be in league with the stones of the field and the beasts of the field shall be at peace with thee.

And it might be that it isn't only an ox and an ass who will breathe warmth upon you.

Coming from savannah and ocean, here they come, Behemoth and Leviathan.

I imagined it: Lucy's first child lying loved and tucked up in a Navajo cradle, Leviathan and Behemoth breathing blessings upon her.

A splendid denouement, surely?

Yes. But there isn't only healing of the psyche. There is also healing from it. Sooner or later we must cross the Kedron. Sooner or later we must look down, as Christ did, into Adam's empty skull.

The deer's cry or Christ's unshieldedness.
His total unshieldedness in Gethsemane.
His total unshieldedness on Good Friday.

I thought about Job. Job's exposure to the extramural. His exposure to what, within and without, is beyond our wall.

It was another kind of exposure I was suffering from. Exposure to the impulse that had me walking these roads looking for a field in which I would plant the groundplan of a temple that would, God willing, good-shepherd through our most dangerous transitions. It was, I believed, only with God's authority that I should be doing it. I didn't sense that I had God's authority. Yet here I was, doing it. That was the killer.

Walking the songline of Red Kangaroo.
Walking the songline of the Lamb who was slain from the foundation of the world.

A little way up the road a car drew level with me and stopped. So down and out did the couple look, so at the end of its ways was their car, that I couldn't bring myself to refuse their offer of a lift. The first cross-roads we came to, they turned right. Not very promising I thought, looking at the fields. Then, quite unexpectedly, there it was, the wild field I had been looking for, a field with birch trees and bracken and heather and white-thorns. Offering them an excuse that amounted to a lie, I asked them to let me out. Cantankerously opposed by it, I broke my way through a hedge. Having a kind of false courage now, I crossed a patch of marsh to higher ground. Within a few minutes I had dug a short but shallow trench with the heels of my boots. Retrieving the groundplan from a satchel, it occurred to me that maybe I should go to Clonmacnoise and ask for a blessing. Re-emerging, not a little the worse for wear, through the hedge, I set off walking, and in less than an hour, I was entering the walled enclosure, the *cluain*.

For however long it would last, it was good to be intramural.

Our city wall it was, built against savannah and steppe. Wall that was broken down in Job.

Our biblical bars and doors it was, built against the abyss, that were washed away within Jonah.

Within this monastery wall, low though it was, I could sense the Psalmist's joy:

Blessed be the name of the Lord, for he hath showed me his marvellous kindness in a strong city.

Strong against Enkidu. Strong against Behemoth.

Labdacidae wall.

Atreidae wall.

High and mighty wall that didn't protect Agamemnon when, home from the war, he walked through its lion gate into bloody encounter with the conjugal axe.

Way of the strong city or Uvavauk's way:

> The great sea has set me in motion,
> Set me adrift,
> Moving me as a weed moves in the river.
> The arch of sky and mightiness of storms
> Have moved the spirit within me
> Till I am carried away
> Trembling with joy.

Did you ever have second thoughts, Gilgamesh?

And you Kadmus, and you Pericles, did either of you ever have second thoughts?

Sitting against the pillaged wall of the pillaged cathedral, I recalled my own quite terrible encounters with the extramural.

At last, after all the waiting, the great day had come. It was Christmas Eve. I was four or five at the time. Jack Scanlon or Mick McGrath or Mick Quinn or Joe Mahony or Jameen Kissane wouldn't come to our house tonight. But I wasn't sad about that. No, not tonight. Tonight was a great night. Sitting high on their camels, the three Wise Men might come to our house tonight. Following a star, they might pass through our yard. Certainly a man with a bag of miracles on his back would come. He surely would come. Last year, first thing on Christmas morning, our father had called us out to see the hoof-tracks of the reindeer on the lawn. At all other times of the year our front window was just a transparence between inside and outside. This evening, the crib set up in it, there was a radiance of angles in it. Strung between the walls there were paper decorations and over the holy pictures other decorations. And what was entirely wonderful, after it got dark there would be a candle lighting in every window. And picked from a tree in our own haggard, there was lots of holly. In a glow of fellow-feeling I crossed the yard to the cow stall. In I went, and I was devastated. No candles, no holly, no radiance of angels. Our cows not expecting the Wise Men to call. It took me a long time to take it in. Ordinary cows eating ordinary hay. And the night ordinary. And the stall ordinary. And the glow of fellow-feeling quenched. It was only in our house that it was Christmas. As sad for myself as I was for the animals, I looked, walking back towards the fowl-house and the piggery. Yes. It was only in our house that it was Christmas. Walking through our door, I walked into the sights of it but not into the glow of it. If it wasn't Christmas for our cows and our hens and our pigs and our horse and our ass, how could it be Christmas for me? Didn't the first Christmas happen in a stable?

Sixteen years or so later I had come home on holidays from university. It was Christmas Eve and to make sure that the fire wouldn't only look good but would also sound good I went out to an outhouse, took down a rope, walked down the road and crossing a fence into Mikie Fitz's fields I began to collect dry sticks. I was tightening the rope on a great bearth of them when, right there beside me in a hawthorn bush, I saw a robin settling down to roost for the night. Looking at her, the old desolation returned. Like the cows years ago in the stall, she wasn't aware that it was Christmas. She hadn't hung her world with sprigs of holly. She hadn't hung a wreath on her door. And there it was, the moon coming up, no crib in its window, no season's greetings to earth or star. For me that evening the conclusion was brutal; the universe wasn't an astral oratorio. And it wouldn't end, everyone and everything joining in, with a great Hallelujah chorus, going on and on and on, singing itself yet once again into the bliss of starless self-loss in Divine Ground. And now, remembering, I could put words on it: the boy crossing the yard walked in a cosmology where 'we' was the collective word; crossing it, coming back, he walked in a cosmology where 'us-and-them' was the collective word. A gulf or wound had opened in our yard, leaving us on one side, everything else on the other. It was Christmas Eve, and we, now meaning us human beings, were alone in our story.

I hadn't yet come across the Blackfoot story of how humanity had acquired the song and the dance of commonage consciousness. When I did come across it, I imagined the Blackfoot singing it, dancing it, there in our yard. By the end of it, the wound that had opened between the house and the stall would have closed. By the end of it, the wound that would have opened in the word 'we' – a wound as wide as 'us-and-them' – that wound would have closed.

There was another night in that yard. I had been reading the geological chapters in Darwin's *Origin of Species*. Long before I came to the end of them, I was man-overboard. As a man might fall out of a boat, I had, quite literally, fallen out of my story, the biblical story which saw the six-thousand-year-old universe as a play in five acts, they being, creation, fall, revelation, redemption and last things. It was, very likely, a play I would walk out of into a life of glory in eternity. For me now, this evening, that play and its scenery were rolled away. I put down the book and saying nothing to my father who was bent forward in his chair talking to the dog, I went out into the night. It was a wild night and for the first time in my life I experienced vertigo, hanging as I was, somewhere, maybe nowhere, in infinite Godlessness. Years later it would be a consolation of sorts to me to learn that Pascal experienced something similar:

Le silence éternel de ces espaces infinis m'effraye.

Tonight, however, there was no such companionship in terror. And so suddenly destructive of all sense of cosmic security was the experience, that I had no hope that a lifeline could ever be thrown to me. As I came through the field gate, a piece of paper was being blown across the yard. Instinctively, I followed it, across the lawn, out over the wall, across the road, and then, in a gust, it was gone, across the hedge. Standing there, watching it go, I felt that for the rest of my life I'd be following it because one day it would maybe blow back into the yard of a God and the house of a God I could believe in.

Meanwhile, this was the wild night, the night out of doors, in which King Lear went mad.

O nuncle, court holy-water in a dry house, is better than this rain-water out o' door. Good nuncle, in, ask thy daughter's blessing; here's a night pities neither wise men nor fools.

Godless night.

Night when the gods, in this case the planets, have kept to their caves.

Night when I was thirteen and three-quarters British miles deep in a universe that didn't have humanity in mind.

Night when, as it rolled over Ishmael, Saturn's grey chaos rolled over me:

When I stand among these mighty Leviathan skeletons, skulls, tusks, jaws, ribs and vertebrae, all characterized by partial resemblances to the existing breeds of sea-monsters; but at the same time bearing on the other hand similar affinities to the annihilated and antechronical Leviathans, their incalculable seniors; I am by a flood borne back to that wondrous period, ere time itself can be said to have begun; for time began with man. Here Saturn's grey chaos rolls over me, and I obtain dim, shuddering glimpses into those polar eternities; when wedged bastions of ice pressed hard upon what is now the Tropics; and in all the 25,000 miles of this world's circumference, not an inhabitable hand's breadth of land was visible. Then the whole world was the whale's; and king of creation, he left his wake along the present line of the Andes and the Himmalehs. Who can show a pedigree like Leviathan? Ahab's harpoon had shed older blood than the Pharaoh's. Methuseleh seems a schoolboy. I look round to shake hands with Shem. I am horror struck at this antemosaic, unsourced existence of the unspeakable terrors of the whale, which, having been before all time, must needs exist after all human ages are over.

Job's terrifying encounter with inwardness and outwardness continuing into the modern world, showing up all over again in Kepler, Pascal, Melville and Nietzsche.

In our century, for one reason or another, millions and millions of people have fallen out of their traditional story and that is serious because it is above all in a great story that we are housed. And if it is great, the story that houses us will house the stars. Will house our cows, our hens, our pigs, our horse, our ass. Will house Leviathan, will house Behemoth. Will house Tyger, will house Lamb.

The gulf in our yard will close when, emerging from ancient Near Eastern and modern cosmologies, we send season's greetings to brother sun and sister moon.

It is time, isn't it, that a new Moses led us in a new exodus – and exodus from a cosmology in which the ur-word is 'us-ruling-over-and-subduing-them' to a cosmology in which the ur-word is 'we'.

We won't, in that exodus, bring Psalm eight with us. Neither will we bring the second stasimon.

Better altogether would it be to bring the *mo-wei* and the *wu-wei* of Taoist cosmology. Or, amounting to the same thing, the lily of the field.

Jesus didn't need to destroy an old world in order that a new world might emerge. He needed only to destroy an old works-and-days cosmology in order that a new lily-of-the-field cosmology might arise in its place.

It wasn't the cosmos he fought. It was our inherited logos about it he fought.

Fighting the cosmos had come to an end in Job. After Job the lily of the field.

And this brings us back to the Navajo cradle:

> I have made a cradleboard for you, my child,
> May you grow to a great old age.
> Of the sun's rays I made the back,
> Of black clouds I have made the blanket,
> Of rainbow I have made the bow,
> Of sunbeams have I made the side-loops,

> Of lightnings have I made the facings,
> Of river mirrorings have I made the footboard,
> Of dawn have I made the covering,
> Of earth's welcome for you have I made the bed.

It brings us back to Uvavnuk's song:

> The great sea has set me in motion,
> Set me adrift,
> Moving me as a weed moves in the river.
> The arch of sky and mightiness of storms
> Have moved the spirit within me,
> Till I am carried away
> Trembling with joy.

Uvavnuk rocking the cradle of the new humanity. But there is of course for most people life after the cradle. And like seals needing to keep breathing-holes open in the icecap, we need to keep breathing-holes open in nature. We need to breathe transcendentally. We need sacraments. We need a temple.

The cradle, the song and, our temple giving it good shepherding shape, the mystical journey. The three stasima from which a culture might grow.

Catching sight of a dressed stone in the cathedral wall, I thought of Bulkington in *Moby-Dick*. No sooner had Bulkington come home from a voyage of three or four years in a whale ship, than he was back at sea again bound for the lonely latitudes and longitudes of the southern oceans where for thousands of leagues around there was no chiselled hearthstone.

Who, coming home from what vast voyage, will sit by our chiselled hearthstone and tell us the great story or, they having lived themselves in him, any fragments of it that he knows? A Narada reach of it. A Job or a Jonah reach of it. A Catherine of Genoa reach of it. A Teresa of Ávila reach of it. The reach of it that sufis call *fana*. The reach of it they call *baqa*.

The chiselled hearthstone, the cradle, the song, the story, the temple: it is time maybe that another Kadmus walked behind another cow.

St Kieran and Kadmus.

St Kieran in his cell. The saint and the cell about which this monastic city grew.

Kieran the new Kadmus. Kieran the Christian Kadmus.

Out of Asia, following a cow, Kadmus came. Where the cow would lie down, there he would build his city. The cow lay down by a dragon's lair. Giving life to the old disaster, Kadmus slew the dragon and built his city. A city of trouble and strife in its seven gates. Of war in its gates. A city polluted in its bedrooms by bad dragon smells, by bad dragon dreams. And Kadmus died and Greek civilization died not having learned that it isn't good, taking a sword to it, to lobotomize the earth or the psyche. The lobotomized earth breeds disasters. So does the lobotomized psyche.

Job and the God who spoke to him out of the whirlwind were wiser. Having seen Leviathan and Behemoth, neither Job nor his God reached for his sword. As between integration and repression, they chose the former. As between the sanctity of inclusion and integration and the sanctity of exclusion and repression they chose the former.

Jesus commanded St Peter to put up his sword. He in other words commanded all dragon-slaying heroes to put up their swords, and on the following day, on Good Friday, all the old slayings, all the old wounds we inflicted on all the old dragons – coming out of our collective depths that day, they came to the surface in Jesus. Jesus expiated them. He atoned for them. In mind and body, he paid the price.

No, Christ's wounds weren't spike wounds from without. They were dragon wounds from within. Wounds we had hoped to suppress and forget. But repression doesn't work.

It would be good if Christianity could catch up with Gethsemane and Good Friday.

It would be good if the West, religious and secular, could catch up with Gethsemane and Good Friday.

It would be good if, without coercion or conversion, humanity everywhere could catch up with Gethsemane and Good Friday. What was won for humanity, what was won for earth and universe, in Gethsemane and on Golgotha, isn't Christian property. Lucy is heir to it. So is the primrose. So is Sirius.

It was during the darkness of Good Friday that beings in other galaxies became aware of our existence and they were glad knowing that something that had happened elsewhere in the universe had happened now again.

It isn't technologically that we communicate with such beings. It is in spirit that we communicate with them. It is in *samadhi* that we communicate with them.

And there's something more: the piece of paper that was blown across a yard one night – still blowing in the wind, it will come again, through an igloo door maybe. Inscribed on it, front and back, will be the score of a great opening phrase and the score of a great closing phrase – of what? we will ask – and from the heath, his mind restored, King Lear will call out

TURTLE WAS GONE A LONG TIME

Of the great oratorio the universe is

Yes! There is no greater task humanity could set itself than to seek to catch up with Gethsemane and Golgotha. We must choose between Kadmus and Christ. Or, as someone who sat in the ruins of both cities might say, we must choose between Thebes and Clonmacnoise.

At the heart of Thebes there was a cave called the Kadmeia. Until Kadmus came and killed him, it was the dragon's den. At the heart of our city which shall it be? A Kadmeia or a Kieraneia, the den of a slain dragon or the cell of someone who, hearing Christ's command, has put up his dragon-slayer's sword.

Kadmeia or Kieraneia?
Kadmus or Kieran?

Hydra with one head or Hydra with nine heads?

The history of humanity in the West is the history of a people multiplying their problems, not solving them.

We find it so hard to learn the lesson Job learned so long ago.

Shema Israel
Hear, O Israel

Shema Europa
Hear O peoples of Europe

Hear the Book of Job

The Book of Job should be the first book of our Holy Book. The Book of Noah, the Book of Job, the Book of Daniel and the Song of Songs — these are neither an old nor a new testament, neither an old nor a new testimony. They are a perennial testimony. For as long as human beings remain human, they will give life and light. In them, relived in the passion narratives, our past is healed. With them, relived in the passion narratives, we can enter the future.

These, and not Psalm eight or the second stasimon.

Having these and the writings of the mystics we have a songline of Upanishads and Gitas.

How happy Aruni would be reading *The Mystical Theology*.
How happy Yajnavalkya would be reading *The Cloud of Unknowing*.
How happy Shandilya would be reading *The Sermons of Eckhart*.
How happy Maitreyi would be reading *The Mirror of Simple Souls*.
How happy Shvetaketu would be to read *The Ascent of Mount Carmel*.
How happy Radha would be to read *The Life of Teresa of Ávila*.

ANACONDA CANOE

How happy Uddalaka would be to read *The Sparkling Stone*.
How happy Nacitekas would be to read *The Dialogues of Boehme*.
How happy Raikva would be to read *The Poems of Hadewyjck*.
How happy they would all be to hear:

Heyly owe we to enioyen that God wonyth in our soule and mekil more heyly owe enioyen that our soule wonyth in God. Our soule is made to be God's wonyng place, and the wonyng place of the soule is God, which is onmade. And hey understondyng it is inwardly to sen and to knowen that God which is our maker wonyth in our soule; and an heyer understondying it is inwardly to sen and to knowen our soule, that is made, wonyth in God's substance; of which substance, God, we arn that we arn.

If it is Upanishads and Gitas we are looking for we needn't leave home.

I remembered a story Martin Halloran told me. It is a story about a man called Feshtus O'Malley from Oorid in Connemara. One night Feshtus dreamed that there was a great hoard of treasure buried beside O'Brien's Bridge in Limerick. Off Feshtus went the next day and three days later he was there. All morning long he walked up and down and in and out and back and forth, looking all the time for the treasure. A cobbler working in his house near the bridge saw the goings-on of Feshtus. In the end he came out and greeted him and asked him was it how he had lost something. No, Feshtus said, but 'tis how I dreamed four nights ago that great treasure is buried here. 'And what's your name?' the cobbler asked. 'My name is Feshtus O'Malley.' 'And you're from where?' 'From a place called Oorid in Connemara.' 'That's awful strange,' the cobbler said, 'because didn't I dream myself last night about you and your house, and what the dream told me was that under a flagstone inside your door there is more treasure than the Vikings, for all their raiding, ever laid their hungry hands on.' In less than three days Feshtus was home and sure enough there it was. All his life long, walking in and out through his own door he had been walking on top of it.

And there's the story of the man who despaired of the West. Going to the East he lived in a Zen monastery for years. In the airport coming home his teacher, who was a great master, gave him a present. In the plane waiting for take-off, the young man unwrapped the gift and to his great surprise and annoyance it was a copy, very beautifully bound, of the Bible.

The master telling him, find it in your own tradition.

The master telling him, walk your own songline.

The master telling him, you don't need to go to O'Brien's Bridge. It is under the flagstone inside your own door.

Since it is the mystical journey we are talking about, it isn't of course as simple as lifting a flagstone. Under the flagstone might be a labyrinth or under it might be very great treasure indeed, the writings of the Christian mystics, among them *The Dark Night of the Soul* and *The Ascent of Mount Carmel* by St John of the Cross. Reading these latter at random most people will soon know whether to drop the flagstone back down on top of them or to continue the quest.

If we continue, and if God is gracious, there will be nights when, like a saucepan of milk on a fire, we will come to the boil. Karmically, we will boil over. And there will be mornings when, boiled out of us while we slept, our room will be filled with moral pollution. If by chance we think of the witches in *Macbeth*, it will be clear to us now that the fog and filthy air they hover in is out of themselves. The vapours of their inner perversity of imagination and will have become their outer element.

Sometimes we will find ourselves thinking that just as there is a physical appendix so is here a karmic appendix. Filling up over innumerable lifetimes, incarnate and disincarnate, it is now ripe and, as soon as we walk in the fire, it bursts, and we are swamped, in our senses swamped, in our minds and imaginations swamped. It sometimes seems that in us there is nothing that isn't swamped:

Fifteen cubits upwards did the waters prevail; and the mountains were covered.

Out of ourselves our *Walpurgis Nacht*. And out of that *Walpurgis Nacht* we send the raven and the dove.

> Come back dove, come back as Paraclete.
> Come back raven, come back as Pentecost.

This is our purgatory, our passage into and through the purifying fire. And a chief source of anguish and suffering in that fire is our deeply felt inability to co-operate with it, for this isn't a dark fire or a wrathful fire or an averaging fire or a vindictive fire. For all its apparent savagery, it is a fire of love. The savagery we experience is the ferocity of our own resistance reflected back upon us.

Nights there will be when, sitting there, a person will think: I won't be here in the morning. Body and soul I will have evaporated. Even the vapours will be gone.

Now, having no way out is our only way.

This is our Gethsemane. Like Jesus, we are sore amazed. And it wouldn't surprise us if, looking in a mirror, we saw not ourselves but Coatlicue.

Nietzsche's discovery has rediscovered itself in us:

ANACONDA CANOE

I have discovered for myself that the old human and animal world, indeed the entire prehistory and past of all sentient being, works on, loves on, hates on, thinks on in me.

Silurian sea-floors at work in me.
Dinosauric life thinking in me.
Australopithecine life loving and hating in me.

Whether we ever heard of it or not, whether we ever set foot on it or not, we are now at the end, below, of Bright Angel Trail. This is *passio pura*, and any other response than total surrender to these divine operations in us and upon us will only add to our hurt.

Here, whoever is watching with us will need to tell us over and over and over again that the good-shepherding and grace that have brought us this far will bring us through.

Bright Angel Trail is a reach of the Christian songline and many indeed are they who, going down and coming up, were given the grace to participate in the unfinished symphony of Christ's passion and death and resurrection.

Any religion that cannot watch with Jesus in Gethsemane and on Golgotha has a lot of growing to do. Any religion that cannot watch with any one of us at the end below of Bright Angel Trail or on the Hill of the Koshaless Skull has a lot of growing to do.

Tenebrae is the ritual in which Christianity watches.

The reason for Tenebrae both as a phase of the mystical journey and as a ritual isn't far to seek. St John of the Cross is forthright in his estimation of our human condition:

Oh, miserable is the fortune of our life, which is lived in such great peril and wherein it is so difficult to find the truth! For that which is most clear and true is to us most dark and doubtful; wherefore, though it is the thing that is most needful for us, we flee from it. And that which gives the greatest light and satisfaction to our eyes we embrace and pursue, though it be the worst thing for us, and make us fall at every step. In what peril and fear does man live, since the very natural light of his eyes by which he has to guide himself is the first light that dazzles him and leads him astray on his road to God. And if he is to know with certainty by what road he travels, he must perforce keep his eyes closed and walk in darkness, that he may be secure from the enemies who inhabit his own house – that is, his senses and faculties.

In this interpretation of them, the candles of the Tenebrae harrow are our senses and faculties. It is only when all its candles are quenched that the Tenebrae harrow lights our way. The quenched Tenebrae harrow is in other words the ritual equivalent of the Koshaless Skull.

The harrow and the skull are a humanist's nightmare. Almost everything that a humanist of the Renaissance kind stands for is anulled by them.

In the quenched Tenebrae harrow we have moved from metaphysics to metanoesis, or as Buddhists in India might say, to *acittatva*, or as Buddhists in China might say, to *wu-hsin*.

Buddhists talk not only about *klesa-avarana*, the eclipse of ultimate reality by our passions. They talk also about *jneya-avarana*, the eclipse of ultimate reality that has its source in thinking, as if all we do when we think is project a snake into the rope, or in language more familiar to Europeans, what we do when we experience things and think about things is project the forms of our sensibility and the categories of our understanding onto the undifferentiated Divine One.

In more homely terms: conscious and unconscious, psyche is the blind not the window.

Or yet again: the light of the fully lighted harrow is a full eclipse.

A Copernican revolution in philosophy ought to issue in a Copernican revolution in religion.

A Copernican revolution in Christianity didn't have to wait for Kant. That revolution reached its '*consummatum est*' on Golgotha.

Jesus is the great Thales of the great Western tradition that runs through *Mystical Theology*, *The Cloud of Unknowing*, *The Dark Night of the Soul*, *The Ascent of Mount Carmel*, to choose but a few, all of which works have their ritual correlative in the nocturnes of Tenebrae.

Tenebrae is Christianity doing philosophy and, having the passage from *The Dark Night of the Soul* quoted above as its introit, it is surely the ritual in and through which Christianity, bringing the Evangel with it, can cross over into Evangelanta.

Tenebrae isn't, of course, Kant's philosophy in sacramental mode. And although vast philosophic illuminations flow from it, the Golgotha experience isn't primarily an exercise, however brilliant and profound, in philosophic speculation. There is nothing in Kant that corresponds to:

God felt, God tasted, and enjoyed, is indeed God but God with those gifts that flatter the human soul. God in darkness, privation, forsakenness and insensibility is so much God that it is as it were God bare and alone.

Kant's philosophy, however helpful in other respects it might be, isn't the dark night of the soul. As St John of the Cross so frequently implies, the dark night of the soul is a divine operation:

And it is clear that this dark contemplation is in these its beginnings painful likewise to the soul, for as this Divine infused contemplation has many excellences that are extremely good, and the soul that receives them, not being purged, has many miseries that are likewise extremely bad, hence it follows that, as two contraries cannot coexist in one subject – the soul – it must of necessity have pain and suffering, since it is the subject wherein these two contraries war against each other, working the one against the other, by reason of the purgation of the imperfections of the soul which comes to pass through this contemplation.

No. The nocturnes of Tenebrae aren't a *Critique of Pure Reason* much as this latter might help us to understand why it is we must walk in darkness.

On this road therefore to have our own faculties in darkness is to see the light.

And this is so because on our return to Divine Ground, the forms of our sensibility and the categories of our understanding are the blind not the window. To seek God with our senses and understanding is to seek God with that which eclipses God. And yet, in some strange way, it is in closing our eyes to the world that we open them to it. When we reopen them, emerging from Tenebrae, we see that the world itself isn't outside or beyond or below the Ground it continually emanates from. There is evening and morning a first day. A day altogether different from the biblical first day. In this first day there is no us and them. There is now in the world nothing that corresponds to the word 'it'. As Blake might have it, the 'it-world' is a delusion of Ulro. A rock that Gorgon sees as Ulro, an Australian aborigine sees as Uluru. Having said to be is to be perceived, Berkeley might, if only by way of challenge, have gone on to say, as the perceiver so the perceived.

Returning to the great first day we come forth into when we open our eyes on the far side of Tenebrae: not only is there now in the world nothing that corresponds to the word 'it', there is in it nothing that corresponds much to language generally.

It is time for the Buddha's flower sermon
It is time for direct beholding.

There is an egoless beholding. A beholding that isn't reducible to 'I see'. A beholding that isn't blinded by seeking eyesight.

There is a rare state of mind in which the head with all its senses and faculties is the blindspot. There is a rare state of mind that makes the head obsolete.

Paradise Regained, Christians might call it.

Pert Em Hru or Coming Forth by Day, ancient Egyptians called it.

Coming forth by day as ancient Egyptians emerging from the Duat experienced it.

Coming forth by day as Christians emerging not only from the Duat but also from Tenebrae experience it.

Ancient Egyptians performed a ceremony called Opening the Mouth on behalf of their deceased who, having died to this world, were now thought to be wayfarers into the immortal world. Ritually, in this ceremony, their senses and faculties were restored to these wayfarers. There are questions concerning this: was it the old senses and faculties, clay-shuttered all their lives, that were restored? Was the restoration premature? Did this restoration to them of their senses and faculties mean that these wayfarers didn't cross into Tenebrae?

At a climactic moment in the ancient Egyptian ceremony, an adze was ritually advanced towards the mouth of the deceased, now a mummy. So perhaps we should ask, which shall it be?

> The ritual adze
> or
> The ritual harrow
>
> Opening the mouth
> or
> Tenebrae

Given what passes for talk about the universe in Europe these days, there can be no doubt about our need for a restoration to us of our senses and faculties. To begin with, a restoration to us of our Pleistocene senses and faculties would be a marvel.

> Come White Buffalo Calf Woman, come.

Come and restore to us our ability to be alive in a living universe.

Come and restore to us our old intuitions of commonage consciousness.

Come and restore to us a sense and a knowledge of the earth as big medicine.

Come and restore to us a sense of things that will enable us to send morning and evening greetings to Brother Sun and Sister Moon.

We need the adze because, locked up as we are in civilization, we have died to the pristine, wide, wild world that Uvavnuk, a survivor from the Pleistocene, sings of in her song.

And we need the harrow because, as Pico tells us, there will always be those who, happy in the lot of no created thing, will desire to retrace their steps back into the solitary darkness of God and sooner or later this means the dark night of the senses and the soul, it means Tenebrae.

ANACONDA CANOE

On this road a day comes when, yes, we will ask the blackbird to shut up. But an altogether greater day comes when, both of them at work in our lives, harrow and adze aren't a contradiction, the one of the other.

Day when the blind doesn't blind the window. Day when blind and window are one divine beholding.

Paradise Regained, Christians call it.

Prematurely or otherwise, ancient Egyptians called it *Pert em hru*, and although doing not a little violence to it, maybe we could appropriate this so hopeful conception to our own desires and needs and translate it as

>Coming Forth into the Great World,
>World at all times great,
>World great by day, World great by night.

Imagine it, that perfect evening in the Dingle peninsula: after listening for a while to the sound of a stream coming down Sliabh an Fhiolair one man says to another:

Tá sé ag glaoch orainn isteach sa tsíoraíocht as a bhfuil sé féin ag teacht
It is calling us into the eternity out of which it is itself flowing.

We don't of course need to walk into that eternity. We are already in it, for what else is time but eternity living temporally?

Out of doors on a wild night in that same peninsula, however, a person might be inclined to suggest that time isn't only eternity living temporally, it is eternity living dangerously.

And nowhere more dangerously perhaps than in the mind of man.

Out of doors that wild night, King Lear didn't sing as Uvavnuk sings:

>The great sea has set me in motion,
>set me adrift,
>Moving me as a weed moves in the river.
>The arch of sky and mightiness of storms
>have moved the spirit within me,
>till I am carried away
>trembling with joy.

World in which Uvavnuk sings.

World of which, for two hours, Pascal had no awareness:

>*L'an de grace 1654*
>*Lundi, 23 Novembre, jour de saint Clément, pape et martyr et autres au martyrologe,*
>*Veille de saint Chrysogone, martyr, et autres,*

TURTLE WAS GONE A LONG TIME

Depuis environ dix heures et demie du soir jusques environ minuit et demie,
Feu.
Dieu d'Abraham, Dieu d'Isaac, Dieu de Jacob,
Non des philosophs et de savans.
Certitude. Certitude. Sertiment. Joie. Paix. (...)
Oubli du monde et de tout, hormis Dieu. (...)

Uvavnuk's song, Pascal's memorial: isn't the contradiction between them too glaring to be ignored, too deep to be reconciled? To someone seriously seeking home, isn't Uvavnuk's song a Siren's song?

Uvavnuk isn't Calypso, her world isn't a bower of bliss, yet surely, if we are ever to reach home, we must, most resolutely, sail away from her song and her world.

Experience of Silam Inua in blizzard and breaker isn't enough. It isn't surely the end of our faring? Indeed there is no reason to believe that it is either a necessary or an inevitable stage on the way. And yet when, at the end of a stupendous journey, we finally reach home, how surprised we will be to discover that we hadn't in fact ever left home.

Within our eternal home it was that we were homesick.

It was for where we already were that we yearned.

To be in the world is not to be outside of God.

Nothing that exists or doesn't exist is outside of God.

God as Ground grounds all that exists.

Divine Ground isn't only under our feet. It is everywhere in us. It is everywhere in everything.

Even if the world is a dream, we shouldn't on that account despise it, because God is in the dream.

Even if the world is a veil, we shouldn't on that account despise it, because God is in the veil that veils him from us.

Walking out of history and culture into nature, Emily Brontë asks and answers her own question:

> What have those lonely mountains worth revealing?
> More glory and more grief than I can tell:
> The earth that wakes one human heart to feeling
> Can centre both the worlds of Heaven and Hell.

But maybe we should allow her her full say:

> Often rebuked, yet always back returning
> To those first feelings that were born with me,
> And leaving busy chase of wealth and learning
> For idle dreams of things that cannot be:

ANACONDA CANOE

Today, I will not seek the shadowy region,
    Its unsustaining vastness waxes drear;
And visions rising, legion after legion,
    Bring the unreal world too strangely near.

I'll walk, but not in old heroic traces,
    And not in paths of high morality,
And not among the half-distinguished faces,
    The clouded forms of long-past history.

I'll walk where my own nature would be leading –
    It vexes me to choose another guide –
Where the grey flocks in ferny glens are feeding,
    Where the wild wind blows on the mountainside.

What have those lonely mountains worth revealing?
    More glory and more grief than I can tell:
The earth that wakes one human heart to feeling
    Can centre both the worlds of Heaven and Hell.

How good it is and how thrilling it is to walk out of culture into nature. How good it is, immersing your head in a stream, to baptize yourself out of culture into nature. How good it is to begin again and live a life of pure sensation. As though the individual sensations were individual *tesserae,* we gradually build up an inner pristine picture of the outer pristine world. In none of its *tesserae* is our picture distorted by language or culture.

One day we are sitting on a rock downstream from a cascade. Closing our eyes, we begin to get to know it in pure hearing. Every tumble and plunge and swirl and gurgle and gasp of it we get to know. All its little side runs and all its pool boilings we come to know. Gradually, however, we shift our attention from them to the pure experience of hearing. It isn't them we are now listening to. It is hearing itself we are listening to. We are getting to know not things heard but hearing. How strange an experience it is, the experience of hearing. Opening our eyes, we begin the process all over again, only this time our purpose is to get to know the cascade in pure visual experience. Again we shift our attention from the thing seen to seeing itself. In the end it is seeing we are seeing. How unaccountably strange seeing is. How unaccountably strange hearing is. And the world as we experience it in seeing and the world as we experience it in hearing are so different one from another that it is only by some lazy, innate habit of mind that we put them together and call them one.

What has now happened in this ferny glen is not without possible vast consequences. Consequences that flow from a simple shifting of attention from the perceived to the perceiver. Soon we might conclude that the sensations we experience awake have as little claim to be reflective of objective reality as the sensations we experience asleep. The metaphor which assimilates the relationship between mind and object to the relationship between mirror and object is beginning to look like a bad habit. And at this point perhaps the philosophy of Kant will begin to make sense. Or it could be that we are on the way into frightful Good Friday desolation. Desolation in our Temple. In our Academy desolation. As the sole surviving wall of Solomon's Temple is a wailing wall so also now is the sole surviving wall of Plato's Academy a wailing wall. Going to it, we take down the mirror and in its place we hang up the new totem:

> A ropesnake

We have walked ourselves into trouble. And it won't come as any big surprise to us if we now baptize ourselves back into culture, or even back into religion. Desperately now, we need the wisdom of humanity. Glad indeed are we now that we are heirs to the teachings of Aruni, the Buddha, Lao Tzu, Al Junayd, Eckhart, Marguerite Porete, St John of the Cross and Teresa of Ávila, to name but a few. How precious an inheritance these teachings are. And how good it is, when we run into trouble out in nature, that there is a culture we can walk back into.

And, now that Kant has helped to dis-illusion us as Vishnu dis-illusioned Narada, how good it is that we have a ritual adequate to our crisis. How good it is that we have Tenebrae.

How good it is that St John of the Cross wrote a book called *The Dark Night of the Soul* before Kant wrote a book called *Critique of Pure Reason*. The remedy preceded the trauma.

> I'll walk, but not in old heroic traces,
>   And not in paths of high morality,
> And not among the half-distinguished faces,
>   The clouded forms of long-past history.
>
> I'll walk where my own nature would be leading –
>   It vexes me to choose another guide –
> Where the grey flocks in ferny glens are feeding,
>   Where the wild wind blows on the mountainside.

How like a Romantic manifesto it reads.

And yet, for all its loveliness, Coleridge, who had read Kant, the *alleszermalmender*, might well have written his 'Ode on Dejection' in that ferny glen.

Like it or not we are dis-illusioned.

The dis-illusioning didn't begin with Kant, however. Listen to Newton:

If at any time I speak of light and rays as coloured or endued with colours, I would be understood to speak, not philosophically and properly, but grossly and accordingly to such conceptions as vulgar people in seeing all these experiments would be apt to frame. For the rays, to speak properly, are not coloured. In them there is nothing else than a certain power and imagination to stir up a sensation of this or that colour. For as sound in a bell or musical string, or other sounding body, is nothing but the trembling motion, and in the air nothing but that motion propagated from the object, and in the sensorium it is a sense of that motion under the form of sound, so colours in the object are nothing but a disposition to reflect this or that sort of rays more copiously than the rest; in the rays they are nothing but their dispositions to propagate this or that motion into the sensorium, and in the sensorium they are sensations of those motions under the form of colour.

A couple of centuries down the road from this, Arnold will listen to the grating roar of pebbles on Dover Beach and, hearing a kind of godlessness in it, he will turn away, seeking meaning and consolation in his relationship with his wife.

The ferny glen is beginning to look like the Kedron Valley. And the cloud coming over the moors might not be a raincloud. The Good Friday Cloud, the cloud of unknowing, has been a long time coming.

It is therefore likely that it is on the far side of Tenebrae that we will once again hear Uvavnuk singing. Likely also it is that, hearing her song, a European father and mother will make for their child a Navajo cradle.

And yet, having passed through Tenebrae with us, neither the song nor the cradle will much resemble what they previously were. In them, for one thing, divine transcendence will be given as much recognition as divine immanence.

To quote Emily again:

> Though earth and man were gone,
>   And suns and universes ceased to be,
> And Thou were left alone,
>   Every existence would exist in Thee.

Indeed, enduring a storm too many in any one year, Uvavnuk might find more solace in the first and last verses of Emily's song than she would in her own:

> No coward soul is mine,
>   No trembler in the world's storm-troubled sphere;

TURTLE WAS GONE A LONG TIME

> I see heaven's glories shine,
>   And faith shines equal, arming me from fear.
>
>   * * *
>
> There is not room for Death,
>   Nor atom that his might could render void;
> Thou – Thou art Being and Breath,
>   And what Thou art may never be destroyed.

Our song has become a Gita.

We can sing it before, between and after the geological chapters. Going out into the yard on a wild night we can sing it antiphonally to Kepler's horror, to Pascal's terror and to Ishmael's canticle from the belly of Zeuglodon.

We might even be ready for a theophany in which, right here before our eyes, God reveals himself, manifests himself, as Vishvarupa.

And yet it is possible, even while acknowledging the divinity of immanence, to despair of immanence. Listen to D.H. Lawrence:

> I lift up mine eyes unto the hills
> and there they are, but no strength comes from
> them to me.
>
> Only from darkness
> and ceasing to see
> strength comes.

I sometimes imagine it:

> Emily, sea-racked like the Ancient Mariner,
> coming home from her romantic manifesto.
> Emily, sea-racked like the Ancient Mariner,
> coming home from the ferny glen.

Emily coming home and, Saturn's grey chaos having rolled over him, Ishmael coming home.

'All the poems of poets who have entered their poethood are poems of homecoming,' Heidegger says.

It sounds good.

But a fog comes down in the ferny glen and the question is, how about Sylvia? Did Sylvia come home?

> The hills step off into whiteness.
> People or stars
> Regard me sadly, I disappoint them.

ANACONDA CANOE

> The train leaves a line of breath.
> O slow
> Horse the colour of rust,
>
> Hooves, dolorous bells –
> All morning the
> Morning has been blackening,
>
> A flower left out.
> My bones hold a stillness, the far
> Fields melt my heart.
>
> They threaten
> To let me through to a heaven
> Starless and fatherless, a dark water.

All of this, even though, unlike Ahab, Sylvia didn't of set purpose strike through the mask, didn't of set purpose launch a diabolically baptized lance at the world-illusion. And yet, less luridly loud than Christ's, there it is, our modern Good-Friday cry of dereliction. And it echoes, echoes, echoes. Like the last lap of the dark water, it echoes back to us off our wailing wall. Wall we built against the final dark. Wall we built from the *res-extensa* shingles of our *res-extensa* world.

And the *Pequod* is bare-poled.

And Ahab is old:

But do I look very old, so very, very old, Starbuck? I feel deadly faint, bowed, and humped, as though I were Adam, staggering beneath the piled centuries since paradise.

It was beneath him that Jesus staggered downwards one night into the final karmic depth and staggered upwards the next day into the final derelict height, and now Bright Angel Trail has taken over from the wake of the *Pequod,* and where our wailing wall stood, there now, stands a Terebrae harrow:

> Harrow of lighted candles
> Harrow of lighted koshas
>
> Harrow of quenched candles
> Harrow of quenched koshas
>
> When it is quenched we sing:
>
> *Oh noche, que guiaste,*
> *Oh noche amable mas que el alborada.*

> Oh guiding night
> Oh night more lovely than the dawn.

The Tenebrae harrow means nothing less than letting the Triduum Sacrum happen to us as it happened to Jesus.

There are Zen Buddhists who say that the mystical journey falls into three stages which, in a lovely formula, they describe as: first there is a mountain, then there is no mountain, then again there is a mountain. The stage when there is no mountain they call sunyata or emptiness. Speaking to Chariputra about *sunyata* the Buddha says:

Tasmac, Chariputra, sunyatayam na rupam na vedana na samjna na samskarah, na vijananam.

Therefore, O Chariputra, in emptiness is neither form nor feeling, nor perception, nor karmic formations nor thinking.

It sounds like something the Golgotha skull might say. Except, most emphatically, it isn't. What the Golgotha skull has to say is wholly positive. As positive as the Chandogya Upanishad when it says:

Yatra na anyat pasyati, na anyat srinoti, na anyad vijanati, sa bhuma.

Where nothing else is seen, nothing else is heard, nothing else is thought about, there's the Fullness.

And we can say of that Fullness what the Mandukya Upanishad says of Turiya: it is *shantam, shivam, advaitam* – it is utterly tranquil, peaceful-blissful, beyond duality.

A Christian, however, can only be happy when God is directly acknowledged, as he is in Fénelon's great statement:

> God in darkness, privation, forsakenness and insensibility
> is so much God that it is, as it were, God bore and alone.

For all its terribleness, with or without a crucifixion, Golgotha is Good News. And it isn't Good News because it will shortly be followed by Easter. In and of itself Golgotha Good News is altogether more stupendous than Easter Good News as we have traditionally understood it.

Calvary is the place of the crucifixion, the place of the atonement. Golgotha is the place of our coming home to Divine Ground.

The Last Supper and Calvary gave us the mass. Golgotha gave us Tenebrae.

A religion that is heir to the Gethsemane experience and the Golgotha experience can, quite literally, take over from nature and guide it through its final evolutionary transitions.

The end of evolution is to cross back into ground that doesn't evolve, and that took place on Golgotha:

Comes then the soul into the unclouded light of God. It is transported so far from creaturehood into nothingness that of its own powers it can never return to it faculties or its former creaturehood. Once there, God shelters the soul's nothingness with his uncreated essence, safeguarding its creaturely existence. The soul has dared to become nothing and cannot pass from its own being into nothingness and back again, losing its own identity in the process, except God safeguarded it.

Gethsemane and Golgotha: two vast steps for Jesus, two vast steps in the evolution of the living earth.

On the spot where the Buddha won enlightenment there is a temple called Buddh Gaya.

When we look at the earth with enlightened eyes what else can we call it but Buddh Gaia?

That does not of course mean that we can now take a hammer and chisel to Coatlicue, the Earth Mother as Aztecs imagined her, and re-sculpt her as a Buddha in *samadhi*.

It wasn't by pretending that Behemoth doesn't exist, nor was it by pretending that bad dreams don't exist, that Job found peace.

It wasn't by avoiding Bright Angel Trail that Jesus came so gloriously through his Triduum Sacrum.

Jesus did come through and that means we can now look at the earth with a hope as deep and as real, if sometimes also as sore amazed, as Gethsemane.

Everything Job saw notwithstanding, it cannot but be good for the earth to imagine it as Buddh Gaia.

Much easier it would be of course to imagine it as Buddh Gaia in the ferny glen than in the Grand Canyon.

Emily with the grey flocks in the ferny glen.

Jesus geological ages below the flight of Archaeornis in the Grand Canyon.

Emily in her ferny glen. The New England colt in his peaceful valley in Vermont:

Tell me why this strong New England colt, foaled in some peaceful valley of Vermont, far removed from all beasts of prey – why is it that upon the sunniest day, if you but shake a fresh buffalo robe behind him, so that he cannot even see it, but only smells its wild animal muskiness – why will he start, snort, and with bursting eyes paw the ground in phrensies of affright? There is no remembrance in him of any gorings of wild creatures in his green northern home, so that the strange muskiness he smells cannot recall to him anything associated with the experience of former perils; for what knows he, this New England colt, of the black bisons of distant Oregon?

What a day it was the day Melville shook that fresh buffalo pelt behind Rousseau's Noble Savage.

What a day it was the day Melville shook that fresh buffalo pelt behind Uvavnuk in the tundra, behind Emily in the ferny glen.

What a day it was the day Melville shook that fresh buffalo pelt behind recent European history, behind our attempts to rationally engineer a secular heaven on a secular earth.

Shelley of course smelt nothing of it in his winnowing, wild west wind, wind that would winnow everything except Promethean humanism out of human affairs.

Emily smelt little or nothing of it in her ferny glen. Had she in fact smelt something more than an evanescent whiff of it, that pastoral Yorkshire glen would have yawned Grand-Canyon-deep about her and beneath her, and there was then a chance that her Romantic manifesto might have given way to the Passion Narratives:

> I'll walk, but not in old heroic traces,
>   And not in paths of high morality,
> And not among the half-distinguished faces,
>   The clouded forms of long-past history.
>
> I'll walk where my own nature would be leading –
>   It vexes me to choose another guide –
> Where the grey flocks in ferny glens are feeding
>   Where the wild wind blows on the mountainside.
> What have those lonely mountains worth revealing?
>   More glory and more grief than I can tell:
> The earth that wakes one human heart to feeling
>   Can centre both the worlds of Heaven and Hell.

From that to this:

Then cometh Jesus with them unto a place called Gethsemane, and saith unto the disciples, Sit ye here while I go and pray yonder. And he took with him Peter and the two sons of Zebedee and began to be sorrowful and very heavy. Then saith he unto them, My soul is exceeding sorrowful, even unto death: tarry ye here, and watch with me. And he went a little further, and fell on his face, and prayed, saying, O my Father, if it be possible, let this cup pass from me: nevertheless not as I will, but as thou wilt. And he cometh unto the disciples, and findeth them asleep, and saith unto Peter, What, could ye not watch with me one hour? Watch and pray, that ye enter not into temptation: the spirit indeed is willing, but the flesh is weak. He went away again the second time, and prayed, saying, O my Father, if this cup may not pass away from me, except I drink it, thy will be done. And he came and found them asleep again: for their eyes were heavy. And he left them, and went away again, and prayed the third time, saying the same words. Then cometh he to his disciples, and saith unto them, Sleep on now, and take your rest: behold the hour is at hand ...

From the glen to Gethsemane.

Songs of the songline between the glen and Gethsemane:

In man is all whatsoever the sun shines upon or heaven contains, as is also hell and all the deeps.

> ... Not Chaos, not
> The darkest pit of lowest Erebus,
> Nor aught of blinder vacancy, scooped out
> By help of dreams – can breed such fear and awe
> As fall upon us often when we look
> Into our Minds, into the Mind of Man.

> O the mind, mind has mountains; cliffs of fall
> Frightful, sheer, no-man-fathomed. Hold them cheap
> May who ne'er hung there.

> The mind of man is capable of anything – because everything is in it, all the past as well as all the future.

The buffalo pelt. In a moment of Rousseauistic optimism, we believed we could obliterate both it and its smell by writing our Rights of Man on it, yet there it is now, the mainsail, the only sail, of our *Polla ta deina* Voyage, and filled as it is with Shelley's wild west wind, it is after all to Utopia, to no place, that it is taking us.

The voyage of *Pequod* culture.

Time to jump ship, even if for the moment the only shelter in sight is the foundered nave of the foundered monastery of Clonmacnoise.

Not that Christianity has foundered. It is only the ark of ancient cosmologies, theologies, philosophies, mythologies and rituals it housed itself in that has foundered. The Triduum Sacrum hasn't foundered and, unlike the hermit crab, it doesn't need to scurry about the shore of Turiya-Tehom taking refuge in the first half-suitable cosmology or theology it comes upon. Galileo can look through his telescope, Leuwenhoek can look through his microscope, Darwin can board the *Beagle,* Einstein can elaborate his formula, none of this either negatively or positively affects the Triduum Sacrum, it being independent of culture and history, it being independent even of biblical culture and history, of Christian culture and history. But eye hasn't yet seen or ear heard the splendours of history and culture that can, and very likely will, continue to flow from it.

Standing in the ruined nave, I remembered some of the old Gregorian dignities of Tenebrae, coming as they do to a terrible climax in its Good Friday nocturnes:

> *Astiterunt reges terrae, et principes convenerunt in unum, adversus Dominum, et adversus Christum ejus.*
>
> *Deus, Deus meus, respice in me: quare me dereliquisti?*
>
> *Anxiatus est in me spiritus meus, in me turbatum est cor meum.*
>
> *Ecce lignam crucis in quo salus mundi pependit.*

In Greece, an ancient tradition had it that the sufferings of Dionysus, and they alone, were the subject-matter of the first staged tragedies. Dionysus himself was the only character on stage.

In Athens, in classical times, it was during the Dionysia, the great festival in honour of Dionysus, that new plays were shown. It was as if everyone who participated in the sufferings of Antigone participated sacramentally in the sufferings of Dionysus.

As Athenians had their Dionysia so, during Holy Week, do Christians have what we might call their Christysia. They in other words have Tenebrae, a ritual reliving of Christ's passion and death.

From St John's Gospel comes one of the Good Friday readings:

In illo tempore: Egressus est Jesus cum discipulis suis trans torrentem Cedron ...

A religion that incorporates those three words, *trans torrentem Cedron*, or rather a religion that incorporates the realities they indicate, will graciously create its own culture, a culture of glories and splendours not yet imaginable. It is only when we see them that we will imagine them, but then only barely.

And it could be that Vishvakarman, his tool bag slung over his shoulder, is already walking our roads, waiting for the morning when we are ready. The sow and her *bonavs* are his way of saying, I'm in the world. Dare we imagine it? The sow and her *bonavs* are his way of saying that the impulse from below will, when it is in the grain of things, evoke a corresponding impulse from above.

Trans torrentem Cedron.

Trans torrentem culture.

Trans torrentem religion.

ANACONDA CANOE

Trans torrentem Christianity crosses the Kedron in both directions, into the past and into the future. It doesn't have a final solution for the past in the way that Milton has in his 'Hymn on the Morning of Christ's Nativity'. In this poem, he has loaded up his *nacht-und-nebel* train with all the divinities of the ancient world, he has loaded it with all their mythologies, rituals and oracles and sent them to an infernal Auschwitz. Among them is Osiris:

> Nor is Osiris seen
> In Memphis Grove, or Green,
>   Trampling the unshowr'd Grasse with lowings loud:
> Nor can he be at rest
> Within his sacred chest,
>   Naught but profoundest Hell can be his shroud;
> In vain with Timbrel'd Anthems dark
> The sable-stole'd Sorcerers bear his worshipt Ark.
>
> He feels from Juda's land
> The dreaded Infant's hand,
>   The rayes of Bethlehem blind his dusky eyn;
> Nor all the gods beside,
> Longer dare abide,
>   Not Typhon huge ending in snaky twine:
> Our Babe to shew his Godhead true,
> Can in his swadling bands controul the damned crew.
>
> So when the Sun in bed,
> Curtained with cloudy red,
>   Pillows his chin upon an Orient wave,
> The flocking shadows pale,
> Troop to th'infernall jail,
>   Each fetter'd Ghost slips to his severall grave,
> And the yellow-skirted Fayes
> Fly after Night-steeds, leaving their Moon-lov'd maze.

To which Blake might well retort:

> The Vision of Christ that thou dost see
> Is my Vision's greatest enemy.

It used to be believed that Jesus harrowed hell. And we shouldn't maybe set any limits to that harrowing. We shouldn't go down into hell and say to Jesus, thus far shalt thou harrow and no farther.

And anyway, it is time perhaps to reformulate the belief: Jesus crossed the Kedron and in him, he consenting, the hell in us all was harrowed.

This being so, it is less likely that we will visit our hell upon others, or make life a hell-upon-earth for others.

Who knows! Maybe one day we won't feel a need, as Milton did, to put a *malleus maleficarum* in the Infant's hand.

A good thing it would be too if, setting foot on Bright Angel Trail, our Rousseauistic optimism were to give way to Christian faith which, coming to us as it does from the floor of the Grand Canyon, is altogether more hopeful.

Odd though it might seem to say so, it is Christ in Gethsemane who has made the Navajo cradle possible for us. It is Christ in Gethsemane who enables St Patrick to believe that the floor of the ocean will protect him.

In the Book of Job is the promise:

For thou shalt be in league with the stones of the field and the beasts of the field shall be at peace with thee.

The Book of Job is, among other things, our way back into the shamanic world. Even in its terrors, the earth is big medicine. Imagine it:

> Job, our medicine man, sitting in a Blue Thunder Tipi.

Imagine him:

> A Christian evangelist whose symbol is archaeornis.

Imagine him:

> A Saint Francis who, singing his song, invites us to choose between
> Herakles and his club,
> Orpheus and his lyre.

So which will it be, John, the lyre or the club, which will you place in the hand of the Christ child? Christ playing the lyre in the Palaeozoic.

Lyre with which he harrows our inner phylogenetic hell, the hell of superseded life that Lawrence talks about:

The abyss, like the underworld, is full of malefic powers injurious to man. For the abyss, like the underworld, represents the superseded powers of creation.

The old nature of man must yield and give way to a new nature. In yielding, it passes away down into Hades, and there lives on, undying and malefic, superseded, yet malevolent-potent in the underworld. This very profound truth was embodied in all the old religions and lies at the root of the worship of the underworld powers. The worship of the underworld powers, the *chthonioi*, was perhaps the very basis of the most ancient Greek religion. When man has neither the strength to subdue his underworld powers which are really the ancient powers of his old superseded self; nor the wit to placate them with sacrifice or the burnt holocaust; then they come back at him, and destroy him again. Hence every new conquest of life means a 'harrowing of hell'.

If only Nietzsche had put down the hammer he philosophized with, if only, putting down his club, he picked up the lyre, he might have survived his discovery:

I have discovered for myself that the old human and animal world, indeed the entire prehistory and past of all sentient being, works on, loves on, hates on, thinks on in me.

Oddly enough, Milton hasn't only chosen Herakles and his club, he has, almost ecstatically, chosen Orpheus and his lyre:

> Ring out ye Crystall sphears,
> Once bless our human ears,
>   (If ye have power to touch our senses so)
> And let your silver chime
> Move in melodious time;
>   And let the Base of Heav'ns deep Organ blow
> And with your ninefold harmony
> Make up full consort to th'Angelike harmony.
>
> For if such holy song
> Enwrap our fancy long,
>   Time will run back, and fetch the age of gold,
> And speckl'd vanity
> Will sicken soon and die,
>   And leprous sin will melt from earthly mould,
> And Hell it self will pass away,
>   And leave her dolorous mansions to the peering day.

Somehow preserved in the stones of this old nave at Clonmacnoise, I imagined I could hear, if only as echo, the great Easter *introit:*

Resurrexi, et adhuc tecum sum, alleluia; posuisti super me manum tuam, alleluia; mirabilis facta est scientia tua, alleluia, alleluia.

Although I was now ready to go down into St Kieran's cell I held back, waiting until some visitors who were in it would go. When one of them, an elaborately confident young man, launched into a detailed history of the place, I thought to myself, this is going to take longer than I at first anticipated, so I sat down.

Below me, beyond the outer, surrounding wall, the Shannon was a great blue snake, bent and bent and bent again, in the reedy, green world of the callows. It could, I thought, be Jarapiri, the great Dreamtime snake.

Singing it into myself, sitting there, I sang the only fragment of his songline that I knew:

> Jarapiri's ribs move him along
> He leaves a meandering track
> Jarapiri's ribs move him along
> He leaves a meandering track.

I imagined it: Anaconda Canoe ascending the Shannon when the Shannon itself was a primordial river.

The Shannon and the Congo.

Speaking through Marlow in *Heart of Darkness,* Conrad tells us about his fascination with the Congo:

Now when I was a little chap I had a passion for maps. I would look for hours at South America or Africa or Australia, and lose myself in the glories of exploration. At that time there were many blank spaces on the earth, and when I saw one that looked particularly inviting on a map (but they all look that) I would put my finger on it and say, When I grow up I will go there. The North Pole was one of those places, I remember. Well, I haven't been there yet, and shall not try now. The glamour's off. Other places were scattered about the Equator, and in every sort of latitude all over the two hemispheres. I haven't been to some of them, and ... well, we won't talk about that. But there was one yet – the biggest, the most blank, so to speak – that I had a hankering after.

True, by this time it was not a blank space any more. It had got filled since my boyhood with rivers and lakes and names. It had ceased to be a blank space of delightful mystery – a white patch for a boy to dream gloriously over. It had become a place of darkness. But there was in it one river especially, a mighty big river, that you could see on the map, resembling an immense snake uncoiled, with its head in the sea, its body at rest curving afar over a vast country, and its tail lost in the depths of the land.

When he came to realize his dream of course, it wasn't the glorious adventure he imagined it would be:

Going up that river was like travelling back to the earliest beginnings of the world, when vegetation rioted on earth and the big trees were kings. An empty stream, a great silence, an impenetrable forest. The air was warm, thick, heavy, sluggish. There was no joy in the brilliance of sunshine. The long stretches of waterway ran on, deserted, into the gloom of overshadowing distances. On silvery sandbanks hippos and alligators sunned themselves side by side ...

Nietzsche has been here.

And Job also, he has been here. Inwardly and outwardly, Job's songline carried him all the way back to Lucy's savannah. It was as though the Vermont colt woke up one morning in distant Oregon.

And like no one before him or after him Jesus has been here. The primordial river he ascended brought him into canyon country.

In Job, Jonah and Jesus our Congo is our songline, and it didn't lead to Kurtz.

... How can you imagine what particular region of the first ages a man's untrammelled feet may take him into by way of solitude.

Living, to begin with in solitude, here in this clearing, here in this *cluain,* did Kieran encounter the primeval in himself?

Of course you may be too much of a fool to go wrong – too dull even to know you are being assaulted by the powers of darkness – Or you may be such a thunderingly exalted creature as to be altogether deaf and blind to anything but heavenly sights and sounds. Then the earth for you is only a standing place – and whether to be like this is your loss or gain I won't pretend to say. But most of us are neither one nor the other. The earth for us is a place to live in, where we must put up with sights, with sounds, with smells, too, by jove – breathe dead hippo so to speak, and not be contaminated.

St Kieran and Kurtz.

St Kieran's *cluain.* Kurtz's clearing.

Likely it is that St Kieran lived in his cell much as Eo Fis lived in Linn Feic. He lived within the protections of the Celtic-Christian Dreamtime.

Time when, returning to convert them to Christianity, St Patrick walked inland along the Boyne. It was within a couple of days of the great fire ceremony at Tara, seat of Laoghaire, the high king. This fire Laoghaire himself would light and, until he had done so, no other fire must be lighted on any other hill-top, no matter how sacred. It being Easter-tide, St Patrick, in direct provocation and challenge, lit a paschal fire not far away on the Hill of Slane. Outraged, Laoghaire and his druids and his warriors rushed to the scene. Intending to kill Patrick and his companions, they drew their swords but instantly there was an earthquake, darkness fell upon them and in the confusion that followed it was among and against themselves that they fought. Discomfited, but still intent on murder, Laoghaire invited Patrick to come and share with him his royal hospitality at Tara. Suspecting treachery, St. Patrick blessed his eight companions, one of them a boy, and by the power of his praying, he transformed both himself and his them into deer, the boy into a fawn. Minutes later they ghosted past the king and his druids and vanished into the wilderness.

In an alternative interpretation of the incident, Patrick is a great mayin, a great master of illusion, an inducer of illusion in others. In this case he so alters Laoghaire's perceptions that he sees nine deer and a fawn where in his normal state of mind he would see nine men and a boy.

Either way we are in the presence of powers which, the Inuit say, nature was instinct with in the beginning:

> In the very earliest time
> when both people and animals lived on earth
> a person could become an animal if he wanted to
> and an animal could become a human being.
> Sometimes they were people
> and sometimes animals
> and there was no difference.
> All spoke the same language.
> The human mind had mysterious powers.
> A word spoken by chance
> might have strange consequences.
> It would suddenly come alive
> and what people wanted to happen could happen –
> all you had to do was say it.
> Nobody can explain this.
> That's the way it was.

And that's how it still is. At a deeper level of earth and psyche than we normally choose to live from, or better, in a more open mood of earth and psyche than we are generally willing to cross into, that's how it still is. And if the lore about him is true, then we cannot but conclude that, irrespective of his actual historical time and place, St Patrick continues to live in the very earliest time.

Time when time itself wasn't yet temporal.
Time when what people wanted to happen could happen –
All you had to do was say it.

Time when, with his God's wand, Aaron could open a path through the sea.

Time when, the world on his side, Merlin could move Stonehenge from Ireland to Britain.

Time when, the world on his side, the Goban Saor would build a monastery between midnight and morning.

Time when every linn was Linn Feic, when every glen was Glen Cush.

Time when even the most ordinary journey could become an *eachtra*, when even the most ordinary voyage could become an *imram*.

Time when mind hadn't pooled into private minds.

ANACONDA CANOE

Time when mind had mysterious powers.
Time when words spoken by chance could have strange consequences.
Time when incantations worked, when spells worked, when prayers worked.
St Patrick was given to praying a great prayer called the Deer's Cry. Praying it, he was doing what St Patrick instructed his converts to do:

Put on the whole armour of God, that ye may be able to stand against the wiles of the devil. For we wrestle not against flesh and blood, but against principalities and powers, against the rulers of the darkness of this world, against spiritual wickedness in high *places*.

In the Deer's Cry, St Patrick invokes and puts on the protection of the Trinity, Christ and the angels. In it, astonishingly, he invokes and puts on the protection of things natural:

>*Atomriug inidiu*
>*niurt nimhe*
>*soilse grene*
>*etrochtae esci*
>*ane thened*
>*dene lochet*
>*luathe gaethe*
>*fudomnae maro*
>*tairismige thalman*
>*cobsaide ailech*
>
>I dress myself today in
>the strength of the heavens
>the light of the sun
>the clarity of water
>the vehemence of fire
>the swiftness of lightning
>the speed of wind
>the stability of the earth
>the endurance of rock

The Deer Cry and the Navajo cradle:

>I have made a cradleboard for you, my child,
>May you grow to a great old age.
>Of the sun's rays I made the back,
>Of black clouds I have made the blanket,
>Of rainbow I have made the bow,
>Of sunbeams I have made the side-loops,

> Of lightning I have made the lacings,
> Of river mirrorings I have made the footboard,
> Of dawn I have made the covering,
> Of earth's welcome for you I have made the bed.

The Deer's Cry, the cradle and the canoe: evolution is with them in a way that it isn't with Sputnik. It is with the Mesektet boat of ancient Egyptians in a way that it isn't with Mir.

St Patrick and Kurtz.

The Boyne and the Congo.

For Muirchu, who in the seventh century wrote a life of St Patrick, the Boyne was a kind of Congo, and the great Eosphoros, the great bringer of light, followed its course into the heart of heathen darkness:

> While these events were taking place in the regions already mentioned, there was reigning at Tara, which was the capital of the Irish, a great king, fierce and pagan, an emperor of barbarians, whose name was Loighuire son of Niall. He belonged to the lineage that held the kingship of almost all of this island. He had druids and learned men, soothsayers and enchanters and inventors of all the black arts who by the practice of heathenism and idolatry were able to know and foresee all things in advance ....
>
> Now it happened that the heathen that very year were holding a ceremony with many spells and conjurings and other idolatries. The kings, governers, leaders, princes and nobility of the nation gathered. And as Nebuchadnezzar was wont to do, Loighuire had summoned the druids, magicians, soothsayers, clairvoyants and teachers of every art and skill to assemble at Tara, a veritable Babylon. Knowing the threat this Christian missioner posed, they planned to take action.

Muirchu and Marlow.

Patrick and Kurtz.

The Boyne and the Congo.

Clearly, it was Muirchu's view of him that Patrick was a man who had tackled a darkness. And for this, as Marlow would remind us, principles won't do. In order not to succumb, as Kurtz succumbed, Patrick needed to be dressed in the whole armour of God. Much as ancient Egyptians needed their coffin texts, he needed his Deer Cry:

> Críst lim, Críst reum, Críst im degaid,
> Críst indium, Críst issum, Críst uasam,
> Críst dessum, Críst túatham,
> Críst illius, Críst isius, Críst inerus.
>
> Críst i cridu cech duini rodomscrutadar,
> Críst i ugin cech óin rodomlabrathar,

ANACONDA CANOE

> Críst hi cech rusk nomdercaeder,
> Críst hi cech clúais rodomcloathar.
>
> Christ by me, Christ before me, Christ behind me,
> Christ in me, Christ beneath me, Christ above me,
> Christ on my right side, Christ on my left side,
> Christ where I lie, Christ where I sit, Christ where I rise
> Christ in the heart of everyone who thinks of me
> Christ in the mouth of everyone who talks of me
> Christ in every ear that hears me.

    By the hermetic totality of the armour he wore can we guess the dangers he faced.
    Thinking of Kurtz, Marlow has no instant answers, but,

The thing was to know what he belonged to, how many powers of darkness claimed him for their own.

    Powers of darkness that sometimes claim some of us in the primeval place can sometimes also of course claim some of us in the civilized place.
    Notwithstanding the churches they mirror, the Tiber is a current in the Colorado, the Boyne is a current in the Congo.
    And yet human inwardness is not so dark, so unexplored and so unknown as D.H. Lawrence would have us believe it is:

> There is the other universe, of the heart of man
> that we know nothing of, that we dare not explore.
> A strange grey distance separates
> our pale mind still from the pulsing continent
> of the heart of man.
>
> Fore-runners have barely landed on the shore,
> and no man knows, no woman knows
> the mystery of the interior
> when darker still than Congo or Amazon
> flow the hearts' rivers of fullness, desire and distress.

    Linn Feic in the Boyne, in the Congo. Linn Feic in the psyche.
    Freud looked into the psyche and in it he found an unconscious and in the unconscious he found more or less what Nietzsche found. He called it the Id. Blinded by nineteenth-century scientific eyesight, he didn't find Linn Feic. He didn't find that ever-ancient, ever-contemporary, mood of earth and psyche that Australian Aborigines call the Dreaming. He didn't chant a trout cry as St Patrick chanted a deer cry. Swimming in the wake of Eo Fis, he didn't ascend the river to the otherworld well.

White Man got no dreaming, Aborigines say. If by this they mean that instead of dreaming its dreams with a dreaming earth, we tend to think scientifically about an independently existing, objective earth, then surely what they say is true. Naïve realists that most of us mostly are, we tend to think of the subjective-objective divide as a kind of absolute. Not for us the attitude of the old Zen master who, retiring for the night, would say, Now I'll let the trees do my thinking for me. Not for us either the attitude of the Zen painter who painted things not as he saw and experienced them but as they saw and experienced themselves. To recover a cultural orientation in any sense similar to this, we would need to go back behind Europa's Europe, all the way back, to the commonage consciousness of Altamira and Lascaux. We would need, sitting in the pit in Lascaux, to call White Buffalo Calf Woman into our world. We would need, like the Sioux, to suffer her tutelage, to suffer the long famine that would predispose us to welcome her gracious ministrations.

Europa or White Buffalo Calf Woman

Europa fleeing from her animal nature, fleeing to disaster in Guernica. Having brought them and taught them the rituals that would enable them to live from commonage consciousness, the Sioux watched White Buffalo Calf Woman walking away: the first time she rolled on the ground she was a red buffalo. Rising up a beautiful woman, she walked away. The second time she rolled on the ground she was a brown buffalo. She rose up a beautiful woman and she walked away. The third time she rolled she was a black buffalo. She rose up a beautiful woman and walked away. The fourth time she rolled on the ground she was a white buffalo calf. She rose up a beautiful woman and walked away.

Europa's Europe or White Buffalo Calf Woman's Europe. Europe during the last three thousand years or Europe during the Pleistocene. The terrible, wounded world of 'I–it' and 'us–them' or the world of commonage consciousness.

World in which it is also Christmas night in the stall.

Yes, it is indeed true: White Man got no dreaming. But if we ever did wish to have a dreaming and if, further, we wished to have a mythic Magna Carta for that dreaming, we haven't far to seek. From India, or should we say, from the eastern extremity of the Indo-European expansion, comes a story of origins in which, asleep on the coils of Ananta, Vishnu dreams the universe. Ananta is the Great Snake. As his name suggests, he is the Endless One. He is, in other words, the pre-cosmic infinity. Recumbent on

Ananta's coils in the beginning, Vishnu dreamed. And to know what he dreamed, we only need to look all about us.

In Sanskrit, Vishnu recumbent on Ananta is called Vishnuanantasayin or Anantashaya.

And there we have it.

> Anantashaya
> The mythic Magna Carta of our dreaming

Our *homo-erectus* shape. Our *anantashaya* shape. And now I could see it: we will only continue to be healthy if we now and then come down from our *homo-erectus* shape to our *anantashaya* shape.

Towards the end of his passion Jesus found his way to pure recumbence.

Not only therefore can we talk about

> *Vishnuanantasayin*

So also can we talk about

> Jesuanantasayin

Jesuanantasayin sponsors our dreaming.

There is, in Jesuanantasayin, a tremendous transvaluing of Western values.

And there they were: half hidden within their reedy, green banks. The bends of the Shannon could, I though, be the coils of Ananta. Looking at them, I wasn't now so sure that I could say, White man got no dreaming.

I knew as little about St Kieran as I knew about Kadmus. It wasn't, I assumed, following a cow that he came here. Neither seeking to destroy them or drive them out, did he draw a sword against the autochthonous energies of the place. And yet, no sooner had he settled here than one of the great monasteries of Early Christian Ireland began to grow up around him. It must be, in this case also, that an impulse from below evoked an enabling grace from above.

Roofless and gaping, the little igloo of stones known as St Kieran's cell has in it, even now, something of the infinite hurt and something of the infinite hope of Christian beginnings.

In it, however humbly, we see Christianity becoming Christian civilization. In it we see the miracles and parables of Christ becoming the forms of a people's sensibility and the categories of their understanding.

This of course was not so momentous an event as it might at first sight seem. It was indeed but a minor migration, if migration it was, from a pagan world of miracle and wonder to a Christian world of miracle and wonder. And given that miracle and wonder continued to be the norm, any severing that did occur was, for the most part, less than terrible.

St Brigit asked a Kildare chieftain for land to build a convent on. Only so much as your cloak will cover, he replied. Not hesitating, Brigit laid her cloak on the ground and it spread and spread and spread until, some say, it covered the plains of Kildare. To the chieftain's great relief, Brigit, being a saint, was content with what would suffice.

So long as miracles such as this continued to happen under its auspices, Christianity would flourish. Only if it robbed the world of wonder would it be in trouble.

Celt that he was, St Kieran would have known that it was only with Aaron's rod that Christianity, coming towards it, could have invoked the land of Ireland. Back across the green-necked waves that protect it from all that is wonderless it would have had to go had it attempted to come here bringing only its commandments and its dogmas.

Celt that he was, it would have been first and second nature to St Kieran to assume that any religion that doesn't sing and celebrate the wonder and terror and danger of the world betrays the world.

In St Kieran's Ireland, a god would be acceptable only if it could be said of him, Thou art the God that doest wonders.

Having so many spectacular wonders to his credit, the biblical God could for that very reason be thought of as the guarantor of wonder, and so both he and his envoy were sure of a favourable hearing:

For ask now of the days that are past, which were before thee, since the day that God created man upon the earth, and *ask* from the one side of heaven unto the other, whether there hath been *any such thing* as this great thing *is*, or hath been heard like it? Did *ever* people hear the voice of God speaking out of the midst of the fire, as thou hast heard, and live? Or hath God assayed to go *and* take him a nation from the midst of *another* nation, by temptations, by signs, and by wonders, and by war, and by a mighty hand, and by a stretched out arm, and by great terrors, according to all that the Lord your God did for you in Egypt before your eyes?

He divided the sea and caused them to pass through; and he made the waters to stand as an heap. In the daytime also he led them with a cloud, and all the night with a light of fire.

He opened the rock, and the waters gushed out: they ran in the dry places like a river.

Wondrous works in the land of Ham and terrible things by the Red Sea.

Tremble, thou earth, at the presence of the Lord, at the presence of the God of

Jacob; which turned the rock into a standing water, the flint into a fountain of waters.

A thousand years after knowledge of him was brought to Ireland, this God was still invoked as

> *A Ri no rend is na reb.*
> O King of stars and wonders.

Nowhere in all of this, though, is there sight or light of the wonder of ordinariness. And yet, of the two Easters, the one in which we awaken to the wonder of what is ordinary is altogether more richly rewarding than the one in which we awaken to the wonder of what is extraordinary.

Of the fact that many early Christian hermits and monks in Ireland did awaken to the wonder of the ordinary, there can be no doubt. And maybe St Kieran, recovering from biblical spectacle, was one of them.

And yet, Aaron's rod is neither a mental nor a cosmological oddity. It embodies something or indeed it is something from deep down in the genius of things:

And the Lord said unto him, what *is* that in thine hand? And he said, a rod. And he said, cast it on the ground. And he cast it on the ground, and it became a serpent; and Moses fled from before it. And the Lord said unto Moses, put forth thine hand and take it by the tail. And he put forth his hand, and caught it, and it became a rod in his hand.

This wouldn't surprise anyone who approaches the universe through fairy story and folktale rather than through Aristotle's logic and metaphysics.

It wouldn't surprise the Inuit:

> In the very earliest time
> when both people and animals lived on earth,
> a person could become an animal if he wanted to
> and an animal could become a human being.
> Sometimes they were people
> and sometimes animals
> and there was no difference.
> All spoke the same language.
> That was the time when words were like magic.
> The human mind had mysterious powers.
> A word spoken by chance might have strange consequences.
> It would suddenly come alive
> and what people wanted to happen could happen –
> all you had to do was say it.

TURTLE WAS GONE A LONG TIME

Nobody can explain this:
that's the way it was.

It wouldn't surprise the Sioux:

Rolling on the ground a first time she was a red buffalo. She rose up a beautiful woman and walked away.

Rolling on the ground a second time she was a brown buffalo. She rose up a beautiful woman and walked away.

Rolling on the ground a third time she was a black buffalo. She rose up a beautiful woman and walked away.

Rolling on the ground a fourth time she was a white buffalo calf. She rose up a beautiful woman and walked away.

It wouldn't surprise St Patrick chanting his Deer's Cry:

> *Niurt nimhe*
> *soilse grene*
> *etrochta saechta:*
> *ane thened*
> *dene lochet*
> *luathe gaethe*
> *fudomna maro*
> *tairirem talman*
> *cobraidecht ailech*

His eyes and mind marinated as they were in Irish folktales, it wouldn't surprise St Kieran. It wouldn't surprise Yeats:

> I went out to the hazel wood,
> Because a fire was in my head,
> And cut and peeled a hazel wand,
> And hooked a berry to a thread;
> And when white moths were on the wing,
> And moth-like stars were flickering out,
> I dropped the berry in a stream
> And caught a little silver trout.
>
> When I had laid it on the floor
> I went to blow the fire aflame,
> But something rustled on the floor,
> And someone called me by my name:
> It had become a glimmering girl,
> With apple blossom in her hair
> Who called me by my name and ran
> And faded through the brightening air.

ANACONDA CANOE

> Though I am old with wandering
> Through hollow lands and hilly lands,
> I will find out where she has gone,
> And kiss her lips and take her hands;
> And walk among long dappled grass,
> And pluck till time and times are done
> The silver apples of the moon,
> The golden apples of the sun.

Aaron's rod. The Deer's Cry. The hazel wand.

Put the peelings of that hazel wand in your pipe, Sir Isaac, and smoke them.

Any cosmology that doesn't allow for the hazel wand to be a principle in things isn't a cosmology of our cosmos.

As a principle in things, the hazel wand is as true of the universe as the laws of gravity.

Putting it bluntly: the hazel wand ought to be a category not just of the poet's understanding, it ought also to be a category of the physicist's understanding.

Rod and wand.

I imagined it: regressed to pre-Christian sleep one night, St Kieran dreamed that rod and wand were his *cliatha fis*.

> *Vishnu Anantasayin*
> *Kieran Cliathasayin*
> Vishnu asleep on the coils of Ananta,
> Kieran asleep on the wattles of vision.

There are more ways of being in touch with the genius of things than is dreamt of now in our philosophy.

It might be that the next great step in human evolution will be a deliberate inheritance of our three shapes: our *homo-erectus* shape, our *anantashaya* shape and, between them both, our *zazen* shape, the shape in which we lay ourselves open to the Transcendent.

Vishnu asleep on the coils of Ananta, Atum asleep on the coils of Iru-To and, giving us a changed past out of which a changed present and future can grow, Jesus asleep on the coils of Leviathan.

> *Jesu Leviathasayin*
> *Leviathashaya*

In other words, there is in our tradition both precedent and permission to dream with the dreaming earth.

Now at last there was no one either in or near the little igloo of stones that is known as St Kieran's cell.

Although not at all like it, it reminded me of the shell at *Sionna Sagara*. Terribly, as shell, as cell, it demanded no less than the mystical death of me.

Given the leaven of terror that was at work in me, it didn't surprise me that I momentarily imagined it to be the waiting maw of the whale that swallowed Jonah. Attempts to dislodge this image with other, more benign images didn't work, and so, hoping that Tehom is Turiya, I crossed its threshold and, taking no bearings, I knelt on the flagstone floor.

In terror, I remembered Jonah's canticle:

I cried by reason of mine affliction unto the Lord, and he heard me: out of the belly of hell cried I, *and* thou heardest my voice. For thou hadst cast me into the deep, in the midst of the seas; and the floods compassed me about; all thy billows and thy waves passed over me. Then I said, I am cast out of thy sight; yet I will look again toward thy holy temple. The waters compassed me about *even* to the soul: the depth closed me round about, the weeds were wrapped about my head. I went down to the bottoms of the mountains; the earth with her bars *was* about me forever: yet hast thou brought up my life out of corruption, O Lord my God.

In hope, I remembered the Maori song of origins:

> Te Kore
> Te Kore-tua-tahi
> Te Kore-tua-rua
> Te Kore-nui
> Te Kore-roa
> Te Kore-para
> Te Kore-whiawhia
> Te Kore-rawea
> Te Kore-te-tamaua
> Te Po
> Te Po-teki
> Te Po-terea
> Te Po-whawha
> Hine-make-moe
> Te Ata
> Te Au-tu-roa
> Te Ao-marama
> Whai-Tua
> Maku
> Mahora-nui-a-rangi
> Rangi-Potiki
> Papa

ANACONDA CANOE

Jonah's descent and ascent.
His Hebrew descent. His Maori ascent.
His Maidu descent and ascent.
As Heidegger has it:

In the age of the world's night, the abyss of the world must be endured. But for this it is necessary that there be those who reach into the abyss.

As Hölderlin has it:

> ... The heavenly powers
> Cannot do all things. It is mortals
> who reach sooner into the abyss. So the turn is
> with these. Long is
> The time, but the true comes into
> Its own.

Like Turtle, like Otter, like Loon, like any of the creatures of the diver myth, Jonah was gone a long time. This time, however, he emerged with a cosmogony that gives the cosmos a chance.

Rising to my feet, I picked four morsels of moss from the cell walls. I did it because I had heard that in the old days people of the locality would take soil from this floor and place it as a blessing on the corners of their wheat fields.

'A serious house on serious earth it is,' I thought, walking away:

> A serious house on serious earth it is,
> In whose blent air all our compulsions meet,
> Are recognized, and robed as destinies.
> And that much never can be obsolete,
> Since someone will forever be surprising
> A hunger in himself to be more serious,
> And gravitating with it to this ground,
> Which, he once heard, was proper to grow wise in,
> If only that so many dead lie round.

An even more serious house on even more serious earth it would be were Vishnu to stand one day in its doorway.

I imagined a tremendous event in Hindu history: Vishnu standing in Narada's doorway.

I imagined a tremendous event in Christian history: Vishnu standing in Kieran's doorway.

It occurred to me, leaving the *cluain,* that the parable which predisposes Hindus to cross over from Veda to Vedanta might yet predispose

Christians to cross over from Evangel to Evangelanta.

There is the Triduum Sacrum as atonement:

> Christ in the Garden of Olives
> Christ on Calvary
> Christ in the Garden of the Sepulchre

There is the Triduum Sacrum as mystical journey:

> Christ in Gethsemane
> Christ on the Hill of the Koshaless Skull
> Christ on the shore of Turiya-Tehom

It is into the fruits of the one and the good-shepherding of the other that we cross over.

It was only when I found myself walking back into Baile na hAbhann that I realized I had taken the wrong road. I felt odd about it. Was there something inauspicious in it, I wondered. I didn't give up, however. I continued walking, out past the church, into the countryside.

I imagined it to be a Dreamtime walking.

Walk with me Rangi-Potiki, I prayed. Walk with me Papa.

I'll shorten the road. I've a story to tell.

I went one day to Galway city to have acupuncture treatment on my back. Listening to the big echoing of my footsteps on it, I climbed the narrow stairs. In a dark bend of it, sitting on a step of it, there was a man.

Have you come for treatment? he asked.

Yes. Is he in?

No. Not yet. What ails you?

A damaged back. And you? What ails you?

I suffer from insomnia, he said.

Coming from him, who was so obviously a countryman, it sounded like a very learned word. Unlike the apple trees behind his house maybe, it had neither mosses nor lichens on it. But that's not all, he said, looking up at me now in awful sadness. In pleading sadness. It could have been one of the caves in Ballybunion when the tide is out that was talking to me.

I also suffer from astral projection, he said.

That can't be easy on you, I said. What I mean is, it can't be easy on you given that it is happening to you in the modern West.

You understand it, do you?

I understand that there is more to being human than my experience of being human.

Could I see you afterwards? he asked.

ANACONDA CANOE

Where?

In the hall downstairs, will that do?

Walking up Shop Street on a crowded commercial day, he told me his story:

It was dreadful for sixteen years. I was in hospital. I prayed for the nurses and doctors who looked after me. They liked me. And then one night it wasn't night at all, it was eternity, and a stone came out of the sun and so vast was the sound of that stone coming out that I knew the whole universe must have heard it. But maybe it didn't. Maybe there wasn't a universe in that eternity. Anyway, you have often heard of something being shattered asunder. Well, that sound shattered me together. And I haven't been in hospital since.

Back at home that night I put down a fire and sat beside it. Leafing through the Tibetan Book of the Dead I soon found the passages, long ago underlined, that I was looking for:

O nobly-born, when thy body and mind were separating thou must have experienced a glimpse of the Pure Truth, subtle, sparkling, bright, dazzling, glorious and radiantly awesome, in appearance like a mirage moving across a landscape in springtime in one continuous stream of vibrations. Be not daunted thereby, nor terrified, nor awed. That is the radiance of thine own true nature. Recognize it.

From the midst of that radiance the natural sound of reality reverberating like a thousand thunders simultaneously sounding will come. That is the natural sound of thine own real self. Be not daunted thereby nor terrified, nor awed.

A stone of total sound coming out of the sun. Sound of a thousand thunders simultaneously sounding coming out of a great radiance, and that radiance and that sound are the sound of our true selves.

William James was right: there should be no premature closing of our account with reality.

Abreast once again of the wild field, I searched for a weakness in the hedge and, finding one, I slipped through, on its far side climbing down to the low-lying patch of marsh. Inattentive to its flora, although not unaware of it, I crossed it, leaping from tussock to tussock, to higher ground. There, among the bracken and furze, I found the trench I had dug. Sinking to my knees, I removed the scraw and the loose soil. I was terrified, thinking that maybe my hands would wither. I persisted, however. Retrieving the groundplan from my shoulder-bag, I placed it in the trench; and then, somehow remembering them, I searched in my trousers pockets for the four morsels of moss. Into each of them in turn I spoke a *mahavakya*:

Yatra na anyat pasyati, na anyat srinoti, na anyad vijanati, sa bhuma.
God in darkness, privation, forsakenness, and insensibility is so much God that it is as it were God bare and alone.

Between me and thee there is an 'I am' that torments me. Through thy 'I am' take away my 'I am' from between us both.

Comes then the soul into the unclouded light of God.

Holding all four of them in my hand I thought of the morsels of soil Turtle brought back from the floor of the abyss.

Into all four of them I spoke, saying,

Oh dichosa ventura

Separating them, I placed one of them on each of the four corners of the groundplan. Then I poured back the soil. I replaced the scraw and, sitting back on my collops, I sensed, or maybe I imagined, a song coming down out of the universe behind me into this *itharuta dil-tata*, this impulse from below.

And then the temptation: thinking of the Maidu story of origins, it excited me to think of this wild field as Ta'doiko.

Thinking of an ancient Egyptian story of origins, it excited me to think of it as *Tai-wer*, the most ancient land, the first mound that emerged from the primordial waters. It excited me to think of this day as *Tep-Zepi*, the first time.

Seeing the implications of these thoughts, I recoiled in terror. In a kind of Actaeon terror. It was as if, in spite of my vigilance, I had momentarily trespassed out of my place in the scale of being. Given the danger in what I was up to, the last thing I needed was the terrible glamour of a tragic flaw in my nature. And yet nature was as perilous in me as it was in everyone else. Like everyone else, I lived in a dangerous place between blessedness and perdition.

I was contrite. I prayed:

Teach me thy way, O Lord, and lead me in a plain path because of mine enemies.

I needed no chorus of Theban or Argive elders to tell me that my enemies were impulses from within.

'Save me from the lion's mouth,' a Psalmist had prayed:

Save me from the lion's mouth, for thou hast heard me from the horns of the unicorns.

And yet, fearful though I was, and contrite, I couldn't but believe that every mound is *Tai-wer*. Its geography and geology notwithstanding, I couldn't but believe that the ground I was standing on was *Tai-wer*. And however far removed from the beginning it might be, this ordinary summer's day in Ireland was *Tep-Zepi*.

It is as much *Tep-Zepi* at the end of the voyage as it is at the beginning of the voyage:

But do I look very old, so very, very old, Starbuck? I feel deadly faint, bowed, and humped, as though I were Adam, staggering beneath the piled centuries since Paradise.

It is as much *Tep-Zepi* in Ahab's day as it is in Adam's day. Adam and Ahab are contemporaries.

The beginning always is. Is now. And so, knowing my place in the scale of being, I can, without hubris or *superbia,* say: wherever it is I am standing, in Belsen or Broadway, it is in *Tai-wer*, it is in Ta'doiko, that I am standing.

Looking back at it as I walked away, I found myself able to believe that the ground I had planted the groundplan in was as cosmically and culturally potent as the first mound out of the waters was.

> O Atum! When you came into being you rose up
> as a High Hill,
> you shone as the Benben Stone in the Temple of
> the Phoenix in Heliopolis.

Leaving the field I prayed:

> As the first mound rose out of the waters, so, in
> the midst of the modern world, may a temple
> rise and, rising, centre us.

Coming through the hedge I remembered the piece of newspaper that was blown across our yard on a wild night. Would it, I wondered, guide us to divine shelter? Would we one day be able to sing with the Psalmist:

Blessed be the name of the Lord, for he hath shewn me his marvellous kindness in a strong city.

By the time we caught up with it, would that stray piece of paper sing other news than daily news to us? Would it be our new holy book speaking in Upanishads and Gitas?

A few hundred yards up the road I went into a pub. I ordered a beer. There were two men sitting on high stools at the counter. They were watching a match on television, a re-run of the Leinster football final between Dublin and Offaly. Recognizing how absorbed they were, I didn't seek to engage them in conversation. Still frightened by what I had done, I finished my beer and left.

Along a stretch of the road I had taken, on either side of it, there was a high wild bog and that, like an ancient piety, calmed me. Preserved in the pre-Christian depths of it somewhere was a landscape that Macha, the Celtic horse goddess, might have walked in or at night neighed in. Below the buried hand-bells and croziers were her hoof marks. Walking this road was like walking in an archaeological dig through the Irish psyche.

As D.H. Lawrence has it:

Man's consciousness has many layers, and the lowest layers continue to be crudely active, especially down among the common people, for centuries after the cultural consciousness of the nation has passed to higher planes. And the consciousness of man always tends to revert to the original levels; though there are two modes of reversion: by degeneration and decadence; and by deliberate return in order to get back to the roots again, for a new start.

Deep as shamanism I walked.

Deep as totemism.

Deep as the hoof marks of the Celtic horse goddess. Deep as the hoof marks of White Buffalo Calf Woman, for as I imagine her, it is to Pleistocene peoples everywhere that she came. Bringing the blessings of commonage consciousness, bringing it as their religion to them, she came to the peoples of Altamira and Lascaux.

Even if we could, it wouldn't be good for us to cross, as though we had no past, into mystical Christianity.

Having gone down Grand-Canyon-deep into the world's karma, Christianity isn't only on the earth. It is of the earth. It is up out of it.

Bright Angel Trail is aisle. Job's safari, inner and outer, is aisle. Jonah's descent is aisle.

From beginning to end, the earth's evolution is aisle.

Even when it enters the wayless way, the mystical journey is aisle.

In his 'Hymn on the Morning of Christ's Nativity' Milton banished our past, cultural and psychological, into deepest Tartarus.

The Miltonic-Cartesian clear sweep hasn't been good for us.

Reversing this calamity, it might be good, in token of our openness towards our own past, to call White Buffalo Calf Woman back into the world. And walking as I now was below the coming of Christianity to Ireland, it would, I thought, be a good thing too to remember the Celtic horse goddess:

So many strange things had been happening to Crunnchu that he wasn't as surprised as he otherwise might be when one day a woman, obviously not of this world, walked through his door and said, I have come to keep house with you.

Although she was in no way casual about it, she lay with him that night.

From then on everything Crunnchu put his hand to prospered.

His wheat fields were a wonder.

A fox had her young in one of his sheds.

Swallows that hatched out in his barn stayed all winter.

Horses that had gone wild on the hills and foaled there came home to his yard. Not that he himself would handle or harness them.

It was to the woman's call they came. At a wave of her hand they thundered away. She ran with them once, all nine of them, she among them, looking down from a high horizon.

Crunnchu went to the Great Assembly.

Loudly unimpressed by their victory, he boasted that his wife could outrun the king's horses.

Taking dangerous offence, the king ordered Crunnchu to be apprehended and his wife brought before him.

Pleading that her labour pains had begun, Crunnchu's wife begged the king, begged his chief warriors, to let her be.

Still outraged, the king insisted. She must race against his horses, now.

Although seeming to run much slower than them, she easily outran the king's team and then, standing there at the winning-post, she gave birth to twins. In a voice neither vengeful nor angry, she calledout a doom upon the king and his warriors: always in their hour of greatest need, foreign armies crossing their borders, they would, to a man, be laid low by her labour pains.

I imagined it:

Men, their swords laid aside, suffering a woman's pains. Warriors laid helplessly low by the screaming contractions of parturition.

And in time some among them gave themselves to the doom, went willingly with the doom, for they felt that in them the earth itself was undergoing a most wonderful and therefore a most perilous transition.

There were some who never again picked up their swords. Becoming hermits, they surrendered in their deepest inwardness to the yearnings of the yearning worlds.

> Yearn in me worlds,
> Be awake in me worlds,
> Be transformed in me worlds.

That was their prayer.

To them, when it came, Christianity wasn't in any way strange. Conversion to them was but a transition from the labour pains of the Goddess to the labour pains of the God.

Christ in Gethsemane gave shape to their yearnings. The passion and death and resurrection of Christ gave them their sufferings in a cup. A cup that wasn't a curse. A cup they could refuse.

Instinctively almost, they understood St Paul:

We are well aware that the whole creation, until this time, has been groaning in labour pains.

Like St Paul, they were happy to give themselves to the unfinished symphony whose three great movements were Gethsemane, Golgotha and the Garden of the Sepulchre. And so it was that within a few centuries an old kind of heroism had yielded ground to a new kind of heroism. Cuchulainn had yielded ground to St Kieran. The hero's sword had yielded ground to God's labour pains. And all of this began on that great day when, appearing as Macha, the Horse Goddess walked through Crunnchu's door.

Phylogenetically, Crunnchu's door is within us all. And that's why medieval Christians were so right to have so often imagined and enacted the Harrowing of Hell.

Think of the scene before Hell's door. Think of the stage direction:

Then shall come Jesus and a clamour shall be made, or a loud sound of things striking together, and let Jesus say: 'Lift up your heads, O ye gates; and be ye lift up, ye everlasting doors, and the King of Glory shall come in.'

Imagine it: Christ-Orpheus singing in our phylogenetic underworld:

> All shall be well
> And all shall be well
> And all manner of thing shall be well

Certainly, during the earlier stages of the spiritual journey, it is surely safer to seek the sanctity of inclusion and integration rather than the sanctity of exclusion and repression. And in this regard, it might be no harm to remember that Christianity didn't only come down from heaven. Coming up through the ages, it came up from the floor of the Grand Canyon. And that means that, from its beginnings, Christianity was already a religion for this side of *The Voyage of the Beagle*. It was already this of course in the Book of Job. Spiritually, the Book of Job is a Galapagos. And the only answer to Galapagos, Job's and Darwin's, is Gethsemane.

Thinking of Jesus in Gethsemane, we might recall Pascal:

We do not show our greatness by touching one extreme only, but by touching both at once, and filling the whole space between.

Within himself, in Gethsemane, Jesus was in touch with the highest heaven and the deepest hell and all the levels of fervent and fallen existence in between.

Thinking of him, we might remember a couple of lines from Psalm eighteen:

> The bed of the seas was revealed.
> The foundations of the world were laid bare.

In Gethsemane these lines might read:

> The Palaeozoic bed of his psyche was revealed.
> The tolmic will to individuation in him was laid bare.

In Gethsemane we are purified in our deepest roots.

In Gethsemane Jesus went back into and came forward from our deepest past.

Having gone back we can go forward. Forward into the second cycle of the Triduum Sacrum. Forward into mystical Christianity.

As D.H. Lawrence has it:

Every profound new movement makes a great swing also backward to some older, half-forgotten way of consciousness.

As Novalis has it:

It is only the look that is turned backward which carries forward as the look that is turned forward leads backward.

Christ in Gethsemane is Christ looking forward from *Tep-zepi*.

Christ on Golgotha is Christ looking forward from *Tai-wer*.

Christ in Gethsemane is Vishvarupa looking forward into our Palaeozoic, Mesozoic and Cainozoic past.

Christ on Golgotha is Vishvayuga looking forward into all we already have been, are and will become.

Having its homeport in the Triduum Sacrum, the Christian nave can, like the *Beagle*, sail out into heavy south-westerlies. It is not to do business in great waters or to bring home a Golden Fleece, nor yet to bring home a new paradigm in our conception of things, that it sails out. It sails out to bring the Tenebrae harrow to the beginning and end of stellar existence.

Imagine it: there are beings elsewhere in the universe. They aren't aware of physical light or of physical sound. They are, however, aware of the light of enlightenment. And it is because of this light of enlightenment in it that they are aware of our galaxy.

Walking this road in the centre of Ireland, I felt that now again I could go back to that Neolithic or Golden Bough house in north Kerry. Sitting by a turf fire and reading them by the light of a double-wick paraffin lamp I would now be able, I thought, for the geological chapters of *The Origin of Species*. This time I wouldn't be man overboard. This time I wouldn't fall out of my world.

Thanks to a lift in his car with a local farmer, I reached Moate that evening. I booked into a hotel. The room I was shown into was a punishment cell. It had in it no remembrance of the wild imagination of the universe. Much too excited to think of sleep, I went back down to the lobby and watched a football match on television. It was one of the World Cup matches being played in Mexico. Listening to the news afterwards, it was, I realized, mid-summer night.

The next day it poured intermittently with rain but, apart from an hour or so waiting under a tree in Tyrrellspass, the lifts were good and I was back at home in Caragh House by early afternoon.

I had yet to complete the journey, however, and that I would do by going back to the baptismal font in the chapel in Coolcarrigan.

It occurred to me that there were two ways I might do this, a symbolic way and an actual way, and both ways, I hoped, would be sacramental.

Symbolically I could, by reading them, immerse my mind in some of the dark sayings of the mystics.

Sayings, written on the weeds of the Great Deep, that Turtle or Jonah might have brought back from their descent into Turiya-Tehom.

Again, momentarily, it excited me to imagine an assimilation of Jonah's descent to the descent described in the diver myth:

In the beginning the was no sun, no moon, no stars. All was dark and everywhere there was only water. A raft came floating on the water. It came from the north, and in it were two persons – Turtle (A'noshma) and Father-of-the-Secret-Society (Peheipe). The stream flowed very rapidly. Then from the sky a rope of feathers, called Po'kelma, was let down, and down it came Earth-Initiate. When he reached the end of the rope, he tied it to the bow of the raft, and stepped in. His face was covered and was never seen, but his body shone like the sun. He sat down and for a long time said nothing. At last Turtle said, 'Where do you come from?', and Earth-Initiate answered, 'I come from above.' Then Turtle said 'Brother, can you not make for me some good dry land, so that I may sometimes come up out of the water?' Then he asked another time, 'Are there going to be any people in the world?' Earth-Initiate thought a while, then said, 'Yes.' Turtle asked, 'How long before you are going to make people?' Earth-Initiate replied, 'I don't know. You want to have some dry land: well, how am I going to get any earth to make it of?' Turtle answered, 'If you will tie a rock about my left arm, I'll dive for some.' Earth-Initiate did as Turtle asked, and then, reaching around, took the end of a rope from somewhere, and tied it to Turtle. When Earth-Initiate came to the raft there was no rope there: he just reached out and found one. Turtle said, 'If the rope is not long enough, I'll jerk it once, and you must haul me up; if it is long enough, I'll give two jerks, and then you must pull me up quickly, as I shall have all the earth that I can carry.' Just as Turtle went over the side of the raft, Father-of-the-Secret-Society began to shout loudly.

Turtle was gone a long time. He was gone six years, and when he came up, he was covered with green slime, he had been down so long. When he reached the top of the water, the only earth he had was a very little under his nails; the rest had all washed away. Earth-Initiate took with his right hand a stone knife from under his left armpit and carefully scraped the earth out from under Turtle's nails. He put the earth in the palm of his hand, and rolled it about till it was round; it was as large as a small pebble. He laid it on the stern of the raft. By and by he went to look at it; it had not grown at all. The third time he went to look at it, it had grown so that it could be spanned by the arms. The fourth time he looked, it was as big as the world, the raft was aground, and all around there were mountains as far as he could see.

When the raft had come to land, Turtle said, 'I can't stay in this dark all the time. Can't you make a light, so that I can see?' Earth-Initiate replied, 'Let us get out of the raft, and then we will see what we can do.' So all three got out. Then Earth-Initiate said, 'Look that way, to the east! I am going to tell my sister to come up.' Then it began to grow light and day began to break; then Father-of-the-Secret-Society began to cry and shout again, and the sun came up. Turtle said, 'Which way is the sun going to travel?' Earth-Initiate answered, 'I'll tell her to go this way and go down there.' After the sun went down, Father-of-the-Secret-Society began to cry and shout again, and it grew very dark. Earth-Initiate asked Turtle and Father-of-the-Secret-Society, 'How do you like it?', and they both answered, 'It is very good.' Then Turtle asked, 'Is that all you are going to do for us?', and Earth-Initiate answered, 'No, I am going to do more yet.' Then he called the stars each by its name and they came out. When this was done, Turtle asked, 'Now, what shall we do?' Earth-Initiate replied, 'Wait, and I'll show you.' Then he made a tree grow at Ta'doiko, the tree called Hu'kimsta; and Earth-Initiate and Turtle and Father-of-the-Secret-Society sat in its shade for two days. The tree was very large and had twelve different kinds of acorns growing on it.

After they sat for two days under the tree, they all went off to see the world that Earth-Initiate had made. They started at sunrise, and were back by sunset …

TURTLE WAS GONE A LONG TIME

Quoting Heidegger yet again:

In the age of the world's night the abyss of the world must be experienced and endured.

Narada-Noah endured it. A'noshma-Jonah endured it. All who enter the darkness of Good Friday on Golgotha endure it.

We mustn't, however, think of the abyss as a chaos of pre-cosmic or prepsychic waters.

With Eckhart we might think of it as an incomprehensible aught:

Everything which has being hangs in the Naught. And this same naught is such an incomprehensible aught that all the spirits in heaven and upon earth cannot comprehend it or sound it.

It is the Divine Ungrund that grounds all merely experienced ground.

It is the Divine Ungrund that grounds all cosmic and extra-cosmic ground.

Blissfully, blissfully, it blissfully grounds.

So we could, or should, rewrite the diver myth:

In the age of the world's night, A'noshma slipped over the side of merely experienced ground into the Divine Ungrund and, after being gone a long time, he came back and now we know that, in or out of the world, we are divinely grounded.

Emily's song could be A'noshma's song:

> Though earth and man were gone,
> And suns and universes ceased to be,
> And thou wert left alone,
> Every existence would exist in Thee.

Turtle has found ground. Ground he doesn't need to come ashore on because, whether here or elsewhere, whether in the world or out of it, he has already always been on it. Indeed, aware of it or not, he has already always lived, moved and had his being in it.

This is the ground that mystics everywhere and in all ages have found. Having found it or having been found by it, Fénelon could say:

God felt, God tasted, God enjoyed, is indeed God, but God with those gifts that flatter the soul. God in darkness, privation, forsakenness and insensibility is so much God that it is as it were God bare and alone.

Dare we say it! Through Fénelon came God's answer to Christ's cry of dereliction on Good Friday.

In it and with it Christianity has caught up with Good Friday.

In it and with it Christianity has caught up with the Hill of the Kosha-less Skull.

In it and with it Christianity has come through the Triduum Sacrum.

The cry and the answer.

Hindus would welcome and celebrate the answer as a *mahavakya*, a great saying. As such, it is the agonistic correlative of the Chandogya great saying:

> *Yatra na anyat pasyati, na anyat srinoti, na anyad vijanati, sa bhuma.*

In and with these two *mahavakyas*, Vedanta and Evangelanta greet each other.

God in dereliction. God in Tenebrae. God in the soul's dark night.

> *O noche amable mas que el alborada.*
> O night more lovely than the dawn.

And that surely is another *mahavakya*.

For Shankara there were six Upanishadic *mahavakyas*.

The question is: how many *mahavakyas* would a Christian Shankara settle for? Indeed, how many Christian Upanishads would he settle for?

Imagine it: a Christianity founded as much on its mahavakyas as on its dogmas. A Christianity founded as much on the writings of its mystics as on the statements of its councils.

Imagine it: a Christianity that continuously draws its life from the Divine Ground the Triduum Sacrum good-shepherds us into.

Imagine it: a good-shepherding temple. A temple that good-shepherds us into and through our Tenebrae.

Comfort ye, comfort ye my people, saith your God.

How extraordinary that 'Gethsemane' and 'Golgotha' are among the most comforting words that Christianity can speak to us.

The anguish we experience in Gethsemane is simple yet manifold. Among the several simultaneous phases of it is an overwhelming sense of our inability to co-operate from our core or with the purifying fire that is invading us. Although we sense a divine compassion in the fire, in neither body nor soul are we tough enough for it. It might well be, we feel, that in the end there will be no ashes to rise from.

Christ in Gethsemane is the Christian Magna Carta of the sanctity of redemptive inclusion and integration.

To advocate the sanctity of redemptive inclusion and integration is not to advocate a kind of Christian psychoanalysis, however helpful that might be. Nor is it to advocate a kind of Christian Tantra. It is, quite simply, to advocate crossing the Kedron with Jesus. It is to advocate Gethsemane and our openness, in Gethsemane, to sanctifying grace.

Nature working on nature will leave us stuck in nature.

In the end, we go beyond all personal attempts to reach sanctity.

We surrender without reserve to pure divine action in us. Someone has called it theopathetic life.

May I be as out of your way awake, God, as I am in dreamless sleep.

Into thy hands I commend my spirit.

It isn't by asserting a natural right but humbly, praying for divine good-shepherding, that we cross the Kedron. It might, as Buddhists suggest, be a gateless gate, but a threshold there is nonetheless. And every such threshold has its guardians.

> O thou who plumed with strong desire
> Wouldst float above the earth, beware!
> A Shadow tracks thy flight of fire!
> Night is coming.

It is not without good reason that Montaigne says:

They want to go out of themselves and escape from the man. That is madness: instead of changing into angels, they change into beasts; instead of raising themselves they lower themselves.

And it is not without good reason that Pascal echoes him:

Man is neither angel nor brute, but unfortunately when he wants to be like an angel he behaves like a brute.

We do well to remember Actaeon: he arrived uninvited and unannounced.

It will offend humanists to say it, but: we need help with out humanity from outside our humanity. And we only need to read St Teresa of Ávila's account of her life to know that such help is available. The divine transcendence condescends to our condition.

As Eckhart has it:

God expects but one thing of you and that is that you should empty yourself in so far as you are a created human being so that God can be God in you.

Eckhart isn't saying: so that God can be you in you. He is saying: so that God can be God in you.

In other words, Eckhart's assertion will in no way justify anyone in saying

> *Aham Brahm'asmi*
> I am Brahman
> or
> *Ana'l-haqq*
> I am the Truth

To say God is in me is not to say I am God.

An offence to our secular sense of human self-sufficiency it also is when Eckhart says:

How blessed are the poor in spirit who leave everything to God now as they did before ever they existed.

Sir Thomas Browne is unapologetic:

Therefore, I say, every man hath a double Horoscope, one of his humanity, his birth; another of his Christianity, his baptism; and from this do I compute or calculate my Nativity ...

Not without a prolonged and sometimes fierce fight will the horoscope of our birth be subsumed by the horoscope of our baptism.

It isn't overnight and without effort that we will find ourselves living under the constellations of the Christian rosary as well as under the signs of the zodiac.

When they came home, Tommy and Charlotte were quite surprised to find me sitting beside the fire. They expected, from what I had said, that I would be away walking the roads of the midlands for at least a few days. And now Tommy, who can be very funny, had all three of us laughing as he continued, in brilliant but good-humoured derision, to joke about my unfittedness for life in the great outdoors. Neither before nor after had I the courage to tell them what it was I was up to.

Later that night after Tommy and Charlotte had gone upstairs to bed I immersed my mind baptismally, marinating it as it were, in four *mahavakyas* I had to hand:

Such at least is the teaching of the blessed Bartholomew. For he says that the subject matter of the Divine Science is vast and yet minute and that the Gospel combines in itself both width and straitness. Methinks he has shewn by these his words how marvellously he has understood that the Good Cause of all things is eloquent yet speaks few words, or rather none; possessing neither speech nor understanding because it exceedeth all things in a super-essential manner and it is revealed in its naked truth to those alone who pass right through the opposition of fair and foul and pass beyond the topmost attitudes of the holy ascent and leave behind them all divine enlightenment and voices and heavenly utterances and plunge into the Darkness where truly dwells, as saith the Scripture, that One which is beyond all things.

Unto this Darkness which is beyond light we pray that we may come and may attain unto vision through the loss of sight and knowledge and that in ceasing thus to see or to know we may learn to know that which is beyond all perception and understanding (for this emptying of our faculties is true sight and knowledge) and that we may offer Him that transcends all things the praises of a transcendent hymnody which we shall do by denying or removing all things that are ...

On this road therefore, to abandon one's own way is to enter on the true way, or, to speak more correctly, to pass onwards to the goal, and to forsake one's own way is to enter on that which has none, namely God. For the soul that attains to this state has no ways or methods of its own, neither does it, nor can it, lean upon anything of the kind. I mean ways of understanding, perceiving or feeling, though it has all ways at the same time as one who, possessing nothing, yet possesseth everything. For the soul, courageously resolved on passing interiorly and exteriorly beyond the limits of its own nature, enters illimitably within the supernatural, which has no measure but contains all measure eminently within itself. To arrive there is to depart hence, going away out of oneself, as far as possible, from this vile state to that which is highest of all. Therefore, rising above all that may be known and understood, temporally and spiritually, the soul must earnestly desire to reach that which in this life cannot be known and which the heart cannot conceive; and leaving behind all possible and actual taste and feeling of sense and spirit must desire earnestly to arrive at that which transcends all sense and all feeling.

I say, then, that the soul, to be rightly guided by faith to this state, must be in darkness, not only as to that part thereof – the sensual and the inferior, of which I have already spoken – which regards temporal and created things, but also as to that part thereof, the rational and the superior, of which I am now speaking which regards God and spiritual things. Because it is clearly necessary for the soul, aiming at its own supernatural transformation, to be in darkness and far removed from all that relates to its natural condition, the sensual and rational parts. The supernatural is that which transcends nature and therefore, that which is natural remains below. Inasmuch as this union and transformation are not recognizable by sense or any human power, the soul must be completely and voluntarily empty of all that can enter into it, of every affection and inclination, so far as it concerns itself. Who shall hinder God from doing his own will in a soul that is resigned, detached and self-annihilated? The soul, therefore, must be emptied of all such feelings; and however great may be its supernatural endowments, it must be as it were detached from them, in darkness like a blind man, leaning upon the obscure faith, and taking it for his light and guide; not trusting to anything it understands, tastes, feels or imagines – for all this is darkness, which will lead it astray, or keep it back; and faith is above all understanding, taste and sense.

Four constellations in the firmament of our Christian horoscope. Constellations whose shinings say:

> God in Tenebrae

The pole star in that firmament should surely be:

> *Oh dichosa ventura*

Walking to Coolcarrigan the next day, I prayed the rosary, the joyful, the sorrowful and the glorious mysteries. I prayed them on what remained of my mother's beads. They were black beads and at times as I prayed them I felt that the mysteries were quenched. Positively not negatively quenched. Quenched as the candles of the Tenebrae harrow might be quenched. Quenched into surer guidance:

> *Oh noche que guiaste*

Quenched so that Turiya might shine. Quenched so that the Divine Ground out of which all things emanated might shine. It was, for the moment, a Good-Friday rosary beads.

> *Oh noche que guiaste*
> *Oh noche amable mas que el alborada*

In a field two fields away from the road a cow lowed. I recognized that lowing, or rather I recognized the huge high horizon-wide calling in it. It was for her calf she was calling. Very likely, her calf had been taken from her that morning and sold at the mart in Maynooth.

All day and all night she would call. She would call tomorrow. By evening, however, she would be grazing.

Sometimes in Connemara a cow calling in the night would wake me, and lying there I would imagine that she was calling White Buffalo Calf Woman back into the world.

As I imagined her, White Buffalo Calf Woman was a manifestation of the immanent Divine, and she didn't only come to the Sioux of the American Great Plains. She came to Pleistocene peoples everywhere. To heal them, she came to the people who, in the crypt in Lascaux, depicted the terrible, prostrating calamity that had overtaken them. On her way to them, she left both buffalo and human footprints in the snow.

Dressed in a Sioux star-blanket, I prayed one night that she would come back, back to that yard in north Kerry where, a long time ago on Christmas Eve, a wound had opened between us who lived in the dwelling house and the cows who lived in the stall. She being both buffalo and woman, both animal and human, the wound hadn't opened in her, and so, reinstituting commonage consciousness among us, she would heal us. And that would mean the end of Europa's Europe. It would mean an exodus within Europe from us-and-them-awareness to we-awareness. Folding the star-blanket at dawn, I felt I could believe that the earth had a chance.

> *Ultima Cumaei venit iam carminis aetas;*
> *Magnus ab integro saeclorum nascitur ordo.*

We have other than mystical needs. We need to be incarnate. We therefore need a world to be incarnate in. And however apocalyptically at odds with the world Early Christians might have been, they nonetheless believed that, on Easter morning, incarnation and salvation are the same thing.

In Christ, we have stood Grand-Canyon-deep in the earth. That is the great apocalypse. That is the great new day. And it will indeed be a vast misfortune if we cannot learn to say 'we', meaning not only all that does exist, but all that has existed and will exist. Or saying the same thing in a picturesque way: it will indeed be a vast misfortune if, come Christmas Eve, we will not light candles in our cow stalls.

As I walked to Coolcarrigan, this yearning for a lost way of being in the world evolved into a fantasy: the Magi were Australian Aborigines. They came to Bethlehem following, not a star, but Red Kangaroo. They had one gift, and that was an intuition: the oneness, in Dreamtime dreaming, of medulla and mountain. I thought of the old Zen master who, retiring to sleep, would say, now I'll let the rocks and the trees do my thinking for me.

The church in Coolcarrigan is surrounded by a dry moat or fosse. Consciously, sensing defeat, a defeat that might yet turn out to be a kind of victory, I crossed the little bridge that spans it. I was coming home to the story I had fallen out of almost thirty years earlier. In my case it was Darwin who had shot the albatross. Out of doors it was a wild night and a piece of paper blowing in the wind was the only thing there was to follow.

In time I would find my way to the shamanic north.

I found my way to Uvavnuk's song:

ANACONDA CANOE

>The great sea has set me in motion
>Set me adrift
>Moving me as a weed moves in the river.
>
>The arch of sky and mightiness of storms
>Have moved the spirit within me
>Till I am carried away
>Trembling with joy.

I found my way to the Navajo cradle:

>I have made a cradleboard for you, my child.
>May you grow to a great old age.
>Of the sun's rays I have made the back,
>Of black clouds I have made the blanket,
>Of rainbow I have made the bow,
>Of sunbeams have I made the side-loops,
>Of lightning have I made the lacings
>Of river mirrorings have I made the footboard,
>Of dawn have I made the covering,
>Of earth's welcome for you have I made the bed.

I found my way to nature:

>I'll walk where my own nature would be leading –
> It vexes me to choose another guide –
>Where the grey flocks in ferny glens are feeding,
> Where the wild wind blows on the mountain side.
>
>What have those lonely mountains worth revealing?
> More glory and more grief than I can tell:
>The earth that wakes one human heart to feeling
> Can centre both the worlds of heaven and hell.

I found my way to the ancient Irish equivalent of this cradle. I found my way to the deer's cry. To protect me today I call upon:

>*Niurt nimhe*
>*Soilse grene*
>*Etrochta snechtar*
>*Are thened*
>*Dene locket*
>*Luathe gaethe*
>*Fudomra mara*
>*Tairirem talmain*
>*Cobraidecht ailech*

The deer's cry and the cradle. Protected by both in both culture and nature.
 Protected it would seem by neither, Emily walked out.
 Wonderful, and most laudable. Yet I cannot but think of Kurtz.
 Wonderful, and most laudable. But in my case, somehow, not enough. Not enough if only because it wasn't only Uvavnak's song that followed me into the ferny glens. Into them with me also came two old European desolations – Kepler's horror and Pascal's terror.
 Aware of an infinite universe without centre or circumference, Kepler was, to say the least, perturbed:

> This very cogitation carries with it I don't know what secret, hidden horror; indeed one finds oneself wandering in this immensity, to which are denied limits and centre and therefore also all determinate places.

 Similarly aware, Pascal was no less distressed:

> The eternal silence of those infinite spaces terrify me.

 And so it was that I crossed the footbridge. Defeated, but seeking, acknowledging my need for the Transcendent Divine, I was walking back into Christianity.
 Immersing my head down into the emptiness of the baptismal font was like immersing it into the emptiness of the shell on the shingle shore of *Sionna Sagara*.
 I sat in the nearest pew.
 The shell and the cell, both of them empty, I thought.
 On the shore at *Sionna Sagara*, the shell. In a *cluain* beside *Sionna Ananta*, the cell.
 And on a calm evening in the Dingle peninsula the sound of a stream coming down Sliabh an Fhiolair.

> *Tá sé ag glaoch orainn*, Mike File said …
> *Tá sé ag glaoch orainn isteach sa tsíoraíocht as a bhfuil se fein ag teacht.*
> It is calling us into the eternity out of which it is itself flowing.

 To us who live in time, eternity – even the thought of it – is almost annihilating. How can we encounter it and not end up like Actaeon? How can we encounter it and not end up like an empty shell, or empty cell?

> A starlit or a moonlit dome disdains
> All that man is,
> All mere complexities,
> The fury and the mire of human veins.

 The ancient Irish didn't talk at all about eternity. They talked rather about the otherworld. Throughout the land there were entrances to this otherworld. Many of them were known, but always there were those that were not yet known, and so it would sometimes happen that your journey home from a fair would become an *eachtra* or that your voyage to your island would become an *imram*. A glen you went into might be your Glen Cush. And a gap well known to you in the mountains – coming through it on a summer morning, the sun coming up behind you, it might turn out to be your Bealach Oisín. And loveliest thought of all, the ancient Irish believed that the seven rivers of Ireland had their source in an otherworld well.

I had crossed by a footbridge into a Christian church, yet here I was Boyne-valley-deep in Iath nAnann, Linn-Feic-deep in Ireland's Dreamtime.

Or Linn-Feic-deep in my psyche.

And the thought occurred to me that whoever you are, if you are Linn-Feic-deep in your psyche, then at that depth of yourself you are Eo Fis. At night, at that depth of yourself, you swim upstream to the otherworld well. At that depth of yourself a hazel overgrows your own inner Nechtan's Well and sometimes, as though dropping a hazel nut, it drops wisdom down into you.

In the end it wasn't Eo Fis I heard – Eo Fis asking me, Can you hear it, the wisdom of this world and the otherworld falling down into your mind? It was Vishnu I heard, Vishnu asking me, Did you bring the water?

Eo Fis under a hazel.

A Christian under a Byzantine dome.

> A starlit or a moonlit dome disdains
> All that man is,
> All mere complexities,
> The fury and the mire of human veins.

The hope was that the horoscope of my birth would be subsumed by the horoscope of my baptism.

In the firmament of my baptism, shining among the shining *mahavakyas*, were three great constellations: Christ in Gethsemane, Christ on the Hill of the Koshaless Skull and Christ on the shore of Turiya-Tehom.

It occurred to me sitting there that there are two kinds of telescope, the ordinary optical or radio telescope and, when it is quenched, the Tenebrae harrow.

And it might be that the only answer to Kepler's horror and Pascal's terror is that they would look once again at the universe, this time through the quenched harrow.

Whoever looks at the universe through the quenched harrow sees farther and deeper.

Sees with a seeing that isn't blinded by eyesight.

And it might be that we too will one day be aware of galaxies not by the physical light and sound they emit but by the light of enlightenment in them. Maybe that's the way we are evolving. Maybe that's the way all galaxies and stars are evolving. And since both have emerged from Divine Ground, maybe the horoscopes of our birth and our baptism have been and are, and will be, the one night sky we already know.

We need to change direction.

It isn't more and more and more Mount Palomar seeing we need. What we need is a Tenebrae Temple.

Architecturally and ritually, a Tenebrae Temple will know that the Triduum Sacrum is the great frontier of human seeking.

We seek more profoundly on the Hill of the Koshaless Skull than we do on Mount Palomar.

And, although it is indeed the great frontier, the Triduum Sacrum isn't a frontier between worlds. Rather is it the frontier between all possible worlds and the Ground, blissful and Divine, out of which they have emanated.

Sitting in it, I didn't sense that this particular little church had ever sailed out into heavy south-westerlies. There was in its walls no obvious awareness of ancient sea-floors. Dead level, dead straight, and short, its aisle was not a reach of Bright Angel Trail. And yet, having a baptismal font in it, this church was a stupendous place. That font meant seas the *Beagle* never sailed into. It meant and means a Galapagos Darwin never came to, not in his official account of himself.

The Galapagos the *Beagle* brings us to involves us in an ideological enantiodromia, in a change of paradigm.

The Galapagos our baptism brings us to involves us in what Mahayana Buddhists call an *ashraya paravritti*. It involves us in the most shattering of all discoveries, the discovery that; conscious and unconscious, psyche is the blind not the window.

In other words: thinking of it as the Hill of the Koshaless Skull, Golgotha is our Christian, our mystical, Galapagos. Further than this I didn't need to go in order to realize that I was sitting in what Philip Larkin would call

ANACONDA CANOE

> A serious house on serious earth

But could it be, I wondered, that it is serious for yet other reasons than those his poem called 'Church Going' enumerates?

> A serious house on serious earth it is,
> In whose blent air all our compulsions meet,
> Are recognized, and robed as destinies.
> And that much never can be obsolete,
> Since someone will forever be surprising,
> A hunger in himself to be more serious,
> And gravitating with it to this ground,
> Which, he once heard, was proper to grow wise in,
> If only that so many dead lie round.

On Galapagos we acknowledge evolution. On Golgotha we are liberated from it into what, in apophatic mood, the Mandukya Upanishad calls Turiya, unchanging Divine Ground in which all development comes to an end, unchanging Divine Ground in which we are no longer identified with that in us which undergoes evolution or regression.

It wasn't just wishfully that Sir Thomas Browne was thinking when he said:

There is surely a piece of Divinity in us, something that was before the Elements, and that owes no homage unto the Sun.

It is only *koshas* in us that undergo evolution or regression. And, in the sense of mental activity or consciousness-of, mind in us is *kosha*. It veils. It is the blind not the window.

Sitting there, I imagined a fish-fin evolving into a foot. I imagined the foot evolving into a wing, into a hand. As I pictured it, the hand evolved from a hand holding a tool into a hand holding a Tenebrae harrow. And that was *eschaton*. That was evolution holding the possibility of liberation from evolution in its own prehensile fin-bones.

I felt like Sir Gawain in Chapel Perilous. Only there was a difference. It wasn't a hand holding a dagger that confronted me. It was a hand holding a quenched Tenebrae harrow that invited me to follow as, a long time ago now, I have followed a scrap of old newspaper on a wild night, our night of heavy south-westerlies.

Old news.
New news.
News then:

> *Yatra na anyat pasyati, na anyat srinoti, na anyad vijanati, sa bhuma.*

News now:

God felt, God tasted, God enjoyed is indeed God, but God with those gifts that flatter the soul, God in darkness, privation, forsakenness and insensibility, is so much God that it is as if it were God bare and alone.

The whyght samyte that veiled it removed, we can now see that the Tenebrae harrow is the Grail of our day. In our day the Grail Castle is a Tenebrae Temple. In it we are good-shepherded into the Light:

Comes then the soul into the unclouded light of God. It is transported so far from creaturehood into nothingness that of its own powers it can never return to its faculties or its former creaturehood. Once there, God shelters the soul's nothingness with his uncreated essence, safeguarding its creaturely existence. The soul has dared to become nothing, and cannot pass from its own being into nothingness and back again, losing its own identity in the process, except God safeguarded it.

And this brings us back to where we began, to Sionna Sagara.

At Sionna Sagara, at Congo Sagara, at Colorado Sagara – at Sushumna Sagara – we sing, with Eckhart we sing:

Oh wonder of wonders, when I think of the union of the soul with God! He makes the enraptured soul to flee out of herself, for she is no more satisfied with anything that can be named. The Spring of Divine Love flows out of the soul and draws her out of herself into the unnamed Being, into her first source, which is God alone.

The Groundplan

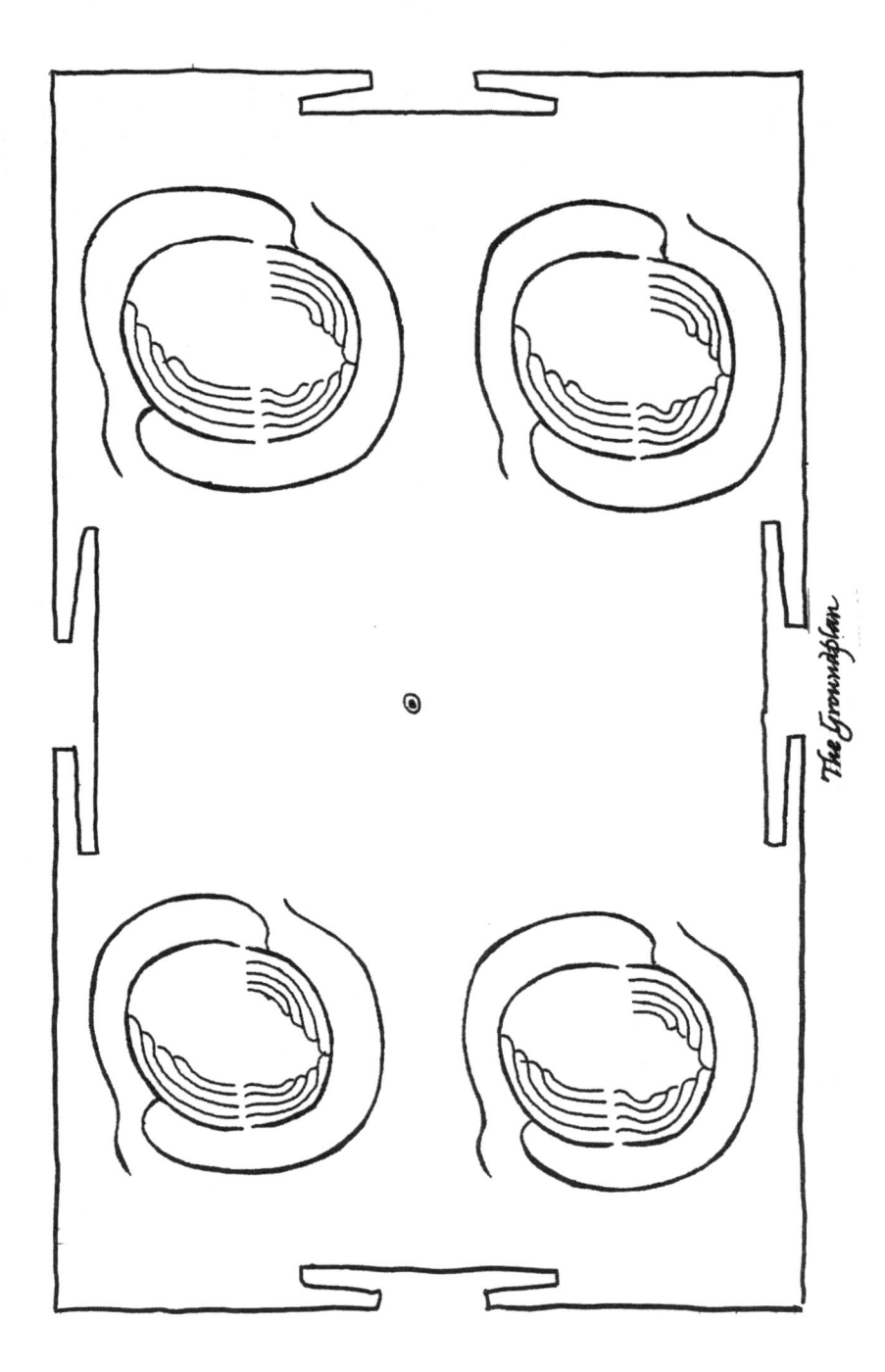

GLOSSARY

Abhaya Mudra In the Hindu tradition mudra denotes meaningful gesture, for instance, the hand and finger gestures of a dancer. The Abhaya Mudra is the fear-not gesture of Shiva Nataraja. Among the catastrophes it invites us to think of with equanimity is the end of the world.

Actaeon In Greek mythology, a hunter who surprised the virgin goddess Artemis bathing with her nymphs in a pool. In punishment Artemis turned him into a stag; not recognizing him, his hounds gave chase and tore him asunder.

Adi Varaha The Hindu god Vishnu in his incarnation as the primal boar.

Adityas In Indo-European mythology adityas are releasers, while danavas are restrainers.

Advaitavedanta A Hindu philosophical system proclaiming the non-dual nature of reality.

Aeon Greek word meaning an age.

Agon A conflictive dialogue as encountered in Greek tragic drama. The Christian word agony derives from it.

Alles-zermalmander All-shattering, or world-shattering.

Altamira Palaeolithic limestone cave near Santander in northern Spain containing rock art *c.* 13,500 BC.

Amfortas The name of the Fisher King, particularly in medieval German literary tradition. See Wolfram Von Eschenbach's *Parzival*.

Anadyomene From the Greek, rising, or coming in from, the sea.

Anaconda A constrictor snake, reaching in some cases a length of thirty feet, that inhabits the Amazonian rainforest.

Anamnesis The remembering of our lives beyond the boundaries of birth and death.

Anantasayin Recumbent on the coils of the great snake Ananta, a figuration of infinity.

Anima Mundi The world's soul.

Anodos The way back up from the underworld. Opposite of kathodos (*q.v.*).

A'noshma Turtle, in the Maidu story of origins.

Antarabhavic Sanskrit word meaning the state between death and rebirth.

Anthropus The Greek word for humanity.

Apophis The great serpent enemy in the Egyptian underworld.

Archaeornis First or most ancient bird as it evolved out of Mesozoic reptile.

GLOSSARY

Areopagus Rock Rock of the Acropolis in Athens where a famous court was held.

Argo Ship in which many Greek heroes, including Orpheus and Herakles, sailed to Colchis to bring home the Golden Fleece.

Arjuna Character in the great Indian epic *The Mahabharata*.

Asparsaya Sanskrit word meaning without contact or touch.

Atreus King of Mycenae, a lion-gated citadel of the Argolid in the Peloponnese. He and his descendants were known as the Atreidae, a family doomed in its generations. Aeschylus, Sophocles and Euripides tell portions of the story in their tragic dramas.

Aurignacian A flint culture of the palaeolithic period in Europe, when some of the cave paintings of south-west France (Lascaux) and northern Spain (Altamira) were executed.

Ayahuasca Hallucinogenic drink brewed from the yaje vine in Amazonia.

Baqa Arabic word used by sufis meaning abiding in the godhead.

Beagle Ten-gun brig in which Darwin spent five years as a naturalist sailing around the world, calling at the Galapagos in the Pacific where he made the observations that would finally give rise to the theory of evolution.

Bealach Oisín A valley in south Kerry through the Atlantic end of which Oisín rode away with Niamh Cinn Oir to the Land of the Ever Young.

Behemoth A mythical beast like a rhinoceros in the Book of Job.

Berkeley, George (1685-1753) Irish bishop and idealist philosopher born in Kilkenny.

Bhagavad Gita Sacred book in Hinduism.

Bhakta Passionate devotee of a goddess or god in Hinduism.

Bhuvaneshvar Temple complex in India.

Bit Akitu The temple outside the walls of ancient Babylon in which the New Year festival was celebrated.

Blake, William (1757-1827) English poet, painter and mystic, born in London to an Irish hosier.

Blue Thunder Tipi Tipi that the chief of the Thunder Bears permitted Wolf Collar (*q.v.*) to erect and live in.

Boehme, Jacob (1575-1624) German Protestant mystic.

Borobudur A great Buddhist temple in Java. In shape it resembles a low, stepped pyramid. Architecturally, it is as if the world mountain had accommodated itself to our desire to ascend into enlightenment or nirvana.

Bozeman A settler who led a famous migration across the American prairies to Montana.

Bright Angel Trail One of the winding trails that leads down to the floor of the Grand Canyon in Arizona.

Browne, Thomas (1605-82) English physician and author of *Religio Medici* (1635).

Buddh Gaia Where the Buddha won enlightenment there is a temple called Buddh Gaya. The word *buddh* is from a root suggesting enlightenment.

GLOSSARY

The ancient Greeks thought of the Earth as a goddess called Gaia. Buddh Gaia therefore suggests that the Earth itself is already enlightened, or is capable of being enlightened.

Buraq A strange, magical animal, both woman and mule, on which Mohammad ascended to within a hand's breadth of God.

Buryat A tribe of Siberia.

Byodo-in A famous Buddhist temple in Japan.

Cetus Dei As in Agnus Dei, the lamb of God, Cetus Dei means the whale of God.

Chalcedon Small town on the Bosphorus, where a Christological definition about Jesus's two-natures-in-one-person was elaborated at a Council of the Church in AD 451.

Chandogya Title for one of the great Upanishads (q.v.).

Chateau Merveil Castle of marvels and terrors in the Grail quest.

Choephoroi In Greek, literally 'libation bearers'. It is the title of the second play in *The Oresteia* by Aeschylus.

Chonyid Bardo In Tibetan Buddhism, a phase or state of the soul's journey between death and rebirth.

Chuang Tzu Great sage who gave his name to one of the classics of Taoism.

Cliatha fis The wattles of wisdom. Someone seeking wisdom in ancient Ireland would lie on nine hazel wattles.

Cluain The Irish for meadow or field.

Coatlicue Aztec earth-goddess.

Coconino sandstone One of the strata of the Grand Canyon.

Colonus Grove sacred to the Erinyes in ancient Attica.

Crinoids Plant-like creatures living in the carboniferous seas.

Daedalus The great craftsman and master-builder of the ancient Greek world. Famously, he designed the Cretan labyrinth.

Demeter In Greek religion, the Corn Mother.

Desana A tribe of north-western Amazonian Indians.

Desert of Zin Desert into which the children of Israel came, having passed through the Red Sea. See Book of Numbers, 20.

Deucalion In Greek mythology, the survivor of the Flood.

Dichosa Ventura Line from a poem by St John of the Cross (q.v.), meaning 'Oh happy venture'.

Die Jungfrau Schiller's name for Joan of Ark, about whom he wrote a famous tragedy.

Dike The immutable, almost impersonal, order and law of things in Greek thinking.

Ding an sich The thing in itself – as it exists independent of our perception and understanding.

GLOSSARY

Dionysus Greek god of wine, called Bacchus by the Romans. Son of Zeus.

Diotima Wise woman from Mantineia (*q.v.*) quoted by Socrates (*q.v.*) in Plato's dialogue, *The Symposium*.

Divine (Un) Grund Ground out of which all things emanate. German word meaning no ground, the no-ground that grounds.

Djed Pillar A symbolic representation of the Egyptian god Osiris, lord of the paradisal underworld.

Docetist One who denied the full humanity of Christ, his suffering, passion and death. The doctrine was declared to be a heresy.

Dover Beach Poem by Matthew Arnold.

Duat Egyptian underworld.

Eachtra An adventure of mythic, or near-mythic, strangeness.

Eckhart (1260-1327) Rhineland mystic.

Eleusis A sacred centre not far from ancient Athens where mysteries were enacted.

Enantiodromia A turning around of the road that one is on.

Enso An empty circle with an opening, suggesting the emptiness of all things.

En-Sof A Caballistic name for God meaning the No-Thing.

Enuma Elish The first two words of the Babylonian creation epic, which give its title to the entire text.

Eo Fis The salmon god of wisdom who lives in the river Boyne.

Eohippus Literally 'dawn-horse', the little animal no bigger that a dog from which the modern horse evolved.

Epoptai Greek word meaning viewers of sacred things.

Erebus Greek underworld.

Esagila Great temple in ancient Babylon.

Eschaton The Greek word for 'last things' as Christians understand them: hence 'eschatological'.

Etymon The Greek root word from which 'etymology' comes.

Eurydice Wife to Orpheus (*q.v.*), who when she died descended to Hades in an effort to bring her back.

Evangelanta Newly coined word. In Hinduism there are collections of sacred texts called the Vedas. They are, so to speak, a first revelation, heard in times long past. Other texts, called the Upanishads, constituting a further 'revelation', were written later. Collectively these latter texts are called Vedanta, a compound of veda and anta, literally 'after the Vedas'. In Christianity we have the initial Good News, the Greek word for which is Evangel. As in Hinduism there is Veda and Vedanta, so in Christianity there is Evangel and Evangelanta. Coming as they do, after the Evangel, the writings of the Christian mystics constitute Evangelanta.

Eveshkigal Queen of the Sumerian Underworld.

GLOSSARY

Fana Arabic word used by sufis meaning our passing away into the godhead.

Fénelon, Francois de (1651-1715) French prelate, writer and champion of Madame Guyon (*q.v.*).

Fisher King The wounded keeper of the Grail.

Fodhla One of the triple goddesses (with Eire and Banba) of Irish sovereignity. Like the others, she gave her name to the country.

Garbhagriha The womb-chamber in a Hindu temple.

Gayatri A Hindu morning prayer.

Ghora murti Terrible face or form of the goddess or god in Hinduism.

Gilgamesh A Sumerian king, a bringer of culture and founder of many great cities. See the *Epic of Gilgamesh*.

Ginnungagap In Norse mythology, the great yawning emptiness or void.

Golgotha-Borobudur Literally, a place of the skull, the hill on which Christ was crucified on Good Friday; and a Buddhist temple in Java: an amalgamation of the Christian and the Buddhist pyramidal temple.

Gundestrup cauldron A famous cauldron of Celtic provenance found in Denmark, the central decorated figure of which is an antlered god.

Gunflint cherts Rock on the northern shores of Lake Superior, in which are found the most ancient algae fossils.

Guyon, Madame (1648-1717) French Christian mystic.

Gyrans gyrendo spiritus radit Spiralling in a spiral, the spirit moves.

Harrowing of Hell Medieval belief that on the night of Good Friday, Jesus went down into Hell and led out all souls of the pre-Christian dispensation who had lived good or exemplary lives. This episode in the great drama of Christian redemption was frequently enacted on the medieval stage. The version quoted here is from the Chester cycle of mystery plays.

Heidegger, Martin (1889-1976) German philosoper, born in Messkirch, Baden, to a Catholic sexton.

Hellvellyn A German Romantic poet.

Hippolytus In Greek mythology, the young hunter who, as he refused Aphrodite and the passions she was the divinity of, was destroyed by a beastly eruption from the sea.

Hölderlin, Johann (1776-1843) Romantic poet and Hellenist, born in Lauffen, Germany.

Hozhonji Type of song sung by the Navajo (*q.v.*). It is believed that it transports the singer to the paradisal place it sings of.

Hubble A telescope at present circling the earth.

Immram A voyage of mythic or near-mythic strangeness.

Inis Fáil An ancient name for Ireland, meaning the island of Fáil, or the stone of destiny on which kings were crowned.

GLOSSARY

Ishmael Narrator of Melville's *Moby-Dick*.

Jivanmukta Sanskrit word meaning one who is liberated in this life.
Jneyavarana Obscuration or veiling caused by thought.
Job Fictional protagonist in the biblical Book of Job.

Kadmus A man from western Asia who came, following a cow, into Greece. Where she first lay down he built a city, later famous as Thebes.
Kant, Immanuel (1724-1804) German philosopher and critical idealist born in Königsberg, Prussia, to a saddler.
Kathodos Road going down, or the way down or journey down, into the Underworld.
Kedron Stream in a valley outside Jerusalem. See John, 18:1.
Ketos The beast from the sea that came to attack Andromeda.
Kinosis Greek for self-emptying.
Konarak A famous sun-temple in Orissa in India.
Kosha A Sanskrit word meaning veil or obscuration. According to Hindus our senses are veils, our minds and our passions are veils, veiling ultimate divine reality from us.
Kundalini Some Hindus believe that within us, starting at the base of the spine, there is an ascending series of spiritual centres called chakras. In the muladhara or lowest chakra there is coiled energy, sometimes thought of as a snake and called Kundalini. The awakening of Kundalini, who in most of us is dormant, and her ascent through the other chakras, is an event that many Hindus think of as our ultimate spiritual blossoming.
Kwakiutl Indian people, living on the north-west coast of North America.

Labacidae The ruling royal family of ancient Thebes, of whom Kadmus (q.v.), Laius and Oedipus were most conspicuous.
Lascaux Palaeolithic cave in southern France.
Law, William (1686-1761) English clergyman from Kingscliffe, Northamptonshire, born to a grocer. Refused to take an oath of loyalty to King George I. Disciple of Boehme (q.v.).
Les Trois Frères A palaeolithic cave in southern France.
Leviathan Great monster of the deep in the Bible.
Linn Feic The most sacred pool in the river Boyne.
Liz de la Mervoille Bed of wonders and terrors in Chateau Merveil (q.v.).
Loman, Willie Hero of Arthur Miller's play *Death of a Salesman*.
Lucy Gray Young woman about whom Wordsworth wrote a poem of that name.

Maag Mahony See *Crossing the Kedron*, volume 1 of *Turtle*, pp. 177ff.
Mabinogion, The Collective name for eleven medieval Welsh folktales commemorating ancient strata of Celtic myth and history, first published in

GLOSSARY

English 1838-49.

Mahavakya Sanskrit word meaning great saying. According to Shankara (*q.v.*), there are six such great sayings in the Upanishads (*q.v.*).

Mahayana Buddhism Literally, the greater vehicle or vessel used to designate northern Buddhism, as opposed to Hinayana or lesser-vehicle Buddhism, which is southern Buddhism.

Maidu raft The Maidu are a Indian tribe living in California. The raft in question is the one which appears in their story of origins 'Turtle Was Gone a Long Time'.

Mahivira One of the great openers of the way to the farther shore in Jainism.

Malleus Maleficarum Hammer of witches; name of a medieval treatise on demonology.

Maloca A native communal house of the Amazonian rainforest.

Mantineia Place in ancient Greece from which Diotima (*q.v.*) comes.

Marasena The hordes of Mara, lord of sensual desire and death in Buddhism.

Marathon Plain in ancient Greece on which a decisive battle between Persians and Greeks, Asians and Europeans, was fought.

Marduk One of the great Babylonian gods, slayer of Tiamat (*q.v.*). His name means son of the sun.

Mayashakti Hindu goddess who is the source of maya, or world illusion.

Mayflower Ship in which the Puritan Pilgrim Fathers sailed to the New World, making landfall at Plymouth Rock in Massachusetts, New England.

Mayin A master of illusion in Hinduism.

Medicine River River to which Standing Mouse journeys in a Native American story.

Medulla One of the oldest and deepest lobes of the brain.

Megalonschema The great or angelical habit worn by Greek Orthodox monks, imprinted frontally with the instruments of Christ's passion.

Melpomane One of the nine muses of Greek mythology, the muse of tragedy.

Mesehtiu An adze-shaped sacred instrument used in the ritual called the Opening of the Mouth in ancient Egypt.

Mesektet boat The night barque in which the Egyptian sungod journeyed through the underworld.

Metanoesis As metaphysics means beyond the physical, so does metanoesis mean beyond mental activity, beyond mind.

Minotaur Half-bull, half-man that Pasiphae (*q.v.*) gave birth to.

Mo wei A Chinese doctrine which proposes that nothing or no one has caused, or continues to cause, the universe.

Morgan Le Fay A euhemerized goddess, here equated with Mayashakti (*q.v.*).

Mount Athos Peninsula in northern Greece famous for the number and importance of its monasteries.

Mount Palomar Observatory site of a 5-metre reflector telescope in southern California.

GLOSSARY

Mucalinda The serpent king in Buddhism who, on the night of his enlightenment, coiled himself around the Buddha's body to protect him from the assaults of the great adversary, Kama-Mara.
Muladhara The lowest of the chakras. See *Kundalini*.

Nacht und nabel Literally, 'night and fog' in German: the trains that brought Jews to the concentration camps.
Narada Protagonist in a Hindu parable.
Navajo Tribe of Indians living in the south-west of North America.
Nave Technically, the body of a Christian church, from the Latin word meaning boat, and therefore thought of as the ship, or ark, that would take us through the turbulent waters of time to the shore of Eternity.
Nectan's Well The Otherworld well in which the river Boyne is said to have its source.
Nekuia A Greek word meaning journey to the underworld.
Newton, Isaac (1642-1727) English author of the laws of gravity, his most famous book being *Philosophiae Naturalis Principia Mathematica* (1687).
Nietzsche, Friedrich (1844-1900) German philosopher, born in Röcken, Saxony, to a Lutheran pastor.
Niffari An Egyptian Muslim mystic.
Nirvikalpasamadhi State of contemplation in which there is no object of awareness. In it, we have gone beyond the subjective–objective divide.

Oedipus King of Thebes (*q.v.*) in ancient Greece, who discovered that he had killed his father and married his mother.
Orpheus A great Thracian singer who, singing and playing his lyre, assuaged the savagery of man and beast.
Osiris (Ani) God of the dead in ancient Egyptian religion.

Palambron A mythical figure in Blake's prophecies.
Paramitas The six characteristic virtues of a fully enlightened person.
Pascal, Blaise (1623-62) French philosopher-mystic and mathematician, born in Clermont-Ferrand.
Pasiphae (calving-ground) Wife of Minos, king of Crete. She mated with a bull from the sea and gave birth to the Minotaur (*q.v.*).
Pequod Whale ship in which Captain Ahab and his crew pursued the great white whale called Moby-Dick. Also, a tribe of Indians from the Massachussetts region, massacred by white settlers in 1639.
Pericles The man under whose inspired leadership Athens flourished in the fifth century BC.
Peyote Small desert cactus whose fruits are hallucinogenic. Mescalin is an extract.
Pico della Mirandola, Giovanni (1493-94) One of the first great humanists of the Italian Renaissance, author of *De Hominis Dignitae* (1486), a seminal text on

GLOSSARY

the theme of free will.
Polla ta deina 'Of all the uncanny things': the first three words in the second stasimon of *The Antigone* by Sophocles.
Porete, Marguerite Mystic from Hainault, Belgium, burnt at the stake in 1360.
Prajnaparamita Literally, the wisdom that is gone beyond.
Protarchos ate Greek term meaning the primal act of madness. See *The Oresteia* by Aeschylus.
Psalm eight Psalm in which a biblical definition of man is elaborated.
Psychopompos A Greek word meaning the guide of souls in their after-death journeys.
Punta Alta In geological times, for about seventy million years, the North and South American land-masses were separated, and during this time their faunas evolved in isolation. When the land-bridge was restored, the great predators that had evolved in the north moved south and events ominous unto extinction for many wiped out whole species, among them Megatherium, Megalonyx, Scelidotherium, Toxodon, Mylodon and Machrauchenia. Darwin found fossils of these animals in and at the base of a cliff called Punta Alta on the coast of Argentina.
Pythia Prophetess at the earth oracle in Delphi in ancient Greece.

Queequeg One of the three harpooners on board the *Pequod* (*q.v.*).
Quetzalcoatl The plumed serpent in Aztec religion.

River of the White Hippopotamus One of the rivers of the Egyptian underworld, taken here to be the karmic equivalent of the Colorado.
Ruysbroeck, Johaness (1293-1381) Flemish mystic.

St John of the Cross (1542-91) Spanish mystic.
St Teresa of Ávila (1515-82) Spanish mystic and Carmelite from Old Castile.
Salamis Site of a sea battle in ancient Greece between Persians and Greeks.
Samadhi A Sanskrit word for states of meditation or contemplation.
Saoi The Irish word for seer.
Sea of Typhoons Eastern sea into which the *Pequod* (*q.v.*) sailed and foundered.
Sefirah In the Cabbala, one of the first ten emanations from the Divine.
Serengeti Great plain in Kenya, famous for its wild animals.
Shankara One of the great philosopher-mystics of the Hindu tradition.
Sidpa Bardo In Tibetan Buddhism, one of the states through which the soul journeys between death and rebirth.
Silam Inua An Eskimo or Inuit concept signifying something like the world soul as Plato or Plotinus understood it.
Simeon The man who, when he saw the Christ-child presented in the temple, uttered the words, 'Now lettest thou thy servant depart in peace' – in Latin, *Nunc dimittis*. See Luke 2.

GLOSSARY

Sinan Great architect of mosques in the Ottoman Empire.
Smoking Mirror Aztec god named Tezcatlipoca, meaning smoking mirror.
Socrates (469-399 BC) Founding father of Greek philosophy, born in Athens.
Soma A psychoactive substance used among Hindus in Vedic times, derived, we now think, from the *amanita muscaria* mushroom.
Sophocles (c. 496-05 BC) One of the great Athenian tragedians.
Stasimon A song of the Chorus in ancient Greek tragedy.
Suger (c. 1081-1151) French bishop responsible for the building of St Denis, outside Paris, the inception of Gothic architecture.
Sulcus primogenius The first and sacred furrow that will enclose the new city.
Sundara murti Beautiful face or form, of the goddess or god in Hinduism.
Sunyata The Mahayana Buddhist doctrine of emptiness.
Sushumna In Hindu belief, the channel in the subtle body along which the chakras are located.
Suso, Heinrich (c 1295-1366) Rhineland mystic, a Dominican monk and disciple of Eckhart (*q.v.*).

Ta'doiko First ground onto which, in the Maidu story of creation, Turtle, Earth-Initiate and Father-of-the-Secret-Society, emerged.
Tai-wer In ancient Egyptian mythology, the first land or mound out of primordial waters.
Takanakapsaluk Among the Inuit, the most mother of sea beasts.
Tantra A religious movement within Hinduism and Buddhism, which seeks to utilize rather than to deny the instinctive energies.
Tao Te Ching Translated by Arthur Waley (1934) as *The Way and Its Power*, a Taoist sacred text attributed to Lao Tzu (c. 604-523 BC) consisting of eighty-one short chapters of poetry and philosophical reflection – profound, beautiful, sometimes paradoxical.
Tartarus One of the deepest pits of the ancient Greek underworld.
Tatha A Buddhist word meaning the indeterminate.
Tauler (1300-1361) Rhineland mystic.
Techne Greek word for the manufacture and use of tools.
Tehom Ancient Hebrew word for the Great Deep.
Tenebrae Ritual re-enactment of the darkness of Good Friday, and the passion and death of Christ.
Tep-Zepi In ancient Eyptian mythology, the First Time.
Thebes Troubled city in ancient Greece, which, more than most, illustrates our difficulties in attempting to civilize ourselves, in attempting to live civically. Oedipus (*q.v.*) was the most famous of its kings.
Theriomorphic Having the shape of an animal.
Theriozoic Alive in the way that an animal is alive (a neologism).
Thermopylae In Greece, meaning the hot gates, the famous pass between the mountains and the sea where Greeks under Xerxes (*q.v.*) stood against a horde of

GLOSSARY

invading Persians, led by Leonidas of Sparta, in the fifth century BC.

Thiasas A group of ecstatically worshipping votaries of Dionysus.

Tiamat Primordial female monster or dragoness of the Abyss in Babylonian and Sumerian mythology. Slain by the god Marduk (*q.v.*).

Torrent The brook, otherwise know as Kedron (*q.v.*), Jesus crossed on his way into Gethsemane.

Traherne, Thomas (1637-74) English mystic and poet, born to a shoemaker in Hereford. Author of *Centuries* of prose religious meditations.

Triduum Sacrum Three sacred days of Holy Week, Holy Thursday, Good Friday and Easter Sunday.

Tsetsekia Winter ceremonies of the Kwakiutl (*q.v.*).

Turiya Literally, the fourth, referring in the Mandukya Upanishad to Divine Ground (*q.v.*) which is beyond all duality.

Udana Hymn or song – especially as spoken by Buddha on the morning of his enlightenment.

Uluru The world's largest monolith in central Australia, popularly known as Ayer's Rock.

Upanishads Sanskrit word meaning a sitting-down (at another's feet); sacred Hindu texts on the nature of man and the universe, part of Vedic writings dating back two and a half millennia.

Uuitoto An Amazonian tribe – a forest-dwelling people of south-eastern Colombia.

Uvavnuk Inuit medicine woman.

Vedas Hindu sacred texts. See *Evangelanta*.

Vespucci, Amerigo (1451-1512) Famous Florentine explorer after whom the Americas were named and who coined the phrase *Mundus Novus*, New World.

Viksepashakti Mental power by which we project something illusory onto reality. 'Shakti' signifies female power in a goddess or god.

Vishnu Major Hindu deity, the second member, with Brahma and Shiva, of a triad of gods manifesting cosmic functions of the Supreme Being.

Vishvarupa Hindu god Vishnu (*q.v.*) as Omniform – the form that contains all forms.

Vishvayuga Form that contains all ages.

Vrindavan A bucolic paradise in which Krishna, an incarnation of the great god Vishnu, would play his flute for the Gopis.

Vulture Peak A peak on which the Buddha spoke the lotus of the heart sutra to beings of earth and heaven.

Whaleman's Chapel Located in New Bedford, Connecticut, mentioned in Melville's *Moby-Dick*.

GLOSSARY

Whyght Samyte White silk in which the Grail was covered when it entered the hall of the round table on Pentecost Sunday.
Wolf Collar Blackfoot medicine man.
Wu wei In Taoist philosophy, action by inaction.

Xerxes Persian king. His efforts and those of King Darius to conquer Greece were defeated at the battles of Marathon (*q.v.*) and Salamis (*q.v.*). As a consequence, the Greek Enlightenment could and did continue to flourish.

Yahweh One of the personal names for the god of the Old Testament. See Psalm seventy-four, verse fourteen.
Yaje Woman The woman associated with the yaje vine, a powerful hallucinogenic Amazonian plant.
Yana Vessel, in the sense of ship or ferry. A Sanskrit word in Buddhism.
Yatra na anyat pasyati, na anyat srinoti, na anyad vijanati, sa bhuma Where nothing else is seen, nothing else is heard, nothing else is thought about, there is the Infinite. *Chandogya Upanishad*, vii, xxiv.
Year One Reed In the Aztec calendar, the year in which Cortez came and destroyed their empire and religion (1519, in our calendar).
Yu wei In Taoist philosophy, deliberate, self-conscious action.

Zazen Meditating while sitting in the lotus position in Zen Buddhism.
Zeuglodon Prehistoric whale, a fossil of which was unearthed in Alabama in the 1840s. See *Moby-Dick*, chapter 104. As Job was down-cast by Leviathan, so was Ishmael down-cast by Zeuglodon: 'I am horror-struck at this antemosaic, unsourced existence of the unspeakable terrors of the whale, which, having been before all time, must needs exist after all humane ages are over.'